O9-ABI-876

Tales of the South

WEST GEORGIA REGIONAL LIBRARY SYSTEM
Neva Lomason Memorial Library

Sharp Snaffles accosts Bachelor Grimstead

From "How Sharp Snaffles Got His Capital and Wife," *Harper's New Monthly Magazine*, 41 (October 1870).

Tales of the South

by William Gilmore Simms

Edited with an introduction by

Mary Ann Wimsatt

University of South Carolina Press

Copyright © 1996 University of South Carolina

Published in Columbia, South Carolina, by the
University of South Carolina Press

Manufactured in the United States of America

00 99 98 97 96 5 4 3 2 1

Library of Congress Cataloging-in-Publication Data

Simms, William Gilmore, 1806–1870.
Tales of the South / by William Gilmore Simms ; edited with an introduction by Mary Ann Wimsatt.
p. cm.
Includes bibliographical references (p.).
ISBN 1–57003–086–3. — ISBN 1–57003–087–1 (pbk.)
1. Southern States—Social life and customs—Fiction.
I. Wimsatt, Mary Ann, 1934– . II. Title.
PS2843.W56 1996
813′.3—dc20 95–39437

For Rayburn and Margaret Moore
Scholars Mentors Friends

Contents

Acknowledgments

I owe thanks to my excellent research assistants and proofreaders, Mark Graybill, Virginia Hodges, Kreg Abshire, Mary Jo Tate, Sandra Barrett, Susan Stone, and Jimmy Smith; to Warren Slesinger, Margaret V. Hill, and Thelma Davis of the University of South Carolina Press for their advice; to Judith S. Baughman for her help and encouragement; and to Matthew J. Bruccoli for his extensive assistance with the project.

Chronology of William Gilmore Simms's Life and Works

1806	William Gilmore Simms, Jr., born in Charleston, South Carolina, on April 17, the second and only surviving son of William Gilmore Simms, Sr., and Harriet Ann Augusta Singleton Simms.
1808	Simms's mother dies at the birth of her third child. His father moves to the Gulf South, leaving Simms in Charleston in the care of his maternal grandmother.
1812–18	Simms educated in Charleston public and private schools.
1818	Is apprenticed to an apothecary in order to prepare for a career in medicine.
1824–26	Pays two visits to his father in Mississippi. The men travel on horseback hundreds of miles west of the Mississippi River, observing frontier conditions.
1825	Reads law in Charleston; helps edit and write for *The Album*, a literary magazine. Publishes first book, a pamphlet entitled *Monody, on the Death of Gen. Charles Cotesworth Pinckney* (Charleston: Gray & Ellis).
1826	Marries Anna Malcolm Giles in Charleston.
1827	Admitted to the bar; publishes *Lyrical and Other Poems* (Charleston: Ellis & Neufville) and *Early Lays* (Charleston: A. E. Miller).
1828–29	Co-founds, helps edit, and writes for *The Southern Literary Gazette* in Charleston. Becomes sole editor of the journal during 1829.
1829	Publishes *The Vision of Cortes, Cain, and Other Poems* (Charleston: James S. Burges).

1830 Publishes *The Tri-Color; or, The Three Days of Blood, in Paris*. Title page carries publishing information as London: Wigfall & Davis. Book, however, perhaps actually published in Charleston in 1831. Also buys with a partner and begins editing a daily newspaper, *The Charleston City Gazette*, which he edits until June 1832.

1832 Death of Anna Malcolm Giles Simms from tuberculosis. Simms travels for the first time to New York and New England, making valuable literary and publishing friendships. Publishes long poem, *Atalantis. A Story of the Sea* (New York: J. & J. Harper).

1833 Publishes short novel *Martin Faber; The Story of a Criminal* (New York: J. & J. Harper). In Charleston, co-edits and writes for *The Cosmopolitan: An Occasional*. Publishes *The Book of My Lady* (Philadelphia: Key & Biddle, 1833).

1834 Publishes *Guy Rivers: A Tale of Georgia*, his first Border Romance about the Gulf South (New York: Harper & Brothers).

1835 Publishes *The Yemassee. A Romance of Carolina* (New York: Harper & Brothers), his first novel about colonial South Carolina, and *The Partisan: A Tale of the Revolution* (New York: Harper & Brothers), his first novel about South Carolina's role in the Revolutionary War.

1836 Publishes *Mellichampe. A Legend of the Santee* (New York: Harper & Brothers), about the Revolution in South Carolina. Marries Chevillette Eliza Roach and moves to her father's plantation, Woodlands, in Barnwell District 70 miles inland from Charleston.

1837 Publishes *Martin Faber, The Story of a Criminal; and Other Tales* (New York: Harper & Brothers, 1837).

1838 Publishes *Carl Werner, An Imaginative Story; With Other Tales of Imagination* (New York: George Adlard); *Richard Hurdis; or, The Avenger of Blood. A Tale of Alabama* (Philadelphia: E. L. Carey & A. Hart), a Border Romance; and *Pelayo: A Story of the Goth* (New York: Harper & Brothers), his first novel about Spain.

1839 Publishes *Southern Passages and Pictures* (New York: George Adlard), a volume of poetry, and *The Damsel of*

Darien (Philadelphia: Lea and Blanchard), his first novel about Spanish America.

1840 Publishes *Border Beagles; A Tale of Mississippi* (Philadelphia: Carey and Hart) and *The History of South Carolina* (Charleston: S. Babcock), a textbook for public schools.

1841 Publishes the Revolutionary War Romance *The Kinsmen: or The Black Riders of Congaree. A Tale* (Philadelphia: Lea and Blanchard); later edition titled *The Scout.* Also publishes *Confession; or The Blind Heart. A Domestic Story* (Philadelphia: Lea and Blanchard).

1842 Publishes *Beauchampe, or The Kentucky Tragedy. A Tale of Passion* (Philadelphia: Lea and Blanchard); its first volume later retitled *Charlemont.* Quits writing long fiction for eight years because of economic recession causing problems in the book market.

1843 Publishes *Donna Florida. A Tale*, a long poem based on the Ponce de Leon story (Charleston: Burges & James) and *The Geography of South Carolina* (Charleston: S. Babcock), a companion to *The History of South Carolina.*

1844 Is elected to South Carolina state legislature for 1844-46. Publishes *The Life of Francis Marion* (New York: Henry G. Langley) as well as two short novels: *Castle Dismal: or, the Bachelor's Christmas. A Domestic Legend* (New York: Burgess, Stringer & Co.) and *The Prima Donna: A Passage from City Life* (Philadelphia: Louis A. Godey).

1845 Publishes collection of tales, *The Wigwam and the Cabin*, First and Second Series (New York: Wiley and Putnam) and two volumes of cultural criticism, *Views and Reviews in American Literature, History and Fiction*, First and Second Series (New York: Wiley and Putnam [volumes dated 1845 but were issued in 1846 and 1847 respectively]). Also publishes *Helen Halsey: or, The Swamp State of Conelachita. A Tale of the Borders* (New York: Burgess, Stringer & Co.); *Count Julian; or, The Last Days of the Goth. A Historical Romance* (Baltimore and New York: William Taylor and Co.), a novel largely written in 1838; and *Grouped Thoughts and Scattered Fancies. A Collection of Sonnets*

(Richmond: Wm. Macfarlane). Edits *The Southern and Western Monthly Magazine and Review.*

1846 Publishes *Areytos: or, Songs of the South* (Charleston: John Russell) and *The Life of Captain John Smith. The Founder of Virginia* (New York: Geo F. Cooledge and Brother).

1847 Publishes *The Life of the Chevalier Bayard; "The Good Knight"* (New York: Harper & Brothers).

1848 Publishes *Lays of the Palmetto: A Tribute to the South Carolina Regiment, in the War with Mexico* (Charleston: John Russell) and satiric poem *Charleston, and Her Satirists; A Scribblement* (Charleston: James S. Burges).

1849 Edits *The Southern Quarterly Review* until 1855. Edits *The Life of Nathanael [sic] Greene, Major-General in the Army of the Revolution* (New York: George F. Cooledge and Brother). Publishes *Sabbath Lyrics; or, Songs From Scripture* (Charleston: Walker & James); *The Cassique of Accabee. A Tale of Ashley River. With Other Pieces* (Charleston: John Russell), poems; and *Father Abbot, or, The Home Tourist* (Charleston: Miller & Brown).

1850 Publishes *The Lily and the Totem, or, The Huguenots in Florida* (New York: Baker and Scribner) and *The City of the Silent: A Poem* (Charleston: Walker & James, 1850 [actually published 1851]).

1851 Publishes *Katharine Walton: or, The Rebel of Dorchester. An Historical Romance of the Revolution in Carolina* (Philadelphia: A. Hart) and *Norman Maurice; or, The Man of the People. An American Drama* (Richmond: Jno. R. Thompson).

1852 Publishes *The Golden Christmas: A Chronicle of St. John's, Berkeley* (Charleston: Walker, Richards & Co., 1852); *The Sword and the Distaff; or, "Fair, Fat and Forty," A Story of the South, at the Close of the Revolution* (Charleston: Walker, Richards, & Co. [later retitled *Woodcraft*]); *As Good as a Comedy: or, the Tennessean's [sic] Story* (Philadelphia: A. Hart, 1852); and a blank verse drama, *Michael Bonham: or, The Fall of Bexar. A Tale of Texas* (Richmond: Jno. R. Thompson).

1853 Uniform Edition of Simms's works, published by Justus

Starr Redfield of New York and illustrated by the noted F. O. C. Darley, commences. Simms revises books for inclusion in the edition. Publishes *Poems Descriptive, Dramatic, Legendary and Contemplative* (New York: Redfield; Charleston: John Russell) and *Vasconselos: A Romance of the New World* (New York: Redfield), a novel of Spanish America; *South-Carolina in the Revolutionary War* (Charleston: Walker & James), an answer to Northern disparagement of the state's central role in the winning of the Revolution; and *Marie de Berniere: A Tale of the Crescent City* (Philadelphia: Lippincott, Grambo & Co.).

1854 Publishes *Southward Ho! A Spell of Sunshine* (New York: Redfield), a travel narrative and collection of tales.

1855 Publishes *The Forayers, or the Raid of the Dog-Days* (New York: Redfield), a novel about the closing days of the Revolution in South Carolina.

1856 Pubiishes *Eutaw: A Sequel to The Forayers, or the Raid of the Dog-Days. A Tale of the Revolution* (New York: Redfield).

1857 Lends support to *Russell's Magazine* (1857-60), edited by his friend the poet Paul Hamilton Hayne and published by John Russell in Charleston.

1859 Publishes *The Cassique of Kiawah: A Colonial Romance* (New York: Redfield), his last novel to appear in book form during his lifetime.

1862 Woodlands partly burned from an apparently accidental fire.

1863 Chevillette Eliza Roach Simms dies suddenly at Woodlands of appendicitis. Simms serializes *Paddy McGann; or, The Demon of the Stump*, a humorous backwoods novel, in *The Southern Illustrated News*, a Richmond weekly.

1865 Woodlands burned by stragglers from General William Tecumseh Sherman's troops; Simms's library of over 10,000 volumes destroyed. Living in Columbia, South Carolina, Simms edits newspaper *The Columbia Phoenix* and publishes *Sack and Destruction of the City of Columbia, South Carolina* (Columbia: Power Press of Daily Phoenix), a description of the devastation wrought by Union forces.

Impoverished by the war, edits *The Daily South Carolinian* in Columbia until 1866.

1866 Edits *War Poetry of the South* (New York: Richardson). Travels to the North in largely futile attempt to re-establish his connections with publishers.

1867 Serializes *Joscelyn: A Tale of the Revolution*, his last novel about the conflict, in *The Old Guard*, a New York magazine.

1869 Serializes *The Cub of the Panther; A Mountain Legend*, in *The Old Guard*, and *Voltmeier, or The Mountain Men* in the *Illuminated Western World*, a New York weekly. *Voltmeier, As Good as a Comedy*, *Paddy McGann*, and *Joscelyn* published in book form for the first time in the Centennial Simms textual edition, University of South Carolina Press, 1969–74.

1870 Surrounded by family members, dies on June 6 of cancer in Charleston and is buried in Magnolia Cemetery north of the city. His best-known tall tale, "How Sharp Snaffles Got His Capital and Wife," published posthumously in *Harper's Magazine*. Its companion piece, " 'Bald-Head Bill Bauldy,' " remains in manuscript until it and "Sharp Snaffles" are published in *Stories and Tales* (1974), a volume in the Centennial Simms edition.

Tales of the South

Introduction

William Gilmore Simms (1806–1870) was the leading literary figure of the antebellum South and a major American author before the Civil War obscured his renown. Surpassing even his friend Edgar Allan Poe in popularity, he was widely acclaimed by readers throughout the country: a contemporary critic said that James Fenimore Cooper could not have written Simms's first novel "had he died for it," and Poe himself called Simms the Lope de Vega "of American writers of fiction."[1] Composing at great speed during the forty-five years of his active professional life, Simms produced over eighty books and enough uncollected work to fill perhaps an additional twenty volumes. He wrote poetry, plays, essays, sketches, literary criticism, short fiction, and novels—meanwhile publishing a commonplace book, a history, a geography, several biographies, and many volumes of miscellaneous writing. He also edited newspapers and magazines, served in the South Carolina legislature, penned treatises on Southern agriculture, and in general functioned as a thoughtful, articulate member of the planter class. So influential was he in his numerous pursuits that by midcentury he had become the acknowledged spokesman for the cultural and literary concerns of his region.

For much of his busy career, Simms was also a prominent national author, a self-styled "ultra-American"[2] whose books were issued by major publishing houses in the North such as Harper and Brothers or

---

1. [Henry William Herbert], Review of *Guy Rivers*, *American Monthly Magazine*, 3 (July 1834): 302; [Edgar Allan Poe], Review of *The Wigwam and the Cabin*, *Broadway Journal*, 2 (October 4, 1845): 190.

2. William Gilmore Simms to George Frederick Holmes, *The Letters of William Gilmore Simms*, ed. Mary C. Simms Oliphant, Alfred Taylor Odell, and T. C. Duncan Eaves (Columbia, S.C.: University of South Carolina Press, 1952), 1: 319, hereafter cited as *Letters*.

Wiley and Putnam. Until near midcentury, when increasing sectional strife began to harm the national literary market, Simms's writing was extremely popular in the North, where critics had been quick to recognize and praise his talent. Northern reviewers commended his novels as "truly American";[3] influential Northern editors such as Evert Duyckinck helped him place and publicize his writing; and prominent Northern authors—among them Cooper, Herman Melville, and William Cullen Bryant—welcomed him into literary and social circles.

Despite the harm done Simms's personal and literary fortunes by the Civil War, his books continued to be read in the editions of his work issued frequently throughout the remainder of the century. And although readers steeped in postwar realistic fiction began to criticize his esthetic conventions, which derive from the genre of romance, William Dean Howells—arbiter of postbellum literary taste—praised Simms's "really excellent" historical novels and styled him "much the most considerable" of antebellum Southern writers.[4] In similar manner, influential critics and literary historians of the twentieth century enthusiastically commend Simms and his writing. Vernon L. Parrington in *Main Currents in American Thought* (1927–30) calls Simms "the most virile and interesting" author of the antebellum South; Jay B. Hubbell in *The South in American Literature* (1954) styles him "a national figure" deserving close study; C. Hugh Holman in *The Roots of Southern Writing* (1972) praises the versatility and power of his writing; and John C. Guilds in *Simms: A Literary Life* (1992) claims that because of his numerous, varied, and distinguished accomplishments in letters Simms should be viewed "as a major American writer."[5]

But despite such commendations, the economic, social, and literary changes that the Civil War helped to usher in have for more than a century drastically—and for the most part dismally—affected the way in which both the culture of the antebellum South and the

---

3. "Literary Notices," *New-York Mirror*, 13 (January 23, 1836): 239.

4. William Dean Howells, "Recent Biography," *Atlantic Monthly*, 69 (June 1892): 838.

5. Parrington, *Main Currents in American Thought*, one-vol. ed. (New York: Harcourt Brace, 1930), p. 127; Hubbell, *The South in American Literature, 1607–1900* (Durham, N.C.: Duke University Press, 1954), p. 572; Holman, *The Roots of Southern Writing: Essays on the Literature of the American South* (Athens, Ga.: University of Georgia Press, 1972), p. 16; Guilds, *Simms: A Literary Life* (Fayetteville, Ark.: University of Arkansas Press, 1992), p. 350.

writing of Simms and other authors who were part of that culture have been viewed. For after the war, Northern historians and literary historians, backed by the powerful Northern publishing industry, rewrote American history in a manner fundamentally unsympathetic toward the South and its authors. The prevailing interpretation of the South, which still operates in the late twentieth century, has distorted the national understanding of Southern culture and literature, particularly of antebellum culture and literature, and most particularly of Simms—in part because he was a tireless proponent of slavery and secession whose attitudes toward race offend readers in a somewhat less prejudiced age, and also because he portrayed in his writing a civilization whose sociopolitical principles and achievements in letters have only recently begun to receive the kind of reasoned analyses long since accorded the culture and writing of other American regions.

Making this bad situation worse are the well-substantiated historical facts that the predominantly rural, agrarian South of Simms's time, unlike the South of the late twentieth century, lacked large urban centers and hence, in contrast with the North, also lacked major publishing houses. Well before midcentury, Simms was keenly aware of the difficulties this situation imposed upon him: in the early 1840s, for instance, he wrote a friend, "My residence in South Carolina, is unfavorable to me as an author. I lose $2000 per annum by it."[6] In the distressing story of Simms's career, it is this fact, in conjunction with the extraordinary, and extraordinarily numerous, tragedies in his private and public life—the latter culminating in the enormous national tragedy of the Civil War—that has driven his writing out of public view. For throughout the antebellum era and the four years of the war, successful writers living in the North were able to superintend their publishing interests more readily than Simms could his. The unfortunate result for our century has been that, until recently, a major man of letters who happened to be Southern has been nearly lost from sight, whereas Northern writers whom he, rightly in the main, considered his inferiors—such as Washington Irving and Henry Wadsworth Longfellow—remain fairly widely known.

Happily for people who appreciate Simms's central role in American as well as Southern literature and history, several books that treat the man and his work from enlightened, sympathetic perspectives are beginning to diminish ignorance and to alter long-en-

6. William Gilmore Simms to James Henry Hammond, *Letters*, 2: 385.

trenched negative beliefs about the gifted South Carolinian. In *"Long Years of Neglect": The Work and Reputation of William Gilmore Simms* (1988), *The Major Fiction of William Gilmore Simms* (1989), *Selected Poems of William Gilmore Simms* (1990), and *Simms: A Literary Life* (1992), Simms's achievements in poetry, historical writing, fiction, and other fields have finally begun to receive the informed scholarly scrutiny that they long have merited. We are clearly in the midst of a Simms renascence, a situation to which *Tales of the South* is designed to contribute. The collection is aimed at bringing what is perhaps Simms's best body of writing, his short fiction, back into view in a form accessible to the general reader and suitable for use in college and university classrooms.

The title *Tales of the South* derives from one of Simms's own proposed titles for a volume of his stories that was eventually issued under another title midway through his career. It is an apt designation for the present book because all but one of the tales reprinted are set in his native region (the exception, "Juan Ponce de Leon," makes reference to Florida). The contents of the volume are drawn from three of the six collections of short fiction Simms published during his career: *The Book of My Lady* (1833); *Martin Faber, The Story of a Criminal; and Other Tales* (1837; hereafter called "the 1837 *Martin Faber*"); *Carl Werner* (1838); *The Wigwam and the Cabin*, First and Second Series (1845; 1846); *The Lily and the Totem, or, The Huguenots in Florida* (1850); and *Southward Ho! A Spell of Sunshine* (1854). Each of these books represents a different stage in Simms's development as a writer of short fiction, and each differs from the others in format and contents because of influences affecting Simms at the time of composition, particular circumstances of publication, and changing conditions in the book market. This introduction will explore, in necessarily brief compass, the various contexts—biographical, historical, economic, and literary—out of which Simms's short fiction and other writing emerged.

Simms was born in Charleston in 1806, the second and only surviving son of a mother descended from a good Virginia family and an energetic Irish father who owned a store on Charleston's busy King Street. When Simms's mother died at the birth of her third child, who died also, his grief-stricken father left South Carolina for frontier Mississippi, putting Simms, who was not yet two years old, in the care of his maternal grandmother in Charleston. Simms visited his father, who had built a plantation in Mississippi, during 1824–26 and traveled with him on horseback through the wildest parts of the Gulf or lower South. These travels, together with later trips to the Gulf South, tours of the Carolinas, and journeys through the Appalachian mountain region, provided Simms with material for his writing on which he would draw for the rest of his life.

Simms had meanwhile from boyhood on involved himself in the varied kinds of literary pursuits that would characterize his entire career. At about age nine he had composed patriotic verses on the Battle of New Orleans; at age twelve he had written a play about Native Americans; in his middle teens he had furnished what he would later call doggerel poetry to newspapers; and during his late teens and early twenties he had joined other Charlestonians in founding or editing, between 1825 and 1833, three periodicals and a newspaper. Through these journals he hoped to provide his fellow Southerners with places in which to publish their writing. But because his fellow Southerners were slow to respond, he was forced to fill many pages of the journals with his own poetry, sketches, essays, and fiction. These early pieces mark the commencement of his career as a professional author.

Spurring Simms's literary ambitions and sharpening his awareness of the national book market were the trips to the major publishing centers of the North that he began to make in the early 1830s and continued until the end of his life. In 1832 he went North for the first time, traveling to Philadelphia, New England, and New York, where he soon became friendly with Bryant and other literary men and women. Encouraged by this and later visits to the North in the thirties, throughout the decade he energetically produced volumes of poetry, short fiction, long fiction, and essays—sixteen books in all, most of which were issued by such prominent Northern publishing houses as Harper Brothers.

Among Simms's books were several volumes of poetry, including the noteworthy *Southern Passages and Pictures* (1839); seven long novels, including the popular *Guy Rivers* (1834), *The Yemassee* (1835), and *The Partisan* (1835); and the three collections, already mentioned, of the writing Simms had furnished to periodicals in the 1820s and early 1830s: *The Book of My Lady*, for which he assembled poetry as well as short fiction; the 1837 *Martin Faber*, which contained a short novel, nine stories, and a poem; and *Carl Werner*, which had a long title narrative and seven additional tales. Critical notices of Simms's books of the thirties were overwhelmingly favorable. Reviewers praised his poetry, called *The Yemassee* "the Romance of the Season," hailed the "generous enthusiasm" of *The Book of My Lady*, and styled *Carl Werner* "a production of no common order."[7] Exhilarated by such praise, Simms committed himself to a career as a professional author; and by the late 1830s, widely commended for his talents in long fiction, he had settled on the novel as his major literary genre. Or, more accurately, he had settled on that branch of prose fiction which he, like Cooper, Hawthorne, and Melville, termed the romance.

Simms would produce long fiction until the end of his life; it is the form in which he achieved his greatest contemporary successes and that for which he has been most widely known and praised by critics in the nineteenth and twentieth centuries. But there have long been critics, including an increasing number of critics in this century, who believe that he produced his most impressive work in the genre of short fiction. Sprightly, diverse, and entertaining, Simms's numerous stories and tales reveal certain elements of his talent more directly perhaps than do his novels. This is partly because the forms for long fiction were less firmly fixed in the early nineteenth century than were those of the highly conventionalized long romance; the relative fluidity of the tale or story mode seems to have liberated lively strains of comedy and diablerie in Simms's imagination. In his short fiction he explores the subjects and employs the conventions that are fundamental to American and British romanticism. Central to his tales and stories throughout his life are the legends, superstitions, ghost-lore, and folk beliefs that connect his work to the Romantic movement and, beyond it, to the literary traditions of myth and romance.

Simms's short fiction, like much of his other work, is most readily understood, in fact, if it is viewed as part of that vast, fluid body of writing comprising myth, romance, legend, fable, fairy tales, and folk stories as variously described by Carl Jung, Joseph Campbell, Bruno Bettelheim, and Northrop Frye. In his tales, Simms explores the connections between myths and dreams, between superstition and religious belief, between the rational and non-rational elements in human personality, and between conscious and unconscious mental processes. These concerns pervade his early collections, *The Book of*

7. Review of *The Book of My Lady*, *The Knickerbocker; or, New-York Monthly Magazine*, 2 (December 1833): 480–81; review of *The Yemassee*, *New York Times*, April 16, 1835; review of *Carl Werner*, *New York Review*, 4 (January 1839): 267.

My Lady, the 1837 *Martin Faber*, and *Carl Werner*. The books contain playful discussions of dreams and dreaming, light-hearted portrayals of folk superstitions, serious as well as humorous treatments of legends from foreign history, and tales of the supernatural that are often eerie or macabre until their conclusions, which may be given comic twists by means of dream-vision endings.

Revealing Simms's use of these and other subjects are his stories from the 1820s and early 1830s republished here: "The Fisherman," "Juan Ponce de Leon," "The Plank," and "Logoochie." Except for "The Fisherman," which seems never to have been reprinted since its publication in a journal in 1829, the stories were collected in *Carl Werner* or the 1837 *Martin Faber*—the latter of which incorporates several tales, revised and retitled, from *The Book of My Lady*. (For information about the editions from which the stories in this volume were collected, please see the "Note on the Text.") "The Fisherman," the first story in *Tales of the South*, is a playfully satiric treatment of an indolent Southern planter who vainly fishes for sunken treasure. The light, even whimsical, tone of the narrative, which is flavored by folk beliefs about the devil, may obscure the fact that it is in essence a moral fable of a type familiar from Joseph Addison and Richard Steele's *Spectator* papers.

Similar in tone to "The Fisherman" is "Juan Ponce de Leon," in which Simms parodies the famous legend of the Spaniard's discovery of Florida and the Fountain of Youth—a subject that engaged such other writers of the antebellum era as Washington Irving in his *Voyages and Discoveries of the Companions of Columbus* (1830). Apparently in order to counter Irving's serious approach to the legend, Simms deliberately gives his own account an anti-romantic, mock-heroic cast. Treating every aspect of his subject humorously, he mocks Spain in the chivalric period; warriors, knights, and foreign explorers; old men; young women; and the elaborate conventions of courtly love. In contrast to these playful narratives stands "The Plank," a macabre story of the sea that reveals Simms's skill in portraying the hidden passions made palpable through dreams or visions, the possible psychological bases of the supernatural, and the ocean as a romantic, demonic realm. Quite different from "The Plank" is "Logoochie," a humorous narrative rooted in the widespread folk belief that spirits can inhabit trees. A tale of "the Indian mischief-maker—the Puck," it depicts the likable, grotesque tree-spirit Logoochie befriending two white lovers in a new settlement in Georgia.

Unfortunately for Simms's twentieth-century reputation, one or two of these early stories, like several of his later ones, reveal his often patronizing attitude toward women and, somewhat more directly, his prejudice against African Americans and Native Americans. Although such prejudice was common among Northern as well as Southern writers—Cooper and Melville come immediately to mind—it is Simms who, because of his pro-Southern, secessionist stance, has virtually become a national scapegoat for the practice. Increasingly in this century, Simms has received far too much unenlightened criticism about his attitudes toward race from scholars who ignore the complicated historical, cultural, and sociopolitical conditions influencing his writing. Addressing such criticism, John C. Guilds in "*Long Years of Neglect*" observes: "In attempting in the late twentieth century to evaluate an early nineteenth-century man-of-letters who believed the white race to be morally and intellectually superior to the black, the scholar must communicate with a reading public understandably reluctant to isolate racial issues from literary judgment. . . . For the most part Simms was not a racial propagandist in his fiction or poetry; his best work mirrors the society that he portrays, and that it is a slave society is an unavoidable fact" (p. 4). Guilds goes on to maintain that Simms's "accuracy as a reflector of the mores and manners of the Old South should not *per se* weigh against his literary significance" (pp. 4–5). The implication of such comments is clear. If thoughtful readers of Simms can rehistoricize his fiction, they may be able to appreciate his detailed, colorful portraits of antebellum Southern civilization.

By the middle 1830s, Simms had published so many books and received such warm praise for them that his stature as a prominent national author seemed secure; and, made reasonably affluent by the sale of his works, he had turned his thoughts toward marriage. While still a young man, he had married, been widowed, and been left with a single daughter to rear. In 1836, he wed Chevillette Eliza Roach, the daughter of a wealthy South Carolina planter, and settled with her on one of the Roach family plantations, Woodlands, where he and she enjoyed a life of comfortable domesticity that would end only when she died suddenly during the Civil War. But even though Simms's family relationships were secure and his reputation as a writer was soaring, his literary prospects, and hence his financial security, were beginning to decline. For as developments later in his career would prove, he had committed himself to professional authorship at a particularly hazardous time in antebellum publishing history, only a short while before the recession called the Panic of 1837 would severely cripple the country's economy and help cause permanent changes in the book market. In conjunction with other factors, the recession made Simms's handsomely bound, expensive two-volume novels, like those of Cooper and other antebellum authors, financially impractical.

By the early 1840s, therefore, Simms was facing a different, considerably more difficult situation in publishing from that which he had faced in the previous decade. The sales for long fiction, as he sadly told a correspondent in 1841, "are terribly diminished within the last few years. You will perceive that Irving now writes almost wholly for magazines and Cooper & myself are almost the only ones whose novels are printed—certainly, we are almost the only persons who hope to get anything for them. . . . [I]t is seldom now that the demand for novels carries them to a 2d. Edition."[8] After publishing four novels between 1840 and 1842, Simms reluctantly bowed to the effects of the recession, quit writing long fiction until the early 1850s, and busied himself with other types of literature. During the forties, he produced an astonishing twenty-nine books, among them eight volumes of poetry, a history and a geography, several short novels, four biographies, two volumes of stories, and an important collection of cultural and literary criticism, *Views and Reviews in American Literature, History and Fiction*, First and Second Series.

However bitter the economic situation of the 1840s was for Simms the novelist—and it was far worse than many of his readers have realized—it was ultimately beneficial for Simms the writer of short fiction. It forced him back into the editing of periodicals, at which he was adept, and therefore also back into the production of new tales, which in his hands would usually be linked to periodical publication. While serving as editor of several Southern journals, he published some of the best stories he had yet written in other Southern or in Northern journals, and he also functioned as an active, articulate member of the New York-based Young America circle, a group informally headed by Evert Duyckinck that included Melville and Poe. Throughout much of the forties, the adherents of Young America argued passionately for an indigenous literature based on native materials. Their arguments formed part of their protracted battle

8. William Gilmore Simms to James Henry Hammond, *Letters*, 1: 271.

with members of the Knickerbocker set, who insisted that American writers should imitate British authors. Duyckinck, who was an editor for the powerful publishing firm of Wiley and Putnam, knew that the tales of planters, Native Americans, African Americans, and pioneers that Simms was assembling for *The Wigwam and the Cabin* aptly illustrated Young America's literary-political stance. Hence he secured Simms's work—along with Poe's *The Raven and Other Poems* (1845), Melville's *Typee* (1846), and Nathaniel Hawthorne's *Mosses from an Old Manse* (1846)—for publication in Wiley and Putnam's "Library of American Books," an important series that was part of a larger series, the "Library of Choice Reading." Not surprisingly, given Simms's well-established reputation, *The Wigwam and the Cabin* was warmly praised by readers in America and abroad. The reviewer for *Godey's Lady's Book*, for example, commended the "beauty and grace" of its narratives, and a London critic called "Grayling"—the first tale in the volume—the "best ghost-story of modern times."[9]

Twentieth-century readers may find Simms's *Wigwam and Cabin* stories prolix even by nineteenth-century standards, so a brief explanation of their publication circumstances is in order. It was common throughout much of the antebellum era for short-story collections, like novels, to be issued in two volumes. In order to attain the requisite number of pages for a two-volume format, Simms was forced to expand much of the short fiction he had published in magazines when he assembled it for book publication. This often overlooked fact helps explain the length of such tales reprinted here from *The Wigwam and the Cabin* as "Oakatibbe," which evolved through several versions from a story of a few pages to the present full-length narrative.

In the tales reprinted here from *The Wigwam and the Cabin*—"Grayling," "The Two Camps," "The Last Wager," "The Arm-Chair of Tustenuggee," and "Oakatibbe"—Simms draws more heavily upon his extensive knowledge of the South than he had done in his previous volumes of stories. At one point, in fact, he considered calling the collection *Tales of the South*, a phrase that became the subtitle of at least one edition of the book. He sets his narratives in the parts of the region he knew best, treats the stages of its history with which he was most familiar, and shapes his central characters to represent different

9. Review of *The Wigwam and the Cabin*, *Godey's Lady's Book*, 31 (December 1845): 271; the London reviewer is quoted in *Letters*, 2: 107 n. 317.

racial, ethnic, and social groups. He constructs his tales in a manner that enables him to stress both the ordinary world of work and domesticity and the realm of legends, visions, dreams, and folk experience that had occupied him since the beginning of his career.

For "Grayling" and "The Two Camps," Simms devises an introductory or outer narrative, essentially realistic in emphasis, that he contrasts with a central, more important tale in which he emphasizes the power of supernatural or visionary experience. In the outer narrative, he portrays the concerns of educated characters or indulges in authorial commentary about his subject. In the inner story, he examines the experiences of less educated characters with the supernatural. For "Grayling," this method of construction allows him to contrast the rationalistic attitudes of his educated figures with the ostensible superstitions of his uneducated ones—to the distinct advantage of the latter. The tale's framing narrative is largely autobiographical, based upon an experience of Simms's youth. Its central characters, likewise autobiographical, are a boy-narrator, his grandmother, and his father. The grandmother tells a tale set immediately after the Revolutionary War, in which the leading figure, the young backwoodsman James Grayling, has a vision of the ghost of a murdered friend. The father provides elaborately rationalized (and wordy) philosophical explanations of the experience. But Simms's narrator makes plain his own sympathies, meanwhile attempting to influence the reader's, by insisting, "I continued to believe in the ghost, and, with my grandmother, to reject the philosophy." Similar to "Grayling" in its emphasis on visionary experience is the frame narrative "The Two Camps," whose core story is set in eighteenth-century backwoods North Carolina. After an introduction describing epoch and region, Simms has his leading figure, woodsman Daniel Nelson, tell in vivid dialect a tale of warfare between whites and Native Americans that is complicated by rivalry within a tribe and further complicated by the attraction between Nelson's daughter Lucy and the tribal prince Lenatewá. Central to Nelson's account is his arresting supernatural vision of Lucy in captivity many years before the event actually occurs. In this story, as in "Oakatibbe," Simms acknowledges through his characters the problem of racial amalgamation and ratifies, somewhat reluctantly perhaps, the conclusions that white antebellum culture had already sanctioned.

Like "Grayling" and "The Two Camps," the story called "The Last Wager, or The Gamester of the Mississippi," has an autobiographical base. And as in those stories so in this one Simms contrasts the firmly grounded realistic details of his outer narrative with the extravagant turns of his central tale. In the first of two introductory sections, he discusses the connections between truth and fiction, his theories of literary genres, and his view of the relationship between author and reader. In the second section—as prelude to the inner story and also as validation of its ominous events—he describes in detail his travels in the 1820s through "the then dreary and dangerous wastes of the Mississippi border." The central story, presumably one Simms himself had heard, is narrated by settler Bill Rayner, who describes how he acquired his wife Rachel through a series of card games carefully orchestrated by Rachel's guardian, Mr. Eckhardt. Among the striking features of the tale are the contrast between Rayner's backwoods dialect and Eckhardt's educated speech, the mournfulness of Rachel's dark beauty, the central role gambling plays and has played in Eckhardt's relationship with his ward, and the sober, and sobering, conclusion. Throughout "The Last Wager," Simms nicely modulates tonal qualities across tragedy, humor, realism, and suspense.

The other *Wigwam and Cabin* narratives reprinted in *Tales of the South* reveal Simms's keen interest in Native Americans as well as his skill in portraying them in both mythic comic and realistic tragic modes. In "The Arm-Chair of Tustenuggee," a light-hearted tale with sinister undercurrents, he weaves together two strands of material that derive from well-established strains in folklore. One strand centers on the superstition, already mentioned in connection with "Logoochie," that spirits can inhabit trees; the other involves a man who is hounded by a shrewish wife. Reflecting the two strands, the story has two levels, one mythic, the other domestic—Simms connecting the levels by his emphasis in each upon male figures who are married to unpleasant women.

Contrasting with this humorous story is "Oakatibbe," a serious realistic narrative about the economic and social experiments of Colonel Harris, a planter in the Gulf South who has hired members of the Choctaw tribe to work alongside his slaves in picking cotton. In the story, which like other narratives in *The Wigwam and the Cabin* is partly autobiographical, Simms explores the differences between Native American and white culture, contrasts the admirable Oakatibbe with the dishonest Loblolly Jack, and emphasizes the unfortunate fact that his white characters, despite their efforts to aid the Native Americans, have ultimately no power to alter tribal laws.

By 1850, five years after the publication of *The Wigwam and the Cabin*, the market for long fiction had improved, and Simms had therefore returned to the production of novels. But because the economics of professional authorship remained uncertain, he continued to produce the varied kinds of writing he had trained himself to do in what he had called the "begging times for authordom" of the 1840s.[10] During the fifties, he published a number of books that, taken together, constitute his most impressive achievement in letters. Among these books are four novels about the Revolutionary War—*Katharine Walton* (1851); *The Sword and the Distaff* (1852; reissued as *Woodcraft* in 1854); *The Forayers* (1855); and *Eutaw* (1856); a romance of Spanish America, *Vasconselos* (1853); two lively satiric novels about Charleston, *The Golden Christmas* (1852) and *The Cassique of Kiawah* (1859); two plays; several short novels; a collection of poetry; and two collections of short fiction, *The Lily and the Totem* (1850) and *Southward Ho!* (1854). *The Lily and the Totem*, an intriguing experimental volume, contains lightly fictionalized historical narratives about French Huguenot settlements in Florida that are loosely linked by chapters in which Simms summarizes significant historical events. Because the narratives are closely connected to the chapters of summary, they do not readily lend themselves to anthologizing. Neither do the tales in *Southward Ho!*, which Simms called a "Southern Decameron"[11] designed for the Christmas gift-book market. His narrative centers on a number of people, including figures based on Evert Duyckinck and Simms himself, who while traveling by steamboat from New York to South Carolina amuse crew members and fellow passengers by telling tales.

"Ephraim Bartlett," one of several fine tall tales by Simms in this volume, was published in Evert Duyckinck's magazine *The Literary World* in 1852 and apparently was not collected in book form until 1974, when it appeared in *Stories and Tales*, a volume in the Centennial Simms textual edition issued by the University of South Carolina Press. Like some of *The Wigwam and the Cabin* stories it is a frame narrative, and the fact that it first appeared in a Northern journal is pertinent to both the frame and the inner story. In the frame, Simms-

10. William Gilmore Simms to George Frederick Holmes, *Letters*, 1: 425.

11. William Gilmore Simms to Evert Augustus Duyckinck, *Letters*, 3: 314.

as-cicerone instructs Northern and Southern travelers in South Carolina about the natural beauty and the many local legends of the state. He bases the inner story on one such legend, which derives from a strain of folk material widespread in nineteenth-century literature about a house haunted by the spirit of its wicked owner. He also uses the inner story to explore the connections among liquor, legend, fantasy, and the supernatural. The title character, a whiskey-loving raftsman "whose case . . . would have staggered the temperance societies," takes part in a lavish dinner party hosted by the spirit of a rich, blasphemous Englishman. As in "Grayling," Simms manages to have his realistic cake while eating his supernatural pie. Ephraim's story is so detailed and lively that readers are tempted to believe it. Yet they are rarely allowed to forget the fact that, as Ephraim's servant slyly reminds him, it is his constant drinking that apparently precipitates his vision of the supernatural.

During the later 1850s and the 1860s, Simms experienced many tragedies, including the deaths of friends and family members, plantation debts, illness, and poverty, that tested his fortitude, obscured his renown, and diminished his productivity—without, however, impairing his ability to construct effective, amusing, and highly imaginative tales. During the nearly twenty-seven years of their marriage, Chevillette had borne him fourteen children, only five of whom lived to adulthood. Particularly tragic for Simms the family man were the deaths of two favorite young sons from malaria on the same day in 1858, the loss of a son and daughter during 1861, and the sudden death of Chevillette from appendicitis in 1863. Making matters worse—or at least no better—for Simms were the loss of his close friends and political advisors, James Henry Hammond and David Flavel Jamison, in 1864. (Hammond had been a prominent state and national politician and Jamison the president of the South Carolina Secession Convention.)

Of more drastic consequence for Simms's literary career were the facts that the Civil War severely harmed the sale of books, especially in the South, and that throughout the four years of the conflict Simms was unable to travel North to superintend his publishing interests. Both during and after the war he was forced, as he ruefully told correspondents, to take whatever contracts he could secure and to write at a furious pace in order to support his family. The unstable economic circumstances in the book market during the 1860s forced him to serialize four pieces of long fiction, *Paddy McGann* (1863), *Joscelyn*

(1867), *The Cub of the Panther* (1869), and *Voltmeier* (1869), in Southern or Northern journals. Given the precarious financial conditions for book publication, it is scarcely surprising that the sixties were the only decade of Simms's adult career during which he failed to issue a collection of stories. Yet even as he tried to rebuild his literary fortunes while suffering from declining energy and ultimately fatal illness, he produced what was perhaps the best work of his life in the tall tales "How Sharp Snaffles Got His Capital and Wife" and " 'Bald-Head Bill Bauldy' "—the first published posthumously in *Harper's Magazine* in 1870, the second remaining in manuscript until 1974 when it appeared in the Centennial Simms edition.

For the setting, characters, and plots of "Sharp Snaffles" and "Bill Bauldy," which yield impressive evidence of his genius in Southern frontier humor, Simms drew upon a trip he had made during the late 1840s with a group of professional hunters in the Appalachian mountains of North Carolina. Both tales are based upon yarns he had heard from the hunters, and both are embellished with folk material he had picked up on the trip as well as in travels throughout his life in the Southern countryside. The occasion for both tales is the hunters' Saturday Night Lying Camp, a weekly ritual at which truth is prohibited and fantasy encouraged. Both are frame narratives, and both combine two persistent elements in antebellum Southern humor, the homely realism of the domestic story and the fabulous flights of the tall tale.

Simms achieves this mixture in "Sharp Snaffles" by yoking the frontier courtship yarn to the tale of a magical hunt. He achieves it in "Bill Bauldy" by grafting a story of failed courtship and military malingering upon a narrative of an enchanted underwater realm peopled by half-human alligators. In "Sharp Snaffles," the title figure and his fiancée, Merry Ann Hopson, represent true love, perseverance, and common sense, whereas John Grimstead, Sharp's rival for Merry Ann, and Squire Hopson, her father, represent the calculating world of materialism and financial gain. That for the inner story of "Sharp Snaffles" Simms wove together three persistent elements in folklore—the wonderful hunt, the man borne into the air by geese, and the man pulled from a hollow tree by a bear—has been shown by scholars.[12] That it is folklore tending toward myth is indicated by Sharp's vision of the goddess-figure who points him toward his treasure and also by

12. Notably by James E. Kibler, Jr., in "Simms's Indebtedness to Folk Tradition in 'Sharp Snaffles,' " *Southern Literary Journal*, 4 (Spring 1972): 55–68.

the roles played by magic animals in aiding the hero—an action emphasizing the interdependence of the animal and human worlds that is found in most Western myths.

Bill Bauldy, the hero of the second story, is a cook and soldier during the Second Seminole War who like Ephraim Bartlett is a lover of the whiskey bottle. In the story centering on Bill's adventures, Simms emphasizes his own comic treatment of mythic material by deliberately evoking central elements of Homer's *Odyssey*. Among the mythic elements in the story are Bill's magical alligator steed, his visit to the underworld, and his enforced captivity by a powerful, alluring woman—beautiful but deadly—who recalls such figures in literature before Simms as Homer's Circe and John Keats's La Belle Dame Sans Merci. In both "Sharp Snaffles" and "Bill Bauldy," Simms stresses the erotic elements central to myth, folklore, and the Southern humor that derives from them by references to Merry Ann's "stitch of clothing," Bill Bauldy's dalliance with Sarah Grimes, and a soldier's playing "Cock Horse, with a Doodle Doo" with Bill's erstwhile sweetheart, comely Susannah Sykes.

From "The Fisherman" and "Logoochie" to "Sharp Snaffles" and "Bill Bauldy," Simms's short fiction sparkles with energy, humor, and charm. It is memorable for its varied subjects, characters, and settings, its comprehensive portrait of antebellum Southern civilization, and its persistent use of legends and folk tales as a means of bringing that multiracial, multicultural civilization alive. Given these merits, the neglect of Simms's tales is puzzling until one reviews the causes: the economic recession in the 1830s and 1840s that crippled the national book market, particularly its Southern wing; the harm done Simms's ability to publish, and consequently his reputation, during the Civil War and its aftermath; and the uninformed criticism leveled by nineteenth- and twentieth-century scholars at Simms's unfortunate attitudes, which of course were the attitudes of many white Americans of his time, toward race. The winds of change are blowing, however, and there is every likelihood that they will continue to rise. The substantial revisionist scholarship devoted to Simms's life and work in recent years together with the growing acclaim for his short fiction bids fair to renew interest in one of the antebellum South's most gifted and also most unjustly neglected authors.

A Note on the Text

There has long been a need for a modern textual edition of Simms's short fiction, but such an edition is costly to produce. Because *Tales of the South* is priced for use in college and university classrooms, I have edited Simms's stories lightly, retaining his long paragraphs while silently correcting such obvious printers' errors as "upou" for "upon." It should probably be noted that conventions of spelling in the early nineteenth century were fluid by twentieth-century standards: a particular printer, for instance, might decide to give such words as "honor" and "favor" the British spellings "honour" and "favour." In *Tales of the South*, I have regularized the spelling of these and similar words to the more familiar American versions. But I have retained Simms's habitual two-word rendition of "any thing," "every thing," and similar expressions.

While on the subject of spelling, I should probably remark that antebellum authors talented in reproducing archaic or dialect terminology knew that "skillful," for instance, might also be rendered as "skilful" or that "scalp" might be spelled as "sculp." When Simms employed, as he frequently did, variant versions of such words, I have retained the variants instead of regularizing them. Frequently, too, Simms or his printers glossed dialect terms by explaining them in parentheses. This practice explains why one finds in several of Simms's stories such constructions as "potetters (potatoes)."

Conventions of nineteenth-century punctuation were also fluid by twentieth-century standards. In Simms's writing, therefore, apostrophes, commas, and semicolons often appear where today's readers do not expect to find them. I have for the most part followed Simms's or his printers' conventions. When contractions such as "didn't," for example, were punctuated "did'nt," I have retained the punctuation.

Six of the stories collected in *Tales of the South* are reprinted from the first editions of volumes published during Simms's lifetime. "Logoochie" is reprinted from *Carl Werner, An Imaginative Story; With Other Tales of Imagination* (1838); "Grayling," "The Two Camps," "The Last Wager," "The Arm-Chair of Tustenuggee," and "Oakatibbe" are reprinted from *The Wigwam and the Cabin*, First and Second Series (1845). Of the other tales, "Juan Ponce de Leon" and "The Plank," which had appeared under different titles in *The Book of My Lady* (1833), are reprinted from *Martin Faber, The Story of a Criminal; and Other Tales* (1837). "The Fisherman" is reprinted from *The Southern Literary Gazette*, a journal Simms helped found and edit. "Ephraim Bartlett," "How Sharp Snaffles Got His Capital and Wife," and " 'Bald-Head Bill Bauldy' " are reprinted from *Stories and Tales*, Volume Five in *The Writings of William Gilmore Simms: Centennial Edition*, ed. John Caldwell Guilds (Columbia, S.C.: University of South Carolina Press, 1974). I am grateful to the University of South Carolina Press for its permission to republish these tales.

I should perhaps add in conclusion that in the three stories reprinted from the Centennial Simms edition I have retained the conventions of textual editing used there, except when it was necessary to correct obvious errors (such as "you're are") that had somehow slipped through despite the numerous careful proofreadings accorded that volume.

Selected Bibliography

Butterworth, Keen, and James E. Kibler, Jr. *William Gilmore Simms: A Reference Guide*. Boston: G. K. Hall and Co., 1980.

Guilds, John Caldwell, ed. *"Long Years of Neglect": The Work and Reputation of William Gilmore Simms*. Fayetteville, Ark.: University of Arkansas Press, 1988.

Guilds, John Caldwell. *Simms: A Literary Life*. Fayetteville, Ark.: University of Arkansas Press, 1992.

Holman, C. Hugh. *The Roots of Southern Writing: Essays on the Literature of the American South*. Athens, Ga.: University of Georgia Press, 1972.

Hubbell, Jay B. *The South in American Literature, 1607–1900*. Durham, N.C.: Duke University Press, 1954.

Kibler, James Everett, Jr., ed. *Selected Poems of William Gilmore Simms*. Athens, Ga.: University of Georgia Press, 1990.

Parrington, Vernon L. *Main Currents in American Thought*. One-vol. ed. New York: Harcourt, Brace and Co., 1930.

Ridgely, J. V. *William Gilmore Simms*. New York: Twayne, 1962.

Rubin, Louis D., Jr., et al. *The History of Southern Literature*. Baton Rouge, La.: Louisiana State University Press, 1985.

Trent, William P. *William Gilmore Simms*. Boston: Houghton Mifflin, 1892.

Wimsatt, Mary Ann. *The Major Fiction of William Gilmore Simms: Cultural Traditions and Literary Form*. Baton Rouge, La.: Louisiana State University Press, 1989.

Tales of the South

The Fisherman—A Fact

There are few men indeed, who do not at times look forward sanguinely to some friendly interposition of Fortune for a sudden and mighty windfall of wealth, by which the slow process of laboring for it through a course of years may be avoided. Such men are always flattered by some airy nothing or other, into the belief that they are Fortune's special favorites. They depend on the slightest casualties for hopes, and the sternest assurances of truth and reason, (so highly are they wrought upon by their ductile fancies,) are seldom altogether sufficient to awaken them from their dreams.—They never reflect that while they all have the same expectations, these expectations are so lavish and excessive, that but very few of them, if any, can be satisfied, and so they proceed according to the dictates of their several imaginations, to procure them. One man pursues for days the bed of some narrow rivulet, where a grain of gold has been found. He dreams at night of the discoveries of the ensuing day: his head is filled with mines, veins of pure ore, shafts, diggers and miners: his life appears a walking dream, attended by all the phantasmagoria of fortune. He has recourse to the turning of the witch-elm—goes astray from his family at night, with his divining rod, and from the multiplicity of his anticipated discoveries, gathers up some encouragement for a few weeks more of labor, to be defeated at last. In the meanwhile, if he be a farmer or planter, the gradual, but certain support arising from a good crop, has been sacrificed by the weakness of his understanding, in his visionary pursuits, and himself and family exposed to beggary and indigence. It is more than probable, too, that the final overthrow of his hopes produces melancholia, and he either becomes a drunkard or commits suicide. With the same, or a very similar fate is he attended who dreams of sudden fortune by the *lottery ticket.* The merest trifles lead and encourage. If he dreams of a number he buys it the next day—if it proves a blank, he charges some mistake upon his memory, and is satisfied that his fortune intended the very best by him, if his cursed memory had not made him choose a different number. An accidental multiplication of figures, or the appearance, in one or two instances, of a collection of the same numerals, creates the idea of a singular coincidence, which does not occur for nothing. He must have a ticket with the identical numbers. None of these visionaries are ever so hardy as to believe that they will not, some time or other, make a fortune by one or another of these means.

Another mode offers itself to the American dreamer, which is not to be had by the present generation in any other country: the large masses of treasure—plate and jewels—concealed during the troubles of the Revolution by those who have been kind enough to allow themselves to be slain, without making any disclosure of the deposit; as well as the immense wealth affirmed to have been hidden by the Buccaneers who frequented our coast, and made it the hiding-place for their ill-gotten treasure—an additional prospect to such as may have lent themselves to the hope of gaining wealth in lump, without sparing their lives in the humiliating and laborious toil of acquiring it by slow and imperceptible degrees. Wealth, like the dew which falls nightly and noiselessly upon the plants, is seldom seen, except from its effects—the improvement of the plant itself indicates the influence of the silent blessing. A storm would destroy the flower: as sudden and unexpected wealth often overthrows the reason—more frequently the affections and good feelings of men.

I once heard a story related of a poor man, who was affected with many of these dreams of good fortune. He was a tall boy in the Revolution, and born under auspices rather friendly than otherwise: that is to say, he had parents who were in such good circumstances, that they could not think of their dear Tommy becoming either mechanic or tradesman; if he pursued any occupation, it must be some honorable profession; but their innate determination was to make him a gentleman. But how was this to be done? Why, nothing could be *done* towards such an object. The process by which so delightful an end was to be brought about, was to leave *undone* many things which, if he had been made a decent laborer or mechanic, should have been done. He was, in fact, to do nothing: all education was denied him, because, as the sage father gravely said, 'If he (Tommy) be the great genius that I believe him to be, education will be of no use to him; he will be utterly independent of it: if he be a dunce, he does not deserve education; it would only be thrown away upon him.' Left, therefore, to his natural parts, they were very soon decided and developed. Master Tommy very soon bade papa and mamma defiance, ridiculed their authority, transgressed their commands, and did precisely what he ought not to have done, but just what his education had fitted him to do. This conduct, it is true, sometimes worried the good and sagacious parents no little, but then it indicated the spirit and forwardness of the boy—and then there was something so manly in it!—This, however, could not last long. Papa and mamma died at last, as all good papas and mammas are in duty bound to do, and Tommy was left with a few negroes and a small planting interest, which he knew not how to manage, and did not, in fact, care to learn. His parents had always supplied his demands and their own from the plantation, and he could conceive of no reason why it should not be perfectly adequate to his necessities now. About this time, the Revolution took place, and after two years' escape, South Carolina was inundated. Tommy, the gentleman, had got on by mere good luck, (for he bestowed not the slightest care upon his interests, leaving them all to his driver,) and had not dissipated as much as might have been expected of his patrimony. He had, however, made a commencement in habits entirely brought about by idleness. He took his *gin slings* every half hour in the day; his *phlegm-cutter* and *anti-fogmatic* before breakfast, and his *toddy* at bed time. These were the *special* drinks. Independent of these, he had his irregulars, or occasionals, which might be calculated on at the *entree* of a neighbor, his departure, and every five or ten minutes during his stay. The little crops which had been previously made now failed him entirely, and he drew from the bank the little cash which a sometimes considerate parent had put up, as he did his umbrella, for a rainy day. This soon went—his negroes began to grow insubordinate, and on the appearance of the British army in the low country of South Carolina, Tommy, the gentleman, was surprised to perceive one morning early, the whole of his field negroes, with his driver at their head, dressed in British uniforms, and going through the manual. His meditations upon this subject were soon broken in upon, as he beheld them bending their way to the mansion, deeming, no doubt, that the death of a gentleman would do no discredit to their first enterprise. But Tommy thought quite otherwise, and without stopping to have his coat brushed, he made his escape into the adjoining woods, and bent his way to town. He did not run fast enough, however, to avoid seeing his paternal mansion in flames; and with but a small lot of land

and dwelling in the city, Tommy was for the first time struck with the difficulty, as well as the necessity, of getting his dinner. It even troubled him to ascertain how, with the little property he had left, he should be able to make out at all. These afflictions served for the first time in his life to occupy his mind with serious reflection.—He reached town in a very bad humor; sought his town house, got something to eat, and more to drink, and was immediately restored to good humor and his own esteem.

Peace was at length restored, and Tommy's patrimony almost gone. He had been dreaming for some time how he should be able to procure money enough to answer his demands. He had (a particular of which we had forgotten to advise the reader,) taken a wife towards the close of the war, as he did every thing else, without any reflection; had a fine child, without any consideration; and was utterly ignorant of the means by which their support could be obtained. In vain had he dreamed of fortunate chances, luck and so forth: he had failed at all of them, and now wanted bread for his family. One night, as he lay in his bed, cogitating upon the many hopes that afflict the unfortunate, he beheld a grave and dignified figure arise slowly before him, seemingly from the earth. She had a stern, but beautiful expression of countenance. In one hand she bore an oaken branch, covered with leaves—in the other a cup of the lotus. A broad sheet of water, crowned with a star, seemed to encircle her forehead, and her right foot appeared to rest upon a rock. By this, Tommy knew that he was in the presence of nature, the great mother of men. This good lady, after announcing herself with all due decorum, to the awe-struck and wondering destitute, and giving him a long harangue, in the form of a lecture, a trial to which Tommy's own papa and mamma had never gone so far as to subject him, and who now bore it with a very ill and scarcely patient grace, concluded with presenting him with a large and new fishing line, having three decent fish-hooks, properly baited, and all ready for use. This having done, she retired as she came, without taking leave, or seeming to care for it. Tommy was struck, as well he might be, at such a visit, and for a long time, altho' well disposed to confide in its reality, he could not altogether hesitate in believing it a dream—a belief that was entirely discarded in the morning, when, upon leaving his room, the first object he laid his eyes upon, was the identical fishing line which had been given him in the night. It lay upon a high shelf in the library, and had probably been in the service of some old proprietor of the house. Tommy made, however, inquiries as to the *where* and *how* of its origination; but taking the advice in good part, breakfast over, he went off, properly armed and accoutred, upon his new employment. A small fishing-boat was soon procured, and in company with a negro fellow, named Quash, he proceeded out as far as the old hulk of a Dutch logger, which had been sunk during the war, in order to arrest the advance of the British fleet upon the town.

Tradition is altogether silent as to the sport at angling which attended our hero upon the first days of his adventure. It is more than probable that for some time his inexperience in the 'divine art' stood greatly in the way of his success. But this did not greatly distress Tommy. It was not fish that he angled for; it was gold that he sought—large boxes of the precious metal, that by some overruling agency was to become attached to his hooks, and drawn securely by him into his own possession. What fish he caught he either threw aside, made bait with, gave to the negro, or returned to the water. He sometimes ate some of them, cooked by the negro, when hungry, but the idea never entered the brain of the dreamer to carry home his catchings. At last this conduct excited the surprise and observation of his negro companion. He could not conceive the motive which brought Mass Tommy out to catch fish, when he made no manner of use of them. His astonishment increased every day more and more—and from being unable rationally to determine upon the cause of this strange course of conduct, his imagination kindly stepped in, and relieved his mind of many doubts. He was now able to perceive it all. The case was sufficiently clear—the whole mystery elucidated. Tommy was dealing with the devil—was probably the devil himself.—This conjecture threw the poor negro into a fit of despair. How should he atone for the association which for so long a time he had held with his dangerous companion! How escape the torments of the wrath to come! His feelings upon the subject of his apprehensions were still more increased and heightened by a sermon which, during the extremest of his sufferings, he heard from his class-reader. This homily was delivered in the most horribly applicable language.—It came directly upon his late connection with 'Mass Tommy,' but the portion which most affected him ran thus: 'Ah, my poor breddren, yerry de word dat I speak, and gib 'tention. De cloben foot and de long tail is 'side you, dough you no see um. He ten by you night and day, wid a big fishing line in 'e hand, ready for hook your poor spirit, 'fore 'e tef your body. Gib 'tention: 'e hook is bait wid lies and deceptions. Da him dat tan by you on lan and on de water, and he make no bone ob taking you whereber you is,' &c. &c. &c.

Nothing could be more in point—no illustration more clear or satisfactory, and the mind of the wretched negro, though torn and distracted by his close connection with the great master of evil, was sufficiently cool to make one determination—not to go fishing again with the devil. It is true, he reasoned with himself, I have but little to do, and get well paid for doing little. The fish I sell, thought he, pays my wages, and gives me enough to eat; besides, I receive something every Saturday night in silver, which passes very well: nobody refuses to take it, and it feels heavy; but then it all comes from the devil. When, thought the distracted African, did good come out of evil: it was in vain to think it. If I get good by my labors to-day, ten chances to one but to-morrow I get a double portion of evil. Thus deliberating, his fears very soon got the better of his desires. The struggle was, however, maintained for a long time by his sense of the pecuniary interest which his body would necessarily sacrifice for the good of his soul. He thought long upon the money at Saturday night—the good fish which in saleable strings it was his work of an afternoon to hawk through King-street, to the internal delight of good old landladies who loved late suppers—he no longer perceived the salutation smile of his good spouse Dinah, on his entry into the kitchen with the unsold string, still floundering in his tray: he saw all these evils at a glance, and for a long time was in doubt whether such productive employment could be considered devilish; but the spiritual triumphed over the worldly man, and Quash left off fishing. Tommy, the gentleman, did not exactly know how to account for the defection of his attendant, and for a long time found it difficult to procure a proper substitute. This he did, however, and pursued, as before, his novel and ill-directed employment. The same surprise was excited by his occupation in the mind of his new assistant, which before surprised and terrified his countryman. Sambo (for that was the name of Tommy's new assistant,) was soon observed by the watchful Quash in the employ of his late master; and being acquainted, an opportunity was not long wanting, in order that a mutual communication and comparison of notes might be made. Selling his lot of fish one Saturday evening in town, the two Africans met, and after mutual civilities Quash began:

'Well, Sambo, you taking bizness, enty? All de harm I wish you, my boy, is dat you no come to wusser sport dan you hab now, my fren.'

'I tank you, brudder, de same to you. But what make you talk so 'bout Mass Tommy?'

'Me talk 'bout Mass Tom!' said Quash hastily, and turning as pale as the soot of his complexion would permit; 'God forbid! Me nebber talk 'bout em 'tall.'

'You seem scare, brudder; you must know someting; let's yearres what you hab for say, for ole time sake,' said Sambo in return, something alarmed by the evident fear and terror with which his companion appeared so suddenly assailed.

Quash. (with a significant gesture, pointing to his feet,) Buckra man no hab cow-heel.

Sambo. Dat true. Who da say 'e hab?

Quash. (pointing to his head) Buckra man no hab horn like goat.

Sambo. Well, who da say 'e hab?

Quash. (putting his hand familiarly and significantly on the shoulder of his companion,) Sambo, *Old Harry* hab horn an hoof.

Sambo. You no say so?

Quash. I say so, for true. Take my word: look 'pon dis fish; you call 'em sheephead, a'nty?

Sambo. To be sure;—what him but sheephead?

Quash. Ah, Sambo, t'ant sheephead, t'ant fish; 'tis all cheat. Look at me, brudder. What make me leff Mass Tom, as you call 'em, you tink?

Sambo. 'Cause you choose to, I 'spose.

Quash. Berry true: tak my word, and choose yousef.

In much the same manner the dialogue continued, until Sambo was finally and completely satisfied that he had been working for no less a person than the devil, and came to be acted upon in much the same manner, and by a similar course of reflection, as influenced the determination of his quondam friend. To give up so lucrative a business as that which he at present pursued, was not the desire, however, of Sambo; and some further arguments were deemed necessary to his conversion. His interest being the principal obstacle in the way, it was only necessary that he should lose nothing by the change. Accordingly, a lucky chance led them both to express their regrets at being obliged to give up a pursuit so productive as that lately held;—and it came to be a question, why they should not unite their labors and fortunes in that profession which, in company with gentleman Tommy, they had both declined. They formed a co-partnership, and the next day saw them in a boat of their own, and steering along past that in which sat the astonished and wondering form of Tommy, the gentleman. To overhaul them, and ascertain the cause of their connection, by which he was like to suffer, was the first impulse of our hero.—Seeing his approach, the trembling Africans changed the direction of their skiff, and lusty sinews plied their way, without waiting to respond to the numerous halloos of their late master, to the city they had left; satisfied that the spiteful devil would no longer permit any laborers in the same vineyard, who did not join interests with himself.

This singular conduct perplexed and astonished our hero; but as he was not apt to let any thing occupy his attention over long, he dismissed it from his thoughts, and returned with redoubled diligence to his pursuit. He had now less need than before of an attendant. He found out how to scull the little boat he used in his employment, and he had made some discoveries, which he thought better known only to himself. For several days his hook had become attached to a heavy something, which he always lost hold of by a variation of position. His hooks had sometimes been broken—at others bent and strained, and at other times had brought up splinters of wood. He provided himself, however, with some stronger and longer hooks, and at length perceived that they were strongly attached to something of considerable weight below. This, with some difficulty, he was enabled to draw from its secret abodes. It was a small square box, tightly hooped with iron, and fastened with screws. He scarce contained himself for joy. Concealed in the bottom of the boat, and beneath his cloak, he pursued his way to town. He entered the city half beside himself, with the excess of his emotions. He had scarce penetrated midway to his dwelling, when he felt himself tapped upon the shoulder. He turned, and in the unwelcome intruder he beheld a sheriff's officer, who pleasantly informed him that he was in his custody, and marched him deliberately off to jail. Nothing could equal the indifference of gentleman Tommy to this event. He flattered himself that all he had to do was to open the box, and satisfy the debt. Ushered into a low, dark room, fenced in by iron bars, and studded with but few windows, he called authoritatively for hammer and chisel. They were brought him, and the gaolor retired. The box was opened in an instant. The gaolor in a little while returned. He called to Tommy, but received no answer—looked in, and to his surprise beheld the gentleman suspended by his own line from a beam that ran across the apartment. On the bed lay the box, broken open, at the bottom of it lay a large book, much saturated with water, open at the title-page. It seemed to be written in low Dutch characters. Tommy was cut down, but life had utterly departed. A note to his wife had these words:

'Dear Nell—By hook and line—let me have a tombstone, stating the place of my birth, and that I was a Southern planter. I leave the book to our neighbor Jansen, the tinplate worker: he will probably understand it. Do as you please, however. Kiss Malvina for me. Good bye.'

Thus terminated the adventures of a gentleman. The widow did not give the book to her neighbor Jansen, but in course of time, gave herself. The volume, upon occasion being referred to, proved to be more valuable than had been supposed. Large amounts, acknowledged and payable by the Bank of England, presented themselves to reward the meritorious. Had the laziness of the gentleman permitted him to turn the leaves of the water-soaked volume, he had lived. Nature wished no drones, however, and made him but an instrument for the benefit of others. In the prominent labors of his life, and the manner of his death, gentleman Tommy had made use of the same utensils—*the hook and line.*

Juan Ponce de Leon

I

The lover of Spanish story is not likely to forget that of John Ponce of Leon. The American reader should not be ignorant on the subject. The narrative has charmed the one often and over; it should be no less familiar, even if less charming, to the other. His story is a rich one for the romancer—the moralist may also gather no little for "grave saw" and sage apothegm from its consideration. His narrative,—the boldness of his achievements, in Old and New Spain alike, have won for him no small share of that renown which, at one period, the Spanish cavaliers seemed to have divided among themselves to the exclusion of all other nations. To those who are at all conversant with the stirring period in which he lived, there is no danger of that oblivion, in his case, which has shadowed the greatness of so many of his contemporaries. Irving, with a pen that charms wherever it touches, has furnished us with a very pleasant and interesting sketch of his life, the perusal of which will amply compensate for the idle hour which it employs; and, though differing greatly from that distinguished writer in his estimate of the *character* of the Spanish adventurers, who seem to us to have been a pack of the greatest scoundrels that ever lived, we are not unwilling to derive our interest from a source from which we never hope to gather many lessons.

Ponce de Leon, like Basco Nunez, was rather a better gentleman than the greater number of his neighbors. He was neither so brutal nor so reckless as the rest, though quite as great a rogue; and, as a knight of romance, we find him fulfilling, to the card, all the dues and duties of the courts and codes of chivalry in its most elevated periods. He was a cavalier after the best fashion, and did no discredit to his order. He was brave and daring to a proverb—strong in person, fiery in spirit—true to his affections—earnest in his devotions—a lover of valorous deeds for valor's sake, and fond of the sex, as became a distinguished disciple in the schools of that gallantry which made woman a goddess or a creature, according to the fancy and caprice of a most unprincipled order, whom a long period of warfare had made vicious and licentious to the last degree. It may not be necessary, however, to dwell longer upon this head; for, I take it, these things are quite as well known to my readers as to myself. I only propose to tell them what Irving has omitted, and which they could not so readily have hunted up for themselves.

II

The wars of Granada had now for some time been over—the Moors expelled for ever the delicious country in which their elysium had, perhaps, been quite too much entertained; and but for the strife and wild adventure which followed the unveilment of the New World to European eyes, the whole kingdom of Spain would have fallen into a most unseemly, and, at that period, unnatural and unbecoming quiet. The hum and hurry of war had ceased to keep awake the cities; and the spirit-stirring blast of the trumpet gave way at nightfall to the gentle, and more delicate, and seductive notes of the guitar—

> "At evening, by some melancholy maid,
> To silver waters."

Knighthood, if not positively unfashionable, began to be somewhat cumbersome, at least; and, if the coat of mail did here and there continue to be worn by the warrior more solicitous of former than of present times, it was not unfrequently concealed by the vestment of gorgeous and embroidered silk. In fact, the entire nation, even at the moment of its greatest glory and true regeneration, had begun to adopt that peculiar languor of habit, the consequence of a sudden flood of prosperous enterprise, which, in after times, when a superabundant wealth provided them with the means of a boundless and luxurious indulgence, has made them a very by-word and a mockery among the nations. This condition of the national character was not then perceptible, however; certainly not to themselves, and perhaps not to the surrounding powers; and the repose in which the nation lay had become particularly irksome to those brave adventurers who looked to carve out their fortunes with their weapons. "The world was their oyster;" and with them the thought, if not the speech, of ancient Pistol, must have been of favorite and frequent application. Peace was not only inglorious, but unprofitable; and the discovery of America was a Godsend quite as necessary to the kingdom of Old Spain, in ridding it of the excess and idle population made by the sudden termination of its protracted warfare, as in extending its dominions and increasing its treasures.

Though fully as renowned as any of the brave spirits of his age and country for every accomplishment of arms, and every requisite of adventure, Ponce de Leon did not, however, at this time, take part in the new crusade for the conquest of the Indian regions. There were, indeed, sundry good and sufficient reasons why such a step would be unnecessary, and might have been imprudent. Ponce was now getting rather old—he had been fighting the good fight for his king and his faith, from boyhood up, against the infidels, and quite long enough to render unquestionable his loyalty to both. Beyond all this, however—although we shame to say it of so brave a knight, yet the truth had better be known than not—Ponce had of late suffered some strange sensations of weakness in regard to a certain capricious damsel, the daughter and only heir of a neighboring Castellan—or, as it now runs, Castilian—a knight of the noblest stock, who could, without any interregnum, trace his genealogical tree, in all its branches, from a time equally beyond man's memory and the deluge. Some may find, also, a sufficiently good reason for the supineness of our hero in the fact of his being now well to do in the world. He had been any thing but a loser in the wars; had been at the sacking of not a few among the Moorish cities: and the spoils thus acquired had been well employed, and with no sparing hand, to enrich and adorn a couple of fine castles on the marches, which the liberality and favor of the queen had committed to his keeping. These, perhaps, were each and all of them strong enough, as reasons, why he should not any more adventure his life for gain or glory. But his amour, his new passion—the feeling which swallowed up all others—had got completely the better of the knight's understanding; and he did nothing but think, talk, and dream, from morning till night, and night till morning, of the beautiful but capricious Leonora D'Alvarado. It was a "gone case" with Don Ponce; and he now had more barbers and friseurs in his pay than he ever knew in his young days, or should have known in his old. But all in vain—the loves of our knight were unfortunate—the course of true love did not run smoothly with him. Leonora was quite too young, beautiful, and wealthy, not to be most fashionable, and most fashionably capricious and coquettish. She laughed at the old knight, made merry with his awkwardnesses, ridiculed his gallantries, which, indeed, did not sit particularly well upon him; and, with much hardness of heart, denied him her attention whenever he sought to be very manifest with his. She was a gay and wild creature; and with so much grace and winningness did she play the despot, that, while the old knight absolutely shrunk and trembled beneath her frown, he loved still more the tyrant, and became still more deeply the victim of the despotism. It was, as we have already remarked, a gone, and, we regret to add, a hopeless case, with our hero. Nor was it with him alone, we do her the justice to say, that the wanton baggage so toyed and trifled. She had a thousand admirers, all of whom she treated and trampled upon in like manner—feeling, and never hesitating to make use of her power, without pause or mercy, till some cut their own throats or the throats of one another, while she, who made all the mischief, cut each of them in turn. No sooner, however, did one array leave the field, than another came into it—such were her attractions—the new-comers destined, however, to experience like treatment, and be driven away in turn by other victims. She was indifferent to the fate so hourly experienced; and many are the epithets of indignation and despairing love which they bestowed upon her; song, sonnet, sigh, and serenade, alike failing to find in her bosom a single accessible or pregnable point; and knight after knight came and saw, and went away hopelessly in his chains.

III

Don Ponce was not one of those who so readily despair. He had sat down too often before the Moorish castles, from one year's end to the other, not to have acquired certain valuable lessons from patience, which stood him in stead in the present strait; and, looking upon the conquest of the lady in question, and with much correctness of analogy, as not unlike those to which, in the Moorish wars, he had been so well accustomed, he concluded that, though he might be able to do nothing by sudden storm, he certainly could not altogether fail of success in the course of a regular blockade. The indefatigable patience and perseverance of the besieger, he well knew, not unfrequently wore out both these qualities in the besieged; so he sat down before the fair fortress, and regularly commenced his approaches.

Never kept besieging army so excellent a watch. Ponce was, and had been at all times, an excellent general; the Moors had taught him the nature of strategy, and he taught it to his retainers. They knew their duty, and did it. Not a messenger entered the castle of the beleaguered damsel that was not overhauled. He permitted no succor to be thrown into the walls, and the unfortunate waving of a handkerchief from any of the lattices did not fail to bring out the whole array of the beleaguering force, ready to put to death any auxiliar, or arrest any supplies that might be going to the succor of the besieged.

At length, all his outworks having been completed, his own courage roused to the sticking-point, the preparations for a final attack made perfect, and believing that his antagonist would now be willing to listen to reason, our knight sounded a parley, and the fair defender of the fair fortress readily, and without pause or seeming apprehension of any kind, gave him the desired interview.

Nothing, of course, could have been more delightfully pleasant or pacific. The knight, as had been his wont on all great and trying occasions, appeared in full armor; and the damsel, conscious of her true strength and the legitimate weapons of her sex, wore, Venus-like, her own graces, set off and exquisitely developed by the voluptuous freedom of the Moorish habit.

As there was now no necessity for any farther delay, the preliminaries having been well passed on both sides, our hero began. Half dignity, half despair, he made a desperate exposition of his case. He described his love, its inveteracy and great irritability, in moving language; now in prose, now in verse, and all in the spirit of that artificial period when love wore wings and worshipped sunbeams, and chivalry carried a lyre in one hand and a lance in the other, ready, in the event of a failure on the part of either, to supply its place with a more faithful auxiliar—for it was not unfrequently the case, that the fair but fickle damsel, having bidden defiance to the persuasive melodies of the first, was borne away triumphantly by the discords and terrors of the last.

Don Ponce was terribly eloquent on the present occasion. Never amorous knight more so. He narrated all his endeavors at her attainment; his labors, more numerous and magnificent than those of Hercules; he detailed at length, and with no little glow in the way of coloring, his various visitations by day, long watchings by night in the perilous weather; described the curious presents, procured at infinite trouble and expense, solely for her gratification; the thousand and one new songs made purposely in her honor, and at his instance, by the most celebrated minstrels, several dozen of whom he kept in pay solely for the purpose. He then proceeded to describe the honors of his state, his great wealth, substance, dignity, and so forth; and, with all due modesty, he referred to the noise and notoriety of his deeds of arms, and the fame, name, and glory which he had thereby acquired. He dwelt with peculiar force and emphasis upon the nature of the establishment, which, upon marriage, he designed her; and, with much, and in the eye of the maiden, tedious minuteness, entered upon an enumeration at large of the manifold sources of delight and comfort which such an event would necessarily occasion—particularly to her. Having, by this time, exhausted all his *materiel* of speech, he wisely determined upon coming to the point; and, in a fine string of verse prepared for the occasion, and rounding off his speech admirably, as the distich is made to do the scene in the old English drama, he concluded by making her the offer of his hand, heart, and substance, little expecting that, after all said and done, such a young maiden should still have the hardihood to refuse. But so she did. Looking archly in his face for a few seconds, she placed her slender and beautiful fingers upon the few small specks of grizzly hair that still condescended to adorn his temples, and laughingly exclaimed—

"Why, bless me, Don Ponce, at your years, how can you talk of such a matter? You are quite bald, and so wrinkled, that it's wonderful to me how you can possibly think of any thing but your prayers."

This was answer enough, in Heaven's name; and, boiling with indignation, yet full of undiminished ardor and love, the worthy knight hurried home to his castle, immersed and buried in the utmost despair and tribulation.

IV

The indifference, not to say ill treatment, of Donna Leonora, was not enough, however, to efface from the mind of our hero the many deep impressions which it had imbibed in favor of that capricious beauty. The very sportiveness of her rejection, while it necessarily increased, could not fail, by the seductiveness of her peculiar manner, in lightening its severity; at least, it gave an added charm to her loveliness in the grace of its expression. He now thought more of the coquettish creature than ever; and the apprehensions—indeed, the now seeming certainty of her loss—threw him into a fever, which was, of course, duly and professionally heightened by the great number of his attending physicians.

The Sangrado principle was at work upon him, and, but that the fates had determined he should be preserved for better things, he had ceased to join in the good cheer of his table, and gone with Polonius, not to eat, but to be eaten! It was on the fourth or fifth day of his malady, history is doubtful which, that, in a moment of interval from pain, his servants brought him intelligence of one below, in the guise of a mariner, who desired sight of his highness, and the royal representative in those parts, the most mighty, and valorous, and wise Don Juan Ponce de Leon, chief of unnumbered titles, and doer of unnumbered deeds, &c. Though not surprised by the application, for Don Ponce was an officer of the king, the knight felt some strange anxieties to see the stranger, for which he could not precisely account; and he did not hesitate, accordingly, to command his appearance.

The new-comer was a Portuguese mariner, seeking permission from the knight, as the king's representative in that section, to make recruits for properly manning his caraval from the province of the knight. He proposed, as was greatly the fashion at that time, to make certain new discoveries on the western continent—the new world which Columbus, a little while before, with unexampled generosity, "gave to Castile and Leon," and which, with still greater generosity, they accepted at his hands. In addition, however, to the lands, and savages, and gold, the articles commonly enumerated among the promises of these adventurers, our Portuguese, reviving an old tradition of his people, pledged himself to the discovery of the far-famed fountain, to the waters of which was ascribed the property of conferring perpetual youth upon those who drank of them.

It had long been a prime article in the fancies of the Portuguese, that such a fountain existed somewhere in the Indian seas; and the singular success attending the enterprise of Columbus, at its time of conception regarded as so visionary, now inspired a large degree of credence in every story, however monstrous or extravagant. Our mariner spoke with singular confidence as to the localities of this fountain, and so very accurately did he describe the features of the spot in which it was to be found, with such a lavish degree of poetical illustration, not to say poetical justice, that, on a sudden, Don Ponce, to the surprise of all about him, who before thought him on his last legs, found himself perfectly restored.

He leaped from his couch, embraced the tarry Portuguese with most unqualified affection; and three of four of his attending physicians happening, most unfortunately for them, at that moment to make their appearance, he gave orders to trundle them from the walls of his castle, in company with all the pills, potions, and purges by which they were usually accompanied; an order, we need not add, almost as soon executed as given. Congratulating himself, with unalloyed pleasure, upon his new acquisition, our hero, to the surprise of everybody, determined upon a voyage of discovery, in proper person, to the newly-found continent.

"I will find these glorious waters, this fountain of youth; I will surprise, I will win this proud lady; I will get rid of this ill-favored complexion, these trenches, this miserable apology for hair."

Such were the broken exclamations of Don Ponce.

"Where's Don Ponce going?" asked the impertinent.

"What's that to you?" said the knight; and, having made a visit P.P.C., he left the sight of the sneering beauty, entered his vessel, and the sails, under a favoring breeze, loomed out gloriously and auspiciously in a balmy atmosphere, as they bore the old veteran, but young lover, in search of the heretofore hidden fountain of perpetual youth.

V

Years had now rolled away, and the world very well knows, or ought to know, that Don Ponce de Leon, after many mishaps, disasters, and delays, discovered the object of his want and search somewhere in the fertile wildernesses of Florida. It answered all his expectations, and had the desired effect upon his form. He grew, upon drinking from it, straightway comely and strong in person and buoyant in mind: and, though tolerably well supplied with the latter characteristic, being already excessively warm and ardent in his temper and affections, his joints grew more supple than ever, and he could feel his blood articulating in his veins perpetually, to the tune of the then new and popular, but now old and unpopular *areyto* of "Oh, 'tis love, 'tis love," &c. The stream, however, which caused all this change in the moral and animal man, was quite a small one; and its virtues having soon made themselves manifest, it only served to supply the first comers, and has been dry to all succeeding. A single draught was quite enough for all his purposes; and, perfectly satisfied with the measure of success which attended his adventure, Don Ponce began again to direct his attention to his native country. He thought of his broad, bright fields, and of his vineyards, and his retainers, and his castles; and then he thought of Donna Leonora, and her fields, and her retainers, and her castles, and all her other charms, personal and contingent; and, so thinking, he commenced his return.

But this was no easy matter. He had to fight his way through troops of naked Indians, and wild woods, and wicked briers, and swamps, that left him half naked; now losing his way, and almost despairing to find it again; now exposed to perils from savage men, and to temptations from savage women; such, indeed, as frequently led his chivalry into singular adventures, and nameless and paralyzing difficulties. But he surmounted them all; as how, in reference to his new acquisitions, could he do otherwise? He had taken, as it were, a bond from fate for life. The gray hairs had fallen from his brow, and had been succeeded by others of a less equivocal complexion, and in less limited quantity. The wrinkles had left his cheek, the dimness his eye; his step was no longer enfeebled and uncertain; he felt himself quite as young as when, in the vigor of his boyhood, he had wrestled with a romping maid of Andalusia, and was not overthrown.

VI

He stood once more, after an interval of many years, upon the deck of his caraval; and, as he proceeded over the mighty waste of waters that lay between him and the land of his nativity, his thoughts grew more than ever active and lively—his spirit more anxiously aroused as to the condition in which he should find all things upon his return. His chief apprehension, however, grew out of his affair of the heart. Should the beautiful Leonora have become the bride of another—and was all his personal beauty to be left upon his hands? This was a damning difficulty, and all in vain did he seek to wrestle with, and to avoid, the reflection. It grew but the stronger as he approached the shore; and when, at his castle's entrance, he put the question to an old retainer, and hastily demanded to know that which his heart yet trembled to learn, how was he rejoiced to hear that all was safe, all as when he had left her, and the capricious damsel quite as open to conviction as ever. He paused at his castle—such was his impatience—but to arrange his habit before intruding himself upon her.

"If," said he, "my gray hairs, my wrinkled face, my infirm gait, were really her objections before, she can no longer entertain them. I will wed her on the spot—she cannot, she dare not, she will not resist me!"

VII

Thus manfully determined, our hero appeared in the halls of his neighbour Castellan, the father of the lady, and, with a view of present prospects, so likely to become the father of the knight. Their meeting was hearty—it could not well be otherwise, though it took the old gentleman some time to understand how Don Ponce could get young while he himself got old. The grateful mystery of his transformation once explained, however, and all matters went well afterward. He did not waste more time upon the father than a proper courtesy actually called for; but, the first proprieties over, hurried, with all a lover's agony of impatience, to the bower in which he had been taught to understand his mistress awaited him. What a moment of delightful anticipation—what funds of love in store—what raptures and felicitations at hand! He was on the threshold—he was in the presence. There she stood—the same sylphlike form, the same figure of consummate symmetry. But why veiled? He rushed valiantly forward, fell upon one knee before her, and oh, unlooked-for condescension, she sank into his arms!

He did not hesitate for a moment; but, tearing away the thick folds of the envious veil, he proceeded to impress upon her lips the kiss of a love so fond, so long treasured with a perfect fidelity—when he beheld—not the Leonora he had left—not the beauty of her girlhood—not the creature of exquisite delicacy and youthful fragrance, that queened it over a thousand hearts—but a superannuated and withered damsel, of wrinkled face, starched features, and lips to which kisses of every kind appeared to have been strangers for a marvellously long season. Don Ponce had never remembered that the term of years employed by him in gaining, was spent by her in losing, both youth and beauty. Nor in this error was our knight alone. To all of us, no changes are so surprising, none certainly so ungracious and painful, as those of the young, and delicate, and gentle, under the hand of time and changing circumstances. Fifteen years had done much for our hero, but much more for our heroine. He could not believe his eyes.

"Nay, lady, there is some mistake here, surely," said he, releasing himself partly from his burden. "I came to see the beautiful Donna Leonora D'Alvarado."

"And I am she, most noble knight—the same Donna Leonora to whom your heart was so perfectly devoted," simpered out the now gracious coquette.

"I must see Don Guzman," said he; "I must learn the facts in this matter;"—and, flying out of the presence of his goddess with far more rapidity than he had ever flown into it, he appeared before the sire of the ancient beauty.

VIII

"Don Ponce, where are you going?" said the old man.

"Home, Don Guzman," said the young one.

"Why this hurry—does my daughter refuse? If she does, Don Ponce, be assured that in your favor I shall constrain her inclinations," was the warm and friendly decision of Don Guzman.

"Not for the world!" was the reply of our hero, "not for the world; and hark ye, Don Guzman; the truth may as well be said now as at another time. I no longer find your daughter as I left her. I am quite too young for her, I perceive. Pray permit me to send, for her use and your own, a bottle of water, which I took from a certain fountain in India. I can assure you that it will do you both great good—you both stand very much in need of it."

Tradition does not say whether the water thus furnished had any effect upon the fair Leonora. One old chronicle insinuates that she brought her action for a breach of promise against the young knight, but failed to recover. The point is apocryphal, however. He, we know, returned to America, and, after losing an eye in a fight with the Indians, and experiencing many other vicissitudes, died of chagrin, from many disappointments, as well in concerns of ambition as in those of love; "without," says the legend from which we borrow our narration, "without losing a single beauty of that youth so marvellously vouchsafed him by Providence, in the discovery of that wondrous fountain in the wildernesses of Florida."

The Plank
A Story of the Sea

I

It was on a pleasant day in the middle of September that I received a grateful intimation from the captain of the Three Cherubs of his intention to sail immediately. My passage in that smart little vessel, for a distant port, had been engaged a week or ten days before. We had been nearly that time delayed on account of wind and weather; and, though still loath, as is natural enough to young travellers, to leave home for the first time in our lives, yet, on the present occasion, the hurrying call of our captain had something in it of a pleasurable relief. There is no bore in the world to the young worse than that of delay when they are ready for a movement, and our impatience at waiting had been such as would have readily reconciled us to a longer voyage, and a more protracted absence from home, than any of us at that time contemplated. The anxiety to be away prompted instant obedience to the requisition of our captain, and but little time was required to complete my preparations. In the course of two hours I was on board, bag and baggage, and an hour had not elapsed before the little swallow-like packet was under weigh, with outspread wings, and rapidly flying from land. All things seemed auspicious—the skies were clear, blue, and beautiful. No shadowing speck lurked like an angry danger on the edge of the horizon; and hope promised us a pleasant voyage, and a speedy return to the anxious friends whose hands and handkerchiefs still waved their adieus; and with fond eyes we still watched the crowded wharves of our native city, now fast melting away in the distance. We were soon far from land, and nothing but the broad ocean, and the curtaining sky, and our own thoughts and feelings, was left us for consolation and survey.

II

There were three of us. We were not only young, but young travellers. Neither of us had seen more than twenty years,—neither of us had ever been before to sea. It was equally a marvel and a mystery to all; and our common inexperience had the effect of bringing us together in a more close communion. We were soon conscious of our mutual dependence, and felt accordingly the necessity of good humor on all hands. This understood, we prepared, each of us, to do the best for the common good and gratification. Thus resolved, it was not difficult to make our little world tolerably comfortable. The sea exacted its dues, and the first day passed slowly, but without our consciousness of any thing but the penalties we were called upon to pay. The next day we were all better, and resolute to make the most of our narrow limits. Every voyager for the first time will readily imagine our employments. We rambled here, there, and everywhere, from the cabin to the caboose; tried to make ourselves familiar with sea-dogs and sea-terms—made the acquaintance of the cook, and listened to one or two long yarns from that important person. In this way we got through a couple of days with tolerable satisfaction. We were now fairly at sea. The land-breeze, with the delicious fragrance of the pine forests, reached us no longer. The plane of ocean was level no longer. Its very voice was changed. The waves grew more elaborate, and seemed to swell up with a greater degree of buoyancy. Broad billows, whose ridges seemed like the backs of tossing giants in some agonizing sleep, bore up our little bark upon their mighty bosoms; then, suddenly shrinking away, left us to struggle and plunge in their deep hollows, until, with like caprice, others of greater weight and volume came to our relief, lifting us in like manner aloft, to leave us again below. Space and density, in glorious contrast and comparison, were all at once before us, in the blue world of vacuity hanging and stretching above, and the immense, seldom quiet, and murmuring mass, spread out below it. The land no longer met our eyes, though strained and stretched to the utmost. The clouds came down and hung about us, narrowing the horizon to a span, and mingling gloomily with the surges that kept howling perpetually around us, growing at each moment more and more threatening and restless. Not a speck beside our own little vessel was to be seen amid the wild infinity, which, admirably consorted, was at once beneath, above, around, and about us. Three days went by in this manner, with scarcely any alteration in the monotonous character of the prospect. Still the weather was fine—the clouds that gathered between, formed a shelter from the intensity of the tropical sun, and, in that warm region and season, were not less a luxury than a relief. But, towards the evening of the third day out, there was a hazy and blood-red crown about the sun as he sank behind the swell in our front—a chiding and increasing motion of the black waters rushing impetuously forward to the wild cavern into which he descended. The wind freshened, and took to itself a melancholy and threatening tone, as it sang at intervals among the spars and cordage; and, while it continued of itself momentarily to change its burden, appeared, with a fine mystery, to warn us of a yet greater change in the aspect and temper of the dread elements all clustering around us. The old seamen looked grave and weatherwise, and shook their heads sagaciously when questioned about the prospect. The captain strode the deck impatiently and anxiously, giving his orders in a tone that left little doubt on my mind of a perfect familiarity on the part of the ancient *voyageur* with the undeceptive and boding countenance of sea and sky. Night came on, travelling hurriedly, and cloaked up in impenetrable gloom. The winds continued to freshen and increase; and but a single star, hanging out like hope, shot a glance of promise and encouragement through the pitchy and threatening atmosphere. The prospect was quite too uncheering to permit of much love, or many looks, on the part of fresh-water seamen. By common consent we went below, and, ransacking our trunks, were enabled to conjure up a pack of cards, with which, to the no small inconvenience of our captain, we sought to shut out from thought any association with the dim and dismal prospect we had just been contemplating. He did not, it is true, request us to lay aside our amusement, but he annoyed us excessively by his mutterings on the subject. He bade us beware, for that we were certainly bringing on a storm. He had seen it tried very often, he assured us, to produce such an effect, and he had never known it fail. His anxiety brought us the very amusement for which he was unwilling we should look to such a devilish instrument as a pack of cards. We had not needed this to convince us that the seaman was rather more given to superstition than well comported with the spirit of the age. He was a Connecticut man, thoroughly imbued with blue-laws, Cotton Mather, &c., and all the tales of demonology and witchcraft ever conceived or hatched in that most productive of all countries in the way of notions. He lectured us freely and frequently upon his favorite topic, on which much familiarity had even made him eloquent.

We encouraged him in his superstition, and derived our sport from its indulgence. Believing fervently himself every syllable he uttered, he could not understand our presumption in doubting, as we sometimes did, many of the veracious and marvellous legends of New-England and the "Sound," which he volunteered for our edification; and when at length convinced of the utter impossibility of overthrowing what, no doubt, he conceived our damnable heresy, he appeared to resign himself to the worst of fates. He evidently regarded each of us as a Jonah, not less worthy of the water and whale than our prototype of old; and, I make not the slightest question, would have tumbled us all overboard, without a solitary scruple, should the helm refuse to obey, or the masts go by the board. His stories, however, I am free to confess for myself, and, I may say, for my companions also, however our philosophy might be supposed to laugh at the matter, had a greater influence upon all of us than we were willing to admit to one another. Upon me, in particular, the impression produced was peculiar in its character. Not that, for a single moment, I could persuade myself, or be persuaded by others, that the mere playing of any game whatever could bring down upon us the wrath of heaven, or hatch a fiendish form upon the deep; but, naturally disposed to live and breathe only in an element of fiction and fantastic change, I drank in every thing savoring of the marvellous with an earnest and yielding spirit. He seemed to have been born and to have lived all his life in the "witch element." He had stories, moved by this agency, of every section of the world in which he had sojourned or travelled. Had seen the "old boy" himself, in the shape of a black pigeon, in a squall off the capes of Delaware; and once, on the night of the 27th June, had himself counted the phantom ships of the British fleet, under Sir Peter Parker, as they were towed over the bar of Charleston, in South Carolina, to the attack of Fort Moultrie. What seemed to vex him most of these things was, that the Carolinians, whom he pronounced a most obstinate and unmanageable race, refused to believe a word of the matter.

But his favorite legend, and one which he believed as honestly as the best authenticated passage in Scripture, was that of the "Flying Dutchman," who was driven out of the German Ocean; and in process of time, and for some such offence, was doomed to a like travail with the wandering Jew. This identical visionary he had seen more than once, and on one occasion had nearly suffered by speaking him. It was only by dint of good-fortune and bad weather that he escaped unseen by that dreadful *voyageur*, to be noticed by whom is peril of storm, and wreck, and utter destruction. It was of this dangerous sail he had now to warn us. We were told that this sea, and almost the very portion which we now travelled, was that in which the Dutchman, at this season, usually sojourned for the exercise, with more perfect freedom, of his manifold vagaries—a power being given to him, according to our worthy captain, for the due and proper punishment of those who, when his spirit was abroad upon the waters, dared to palter and trifle in idle games, sport, and buffoonery. The voyager evidently apprehended much; and, as the gale freshened, his countenance grew more gloomy, and his words were more importunate in reference to those levities and sports which we had fallen into. To pacify him, at length, we forbore our game, and were compelled accordingly to refer to other resources for the recreation we required at such a time.

III

This was no easy matter. Books are dull and difficult things at sea. We tried them, and they soon tired us. Conversation flagged, and we gave it up as soon. We lacked the continual provocation of society to afford us the materials for chat. What were we to do? The question was soon answered; and, with the warm confidence of youth, and forming, as it were, a little community of our own, we determined to relate the story of our several lives. There is no narrative of a life, however short or humble, if related truly and without constraint, which may not be made to interest and instruct the hearer; and our narratives, though void of morbid and romantic interest, were nevertheless more agreeable to us, circumstanced as we were, than the books, written by wise and ingenious heads, which we had often conned before. The story which most pleased and interested me was that of the youngest of our trio. His name was Hubert. He was but nineteen; a tall, slender, graceful youth, eminently handsome in face, possessed of a mind highly taught, and naturally intelligent, and warmed with a spirit at once modest and vivacious. His story was a simple and common one. His manner of telling it, and his earnestness and simplicity of character, gave it the interest which attracted me to him. He was deeply enamored of a maiden of his own age, who requited him with a corresponding love. They were engaged to be married upon his return; and he spoke of his engagement with so much ardor and devotedness, and dwelt with so much hopeful impatience upon the appointed period of his return, that I could have hugged him to my own heart for his whole-souled attachment. He gave us a picture, drawn by a vivid imagination, of the charms of his mistress, narrated the whole history of his fears and hopes, his subsequent avowal of his flame, the approving sanction with which she listened, and the bright prospect which, a few months distant, was to crown, and hallow, and realize all their mutual hopes. I need not say that we were equally communicative. I had no love narrative to unfold, but I had my hopes, my fears, my fortunes. We kept each other awake until a late hour, and retired to dream over what we had heard and related.

IV

That night, in a dream, a singular vision came to my imagination—a vision so much mingled up with the truth, that, in the confusion of my sleeping thoughts, I could not disentangle their united threads, and draw the line of demarcation between the opposing provinces of fact and fancy. Night lay upon the ocean before me—her sable bosom heaving with a tumultuous motion, while the winds were rushing through the white foaming tresses of her hair. A sullen moaning came from the deep abysses, and then a dreadful shriek as of a thousand demons in the agony of a hopeless conflict. Suddenly, the deep opened yawningly before me—the dark bosom of Night seemed to be parted; and, from the wide cavity, a vast volume of uprushing flame swelled and dilated until it covered all the seas upon our track. When, in its diffusion, the light became somewhat subdued, I beheld a terrible form, vague, dark, and imperious in its attributes and its expressions, and, in my thought, I at once knew this dreadful presence to be that of the spirit of the storm. Feebly could mortal tongue describe the terrors of that remorseless spectre; but, as I surveyed, my heart throbbed convulsively, the cold drops of sweat stood like heavy beads upon my clammy forehead, and the hairs upon my head, each endowed, at that moment, with a life and feeling of its own, rose upright in the cold apprehensions which assailed me. While I gazed, other spectres, no less terrible than the first, ascended from the deep abysses, and gathered in attendance upon their chief and master. The whole scene was before me, with all the regularity and method of a melodrame. I saw the demon glare with his meteor eye; I beheld him point with his bony finger; and the awful tones of his voice, though uttered in a foreign language, by a strange intuition, I was at that moment permitted to comprehend.

"Go," he cried, to the forms that glowered and gathered obediently, but in frowns, around him.

"We go, mighty Onesimarchus," was the reverential reply.

"Haste to yon riding hull; it has a victim. Look on its inmates—mingle in with their slumbers—follow the thoughts through their minds—examine the hopes in their hearts, and see if they scorn Onesimarchus."

And with the words there was a general rush of wings, and for a while I saw them around me. A heavy slumber seemed then to possess me, and I was conscious of whispers in my ears—of inquiries proposed to me, and so beguilingly, that I answered as freely as to my best friend, telling all the hopes, and thoughts, and desires of my bosom. When the slumber passed away, I looked once more upon the broad ocean. The terrible demon still sat rocking upon his billowy throne, and lo! one of the returning attendants, who had been despatched for our examination, now stood before him.

"Thou has done?" said Onesimarchus.

"I serve," was the reply.

"What know'st thou?"

"I found one who served thee, mighty Onesimarchus. In the wide world he is alone, yet he is serving thee. He has thoughts of fame and glory. He dreams of conquest. Man's honors glitter before his mind, and he schemes for power. He would sway beyond his sphere, and he must therefore serve thee. I left him still dreaming of empire and a field of strife."

"Let him dream on," exclaimed the exulting demon; "let him work out his dream by daylight. The phantom in his mind shall be still a phantom, though it hurries him to excess in my service. He shall live that he may labor against his proper life, and only awaken to know what his madness hath been when he is lost for ever. He hath chosen his curse—he shall enjoy it."

Scarce had he dismissed the one follower, when a second returning spirit appeared before him.

"And thou?" said the demon.

"I have served thee well."

"What is he whom thou hast seen?"

"A wretch, whose sleep, though troubled, was unbroken, while he dreamed of wealth, of mighty hoards concealed from the rest of mankind, but to him revealed in secret. I left him toying with uncounted millions—gold and jewels, the wealth alike of the city and of the mine, were spread out before his gloating eye, and show the nature of the hopes which rule within him."

"No more," cried the demon, still exultingly. "No more—he too shall live—he labors in my service. How pleasant is it to behold man toiling for the unstayed enjoyment of excess, which is almost the only foe to his perfect happiness. The miser shall not perish—he shall live to enjoy his gains—he shall have all the life and happiness that his narrow and base soul is willing to give himself."

The second spirit disappeared, and a third stood in his place. His reply to the question of his superior was not equally satisfactory with that of his predecessors.

"I sought," he said, "the spirit of a youth—of one whose hopes are few and humble, who asks but little from life, and has no aim which is not easily attainable by the pure and simple minded. Without ambition, he possesses content; without asking for much, he has more than he desires. He is happy in few friends—in fond relations, and he loves, and is beloved by, a maiden having a spirit formed to mate with his own, and requite his love, while confirming him in his pursuits. Returning to his native land for the consummation of his heart's best hope of happiness, he dreams even now that he is upon the threshold of that maiden's home. A disguise conceals him, and he designs to surprise her sweetly with his unlooked-for presence. That cottage in which she dwells contains at this moment the highest object of his ambition, the dearest object in his regards."

"Back and awake him!" cried the demon, in a voice of thunder. "Awake him to the truth. His feet never shall press the threshold of that cottage. Awake him, that he may be no longer blessed with even the dream of happiness. He shall feel the venom of that tooth, which gnaws away the joy from the hope, and leaves a skeleton in its place. Then let him perish. How should he dare thus hope to escape from the allotted curse; pluck joy, as a blessed fruit, from the withered trees of Eden, and thus defraud the destiny which has made him mine? Let him perish. Let the rest live. They serve me in their aims and hopes. They serve me as they gain their wishes,—they die, daily, yet part with no breath—and wake, from their hourly struggles with death, to more acute pain and agonizing life. But he!—Let the maid he loves watch by the seaside—let her start, as on her sharpened ear falls the approaching footstep. She shall see him no more. Her hope is in her dreams. Her love is mine—mine only. Away! The victim is chosen."

V

That victim was Hubert—the youth whose story had so much interested me. I knew it even as the demon spake, and I saw it afterward. Suddenly, when the conference was over, the storm, which had somewhat subsided while it was in progress, was again renewed, and with a tenfold fury. The ready and attending demons each sped away upon his task of terror, and I beheld them approach the ship in which I lay with a feeling of awful horror, that unnerved my faculties and silenced my speech. In a thousand vague but dreadful shapes they assailed us. With their boisterous blows they beat upon the sides of our bark, shattered the cordage, rent the sails, and finally assailed the masts, which they warped and bent, and finally snapped, as if they had been reeds. Methought, as was natural enough, our crew and passengers, in despair, were all assembled upon deck. It was then that I fixed my eyes upon Hubert; he seemed to anticipate his fate, which was not long delayed. A heavy sea came bounding over us, in the billows of which I beheld some terrible and huge forms inwrap themselves. When we recovered from the shock, and the seas had subsided, I no longer beheld the chosen victim among us. The demon had got his prey, and had departed. I awakened from this dreadful dream with awfully exciting sensations. These sensations were not diminished, as I found that the storm which threatened us, as we were about to retire the night before, had burst upon us in reality. That dream had a fearful aspect of truth, to my eyes, in the first glance which I took of the morning prospect. It was a picture of the sublime—fearfully beautiful in its sublimity. I shall never forget the awful splendor—the dreadful, the gorgeous magnificence of the scene. I had not looked for ten minutes before the gale had increased to such a degree as would permit us to hang out but a miserable rag of sail, and the vessel, almost under her bare poles, was driving down upon and through the black and boiling waters. Nothing was now to be seen but the great deep, the vast and ponderous bulk and body of which groaned with its own wild and ungovernable labors. Horrible abysses opened before us—monstrous and ravenous billows rushed after us in uncouth gambols. Mountains gathering upon mountains, clustering and clashing together, threw up from the dreadful collision tall and spiry columns of white foam; which, keeping their position for a few seconds, would rush down towards us like so many demons of the sea, bestriding the billows, and directing their furies for our destruction. Under such impulses we drove on with a recklessness fully according with the dread spirit that presided over the scene which I had witnessed in my vision of the preceding night; at one time we darted through the waters, occasionally rushing beneath them; then, emerging at another, and throwing off the spray that shone upon the black and terrific picture in a contrast as grotesque as the tinsel ornaments upon the robe of a tyrant in the thick of a battle or at the execution of thousands. On a sudden our course was arrested by a mountain of water, under which our vessel labored. She broke through the impediment, however, with a fearful energy. Another sea came on, which we shipped, and the bark reeled without power beneath the surging and swelling mass. The picture of my dream was now dreadfully renewed. I was thrown from my feet, and seized with difficulty upon the side, the water rushing in volumes over me. Again our vessel sprung up and righted, but with a shock that again lost me the possession of my hold. At that moment a shriek of agony pierced my ears; and immediately beside me, a passenger, one of my companions, torn from his hold, was swept over the side into the unreturning ocean. He passed but a foot from me in his progress to the deep. How terrible was his cry of death—it will never pass out of my memory! He grasped desperately at my arm as he was borne along by me. He would have dragged me with him to death, but I shrunk back; and his look—the gleam of his eye—its vacantly horrible expression, will never leave me. The vessel rushed on unheeding; and I saw him carried off by the waves buoyantly for many yards in her wake before he sank. He called upon Heaven—I heard his prayer—and the winds howled in his ears, and the waters mocked his supplications. Down he went, with one husky scream, that the seas half stifled—and the agony was over. That cry brought a chilling presentiment to my heart. Despair was in its tones to all. Though I seemed to live under a like influence, there was a degree of strange recklessness even in our scrupulous captain, for which I could not, and indeed did not, seek to account. I felt assured we could not long survive. Our vessel groaned and labored fearfully; her seams opened, and the waters came bubbling and hissing in as if impatient of their prey. Still she went on, the violence of the storm contributing to the buoyancy of the billows, and aiding her in keeping afloat. But amid all this rage and tumult, this strife of warring and vexed elements, there was yet one moment in which they were under a universal calm—one awful moment, afforded seemingly by the demon who had roused the tempest, that we might be enabled adequately to comprehend our situation. The feeling in this extremest moment was the same with all on board, without exception; and one unanimous prayer went up to Heaven.

VI

The calm was but for a moment. The winds and the waves went forth with redoubled violence and power. There seemed an impelling tempest from every point of the compass. Suddenly, a broad and vivid flash of lightning illuminated the black and boiling surges, lingering upon them sufficiently long to give us a full prospect of the scene. Immediately in our course came on a large and majestic vessel. She had no sails, but pursued a path directly in the teeth of the tempest. She came down upon us with the swiftness of an eagle. Her decks were bare, as if swept by a thousand seas—we were right in her path—there was no veering—no change of course—no hope. The voice of the captain rose above the tempest—it had a horror which the storm itself lacked. It spoke of the utter despair which was the feeling with all of us alike. "The Flying Dutchman," was all he could say, ere the supposed phantom was over us. I felt the shock—a single crash—and crew, cargo, vessel, all were down, crushed and writhing beneath its superior weight, struggling with, and finally sinking beneath, the exulting waters. But where was she, the mysterious bark that had destroyed us—gone, gone! no trace of her progress except our broken fragments—our sinking hopes.

VII

There had been no time for preparation or for prayer. The fatal stranger had gone clean over, or indeed through us; and, though sinking myself, it appeared to me that I could see her keel, with a singular facility of optical penetration, cutting the green mountains behind me with the velocity of an arrow. Around me, scattered and sinking with myself, I beheld the fragments of our vessel, together with the struggling atoms of our crew and company. Among these, floating near me on a plank, I recognised the fair and melancholy features of young Hubert. I had thought him lost for ever. Where had he been in all the interval since the sea we shipped had swept him overboard? I felt myself sinking, and seized upon him convulsively. The plank upon which he rested veered about, and grasping it firmly, I raised my body to the surface. He felt conscious of its inadequacy to the task of supporting both of us, and strove to divert its direction from me. But in vain! Neither of us could prove capable of much, if any, generosity on such an occasion, and at such a time! Our grasp became more tenacious; and while death and desolation, and a nameless horror, enveloped every thing in which we were the sole surviving occupants, we were enemies, deadly and avowed enemies—we who had exchanged vows of the warmest friendship—to whom our several hopes and prospects had been unfolded with a confidence the most pure and unqualified—we sought each other's destruction as the only hope in which our own lives could repose. He appealed to me with tears—spoke of the young girl who awaited him—the joys that were promised him by the future—the possibility of both of us surviving if I would swim off to a neighboring spar, which he strove to point out to me. But I saw no spar; I felt that he strove to deceive me, and I became indignant with his hypocrisy. What was his love to me? I laughed with a fierce fury in his face! I too had loves and hopes, and a wild ambition, and I swore that I would not risk farther a life so precious in so many ways. My dream was surely about to be realized in the most fearful manner.

VIII

The waters seemed to comprehend our situation—a swell threw us together, and our grasp was mutual. My hand was upon his throat with the gripe and energy of despair; his arms, in turn, were wound about my body. I strangled him. I held on, with a demon's clutch, till all his gaspings, all his struggles, and every pulsation, had entirely ceased. My strength, as if in close correspondence and sympathy with the spirit that prompted me, seemed that of a demon. In vain did he struggle. Could he hope to contend with the fiend of self, that nerved and corded every vein and muscle of my body? Fool that he was—but such was not his thought. He uttered but a single name—but a brief word—throughout all our contest. That name was the young girl's who had his pledges and his soul—that word was one of prayer for her and her happiness; and I smiled scornfully, even in our grapple of death, at the pusillanimity of his boyish heart. I had aspirations too, and I mocked him with the utterance of my ambitious hopes. I told him of my anticipated triumphs; I predicted my own fame and future glory, and asked him the value of his worthless life in comparison with mine. He had but one answer to all this, and that consisted in the repetition of the beloved one's name. This but deepened my phrensy, and invigorated my hate. Had he uttered but one ambitious desire—had he been stimulated by one single dream of glory or of greatness, I had possibly spared his life. But there was something of insolence in the humility of his aim that provoked my deepest malignity. I grappled him more firmly than ever, and withdrew not my grasp until, by a flash of lightning, I beheld him blacker than the wild waters which were dashing around us. I felt the warm blood gush forth upon my hands and arms from his mouth and nostrils, and he hung heavily upon me. Would the deed had not been done! Would that I might have restored him—but the good spirit came too late for his hope and for my peace! I shrunk at last from my victim. I withdrew my grasp—but not so he. The paroxysm of death had confirmed the spasmodic hold which, in the struggle, he had taken upon my body. My victory was something worse than defeat. It was not merely death—it was the grave, and its foul associations—its specters and its worms—and they haunt me for ever.

IX

We were supported by the buoyancy of the ocean alone, while under the violence of its dread excitements; and I felt assured that the relaxation to repose of the elements would carry us both down together. Vainly did I struggle to detach myself from his grasp. Freed from one hand, the other would suddenly clasp itself about my neck, with a tenacity only increased by every removal. His face was thrust close into mine—the eyes were lighted up by supernatural fires glaring in my own; while the teeth, chattering in the furious winds, kept up a perpetual cry of death—death—death—until I was mad—wild as the waters about me, and shrieking almost as loudly in concert with the storm. Fortunately, however, I had but little time for the contemplation of these terrors. The agony of long suspense was spared me. The storm was almost over. The plank on which I floated, no longer sustained by the continuous swell, settled, at length, heavily down in its pause; and, without an effort, I sank beneath the waters, the corpse of my companion changing its position, and riding rigidly upon my shoulders. Ten thousand ships had not sustained me under such a pressure. The waters went over me with a roar of triumph, and I felt, with

Clarence, how "horrid 'twas to drown." Even at that moment of dread and death, the memory of that vivid picture of the dramatist came to my senses, as I realized all its intensely fearful features in my own fate. What was that fate? The question was indeed difficult of solution, for I did not perish. I was not deprived of sense or feeling, though shut in from the blessed air, and pressed upon and surrounded by the rolling and yet turbulent waters. For leagues, apparently, could I behold the new domain in which I was now, perforce, a resident; the cold corpse still hanging loosely, but with a firm grasp, about my shoulders. I settled at length upon a rock of a broad surface, which, in turn, rested upon a fine gravelly bed of white sand. Shrinking, and sheltering themselves in innumerable crevices of the rocks around me, from the violence of the storm that had raged above, I was enabled in a little time to behold the numberless varieties of the finny tribe that dwelt in the mighty seas. Many were the ferocious monsters by which I was surrounded, and from which I was only safe through the influence of their own terrors. There were huge serpents, lions, and tigers of the ocean. There roved the angry and ever hungry shark—his white teeth, showing like the finest saws, promising little pause in the banquet on his prey. There leaped the lively porpoise—there swam the sword-fish, and galloped the sea-horse. They were not long in their advances. I saw the sea-wolf prepare to spring—the shark darted like an arrow on my path, and, with a horror too deep for expression, I struck forth into the billows, and strove once more for the upper air. A blow, from what quarter I know not, struck the corpse from my shoulders, and was spent upon my head. My body was seized by a power, in whose grasp all vigor was gone, and every muscle instantly relaxed.

X

On a sudden the entire character of the scene was strangely altered. Where was I? What did I then behold? My enemies now assumed a new guise and appearance, and in place of fish, and beast, and reptile, I perceived myself closely surrounded by a crowd of old and young ladies, busily employed with a dozen smelling-bottles, which they vigorously and most industriously employed in application to my nostrils. Instead of a billowy dwelling in the deeps, I was in possession of the large double family pew in the well-known meeting-house. I had never been to sea—had not killed my companion—was not drowned, and hope never to be; but the whole affair was a vast effort of *diablerie*—a horrible trick of the *incubi*, got up by the foul fiend himself, and none other, for my especial exposure and mortification. The old ladies told me I had been trying to swim in the pew; the young ladies spoke of an endeavor to embrace the prettiest among them; the gauntlike, however, most charitably put all down to a spiritual influence; as—*entre nous*—doubtless, it was. So much for taking late dinners with a friend, drinking my two bottles of Madeira, and going to a night meeting, when I should have gone to bed.

Logoochie; or, The Branch of Sweet Water
A Legend of Georgia

I

With the approach of the white settlers, along the wild but pleasant banks of the St. Mary's river, in the state of Georgia, the startled deities of Indian mythology began to meditate their departure to forests more secure. Tribe after tribe of the aborigines had already gone, and the uncouth gods of their idolatry presided, in numberless instances, only over their deserted habitations. The savages had carried with them no guardian divinities—no hallowed household altars—cheering them in their new places of abode, by the acceptance of their sacrifice, and with the promise of a moderate winter, or a successful hunt. In depriving them of the lands descended to them in trust from their fathers, the whites seem also to have exiled them from the sweet and mystic influences, so aptly associated with the vague loveliness of forest life, of their many twilight superstitions. Their new groves, as yet, had no spells for the huntsman; and the Manneyto of their ancient sires, failed to appreciate their tribute offerings, intended to propitiate his regards, or to disarm his anger. They were indeed outcasts; and, with a due feeling for their exiled worshippers, the forest-gods themselves determined also to depart from those long-hallowed sheltering places in the thick swamps of the Okephanokee, whence, from immemorial time, they had gone forth, to cheer or to chide the tawny hunter in his progress through life. They had served the fathers faithfully, nor were they satisfied that the sons should go forth unattended. They had consecrated his dwellings, they had stimulated his courage, they had thrown the pleasant waters along his path, when his legs failed him in the chase, and his lips were parched with the wanderings of the long day in summer; and though themselves overcome in the advent of superior gods, they had, nevertheless, prompted him to the last, in the protracted struggle which he had maintained, for so many years, and with such various successes, against his pale invaders. All that could be done for the feather-crowned and wolf-mantled warrior, had been done, by the divinities he worshipped. He was overcome, driven away from his ancient haunts, but he still bowed in spirit to the altars, holy still to him, though, haplessly, without adequate power to secure him in his possessions. They determined not to leave him unprotected in his new abodes, and gathering, at the bidding of Satilla, the Mercury of the southern Indians, the thousand gods of their worship—the wood-gods and the water-gods—crowded to the flower-island of Okephanokee, to hear the commands of the Great Manneyto.

II

All came but Logoochie, and where was he? he, the Indian mischief-maker—the Puck, the tricksiest spirit of them all,—he, whose mind, like his body, a creature of distortion, was yet gentle in its wildness, and never suffered the smallest malice to mingle in with its mischief. The assembly was dull without him—the season cheerless—the feast wanting in provocative. The Great Manneyto himself, with whom Logoochie was a favorite, looked impatiently on the approach of every new comer. In vain were all his inquiries—where is Logoochie? who has seen Logoochie? The question remained unanswered—the Great Manneyto unsatisfied. Anxious search was instituted in every direction for the discovery of the truant. They could hear nothing of him, and all scrutiny proved fruitless. They knew his vagrant spirit, and felt confident he was gone upon some mission of mischief; but they also knew how far beyond any capacity of theirs to detect, was his to conceal himself, and so, after the first attempt at search, the labor was given up in despair. They could get no tidings of Logoochie.

III

The conference went on without him, much to the dissatisfaction of all parties. He was the spice of the entertainment, the spirit of all frolic; and though sometimes exceedingly annoying, even to the Great Manneyto, and never less so to the rival power of evil, the Opitchi-Manneyto, yet, as the recognized joker on all hands, no one found it wise to take offence at his tricks. In council, he relieved the dull discourse of some drowsy god, by the sly sarcasm, which, falling innocuously upon the ears of the victim, was yet readily comprehended and applied by all the rest. On the journey, he kept all around him from any sense of weariness,—and, by the perpetual practical application of his humor, always furnished his companions, whether above or inferior to him in dignity, with something prime, upon which to make merry. In short, there was no god like Logoochie, and he was as much beloved by the deities, as he was honored by the Indian, who implored him not to turn aside the arrow which he sent after the bounding buck, nor to spill the water out of his scooped leaf as he carried it from the running rivulet up to his mouth. All these were tricks of the playful Logoochie, and by a thousand, such as these, was he known to the Indians.

IV

Where, then, was the absentee when his brother divinities started after the outlawed tribes? Had he not loved the Indians—had he no sympathy with his associate gods—and wherefore went he not upon the sad journey through the many swamps and the long stretches of sand and forest, that lay between the Okephanokee, and the rapidly-gushing waters of the Chatahoochie, where both the aborigines and their rude deities had now taken up their abodes? Alas! for Logoochie! He loved the wild people, it is true, and much he delighted in the association of those having kindred offices with himself; but though a mimic and a jester, fond of sportive tricks, and perpetually practicing them on all around him, he was not unlike the memorable buffoon of Paris, who, while ministering to the amusement of thousands, possessing them with an infinity of fun and frolic, was yet, at the very time, craving a precious mineral from the man of science to cure him of his confirmed hypochondria. Such was the condition of Logoochie. The idea of leaving the old woods and the waters to which he had been so long accustomed, and which were associated in his memory with a thousand instances of merriment, was too much for his most elastic spirits to sustain; and the summons to depart filled him with a nameless, and, to him, a hitherto unknown form of terror. His organ of inhabitiveness had undergone prodigious increase in the many exercises which his mind and mood had practiced upon the banks of the beautiful Branch of Sweet Water, where his favorite home had been chosen by a felicitous fancy. It was indeed a spot to be loved and dwelt upon, and he who surveyed its clear and quiet waters, sweeping pleasantly onward with a gentle murmur, under the high and bending pine trees that arched over and fenced it in, would have no wonder at its effect upon a spirit so susceptible, amidst all his frolic, as that of Logoochie. The order to depart made him miserable; he could not think of doing so; and, trembling all the while, he yet made the solemn determination not to obey the command; but rather to subject himself, by his refusal, to a loss of caste, and, perhaps, even severer punishment, should he be taken, from the other powers having guardianship with himself, over the wandering red men. With the determination came the execution of his will. He secreted himself from those who sought him, and in the hollow of a log lay secure, even while the hunters uttered their conjectures and surmises under the very copse in which he was hidden. His arts to escape were manifold, and, unless the parties in search of him knew intimately his practices, he could easily elude their scrutiny by the simplest contrivances. Such, too, was the susceptibility of his figure for distortion, that even Satilla, the three-eyed, the messenger of the Indian divinities, the most acute and cunning among them, was not unfrequently overreached and evaded by the truant Logoochie. He too had searched for him in vain, and though having a shrewd suspicion, as he stepped over a pine knot lying across a path, just about dusk, that it was something more than it seemed to be, yet passing on without examining it, he left the breathless Logoochie, for it was he, to gather himself up, the moment his pursuer was out of sight, and take himself off in a more secluded direction. The back of Logoochie was, itself, little better than a strip of the tree bark to those who remarked it casually. From his heel to his head, inclusive, it looked like so many articulated folds or scales of the pine tree, here and there bulging out into excrescences. The back of his head was a solid knot, for all the world like that of the scorched pine knot, hard and resinous. This knot ran across in front, so as to arch above and overhang his forehead, and was crowned with hair, that, though soft, was thick and woody to the eye, and looked not unlike the plates of the pine-bur when green in season. It rose into a ridge or comb directly across the head from front to rear, like the war tuft of a Seminole warrior. His eyes, small and red, seemed, occasionally, to run into one another, and twinkled so, that you could not avoid laughing but to look upon them. His nose was flat, and the mouth was simply an incision across his face, reaching nigh to both his ears, which lapped and hung over like those of a hound. He was short in person, thick, and strangely bow-legged; and, to complete the uncouth figure, his arms, shooting out from under a high knot, that gathered like an epaulette upon each shoulder, possessed but a single though rather long bone, and terminated in a thick, squab, bur-like hand, having fingers, themselves inflexible, and but of single joints, and tipped, not with nails, but with claws, somewhat like those of the panther, and equally fearful in strife. Such was the vague general outline which, now and then, the Indian hunter, and, after him, the Georgia squatter, caught, towards evening, of the wandering Logoochie, as he stole suddenly from sight into the sheltering copse, that ran along the edges of some wide savannah.

The brother divinities of the Creek warriors had gone after their tribes, and Logoochie alone remained upon the banks of the Sweet Water Branch. He remained in spite of many reasons for departure. The white borderer came nigher and nigher, with every succeeding day. The stout log-house started up in the center of his favorite groves, and many families, clustering within a few miles of his favorite stream, formed the nucleus of the flourishing little town of St. Mary's. Still he lingered, though with a sadness of spirit, hourly increasing, as every hour tended more and more to circumscribe the haunts of his playful wandering. Every day called upon him to deplore the overthrow, by the woodman's axe, of some well remembered tree in his neighborhood; and though he strove, by an industrious repetition of his old tricks, to prevent much of this desolation, yet the divinities which the white man brought with him were too potent for Logoochie. In vain did he gnaw by night the sharp edge of the biting steel, with which the squatter wrought so much desolation. Alas! the white man had an art given him by his God, by which he smoothed out its repeated gaps, and sharpened it readily again, or found a new one, for the destruction of the forest. Over and over again, did Logoochie think to take the trail of his people, and leave a spot in which a petty strife of this nature had become, though a familiar, a painful practice; but then, as he thought of the humiliating acknowledgment which, by so doing, he must offer to his brother gods, his pride came to his aid, and he determined to remain where he was. Then again, as he rambled along the sweet waters of the branch, and talked pleasantly with the trees, his old acquaintances, and looked down upon little groups of Indians that occasionally came to visit this or that tumulus of the buried nations, he felt a sweet pleasure in the thought, that although all were gone of the old possessors, and a new people and new gods had come to sway the lands of his outlawed race, he still should linger and watch over, with a sacred regard, the few relics, and the speechless trophies, which the forgotten time had left them. He determined to remain still as he long had been, the presiding genius of the place.

V

From habit, at length, it came to Logoochie to serve, with kind offices, the white settlers, just as he had served the red men before him. He soon saw that, in many respects, the people dwelling in the woods, however different their color and origin, must necessarily resemble one another. They were in some particulars equally wild and equally simple. He soon discovered, too, that however much they might profess indifference to the superstitions of the barbarous race they had superseded, they were not a whit more secure from the occasional tremors which followed his own practices or presence. More than once had he marked the fright of the young woodman, as, looking towards nightfall over his left shoulder, he had beheld the funny twinkling eyes, and the long slit mouth, receding suddenly into the bush behind him. This assured Logoochie of the possession still, even with a new people, of some of that power which he had exercised upon the old; and when he saw, too, that the character of the white man was plain, gentle, and unobtrusive, he came, after a brief study, to like him also; though, certainly, in less degree, than his Indian predecessors. From one step of his acquaintance with the new comers to another, Logoochie at length began to visit, at stolen periods, and to prowl around the little cottage, of the squatter;—sometimes playing tricks upon his household, but more frequently employing himself in the analysis of pursuits, and of a character, as new almost to him as to the people whose places they had assumed. Nor will this seeming ignorance, on the part of Logoochie, subtract a single jot from his high pretension as an Indian god, since true philosophy and a deliberate reason, must, long since, have been aware, that the mythological rule of every people, has been adapted, by the superior of all, to their mental and physical condition; and the Great Manneyto of the savage, in his primitive state, was, doubtless, as wise a provision for him then, as, in our time, has been the faith, which we proudly assume to be the close correlative of the highest point of moral liberty and social refinement.

VI

In this way, making new discoveries daily, and gradually becoming known himself, though vaguely, to the simple cottagers around him, he continued to pass the time with something more of satisfaction than before; though still suffering pain at every stroke of the sharp and smiting axe, as it called up the deploring echoes of the rapidly yielding forest. Day and night he was busy, and he resumed, *in extenso*, many of the playful humors, which used to annoy the savages and compel their homage. It is true, the acknowledgment of the white man was essentially different from that commonly made by the Indians. When their camp-pots were broken, their hatchets blunted, their bows and arrows warped, or they had suffered any other such mischief at his hands, they solemnly deprecated his wrath, and offered him tribute to disarm his hostility. All that Logoochie could extort from the borderer, was a sullen oath, in which the tricksy spirit was identified with no less a person than the devil, the Opitchi-Manneyto of the southern tribes. This—as Logoochie well knew the superior rank of that personage with his people—he esteemed a compliment; and its utterance was at all times sufficiently grateful in his ears to neutralize his spleen at the moment. In addition to this, the habit of smoking more frequently and freely than the Indians, so common to the white man, contributed wonderfully to commend him to the favor of Logoochie. The odor in his nostrils was savory in the extreme, and he consequently regarded the smoker as tendering, in this way, the deprecatory sacrifice, precisely as the savages had done before him. So grateful, indeed, was the oblation to his taste, that often, of the long summer evening, would he gather himself into a bunch, in the thick branches of the high tree overhanging the log-house, to inhale the reeking fumes that were sent up by the half oblivious woodman, as he lay reposing under its grateful shadow.

VII

There was one of these little cottages, which, for this very reason, Logoochie found great delight in visiting. It was tenanted by a sturdy old farmer, named Jones, and situated on the skirts of the St. Mary's village, about three miles from the Branch of Sweet Water, the favorite haunt of Logoochie. Jones had a small family—consisting, besides himself, of his wife, his sister—a lady of certain age, and monstrous demure—and a daughter, Mary Jones, as sweet a May-flower as the eye of a good taste would ever wish to dwell upon. She was young—only sixteen, and had not yet learned a single one of the thousand arts, which, in making a fine coquette, spoil usually a fine woman. She thought purely, and freely said all that she thought. Her old father loved her—her mother loved her, and her aunt, she loved her too, and proved it, by doing her own, and the scolding of all the rest, whenever the light-hearted Mary said more in her eyes, or speech, than her aunt's conventional sense of propriety deemed absolutely necessary to be said. This family Logoochie rather loved,—whether it was because farmer Jones did more smoking than any of the neighbors, or his sister more scolding, or his wife more sleeping, or his daughter more loving, we say not, but such certainly was the fact. Mary Jones had learned this latter art, if none other. A tall and graceful lad in the settlement, named Johnson, had found favor in her sight, and she in his; and it was not long before they made the mutual discovery. He was a fine youth, and quite worthy of the maiden; but then he was of an inquiring, roving temper, and though not yet arrived at manhood, frequently indulged in rambles, rather startling, even to a people whose habit in that respect is somewhat proverbial. He had gone in his wanderings even into the heart of the Okephanokee Swamp, and strange were the wonders, and wild the stories, which he gave of that region of Indian fable—a region, about which they have as many and as beautiful traditions, as any people can furnish from the store house of its primitive romance. This disposition on the part of Ned Johnson, though productive of much disquiet to his friends and family, they hoped to overcome or restrain, by the proposed union with Mary Jones—a connexion seemingly acceptable to all parties. Mary, like most other good young ladies, had no doubt, indeed, of her power to control her lover in his wanderings, when once they were man and wife; and he, like most good young gentlemen in like cases, did not scruple to swear a thousand times, that her love would be as a chain about his feet, too potent to suffer him the slightest indulgence of his rambling desires.

VIII

So things stood, when, one day, what should appear in the Port of St. Mary's—the Pioneer of the Line—but a vessel—a schooner—a brightly painted, sharp, cunning looking craft, all the way from the eastern waters, and commanded by one of that daring tribe of Yankees, which will one day control the commercial world. Never had such a craft shown its face in those waters, and great was the excitement in consequence. The people turned out, *en masse*,—men, women, and children,—all gathered upon the sands at the point to which she was approaching, and while many stood dumb with mixed feelings of wonder and consternation, others, more bold and elastic, shouted with delight. Ned Johnson led this latter class, and almost rushed into the waters to meet the new comer, clapping his hands and screaming like mad. Logoochie himself, from the close hugging branches of a neighboring tree, looked down, and wondered and trembled as he beheld the fast rushing progress toward him of what might be a new and more potent god. Then, when her little cannon, ostentatiously large for the necessity, belched forth its thunders from her side, the joy and the terror was universal. The rude divinity of the red men leaped down headlong from his place of eminence, and bounded on without stopping, until removed from the sight and the shouting, in the thick recesses of the neighboring wood; while the children of the squatters taking to their heels, went bawling and squalling back to the village, never thinking for a moment to reach it alive. The schooner cast her anchor, and her captain came to land. Columbus looked not more imposing, leaping first to the virgin soil of the New World, than our worthy down-easter, commencing, for the first time, a successful trade in onions, potatoes, codfish, and crab-cider, with the delighted Georgians of our little village. All parties were overjoyed, and none more so than our young lover, Master Edward Johnson. He drank in with willing ears, and a still thirsting appetite, the narrative which the Yankee captain gave the villagers of his voyage. His long yarn, to be sure, was stuffed with wonders. The new comer soon saw from Johnson's looks how greatly he had won the respect and consideration of the youthful wanderer, and, accordingly, addressed some of his more spirited and romantic adventures purposely to him. Poor Mary Jones beheld, with dreadful anticipations, the voracious delight which sparkled in the eyes of Ned as he listened to the marvellous narrative, and had the thing been at all possible or proper, she would have insisted, for the better control of the erratic boy, that old Parson Collins should at once do his duty, and give her legal authority to say to her lover—"obey, my dear—stay at home, or," etc. She went back to the village in great tribulation, and Ned—he stayed behind with Captain Nicodemus Doolittle, of the "Smashing Nancy."

IX

Now Nicodemus, or, as they familiarly called him, "Old Nick," was a wonderfully 'cute personage; and as he was rather slack of hands—was not much of a penman or grammarian, and felt that in his new trade he should need greatly the assistance of one to whom the awful school mystery of fractions and the rule of three had, by a kind fortune, been developed duly—he regarded the impression which he had obviously made upon the mind of Ned Johnson, as promising to neutralize, if he could secure him, some few of his own deficiencies. To this end, therefore, he particularly addressed himself, and, as might be suspected, under the circumstances, he was eminently successful. The head of the youth was soon stuffed full of the wonders of the sea; and after a day or two of talk, all round the subject, in which time, by the way, the captain sold off all his "notions," he came point blank to the subject in the little cabin of the schooner. Doolittle sat over against him with a pile of papers before him, some of which, to the uneducated down-easter, were grievous mysteries, calling for a degree of arithmetical knowledge which was rather beyond his capacity. His sales and profits—his accounts with creditors and debtors—were to be registered, and these required him to reconcile the provoking cross-currencies of the different states—the York shilling, the Pennsylvania levy, the Georgia thrip, the pickayune of Louisiana, the Carolina fourpence—and this matter was, alone, enough to bother him. He knew well enough how to count the coppers on hearing them. No man was more expert at that. But the difficulty of bringing them into one currency on paper, called for a more experienced accountant than our worthy captain; and the youth wondered to behold the ease with which so great a person could be bothered. Doolittle scratched his head in vain. He crossed his right leg over his left, but still he failed to prove his sum. He reversed the movement, and the left now lay problematically of the right. The product was very hard to find. He took a sup of cider, and then he thought things began to look a little clearer; but a moment after all was cloud again, and at length the figures absolutely seemed to run into one another. He could stand it no longer, and slapped his hand down, at length, with such emphasis upon the table, as to startle the poor youth, who, all the while, had been dreaming of plunging and wriggling dolphins, seen in all their gold and glitter, three feet or less in the waters below the advancing prow of the ship. The start which Johnson made, at once showed the best mode to the captain of extrication from his difficulty.

"There—there, my dear boy,—take some cider—only a little—do you good—best thing in the world—There,—and now do run up these figures, and see how we agree."

Ned was a clever lad, and used to stand head of his class. He unravelled the mystery in little time—reconciled the cross-currency of the several sovereign states, and was rewarded by his patron with a hearty slap upon the shoulder, and another cup of cider. It was not difficult after this to agree, and half fearing that all the while he was not doing right by Mary Jones, he dashed his signature, in a much worse hand than he was accustomed to write, upon a printed paper which Doolittle thrust to him across the table.

"And now, my dear boy," said the captain, "you are my secretary, and shall have best berth, and place along with myself, in the 'Smashing Nancy.' "

X

The bargain had scarcely been struck, and the terms well adjusted with the Yankee captain, before Ned Johnson began to question the propriety of what he had done. He was not so sure that he had not been hasty, and felt that the pain his departure would inflict upon Mary Jones, would certainly be as great in degree, as the pleasure which his future adventures must bring to himself. Still, when he looked forward to those adventures, and remembered the thousand fine stories of Captain Doolittle, his dreams came back, and with them came a due forgetfulness of the hum-drum happiness of domestic life. The life in the woods, indeed—as if there was life, strictly speaking, in the eternal monotony of the pine forests, and the drowsy hum they keep up so ceaselessly! Woodchopping, too, was his aversion, and when he reflected upon the acknowledged superiority of his own over all the minds about him, he felt that his destiny called upon him for better things, and a more elevated employment. He gradually began to think of Mary Jones, as of one of those influences which had subtracted somewhat from the nature and legitimate exercises of his own genius; and whose claims, therefore, if acknowledged by him, as she required, must only be acknowledged at the expense and sacrifice of the higher pursuits and purposes for which the discriminating Providence had designed him. The youth's head was fairly turned by his ambitious yearnings, and it was strange how sublimely metaphysical his musings now made him. He began to analyze closely the question, since made a standing one among the phrenologists, as to how far particular heads were intended for particular pursuits. General principles were soon applied to special developments in his own case, and he came to the conclusion, just as he placed his feet upon the threshold of Father Jones's cottage, that he should be contending with the aim of fate, and the original design of the Deity in his own creation, if he did not go with Captain Nicodemus Doolittle, of the "Smashing Nancy."

XI

"Ahem! Mary—" said Ned, finding the little girl conveniently alone, half sorrowful, and turning the whizzing spinning wheel.

"Ahem! Mary—ahem—" and as he brought forth the not very intelligible introduction, his eye had in it a vague indeterminateness that looked like confusion, though, truth to speak, his head was high and confident enough.

"Well, Ned—"

"Ahem! ah, Mary, what did you think of the beautiful vessel? Was n't she fine, eh?"

"Very—very fine, Ned, though she was so large, and, when the great gun was fired, my heart beat so—I was so frightened, Ned—that I was."

"Frightened—why, what frightened you, Mary?" exclaimed Ned proudly—"That was grand, and as soon as we get to sea, I shall shoot it off myself."

"Get to sea—why, Ned—get to sea? Oh, dear, why—what do you mean?" and the bewildered girl, half conscious only, yet doubting her senses, now left the wheel, and came toward the contracted secretary of Captain Doolittle.

"Yes, get to sea, Mary. What! don't you know I'm going with the captain clear away to New York?"

Now, how should she know, poor girl? He knew that she was ignorant; but as he did not feel satisfied of the propriety of what he had done, his phraseology had assumed a somewhat indirect and distorted complexion.

"You going with the Yankee, Ned—you don't say!"

"Yes, but I do—and what if he is a Yankee, and sells notions—I'm sure, there's no harm in that; he's a main smart fellow, Mary, and such wonderful things as he has seen, it would make your hair stand on end to hear him. I'll see them too, Mary, and then tell you."

"Oh, Ned,—you're only joking now—you don't mean it, Ned—you only say so to tease me—Isn't it so, Ned—say it is—say yes, dear Ned, only say yes."

And the poor girl caught his arm, with all the confiding warmth of an innocent heart, and as the tears gathered slowly, into big drops, in her eyes, and they were turned appealingly up to his, the heart of the wanderer smote him for the pain it had inflicted upon one so gentle. In that moment, he felt that he would have given the world to get off from his bargain with the captain; but his mood lasted not long. His active imagination, provoking a curious thirst after the unknown; and his pride, which suggested the weakness of a vacillating purpose, all turned and stimulated him to resist and refuse the prayer of the conciliating affection, then beginning to act within him in rebuke. Speaking through his teeth, as if he dreaded that he should want firmness, he resolutely reiterated what he had said; and, while the sad girl listened, silently, as one thunder struck, he went on to give a glowing description of the wonderful discoveries in store for him during the proposed voyage. Mary sunk back upon her stool, and the spinning wheel went faster than ever; but never in her life had she broken so many tissues. He did his best at consolation, but the true hearted girl, though she did not the less suffer as he pleaded, at least forbore all complaint. The thing seemed irrevocable, and so she resigned herself, like a true woman, to the imperious necessity. Ned, after a while, adjusted his plaited straw to his cranium, and sallied forth with a due importance in his strut, but with a swelling something at his heart, which he tried in vain to quiet.

XII

And what of poor Mary—the disconsolate, the deserted and denied of love? She said nothing, ate her dinner in silence, and then putting on her bonnet, prepared to sally forth in a solitary ramble.

"What ails it, child?" said old Jones, with a rough tenderness of manner.

"Where going, baby?" asked her mother, half asleep.

"Out again, Mary Jones—out again," vociferously shouted the antique aunt, who did all the family scolding.

The little girl answered them all meekly, without the slightest show of impatience, and proceeded on her walk.

The "Branch of Sweet Water," now known by this name to all the villagers of St. Mary's, was then, as it was supposed to be his favorite place of abode, commonly styled "The Branch of Logoochie." The Indians—such stragglers as either lingered behind their tribes, or occasionally visited the old scenes of their home,—had made the white settlers somewhat acquainted with the character, and the supposed presence of that playful god, in the region thus assigned him; and though not altogether assured of the idleness of the superstition, the young and innocent Mary Jones had no apprehensions of his power. She, indeed, had no reason for fear, for Logoochie had set her down, long before, as one of his favorites. He had done her many little services, of which she was unaware, nor was she the only member of her family indebted to his ministering good will. He loved them all—all but the scold, and many of the annoyances to which the old maid was subject, arose from this antipathy of Logoochie. But to return.

It was in great tribulation that Mary set out for her usual ramble along the banks of the "Sweet Water." Heretofore most of her walks in that quarter had been made in company with her lover. Here, perched in some sheltering oak, or safely doubled up behind some swollen pine, the playful Logoochie, himself unseen, a thousand times looked upon the two lovers, as, with linked arms, and spirits maintaining, as it appeared, a perfect unison, they walked in the shade during the summer afternoon. Though sportive and mischievous, such sights were pleasant to one who dwelt alone; and there were many occasions, when, their love first ripening into expression, he would divert from their path, by some little adroit art or management of his own, the obtrusive and unsympathising woodman, who might otherwise have spoiled the sport which he could not be permitted to share. Under his unknown sanction and service, therefore, the youthful pair had found love a rapture, until, at length, poor Mary had learned to regard it as necessary too. She knew the necessity from the privation, as she now rambled alone; her wandering lover meanwhile improving his knowledge by some additional chit-chat, on matters and things in general, with the captain; with whom he had that day dined heartily on codfish and potatoes, a new dish to young Johnson, which gave him an additional idea of the vast resources of the sea.

XIII

Mary Jones at length trod the banks of the Sweet Water, and footing it along the old pathway to where the rivulet narrowed, she stood under the gigantic tree which threw its sheltering and concealing arms completely across the stream. With an old habit, rather than a desire for its refreshment, she took the gourd from the limb whence it depended, *pro bono publico*, over the water, and scooping up a draught of the innocent beverage, she proceeded to drink, when, just as she carried the vessel to her lips, a deep moan assailed her ears, as from one in pain, and at a little distance. She looked up, and the moan was repeated, and with increased fervency. She saw nothing, however, and somewhat startled, was about to turn quickly on her way homeward, when a third and more distinct repetition of the moan appealed so strongly to her natural sense of duty, that she could stand it no longer; and with the noblest of all kinds of courage, for such is the courage of humanity, she hastily tripped over the log which ran across the stream, and proceeded in the direction from whence the sounds had issued. A few paces brought her in sight of the sufferer, who was no other than our solitary acquaintance, Logoochie. He lay upon the grass, doubled now into a knot, and now stretching and writhing himself about in agony. His whole appearance indicated suffering, and there was nothing equivocal in the expression of his moanings. The astonishment, not to say fright, of the little cottage maiden, may readily be conjectured. She saw, for the first time, the hideous and uncouth outline of his person—the ludicrous combination of features in his face. She had heard of Logoochie, vaguely; and without giving much, if any credence, to the mysterious tales related by the credulous woodman, returning home at evening, of his encounter in the forest with its pine-bodied divinity;—and now, as she herself looked down upon the suffering and moaning monster, it would be difficult to say, whether curiosity or fear was the most active principle in her bosom. He saw her approach, and he half moved to rise and fly; but a sudden pang, as it seemed, brought him back to a due sense of the evil from which he was suffering, and, looking towards the maiden with a mingled expression of good humor and pain in his countenance, he seemed to implore her assistance. The poor girl did not exactly know what to do, or what to conjecture. What sort of monster was it before her? What queer, distorted, uncouth limbs—what eyes, that twinkled and danced into one another—and what a mouth! She was stupefied for a moment, until he spoke, and, stranger still, in a language that she understood. And what a musical voice,—how sweetly did the words roll forth, and how soothingly, yet earnestly, did they strike upon her ear! Language is indeed a god, and powerful before all the rest. His words told her all his misfortunes, and the tones were all-sufficient to inspire confidence in one even more suspicious than our innocent cottager. Besides, humanity was a principle in her heart, while fear was only an emotion, and she did not scruple, where the two conflicted, after the pause for reflection of a moment, to determine in favor of the former. She approached Logoochie—she approached him, firmly determined in her purpose, but trembling all the while. As she drew nigh, the gentle monster stretched himself out at length, patiently extending one foot towards her, and raising it in such a manner as to indicate the place which afflicted him. She could scarce forbear laughing, when she looked closely upon the strange feet. They seemed covered with bark, like that of the small leafed pine tree; but as she stooped, to her great surprise, the coating of his sole flew wide as if upon a hinge, showing below it a skin as soft, and white, and tender, seemingly, as her own. There, in the centre of the hollow, lay the cause of his suffering. A poisonous thorn had penetrated, almost to the head, as he had suddenly leaped from the tree, the day before, upon the gun being fired from the "Smashing Nancy." The spot around it was greatly inflamed, and Logoochie, since the accident, had vainly striven, in every possible way, to rid himself of the intruder. His short, inflexible arms, had failed so to reach it as to make his fingers available; and then, having claws rather than nails, he could scarce have done any thing for his own relief, even could they have reached it. He now felt the evil of his isolation, and the danger of his seclusion from his brother divinities. His case was one, indeed, of severe bachelorism; and, doubtless, had his condition been less than that of a deity, the approach of Mary Jones to his aid, at such a moment, would have produced a decided revolution in his domestic economy. Still trembling, the maiden bent herself down to the task, and with a fine courage, that did not allow his uncouth limbs to scare, or his wild and monstrous features to deter, she applied her own small fingers to the foot, and carefully grappling the head of the wounding thorn with her nails, with a successful effort, she drew it forth, and rid him of his encumbrance. The wood-god leaped to his feet, threw a dozen antics in the air, to the great terror of Mary, then running a little way into the forest, soon returned with a handful of fresh leaves, which he bruised between his fingers, and applied to the irritated and wounded foot. He was well in a moment after, and pointing the astonished Mary to the bush from which he had taken the anointing leaves, thus made her acquainted with one item in the history of Indian pharmacy.

XIV

"The daughter of the white clay—she has come to Logoochie,—to Logoochie when he was suffering.

"She is a good daughter to Logoochie, and the green spirits who dwell in the forest, they love, and will honor her.

"They will throw down the leaves before her, they will spread the branches above her, they will hum a sweet song in the tree top, when she walks underneath it.

"They will watch beside her, as she sleeps in the shade, in the warm sun of the noon-day,—they will keep the flat viper, and the war rattle, away from her ear.

"They will do this in honor of Logoochie, for they know Logoochie, and he loves the pale daughter. She came to him in his suffering.

"She drew the poison thorn from his foot—she fled not away when she saw him.

"Speak,—let Logoochie hear—there is sorrow in the face of the pale daughter. Logoochie would know it and serve her, for she is sweet in the eye of Logoochie."

XV

Thus said, or rather sung, the uncouth god, to Mary, as after the first emotions of his own joy were over, he beheld the expression of melancholy in her countenance. Somehow, there was something so fatherly, so gentle, and withal, so melodious, in his language, that she soon unbosomed herself to him, telling him freely and in the utmost confidence, though without any hope of relief at his hands, the history of her lover, and the new project for departure which he had now got in his head. She was surprised, and pleased, when she saw that Logoochie smiled at the narrative. She was not certain, yet she had a vague hope, that he could do something for her relief; and her conjecture was not in vain. He spoke—"Why should the grief be in the heart and the cloud on the face of the maiden? Is not Logoochie to help her? He stands beside her to help. Look, daughter of the pale clay—look! There is power in the leaf that shall serve thee at the bidding of Logoochie;—the bough and the branch have a power for thy good, when Logoochie commands; and the little red-berry which I now pluck from the vine hanging over thee, it is strong with a spirit which is good in thy work, when Logoochie has said in thy service. Lo, I speak to the leaf, and to the bough, and to the berry. They shall speak to the water, and one draught from the branch of Logoochie, shall put chains on the heart of the youth who would go forth with the stranger."

As he spoke, he gathered the leaf, broke a bough from an overhanging tree, and, with a red-berry, pulled from a neighboring vine, approached the Branch of Sweet Water, and turning to the west, muttered a wild spell of Indian power, then threw the tributes into the rivulet. The smooth surface of the stream was in an instant ruffled—the offerings were whirled suddenly around—the waters broke, boiled, bubbled, and parted, and in another moment, the bough, the berry, and the leaf, had disappeared from their sight.

XVI

Mary Jones was not a little frightened by these exhibitions, but she was a girl of courage, and having once got over the dread and the novelty of contact with a form so monstrous as that of Logoochie, the after effort was not so great. She witnessed the incantations of the demon without a word, and when they were over, she simply listened to his farther directions, half stupefied with what she had seen, and not knowing how much of it to believe. He bade her bring her lover, as had been the custom with them hitherto, to the branch, and persuade him to drink of its waters. When she inquired into its effect, which, at length, with much effort, she ventured to do, he bade her be satisfied, and all would go right. Then, with a word, which was like so much music—a word she did not understand, but which sounded like a parting acknowledgment,—he bounded away into the woods, and, a moment after, was completely hidden from her sight.

XVII

Poor Mary, not yet relieved from her surprise, was still sufficiently aroused and excited to believe there was something in it; and as she moved off on her way home, how full of anticipation were her thoughts—pleasant anticipation, in which her heart took active interest, and warmed, at length, into a strong and earnest hope! She scarcely gave herself time to get home, and never did the distance between Sweet Water Branch and the cottage of her father appear so extravagantly great. She reached it, however, at last; and there, to her great joy, sat her lover, alongside the old man, and giving him a glowing account, such as he had received from the Yankee captain, of the wonders to be met with in his coming voyage. Old Jones listened patiently, puffing his pipe all the while, and saying little, but now and then, by way of commentary, uttering an ejaculatory grunt, most commonly, of sneering disapproval.

"Better stay at home, a d——d sight, Ned Johnson, and follow the plough."

Ned Johnson, however, thought differently, and it was not the farmer's grunts or growlings that were now to change his mind. Fortunately for the course of true love, there were other influences at work, and the impatience of Mary Jones to try them was evident, in the clumsiness which she exhibited while passing the knife under the thin crust of the corn hoe-cake that night for supper, and laying the thick masses of fresh butter between the smoking and the savory-smelling sides, as she turned them apart. The evening wore, at length, and, according to an old familiar habit, the lovers walked forth to the haunted and fairy-like branch of Logoochie, or the Sweet Water. It was the last night in which they were to be together, prior to his departure in the "Smashing Nancy." That bouncing vessel and her dexterous captain were to depart with early morning; and it was as little as Ned Johnson could do, to spend that night with his sweetheart. They were both melancholy enough, depend on it. She, poor girl, hoping much, yet still fearing—for when was true love without fear—she took his arm, hung fondly upon it, and, without a word between them for a long while, inclined him, as it were naturally, in the required direction. Ned really loved her, and was sorry enough when the thought came to him, that this might be the last night of their association; but he plucked up courage, with the momentary weakness, and though he spoke kindly, yet he spoke fearlessly, and with a sanguine temper, upon the prospect of the sea-adventure before him. Mary said little—her heart was too full for speech, but she looked up now and then into his eyes, and he saw, by the moonlight, that her own glistened as with tears. He turned away his glance as he saw it, for his heart smote him with the reproach of her desertion.

XVIII

They came at length to the charmed streamlet, the Branch of the Sweet Water, to this day known for its fascinations. The moon rose sweetly above it, the trees coming out in her soft light, and the scatterings of her thousand beams glancing from the green polish of their crowding leaves. The breeze that rose along with her was soft and wooing as herself; while the besprinkling fleece of the small white clouds, clustering along the sky, and flying from her splendors, made the scene, if possible, far more fairy-like and imposing. It was a scene for love, and the heart of Ned Johnson grew more softened than ever. His desire for adventure grew modified; and when Mary bent to the brooklet, and scooped up the water for him to drink, with the water-gourd that hung from the bough, wantoning in the breeze that loved to play over the pleasant stream, Ned could not help thinking she never looked more beautiful. The water trickled from the gourd as she handed it to him, falling like droppings of the moonshine again into its parent stream. You should have seen her eye—so full of hope—so full of doubt—so beautiful—so earnest,—as he took the vessel from her hands. For a moment he hesitated, and then how her heart beat and her limbs trembled! But he drank off the contents at a draught, and gave no sign of emotion. Yet his emotions were strange and novel. It seemed as if so much ice had gone through his veins in that moment. He said nothing, however, and dipping up a gourd full for Mary, he hung the vessel again upon the pendant bough, and the two moved away from the water—not, however, before the maiden caught a glimpse, through the intervening foliage, of those two queer, bright little eyes of Logoochie, with a more delightful activity than ever, dancing gayly into one.

XIX

But the spell had been effectual, and a new nature filled the heart of him, who had heretofore sighed vaguely for the unknown. The roving mood had entirely departed; he was no longer a wanderer in spirit, vexed to be denied. A soft languor overspread his form—a weakness gathered and grew about his heart, and he now sighed unconsciously. How soft, yet how full of emphasis, was the pressure of Mary's hand upon his arm as she heard that sigh; and how forcibly did it remind the youth that she who walked beside him was his own—his own forever. With the thought came a sweet perspective—a long vista rose up before his eyes, crowded with images of repose and plenty, such as the domestic nature likes to dream of.

"Oh, Mary, I will not go with this captain—I will not. I will stay at home with you, and we shall be married."

Thus he spoke, as the crowding thoughts, such as we have described, came up before his fancy.

"Will you—shall we? Oh, dear Edward, I am so happy."

And the maiden blessed Logoochie, as she uttered her response of happy feeling.

"I will, dear—but I must hide from Doolittle. I have signed papers to go with him, and he will be so disappointed—I must hide from him."

"Why must you hide, Edward—he cannot compel you to go, unless you please; and you just to be married."

Edward thought she insisted somewhat unnecessarily upon the latter point, but he replied to the first.

"I am afraid he can. I signed papers—I don't know what they were, for I was rash and foolish—but they bound me to go with him, and unless I keep out of the way, I shall have to go."

"Oh, dear—why, Ned, where will you go—you must hide close,—I would not have him find you for the world."

"I reckon not. As to the hiding, I can go where all St. Mary's can't find me; and that's in Okephanokee."

"Oh, don't go so far—it is so dangerous, for some of the Seminoles are there!"

"And what if they are?—I don't care *that* for the Seminoles. They never did me any harm, and never will. But, I shan't go quite so far. Bull Swamp is close enough for me, and there I can watch the 'Smashing Nancy' 'till she gets out to sea."

XX

Having thus determined, it was not long before Ned Johnson made himself secure in his place of retreat, while Captain Doolittle, of the "Smashing Nancy," in great tribulation, ransacked the village of St. Mary's in every direction for his articled seaman, for such Ned Johnson had indeed become. Doolittle deserved to lose him for the trick which, in this respect, he had played upon the boy. His search proved fruitless, and he was compelled to sail at last. Ned, from the top of a high tree on the edge of Bull Swamp, watched his departure, until the last gleam of the white sail flitted away from the horizon; then descending, he made his way back to St. Mary's, and it was not long before he claimed and received the hand of his pretty cottager in marriage. Logoochie was never seen in the neighborhood after this event. His accident had shown him the necessity of keeping with his brethren, for, reasoning from all analogy, gods must be social animals not less than men. But, in departing, he forgot to take the spell away which he had put upon the Sweet Water Branch; and to this day, the stranger, visiting St. Mary's, is warned not to drink from the stream, unless he proposes to remain; for still, as in the case of Ned Johnson, it binds the feet and enfeebles the enterprise of him who partakes of its pleasant waters.

Grayling;
or, "Murder Will Out"

I

The world has become monstrous matter-of-fact in latter days. We can no longer get a ghost story, either for love or money. The materialists have it all their own way; and even the little urchin, eight years old, instead of deferring with decent reverence to the opinion of his grandmamma, now stands up stoutly for his own. He believes in every "ology" but pneumatology. "Faust" and the "Old Woman of Berkeley" move his derision only, and he would laugh incredulously, if he dared, at the Witch of Endor. The whole armory of modern reasoning is on his side; and, however he may admit at seasons that belief can scarcely be counted a matter of will, he yet puts his veto on all sorts of credulity. That cold-blooded demon called Science has taken the place of all the other demons. He has certainly cast out innumerable devils, however he may still spare the principal. Whether we are the better for his intervention is another question. There is reason to apprehend that in disturbing our human faith in shadows, we have lost some of those wholesome moral restraints which might have kept many of us virtuous, where the laws could not.

The effect, however, is much the more seriously evil in all that concerns the romantic. Our story-tellers are so resolute to deal in the real, the actual only, that they venture on no subjects the details of which are not equally vulgar and susceptible of proof. With this end in view, indeed, they too commonly choose their subjects among convicted felons, in order that they may avail themselves of the evidence which led to their conviction; and, to prove more conclusively their devoted adherence to nature and the truth, they depict the former not only in her condition of nakedness, but long before she has found out the springs of running water. It is to be feared that some of the coarseness of modern taste arises from the too great lack of that veneration which belonged to, and elevated to dignity, even the errors of preceding ages. A love of the marvellous belongs, it appears to me, to all those who love and cultivate either of the fine arts. I very much doubt whether the poet, the painter, the sculptor, or the romancer, ever yet lived, who had not some strong bias—a leaning, at least,—to a belief in the wonders of the invisible world. Certainly, the higher orders of poets and painters, those who create and invent, must have a strong taint of the superstitious in their composition. But this is digressive, and leads us from our purpose.

It is so long since we have been suffered to see or hear of a ghost, that a visitation at this time may have the effect of novelty, and I propose to narrate a story which I heard more than once in my boyhood, from the lips of an aged relative, who succeeded, at the time, in making me believe every word of it; perhaps, for the simple reason that she convinced me she believed every word of it herself. My grandmother was an old lady who had been a resident of the seat of most frequent war in Carolina during the Revolution. She had fortunately survived the numberless atrocities which she was yet compelled to witness; and, a keen observer, with a strong memory, she had in store a thousand legends of that stirring period, which served to beguile me from sleep many and many a long winter night. The story which I propose to tell was one of these; and when I say that she not only devoutly believed it herself, but that it was believed by sundry of her contemporaries, who were themselves privy to such of the circumstances as could be known to third parties, the gravity with which I repeat the legend will not be considered very astonishing.

The revolutionary war had but a little while been concluded. The British had left the country; but peace did not imply repose. The community was still in that state of ferment which was natural enough to passions, not yet at rest, which had been brought into exercise and action during the protracted seven years' struggle through which the nation had just passed. The state was overrun by idlers, adventurers, profligates, and criminals. Disbanded soldiers, half-starved and reckless, occupied the highways,—outlaws, emerging from their hiding-places, skulked about the settlements with an equal sentiment of hate and fear in their hearts;—patriots were clamoring for justice upon the tories, and sometimes anticipating its course by judgments of their own; while the tories, those against whom the proofs were too strong for denial or evasion, buckled on their armor for a renewal of the struggle. Such being the condition of the country, it may easily be supposed that life and property lacked many of their necessary securities. Men generally travelled with weapons which were displayed on the smallest provocation: and few who could provide themselves with an escort ventured to travel any distance without one.

There was, about this time, said my grandmother, and while such was the condition of the country, a family of the name of Grayling, that lived somewhere upon the skirts of "Ninety-Six" district. Old Grayling, the head of the family, was dead. He was killed in Buford's massacre. His wife was a fine woman, not so very old, who had an only son named James, and a little girl, only five years of age, named Lucy. James was but fourteen when his father was killed, and that event made a man of him. He went out with his rifle in company with Joel Sparkman, who was his mother's brother, and joined himself to Pickens's Brigade. Here he made as good a soldier as the best. He had no sort of fear. He always was the first to go forward; and his rifle was always good for his enemy's button at a long hundred yards. He was in several fights both with the British and tories; and just before the war was ended he had a famous brush with the Cherokees, when Pickens took their country from them. But though he had no fear, and never knew when to stop killing while the fight was going on, he was the most bashful of boys that I ever knew; and so kind-hearted that it was almost impossible to believe all we heard of his fierce doings when he was in battle. But they were nevertheless quite true for all his bashfulness.

Well, when the war was over, Joel Sparkman, who lived with his sister, Grayling, persuaded her that it would be better to move down into the low country. I don't know what reason he had for it, or what they proposed to do there. They had very little property, but Sparkman was a knowing man, who could turn his hand to a hundred things; and as he was a bachelor, and loved his sister and her children just as if they had been his own, it was natural that she should go with him wherever he wished. James, too, who was restless by nature—and the taste he had enjoyed of the wars had made him more so—he was full of it; and so, one sunny morning in April, their wagon started for the city. The wagon was only a small one, with two horses, scarcely larger than those that are employed to carry chickens and fruit to the market from the Wassamaws and thereabouts. It was driven by a negro fellow named Clytus, and carried Mrs. Grayling and Lucy. James and his uncle loved the saddle too well to shut themselves up in such a vehicle; and both of them were mounted on fine horses which they had won from the enemy. The saddle that James rode on,—and he was very proud of it,—was one that he had taken at the battle of Cowpens from one of Tarleton's own dragoons, after he had tumbled the owner. The roads at that season were excessively bad, for the rains of March had been frequent and heavy, the track was very much cut up, and the red clay gullies of the hills of "Ninety-Six" were so washed that it required all shoulders, twenty times a day, to get the wagon-wheels out of the bog. This made them travel very slowly,—perhaps, not more than fifteen miles a day. Another cause for slow travelling was, the necessity of great caution, and a constant look-out for enemies both up and down the road. James and his uncle took it by turns to ride ahead, precisely as they did when scouting in war, but one of them always kept along with the wagon. They had gone on this way for two days, and saw nothing to trouble and alarm them. There were few persons on the high-road, and these seemed to the full as shy of them as they probably were of strangers. But just as they were about to camp, the evening of the second day, while they were splitting light-wood, and getting out the kettles and the frying-pan, a person rode up and joined them without much ceremony. He was a short thick-set man, somewhere between forty and fifty: had on very coarse and common garments, though he rode a fine black horse of remarkable strength and vigor. He was very civil of speech, though he had but little to say, and that little showed him to be a person without much education and with no refinement. He begged permission to make one of the encampment, and his manner was very respectful and even humble; but there was something dark and sullen in his face—his eyes, which were of a light grey color, were very restless, and his nose turned up sharply, and was very red. His forehead was excessively broad, and his eyebrows thick and shaggy—white hairs being freely mingled with the dark, both in them and upon his head. Mrs. Grayling did not like this man's looks, and whispered her dislike to her son; but James, who felt himself equal to any man, said, promptly—

"What of that, mother! we can't turn the stranger off and say 'no;' and if he means any mischief, there's two of us, you know."

The man had no weapons—none, at least, which were then visible; and deported himself in so humble a manner, that the prejudice which the party had formed against him when he first appeared, if it was not dissipated while he remained, at least failed to gain any increase. He was very quiet, did not mention an unneccessary word, and seldom permitted his eyes to rest upon those of any of the party, the females not excepted. This, perhaps, was the only circumstance, that, in the mind of Mrs. Grayling, tended to confirm the hostile impression which his coming had originally occasioned. In a little while the temporary encampment was put in a state equally social and warlike. The wagon was wheeled a little way into the woods, and off the road; the horses fastened behind it in such a manner that any attempt to steal them would be difficult of success, even were the watch neglectful which was yet to be maintained upon them. Extra guns, concealed in the straw at the bottom of the wagon, were kept well loaded. In the foreground, and between the wagon and the highway, a fire was soon blazing with a wild but cheerful gleam; and the worthy dame, Mrs. Grayling, assisted by the little girl, Lucy, lost no time in setting on the frying-pan, and cutting into slices the haunch of bacon, which they had provided at leaving home. James Grayling patrolled the woods, meanwhile, for a mile or two round the encampment, while his uncle, Joel Sparkman, foot to foot with the stranger, seemed—if the absence of all care constitutes the supreme of human felicity—to realize the most perfect conception of mortal happiness. But Joel was very far from being the careless person that he seemed. Like an old soldier, he simply hung out false colors, and concealed his real timidity by an extra show of confidence and courage. He did not relish the stranger from the first, any more than his sister; and having subjected him to a searching examination, such as was considered, in those days of peril and suspicion, by no means inconsistent with becoming courtesy, he came rapidly to the conclusion that he was no better than he should be.

"You are a Scotchman, stranger," said Joel, suddenly drawing up his feet, and bending forward to the other with an eye like that of a hawk stooping over a covey of partridges. It was a wonder that he had not made the discovery before. The broad dialect of the stranger was not to be subdued; but Joel made slow stages and short progress in his mental journeyings. The answer was given with evident hesitation, but it was affirmative.

"Well, now, it's mighty strange that you should ha' fou't with us and not agin us," responded Joel Sparkman. "There was a precious few of the Scotch, and none that I knows on, saving yourself, perhaps,—that didn't go dead agin us, and for the tories, through thick and thin. That 'Cross Creek settlement' was a mighty ugly thorn in the sides of us whigs. It turned out a raal bad stock of varmints. I hope,—I reckon, stranger,—you aint from that part."

"No," said the other, "oh no! I'm from over the other quarter. I'm from the Duncan settlement above."

"I've hearn tell of that other settlement, but I never know'd as any of the men fou't with us. What gineral did you fight under? What Carolina gineral?"

"I was at Gum Swamp when General Gates was defeated," was the still hesitating reply of the other.

"Well, I thank God, *I* warn't there, though I reckon things wouldn't ha' turned out quite so bad, if there had been a leetle sprinkling of Sumter's, or Pickens's, or Marion's men, among them two-legged critters that run that day. They did tell that some of the regiments went off without ever once emptying their rifles. Now, stranger, I hope you warn't among them fellows."

"I was not," said the other with something more of promptness.

"I don't blame a chap for dodging a bullet if he can, or being too quick for a bagnet, because, I'm thinking, a live man is always a better man than a dead one, or he can become so; but to run without taking a single crack at the inimy, is downright cowardice. There's no two ways about it, stranger."

This opinion, delivered with considerable emphasis, met with the ready assent of the Scotchman, but Joel Sparkman was not to be diverted, even by his own eloquence, from the object of his inquiry.

"But you ain't said," he continued, "who was your Carolina gineral. Gates was from Virginny, and he stayed a mighty short time when he come. You didn't run far at Camden, I reckon, and you joined the army ag'in, and come in with Greene? Was that the how?"

To this the stranger assented, though with evident disinclination.

"Then, mou'tbe, we sometimes went into the same scratch together? I was at Cowpens and Ninety-Six, and seen sarvice at other odds and eends, where there was more fighting than fun. I reckon you must have been at 'Ninety-Six,'—perhaps at Cowpens, too, if you went with Morgan?"

The unwillingness of the stranger to respond to these questions appeared to increase. He admitted, however, that he had been at "Ninety-Six," though, as Sparkman afterwards remembered, in this case, as in that of the defeat of Gates at Gum Swamp, he had not said on which side he had fought. Joel, as he discovered the reluctance of his guest to answer his questions, and perceived his growing doggedness, forbore to annoy him, but mentally resolved to keep a sharper look-out than ever upon his motions. His examination concluded with an inquiry, which, in the plain-dealing regions of the south and south-west, is not unfrequently put first.

"And what mou't be your name, stranger?"

"Macnab," was the ready response, "Sandy Macnab."

"Well, Mr. Macnab, I see that my sister's got supper ready for us; so we mou't as well fall to upon the hoecake and bacon."

Sparkman rose while speaking, and led the way to the spot, near the wagon, where Mrs. Grayling had spread the feast. "We're pretty nigh on to the main road, here, but I reckon there's no great danger now. Besides, Jim Grayling keeps watch for us, and he's got two as good eyes in his head as any scout in the country, and a rifle that, after you once know how it shoots, 'twould do your heart good to hear its crack, if so be that twa'n't your heart that he drawed sight on. He's a perdigious fine shot, and as ready to shoot and fight as if he had a nateral calling that way."

"Shall we wait for him before we eat?" demanded Macnab, anxiously.

"By no sort o' reason, stranger," answered Sparkman. "He'll watch for us while we're eating, and after that I'll change shoes with him. So fall to, and don't mind what's a coming."

Sparkman had just broken the hoecake, when a distant whistle was heard.

"Ha! That's the lad now!" he exclaimed, rising to his feet. "He's on trail. He's got a sight of an inimy's fire, I reckon. 'Twon't be onreasonable, friend Macnab, to get our we'pons in readiness;" and, so speaking, Sparkman bid his sister get into the wagon, where the little Lucy had already placed herself, while he threw open the pan of his rifle, and turned the priming over with his finger. Macnab, meanwhile, had taken from his holsters, which he had before been sitting upon, a pair of horseman's pistols, richly mounted with figures in silver. These were large and long, and had evidently seen service. Unlike his companion's, his proceedings occasioned no comment. What he did seemed a matter of habit, of which he himself was scarcely conscious. Having looked at his priming, he laid the instruments beside him without a word, and resumed the bit of hoecake which he had just before received from Sparkman. Meanwhile, the signal whistle, supposed to come from James Grayling, was repeated. Silence ensued then for a brief space, which Sparkman employed in perambulating the grounds immediately contiguous. At length, just as he had returned to the fire, the sound of a horse's feet was heard, and a sharp quick halloo from Grayling informed his uncle that all was right. The youth made his appearance a moment after accompanied by a stranger on horseback; a tall, fine-looking young man, with a keen flashing eye, and a voice whose lively clear tones, as he was heard approaching, sounded cheerily like those of a trumpet after victory. James Grayling kept along on foot beside the new-comer; and his hearty laugh, and free, glib, garrulous tones, betrayed to his uncle, long ere he drew nigh enough to declare the fact, that he had met unexpectedly with a friend, or, at least, an old acquaintance.

"Why, who have you got there, James?" was the demand of Sparkman, as he dropped the butt of his rifle upon the ground.

"Why, who do you think, uncle? Who but Major Spencer—our own major!"

"You don't say so!—what!—well! Li'nel Spencer, for sartin! Lord bless you, major, who'd ha' thought to see you in these parts; and jest mounted too, for all natur, as if the war was to be fou't over ag'in. Well, I'm raal glad to see you. I am, that's sartin!"

"And I'm very glad to see you, Sparkman," said the other, as he alighted from his steed, and yielded his hand to the cordial grasp of the other.

"Well, I knows that, major, without you saying it. But you've jest come in the right time. The bacon's frying, and here's the bread;—let's down upon our haunches, in right good airnest, camp fashion, and make the most of what God gives us in the way of blessings. I reckon you don't mean to ride any further to-night, major?"

"No," said the person addressed, "not if you'll let me lay my heels at your fire. But who's in your wagon? My old friend, Mrs. Grayling, I suppose?"

"That's a true word, major," said the lady herself, making her way out of the vehicle with good-humored agility, and coming forward with extended hand.

"Really, Mrs. Grayling, I'm very glad to see you." And the stranger, with the blandness of a gentleman and the hearty warmth of an old neighbor, expressed his satisfaction at once more finding himself in the company of an old acquaintance. Their greetings once over, Major Spencer readily joined the group about the fire, while James Grayling—though with some reluctance—disappeared to resume his toils of the scout while the supper proceeded.

"And who have you here?" demanded Spencer, as his eye rested on the dark, hard features of the Scotchman. Sparkman told him all that he himself had learned of the name and character of the stranger, in a brief whisper, and in a moment after formally introduced the parties in this fashion—

"Mr. Macnab, Major Spencer. Mr. Macnab says he's true blue, major, and fou't at Camden, when General Gates run so hard to 'bring the d——d militia back.' He also fou't at Ninety-Six, and Cowpens—so I reckon we had as good as count him one of us."

Major Spencer scrutinized the Scotchman keenly—a scrutiny which the latter seemed very ill to relish. He put a few questions to him on the subject of the war, and some of the actions in which he allowed himself to have been concerned; but his evident reluctance to unfold himself—a reluctance so unnatural to the brave soldier who has gone through his toils honorably—had the natural effect of discouraging the young officer, whose sense of delicacy had not been materially impaired amid the rude jostlings of military life. But, though he forbore to propose any other questions to Macnab, his eyes continued to survey the features of his sullen countenance with curiosity and a strangely increasing interest. This he subsequently explained to Sparkman, when, at the close of supper, James Grayling came in, and the former assumed the duties of the scout.

"I have seen that Scotchman's face somewhere, Sparkman, and I'm convinced at some interesting moment; but where, when, or how, I cannot call to mind. The sight of it is even associated in my mind with something painful and unpleasant; where could I have seen him?"

"I don't somehow like his looks myself," said Sparkman, "and I mislists he's been rether more of a tory than a whig; but that's nothing to the purpose now; and he's at our fire, and we've broken hoecake together; so we cannot rake up the old ashes to make a dust with."

"No, surely not," was the reply of Spencer. "Even though we knew him to be a tory, that cause of former quarrel should occasion none now. But it should produce watchfulness and caution. I'm glad to see that you have not forgot your old business of scouting in the swamp."

"Kin I forget it, major?" demanded Sparkman, in tones which, though whispered, were full of emphasis, as he laid his ear to the earth to listen.

"James has finished supper, major—that's his whistle to tell me so; and I'll jest step back to make it cl'ar to him how we're to keep up the watch to-night."

"Count me in your arrangements, Sparkman, as I am one of you for the night," said the major.

"By no sort of means," was the reply. "The night must be shared between James and myself. Ef so be you wants to keep company with one or t'other of us, why, that's another thing, and, of course, you can do as you please."

"We'll have no quarrel on the subject, Joel," said the officer, good-naturedly, as they returned to the camp together.

II

The arrangements of the party were soon made. Spencer renewed his offer at the fire to take his part in the watch; and the Scotchman, Macnab, volunteered his services also; but the offer of the latter was another reason why that of the former should be declined. Sparkman was resolute to have everything his own way; and while James Grayling went out upon his lonely rounds, he busied himself in cutting bushes and making a sort of tent for the use of his late commander. Mrs. Grayling and Lucy slept in a wagon. The Scotchman stretched himself with little effort before the fire; while Joel Sparkman, wrapping himself up in his cloak, crouched under the wagon body, with his back resting partly against one of the wheels. From time to time he rose and thrust additional brands into the fire, looked up at the night, and round upon the little encampment, then sunk back to his perch and stole a few moments, at intervals, of uneasy sleep. The first two hours of the watch were over, and James Grayling was relieved. The youth, however, felt in no mood for sleep, and taking his seat by the fire, he drew from his pocket a little volume of Easy Reading Lessons, and by the fitful flame of the resinous light-wood, he prepared, in this rude manner, to make up for the precious time which his youth had lost of its legitimate employments, in the stirring events of the preceding seven years consumed in war. He was surprised at this employment by his late commander, who, himself sleepless, now emerged from the bushes and joined Grayling at the fire. The youth had been rather a favorite with Spencer. They had both been reared in the same neighborhood, and the first military achievements of James had taken place under the eye, and had met the approbation of his officer. The difference of their ages was just such as to permit of the warm attachment of the lad without diminishing any of the reverence which should be felt by the inferior. Grayling was not more than seventeen, and Spencer was perhaps thirty-four—the very prime of manhood. They sat by the fire and talked of old times and told stories with the hearty glee and good-nature of the young. Their mutual inquiries led to the revelation of their several objects in pursuing the present journey. Those of James Grayling were scarcely, indeed, to be considered his own. They were plans and purposes of his uncle, and it does not concern this narrative that we should know more of their nature than has already been revealed. But, whatever they were, they were as freely unfolded to his hearer as if the parties had been brothers, and Spencer was quite as frank in his revelations as his companion. He, too, was on his way to Charleston, from whence he was to take passage for England.

"I am rather in a hurry to reach town," he said, "as I learn that the Falmouth packet is preparing to sail for England in a few days, and I must go in her."

"For England, major!" exclaimed the youth with unaffected astonishment.

"Yes, James, for England. But why—what astonishes you?"

"Why, lord!" exclaimed the simple youth, "if they only knew there, as I do, what a cutting and slashing you did use to make among their red coats, I reckon they'd hang you to the first hickory."

"Oh, no! scarcely," said the other, with a smile.

"But I reckon you'll change your name, major?" continued the youth.

"No," responded Spencer, "if I did that, I should lose the object of my voyage. You must know, James, that an old relative has left me a good deal of money in England, and I can only get it by proving that I am Lionel Spencer; so you see I must carry my own name, whatever may be the risk."

"Well, major, you know best; but I do think if they could only have a guess of what you did among their sodgers at Hobkirk's and Cowpens, and Eutaw, and a dozen other places, they'd find some means of hanging you up, peace or no peace. But I don't see what occasion you have to be going cl'ar away to England for money, when you've got a sight of your own already."

"Not so much as you think for," replied the major, giving an involuntary and uneasy glance at the Scotchman, who was seemingly sound asleep on the opposite side of the fire. "There is, you know, but little money in the country at any time, and I must get what I want for my expenses when I reach Charleston. I have just enough to carry me there."

"Well, now, major, that's mighty strange. I always thought that you was about the best off of any man in our parts; but if you're strained so close, I'm thinking, major,—if so be you wouldn't think me too presumptuous,—you'd better let me lend you a guinea or so that I've got to spare, and you can pay me back when you get the English money."

And the youth fumbled in his bosom for a little cotton wallet, which, with its limited contents, was displayed in another instant to the eyes of the officer.

"No, no, James," said the other, putting back the generous tribute; "I have quite enough to carry me to Charleston, and when there I can easily get a supply from the merchants. But I thank you, my good fellow, for your offer. You *are* a good fellow, James, and I will remember you."

It is needless to pursue the conversation farther. The night passed away without any alarms, and at dawn of the next day the whole party was engaged in making preparation for a start. Mrs. Grayling was soon busy in getting breakfast in readiness. Major Spencer consented to remain with them until it was over; but the Scotchman, after returning thanks very civilly for his accommodation of the night, at once resumed his journey. His course seemed, like their own, to lie below; but he neither declared his route nor betrayed the least desire to know that of Spencer. The latter had no disposition to renew those inquiries from which the stranger seemed to shrink the night before, and he accordingly suffered him to depart with a quiet farewell, and the utterance of a good-natured wish, in which all the parties joined, that he might have a pleasant journey. When he was fairly out of sight, Spencer said to Sparkman,

"Had I liked that fellow's looks, nay, had I not positively disliked them, I should have gone with him. As it is, I will remain and share your breakfast."

The repast being over, all parties set forward; but Spencer, after keeping along with them for a mile, took his leave also. The slow wagon-pace at which the family travelled, did not suit the high-spirited cavalier; and it was necessary, as he assured them, that he should reach the city in two nights more. They parted with many regrets as truly felt as they were warmly expressed; and James Grayling never felt the tedium of wagon travelling to be so severe as throughout the whole of that day when he separated from his favorite captain. But he was too stout-hearted a lad to make any complaint; and his dissatisfaction only showed itself in his unwonted silence, and an over-anxiety, which his steed seemed to feel in common with himself, to go rapidly ahead. Thus the day passed, and the wayfarers at its close had made a progress of some twenty miles from sun to sun. The same precautions marked their encampment this night as the last, and they rose in better spirits with the next morning, the dawn of which was very bright and pleasant, and encouraging. A similar journey of twenty miles brought them to the place of bivouac as the sun went down; and they prepared as usual for their securities and supper. They found themselves on the edge of a very dense forest of pines and scrubby oaks, a portion of which was swallowed up in a deep bay—so called in the dialect of the country—a swamp-bottom, the growth of which consisted of mingled cypresses and baytrees, with tupola, gum, and dense thickets of low stunted shrubbery, cane grass, and dwarf willows, which filled up every interval between the trees, and to the eye most effectually barred out every human intruder. This bay was chosen as the background for the camping party. Their wagon was wheeled into an area on a gently rising ground in front, under a pleasant shade of oaks and hickories, with a lonely pine rising loftily in occasional spots among them. Here the horses were taken out, and James Grayling prepared to kindle up a fire; but, looking for his axe, it was unaccountably missing, and after a fruitless search of half an hour, the party came to the conclusion that it had been left on the spot where they had slept last night. This was a disaster, and, while they meditated in what manner to repair it, a negro boy appeared in sight, passing along the road at their feet, and driving before him a small herd of cattle. From him they learned that they were only a mile or two from a farmstead where an axe might be borrowed; and James, leaping on his horse, rode forward in the hope to obtain one. He found no difficulty in his quest; and, having obtained it from the farmer, who was also a tavern-keeper, he casually asked if Major Spencer had not stayed with him the night before. He was somewhat surprised when told that he had not.

"There was one man stayed with me last night," said the farmer, "but he didn't call himself a major, and didn't much look like one."

"He rode a fine sorrel horse,—tall, bright color, with white fore foot, didn't he?" asked James.

"No, that he didn't! He rode a powerful black, coal black, and not a bit of white about him.

"That was the Scotchman! But I wonder the major didn't stop with you. He must have rode on. Isn't there another house near you, below?"

"Not one. There's ne'er a house either above or below for a matter of fifteen miles. I'm the only man in all that distance that's living on this road; and I don't think your friend could have gone below, as I should have seen him pass. I've been all day out there in that field before your eyes, clearing up the brush."

III

Somewhat wondering that the major should have turned aside from the track, though without attaching to it any importance at that particular moment, James Grayling took up the borrowed axe and hurried back to the encampment, where the toil of cutting an extra supply of light-wood to meet the exigencies of the ensuing night, sufficiently exercised his mind as well as his body, to prevent him from meditating upon the seeming strangeness of the circumstance. But when he sat down to his supper over the fire that he had kindled, his fancies crowded thickly upon him, and he felt a confused doubt and suspicion that something was to happen, he knew not what. His conjectures and apprehensions were without form, though not altogether void; and he felt a strange sickness and a sinking at the heart which was very unusual with him. He had, in short, that lowness of spirits, that cloudy apprehensiveness of soul which takes the form of presentiment, and makes us look out for danger even when the skies are without a cloud, and the breeze is laden, equally and only, with balm and music. His moodiness found no sympathy among his companions. Joel Sparkman was in the best of humors, and his mother was so cheery and happy, that when the thoughtful boy went off into the woods to watch, he could hear her at every moment breaking out into little catches of a country ditty, which the gloomy events of the late war had not yet obliterated from her memory.

"It's very strange!" soliloquized the youth, as he wandered along the edges of the dense bay or swamp-bottom, which we have passingly referred to,—"it's very strange what troubles me so! I feel almost frightened, and yet I know I'm not to be frightened easily, and I don't see anything in the woods to frighten me. It's strange the major didn't come along this road! Maybe he took another higher up that leads by a different settlement. I wish I had asked the man at the house if there's such another road. I reckon there must be, however, for where could the major have gone?"

The unphilosophical mind of James Grayling did not, in his farther meditations, carry him much beyond this starting point; and with its continual recurrence in soliloquy, he proceeded to traverse the margin of the bay, until he came to its junction with, and termination at, the high-road. The youth turned into this, and, involuntarily departing from it a moment after, soon found himself on the opposite side of the bay thicket. He wandered on and on, as he himself described it, without any power to restrain himself. He knew not how far he went; but, instead of maintaining his watch for two hours only, he was gone more than four; and, at length, a sense of weariness which overpowered him all of a sudden, caused him to seat himself at the foot of a tree, and snatch a few moments of rest. He denied that he slept in this time. He insisted to the last moment of his life that sleep never visited his eyelids that night,—that he was conscious of fatigue and exhaustion, but not drowsiness,—and that this fatigue was so numbing as to be painful, and effectually kept him from any sleep. While he sat thus beneath the tree, with a body weak and nerveless, but a mind excited, he knew not how or why, to the most acute degree of expectation and attention, he heard his name called by the well-known voice of his friend, Major Spencer. The voice called him three times,—"James Grayling!—James!—James Grayling!" before he could muster strength enough to answer. It was not courage he wanted,—of that he was positive, for he felt sure, as he said, that something had gone wrong, and he was never more ready to fight in his life than at that moment, could he have commanded the physical capacity; but his throat seemed dry to suffocation,—his lips effectually sealed up as if with wax, and when he did answer, the sounds seemed as fine and soft as the whisper of some child just born.

"Oh! major, is it you?"

Such, he thinks, were the very words he made use of in reply; and the answer that he received was instantaneous, though the voice came from some little distance in the bay, and his own voice he did not hear. He only knows what he meant to say. The answer was to this effect.

"It is, James!—It is your own friend, Lionel Spencer, that speaks to you; do not be alarmed when you see me! I have been shockingly murdered!"

James asserts that he tried to tell him that he would not be frightened, but his own voice was still a whisper, which he himself could scarcely hear. A moment after he had spoken, he heard something like a sudden breeze that rustled through the bay bushes at his feet, and his eyes were closed without his effort, and indeed in spite of himself. When he opened them, he saw Major Spencer standing at the edge of the bay, about twenty steps from him. Though he stood in the shade of a thicket, and there was no light in the heavens save that of the stars, he was yet enabled to distinguish perfectly, and with great ease, every lineament of his friend's face.

He looked very pale, and his garments were covered with blood; and James said that he strove very much to rise from the place where he sat and approach him;—"for, in truth," said the lad, "so far from feeling any fear, I felt nothing but fury in my heart; but I could not move a limb. My feet were fastened to the ground; my hands to my sides; and I could only bend forward and gasp. I felt as if I should have died with vexation that I could not rise; but a power which I could not resist, made me motionless, and almost speechless. I could only say, 'Murdered!'—and that one word I believe I must have repeated a dozen times."

" 'Yes, murdered!—murdered by the Scotchman who slept with us at your fire the night before last. James, I look to you to have the murderer brought to justice! James!—do you hear me, James?'

"These," said James, "I think were the very words, or near about the very words, that I heard; and I tried to ask the major to tell me how it was, and how I could do what he required; but I didn't hear myself speak, though it would appear that he did, for almost immediately after I had tried to speak what I wished to say, he answered me just as if I had said it. He told me that the Scotchman had waylaid, killed, and hidden him in that very bay; that his murderer had gone to Charleston; and that if I made haste to town, I would find him in the Falmouth packet, which was then lying in the harbor and ready to sail for England. He farther said that everything depended on my making haste,—that I must reach town by tomorrow night if I wanted to be in season, and go right on board the vessel and charge the criminal with the deed. 'Do not be afraid,' said he, when he had finished; 'be afraid of nothing, James, for God will help and strengthen you to the end.'

When I heard all I burst into a flood of tears, and then I felt strong. I felt that I could talk, or fight, or do almost anything; and I jumped up to my feet, and was just about to run down to where the major stood, but, with the first step which I made forward, he was gone. I stopped and looked all around me, but I could see nothing; and the bay was just as black as midnight. But I went down to it, and tried to press in where I thought the major had been standing; but I couldn't get far, the brush and bay bushes were so close and thick. I was now bold and strong enough, and I called out, loud enough to be heard half a mile. I didn't exactly know what I called for, or what I wanted to learn, or I have forgotten. But I heard nothing more. Then I remembered the camp, and began to fear that something might have happened to mother and uncle, for I now felt, what I had not thought of before, that I had gone too far round the bay to be of much assistance, or, indeed, to be in time for any, had they been suddenly attacked. Besides, I could not think how long I had been gone; but it now seemed very late. The stars were shining their brightest, and the thin white clouds of morning were beginning to rise and run towards the west. Well, I bethought me of my course,—for I was a little bewildered and doubtful where I was; but, after a little thinking, I took the back track, and soon got a glimpse of the camp-fire, which was nearly burnt down; and by this I reckoned I was gone considerably longer than my two hours. When I got back into the camp, I looked under the wagon, and found uncle in a sweet sleep, and though my heart was full almost to bursting with what I had heard, and the cruel sight I had seen, yet I wouldn't waken him; and I beat about and mended the fire, and watched, and waited, until near daylight, when mother called to me out of the wagon, and asked who it was. This wakened my uncle, and then I up and told all that had happened, for it if had been to save my life, I couldn't have kept it in much longer. But though mother said it was very strange, Uncle Sparkman considered that I had been only dreaming; but he couldn't persuade me of it; and when I told him I intended to be off at daylight, just as the major had told me to do, and ride my best all the way to Charleston, he laughed, and said I was a fool. But I felt that I was no fool, and I was solemn certain that I hadn't been dreaming; and though both mother and he tried their hardest to make me put off going, yet I made up my mind to it, and they had to give up. For, wouldn't I have been a pretty sort of a friend to the major, if, after what he told me, I could have stayed behind, and gone on only at a wagon-pace to look after the murderer!

I don't think if I had done so that I should ever have been able to look a white man in the face again. Soon as the peep of day, I was on horseback. Mother was mighty sad, and begged me not to go, but Uncle Sparkman was mighty sulky, and kept calling me fool upon fool, until I was almost angry enough to forget that we were of blood kin. But all his talking did not stop me, and I reckon I was five miles on my way before he had his team in traces for a start. I rode as briskly as I could get on without hurting my nag. I had a smart ride of more than forty miles before me, and the road was very heavy. But it was a good two hours from sunset when I got into town, and the first question I asked of the people I met was, to show me where the ships were kept. When I got to the wharf they showed me the Falmouth packet, where she lay in the stream, ready to sail as soon as the wind should favor."

IV

James Grayling, with the same eager impatience which he has been suffered to describe in his own language, had already hired a boat to go on board the British packet, when he remembered that he had neglected all those means, legal and otherwise, by which alone his purpose might be properly effected. He did not know much about legal process, but he had common sense enough, the moment that he began to reflect on the subject, to know that some such process was necessary. This conviction produced another difficulty; he knew not in which quarter to turn for counsel and assistance; but here the boatman who saw his bewilderment, and knew by his dialect and dress that he was a back-countryman, came to his relief, and from him he got directions where to find the merchants with whom his uncle, Sparkman, had done business in former years. To them he went, and without circumlocution, told the whole story of his ghostly visitation. Even as a dream, which these gentlemen at once conjectured it to be, the story of James Grayling was equally clear and curious; and his intense warmth and the entire absorption, which the subject had effected, of his mind and soul, was such that they judged it not improper, at least to carry out the search of the vessel which he contemplated. It would certainly, they thought, be a curious coincidence—believing James to be a veracious youth—if the Scotchman should be found on board. But another test of his narrative was proposed by one of the firm. It so happened that the business agents of Major Spencer, who was well known in Charleston, kept their office but a few rods distant from their own; and to them all parties at once proceeded. But here the story of James was encountered by a circumstance that made somewhat against it. These gentlemen produced a letter from Major Spencer, intimating the utter impossibility of his coming to town for the space of a month, and expressing his regret that he should be unable to avail himself of the opportunity of the foreign vessel, of whose arrival in Charleston, and proposed time of departure, they had themselves advised him. They read the letter aloud to James and their brother merchants, and with difficulty suppressed their smiles at the gravity with which the former related and insisted upon the particulars of his vision.

"He had changed his mind," returned the impetuous youth; "he was on his way down, I tell you,—a hundred miles on his way,—when he camped with us. I know him well, I tell you, and talked with him myself half the night."

"At least," remarked the gentlemen who had gone with James, "it can do no harm to look into the business. We can procure a warrant for searching the vessel after this man, Macnab; and should he be found on board the packet, it will be a sufficient circumstance to justify the magistrates in detaining him, until we can ascertain where Major Spencer really is."

The measure was accordingly adopted, and it was nearly sunset before the warrant was procured, and the proper officer in readiness. The impatience of a spirit so eager and so devoted as James Grayling, under these delays, may be imagined; and when in the boat, and on his way to the packet where the criminal was to be sought, his blood became so excited that it was with much ado he could be kept in his seat. His quick, eager action continually disturbed the trim of the boat, and one of his mercantile friends, who had accompanied him, with that interest in the affair which curiosity alone inspired, was under constant apprehension lest he would plunge overboard in his impatient desire to shorten the space which lay between. The same impatience enabled the youth, though never on shipboard before, to grasp the rope which had been flung at their approach, and to mount her sides with catlike agility. Without waiting to declare himself or his purpose, he ran from one side of the deck to the other, greedily staring, to the surprise of officers, passengers, and seamen, in the faces of all of them, and surveying them with an almost offensive scrutiny. He turned away from the search with disappointment. There was no face like that of the suspected man among them. By this time, his friend, the merchant, with the sheriff's officer, had entered the vessel, and were in conference with the captain. Grayling drew nigh in time to hear the latter affirm that there was no man of the name Macnab, as stated in the warrant, among his passengers or crew.

"He is—he must be!" exclaimed the impetuous youth. "The major never lied in his life, and couldn't lie after he was dead. Macnab is here—he is a Scotchman—"

The captain interrupted him—

"We have, young gentleman, several Scotchmen on board, and one of them is named Macleod—"

"Let me see him—which is he?" demanded the youth.

By this time, the passengers and a goodly portion of the crew were collected about the little party. The captain turned his eyes upon the group, and asked,

"Where is Mr. Macleod?"

"He is gone below—he's sick!" replied one of the passengers.

"That's he! That must be the man!" exclaimed the youth. "I'll lay my life that's no other than Macnab. He's only taken a false name."

It was now remembered by one of the passengers, and remarked, that Macleod had expressed himself as unwell, but a few moments before, and had gone below even while the boat was rapidly approaching the vessel. At this statement, the captain led the way into the cabin, closely followed by James Grayling and the rest.

"Mr. Macleod," he said with a voice somewhat elevated, as he approached the berth of that person, "you are wanted on deck for a few moments."

"I am really too unwell, captain," replied a feeble voice from behind the curtain of the berth.

"It will be necessary," was the reply of the captain. "There is a warrant from the authorities of the town, to look after a fugitive from justice."

Macleod had already begun a second speech declaring his feebleness, when the fearless youth, Grayling, bounded before the captain and tore away, with a single grasp of his hand, the curtain which concealed the suspected man from their sight.

"It is he!" was the instant exclamation of the youth, as he beheld him. "It is he—Macnab, the Scotchman—the man that murdered Major Spencer!"

Macnab,—for it was he,—was deadly pale. He trembled like an aspen. His eyes were dilated with more than mortal apprehension, and his lips were perfectly livid. Still, he found strength to speak, and to deny the accusation. He knew nothing of the youth before him—nothing of Major Spencer—his name was Macleod, and he had never called himself by any other. He denied, but with great incoherence, everything which was urged against him.

"You must get up, Mr. Macleod," said the captain; "the circumstances are very much against you. You must go with the officer!"

"Will you give me up to my enemies?" demanded the culprit. "You are a countryman—a Briton. I have fought for the king, our master, against these rebels, and for this they seek my life. Do not deliver me into their bloody hands!"

"Liar!" exclaimed James Grayling—"Didn't you tell us at our own camp-fire that you were with us? that you were at Gates's defeat, and Ninety-Six?"

"But I didn't tell you," said the Scotchman, with a grin, "which side I was on!"

"Ha! remember that!" said the sheriff's officer. "He denied, just a moment ago, that he knew this young man at all; now, he confesses that he did see and camp with him."

The Scotchman was aghast at the strong point which, in his inadvertence, he had made against himself; and his efforts to excuse himself, stammering and contradictory, served only to involve him more deeply in the meshes of his difficulty. Still he continued his urgent appeals to the captain of the vessel, and his fellow-passengers, as citizens of the same country, subjects to the same monarch, to protect him from those who equally hated and would destroy them all. In order to move their national prejudices in his behalf, he boasted of the immense injury which he had done, as a tory, to the rebel cause; and still insisted that the murder was only a pretext of the youth before him, by which to gain possession of his person, and wreak upon him the revenge which his own fierce performances during the war had naturally enough provoked. One or two of the passengers, indeed, joined with him in entreating the captain to set the accusers adrift and make sail at once; but the stout Englishman who was in command, rejected instantly the unworthy counsel. Besides, he was better aware of the dangers which would follow any such rash proceeding. Fort Moultrie, on Sullivan's Island, had been already refitted and prepared for an enemy; and he was lying, at that moment, under the formidable range of grinning teeth, which would have opened upon him, at the first movement, from the jaws of Castle Pinckney.

"No, gentlemen," said he, "you mistake your man. God forbid that I should give shelter to a murderer, though he were from my own parish."

"But I am no murderer," said the Scotchman.

"You look cursedly like one, however," was the reply of the captain. "Sheriff, take your prisoner."

The base creature threw himself at the feet of the Englishman, and clung, with piteous entreaties, to his knees. The latter shook him off, and turned away in disgust.

"Steward," he cried, "bring up this man's luggage."

He was obeyed. The luggage was brought up from the cabin and delivered to the sheriff's officer, by whom it was examined in the presence of all, and an inventory made of its contents. It consisted of a small new trunk, which, it afterwards appeared, he had bought in Charleston, soon after his arrival. This contained a few changes of raiment, twenty-six guineas in money, a gold watch, not in repair, and the two pistols which he had shown while at Joel Sparkman's camp-fire; but, with this difference, that the stock of one was broken off short just above the grasp, and the butt was entirely gone. It was not found among his chattels. A careful examination of the articles in his trunk did not result in anything calculated to strengthen the charge of his criminality; but there was not a single person present who did not feel as morally certain of his guilt as if the jury had already declared the fact. That night he slept—if he slept at all—in the common jail of the city.

V

His accuser, the warm-hearted and resolute James Grayling, did not sleep. The excitement, arising from mingling and contradictory emotions,—sorrow for his brave young commander's fate, and the natural exultation of a generous spirit at the consciousness of having performed, with signal success, an arduous and painful task—combined to drive all pleasant slumbers from his eyes; and with the dawn he was again up and stirring, with his mind still full of the awful business in which he had been engaged. We do not care to pursue his course in the ordinary walks of the city, nor account for his employments during the few days which ensued, until, in consequence of a legal examination into the circumstances which anticipated the regular work of the sessions, the extreme excitement of the young accuser had been renewed. Macnab or Macleod,—and it is possible that both names were fictitious,—as soon as he recovered from his first terrors, sought the aid of an attorney—one of those acute, small, chopping lawyers, to be found in almost every community, who are willing to serve with equal zeal the sinner and the saint, provided that they can pay with equal liberality. The prisoner was brought before the court under *habeas corpus*, and several grounds submitted by his counsel with the view to obtaining his discharge. It became necessary to ascertain, among the first duties of the state, whether Major Spencer, the alleged victim, was really dead. Until it could be established that a man should be imprisoned, tried, and punished for a crime, it was first necessary to show that a crime had been committed, and the attorney made himself exceedingly merry with the ghost story of young Grayling. In those days, however, the ancient Superstition was not so feeble as she has subsequently become. The venerable judge was one of those good men who had a decent respect for the faith and opinions of his ancestors; and though he certainly would not have consented to the hanging of Macleod under the sort of testimony which had been adduced, he yet saw enough, in all the circumstances, to justify his present detention. In the meantime, efforts were to be made, to ascertain the whereabouts of Major Spencer; though, were he even missing,—so the counsel for Macleod contended,—his death could be by no means assumed in consequence. To this the judge shook his head doubtfully. "'Fore God!" said he, "I would not have you to be too sure of that." He was an Irishman, and proceeded after the fashion of his country. The reader will therefore *bear* with his *bull*. "A man may properly be hung for murdering another, though the murdered man be not dead; ay, before God, even though he be actually unhurt and uninjured, while the murderer is swinging by the neck for the bloody deed!"

The judge, who it must be understood was a real existence, and who had no small reputation in his day in the South,—proceeded to establish the correctness of his opinions by authorities and argument, with all of which, doubtlessly, the bar were exceedingly delighted; but, to provide them in this place would only be to interfere with our own progress. James Grayling, however, was not satisfied to wait the slow processes which were suggested for coming at the truth. Even the wisdom of the judge was lost upon him, possibly, for the simple reason that he did not comprehend it. But the ridicule of the culprit's lawyer stung him to the quick, and he muttered to himself, more than once, a determination "to lick the life out of that impudent chap's leather." But this was not his only resolve. There was one which he proceeded to put into instant execution, and that was to seek the body of his murdered friend in the spot where he fancied it might be found—namely, the dark and dismal bay where the specter had made its appearance to his eyes.

The suggestion was approved—though he did not need this to prompt his resolution—by his mother and uncle, Sparkman. The latter determined to be his companion, and he was farther accompanied by the sheriff's officer who had arrested the suspected felon. Before daylight, on the morning after the examination before the judge had taken place, and when Macleod had been remanded to prison, James Grayling started on his journey. His fiery zeal received additional force at every added moment of delay, and his eager spurring brought him at an early hour after noon, to the neighborhood of the spot through which his search was to be made. When his companions and himself drew nigh, they were all at a loss in which direction first to proceed. The bay was one of those massed forests, whose wall of thorns, vines, and close tenacious shrubs, seemed to defy invasion. To the eye of the townsman it was so forbidding that he pronounced it absolutely impenetrable. But James was not to be baffled. He led them round it, taking the very course which he had pursued the night when the revelation was made him; he showed them the very tree at whose foot he had sunk when the supernatural torpor—as he himself esteemed it—began to fall upon him; he then pointed out the spot, some twenty steps distant, at which the specter made his appearance. To this spot they then proceeded in a body, and essayed an entrance, but were so discouraged by the difficulties at the outset that all, James not excepted, concluded that neither the murderer nor his victim could possibly have found entrance there.

But, lo! a marvel! Such it seemed, at the first blush, to all the party. While they stood confounded and indecisive, undetermined in which way to move, a sudden flight of wings was heard, even from the center of the bay, at a little distance above the spot where they had striven for entrance. They looked up, and beheld about fifty buzzards—those notorious domestic vultures of the South—ascending from the interior of the bay, and perching along upon the branches of the loftier trees by which it was overhung. Even were the character of these birds less known, the particular business in which they had just then been engaged, was betrayed by huge gobbets of flesh which some of them had borne aloft in their flight, and still continued to rend with beak and bill, as they tottered upon the branches where they stood. A piercing scream issued from the lips of James Grayling as he beheld this sight, and strove to scare the offensive birds from their repast.

"The poor major! the poor major!" was the involuntary and agonized exclamation of the youth. "Did I ever think he would come to this!"

The search, thus guided and encouraged, was pressed with renewed diligence and spirit; and, at length, an opening was found through which it was evident that a body of considerable size had but recently gone. The branches were broken from the small shrub trees, and the undergrowth trodden into the earth. They followed this path, and, as is the case commonly with waste tracts of this description, the density of the growth diminished sensibly at every step they took, till they reached a little pond, which, though circumscribed in area, and full of cypresses, yet proved to be singularly deep. Indeed, it was an alligator-hole, where, in all probability, a numerous tribe of these reptiles had their dwelling. Here, on the edge of the pond, they discovered the object which had drawn the keen-sighted vultures to their feast, in the body of a horse, which James Grayling at once identified as that of Major Spencer. The carcass of the animal was already very much torn and lacerated. The eyes were plucked out, and the animal completely disembowelled. Yet, on examination, it was not difficult to discover the manner of his death. This had been effected by firearms. Two bullets had passed through his skull, just above the eyes, either of which must have been fatal. The murderer had led the horse to the spot, and committed the cruel deed where his body was found. The search was now continued for that of the owner, but for some time it proved ineffectual. At length, the keen eyes of James Grayling detected, amidst a heap of moss and green sedge that rested beside an overthrown tree, whose branches jutted into the pond, a whitish, but discolored object, that did not seem native to the place. Bestriding the fallen tree, he was enabled to reach this object, which, with a burst of grief, he announced to the distant party was the hand and arm of his unfortunate friend, the wristband of the shirt being the conspicuous object which had first caught his eye. Grasping this, he drew the corpse, which had been thrust beneath the branches of the tree, to the surface; and, with the assistance of his uncle, it was finally brought to the dry land. Here it underwent a careful examination. The head was very much disfigured; the skull was fractured in several places by repeated blows of some hard instrument, inflicted chiefly from behind. A closer inspection revealed a bullet-hole in the abdomen, the first wound, in all probability, which the unfortunate gentleman received, and by which he was, perhaps, tumbled from his horse. The blows on the head would seem to have been unnecessary, unless the murderer—whose proceedings appeared to have been singularly deliberate,—was resolved upon making "assurance doubly sure." But, as if the watchful Providence had meant that nothing should be left doubtful which might tend to the complete conviction of the criminal, the constable stumbled upon the butt of the broken pistol which had been found in Macleod's trunk. This he picked up on the edge of the pond in which the corpse had been discovered, and while James Grayling and his uncle, Sparkman, were engaged in drawing it from the water. The place where the fragment was discovered at once denoted the pistol as the instrument by which the final blows were inflicted. "'Fore God," said the judge to the criminal, as these proofs were submitted at the trial, "you may be a very innocent man after all, as, by my faith, I do think there have been many murderers before you; but you ought, nevertheless, to be hung as an example to all other persons who suffer such strong proofs of guilt to follow their innocent misdoings. Gentlemen of the jury, if this person, Macleod or Macnab, didn't murder Major Spencer, either you or I did; and you must now decide which of us it is! I say, gentlemen of the jury, either you, or I, or the prisoner at the bar, murdered this man; and if you have any doubts which of us it was, it is but justice and mercy that you should give the prisoner the benefit of your doubts; and so find your verdict. But, before God, should you find him not guilty, Mr. Attorney there can scarcely do anything wiser than to put us all upon trial for the deed."

The jury, it may be scarcely necessary to add, perhaps under certain becoming fears of an alternative such as his honor had suggested, brought in a verdict of "Guilty," without leaving the panel; and Macnab, *alias* Macleod, was hung at White Point, Charleston, somewhere about the year 178–.

"And here," said my grandmother, devoutly, "you behold a proof of God's watchfulness to see that murder should not be hidden, and that the murderer should not escape. You see that he sent the spirit of the murdered man—since, by no other mode could the truth have been revealed—to declare the crime, and to discover the criminal. But for that ghost, Macnab would have got off to Scotland, and probably have been living to this very day on the money that he took from the person of the poor major."

As the old lady finished the ghost story, which, by the way, she had been tempted to relate for the fiftieth time in order to combat my father's ridicule of such superstitions, the latter took up the thread of the narrative.

"Now, my son," said he, "as you have heard all that your grandmother has to say on this subject, I will proceed to show you what you have to believe, and what not. It is true that Macnab murdered Spencer in the manner related; that James Grayling made the discovery and prosecuted the pursuit; found the body and brought the felon to justice; that Macnab suffered death, and confessed the crime; alleging that he was moved to do so, as well because of the money that he suspected Spencer to have in his possession, as because of the hate which he felt for a man who had been particularly bold and active in cutting up a party of Scotch loyalists to which he belonged, on the borders of North Carolina. But the appearance of the specter was nothing more than the work of a quick imagination, added to a shrewd and correct judgment. James Grayling saw no ghost, in fact, but such as was in his own mind; and, though the instance was one of a most remarkable character, one of singular combination, and well depending circumstances, still, I think it is to be accounted for by natural and very simple laws."

The old lady was indignant.

"And how could he see the ghost just on the edge of the same bay where the murder had been committed, and where the body of the murdered man even then was lying?"

My father did not directly answer the demand, but proceeded thus:—

"James Grayling, as we know, mother, was a very ardent, impetuous, sagacious man. He had the sanguine, the race-horse temperament. He was generous, always prompt and ready, and one who never went backward. What he did, he did quickly, boldly, and thoroughly! He never shrank from trouble of any kind: nay, he rejoiced in the constant encounter with difficulty and trial; and his was the temper which commands and enthrals mankind. He felt deeply and intensely whatever occupied his mind, and when he parted from his friend he brooded over little else than their past communion and the great distance by which they were to be separated. The dull travelling wagon-gait at which he himself was compelled to go, was a source of annoyance to him; and he became sullen, all the day, after the departure of his friend. When, on the evening of the next day, he came to the house where it was natural to expect that Major Spencer would have slept the night before, and he learned the fact that no one stopped there but the Scotchman, Macnab, we see that he was struck with the circumstance. He mutters it over to himself, "Strange, where the major could have gone!" His mind then naturally reverts to the character of the Scotchman; to the opinions and suspicions which had been already expressed of him by his uncle, and felt by himself. They had all, previously, come to the full conviction that Macnab was, and had always been, a tory, in spite of his protestations. His mind next, and very naturally, reverted to the insecurity of the highways; the general dangers of travelling at that period; the frequency of crime, and the number of desperate men who were everywhere to be met with. The very employment in which he was then engaged, in scouting the woods for the protection of the camp, was calculated to bring such reflections to his mind. If these precautions were considered necessary for the safety of persons so poor, so wanting in those possessions which might prompt cupidity to crime, how much more necessary were precautions in the case of a wealthy gentleman like Major Spencer! He then remembered the conversation with the major at the camp-fire, when they fancied that the Scotchman was sleeping. How natural to think, then, that he was all the while awake; and, if awake, he must have heard him speak of the wealth of his companion. True, the major, with more prudence than himself, denied that he had any money about him, more than would bear his expenses to the city; but such an assurance was natural enough to the lips of a traveller who knew the dangers of the country. That the man, Macnab, was not a person to be trusted, was the equal impression of Joel Sparkman and his nephew from the first. The probabilities were strong that he would rob and perhaps murder, if he might hope to do so with impunity; and as the youth made the circuit of the bay in the darkness and solemn stillness of the night, its gloomy depths and mournful shadows, naturally gave rise to such reflections as would be equally active in the mind of a youth, and of one somewhat familiar with the arts and usages of strife. He would see that the spot was just the one in which a practiced partisan would delight to set an ambush for an unwary foe. There ran the public road, with a little sweep, around two-thirds of the extent of its dense and impenetrable thickets. The ambush could lie concealed, and at ten steps command the bosom of its victim.

Here, then, you perceive that the mind of James Grayling, stimulated by an active and sagacious judgment, had by gradual and reasonable stages come to these conclusions: that Major Spencer was an object to tempt a robber; that the country was full of robbers; that Macnab was one of them; that this was the very spot in which a deed of blood could be most easily committed, and most easily concealed; and, one important fact, that gave strength and coherence to the whole, that Major Spencer had not reached a well-known point of destination, while Macnab had.

"With these thoughts, thus closely linked together, the youth forgets the limits of his watch and his circuit. This fact, alone, proves how active his imagination had become. It leads him forward, brooding more and more on the subject, until, in the very exhaustion of his body, he sinks down beneath a tree. He sinks down and falls asleep; and in his sleep, what before was plausible conjecture, becomes fact, and the creative properties of his imagination give form and vitality to all his fancies. These forms are bold, broad, and deeply colored, in due proportion with the degree of force which they receive from probability. Here, he sees the image of his friend; but, you will remark—and this should almost conclusively satisfy any mind that all that he sees is the work of his imagination,—that, though Spencer tells him that he is murdered, and by Macnab, he does not tell him how, in what manner, or with what weapons. Though he sees him pale and ghostlike, he does not see, nor can he say, where his wounds are! He sees his pale features distinctly, and his garments are bloody. Now, had he seen the specter in the true appearances of death, as he was subsequently found, he would not have been able to discern his features, which were battered, according to his own account, almost out of all shape of humanity, and covered with mud; while his clothes would have streamed with mud and water, rather than with blood."

"Ah!" exclaimed the old lady, my grandmother, "it's hard to make you believe anything that you don't see; you are like Saint Thomas in the Scriptures; but how do you propose to account for his knowing that the Scotchman was on board the Falmouth packet? Answer to that!"

"That is not a more difficult matter than any of the rest. You forget that in the dialogue which took place between James and Major Spencer at the camp, the latter told him that he was about to take passage for Europe in the Falmouth packet, which then lay in Charleston harbor, and was about to sail. Macnab heard all that."

"True enough, and likely enough," returned the old lady; "but, though you show that it was Major Spencer's intention to go to Europe in the Falmouth packet, that will not show that it was also the intention of the murderer."

"Yet what more probable, and how natural for James Grayling to imagine such a thing! In the first place he knew that Macnab was a Briton; he felt convinced that he was a tory; and the inference was immediate, that such a person would scarcely have remained long in a country where such characters labored under so much odium, disfranchisement, and constant danger from popular tumults. The fact that Macnab was compelled to disguise his true sentiments, and affect those of the people against whom he fought so vindictively, shows what was his sense of the danger which he incurred. Now, it is not unlikely that Macnab was quite as well aware that the Falmouth packet was in Charleston, and about to sail, as Major Spencer. No doubt he was pursuing the same journey, with the same object, and had he not murdered Spencer, they would, very likely, have been fellow-passengers together to Europe. But, whether he knew the fact before or not, he probably heard it stated by Spencer while he seemed to be sleeping; and, even supposing that he did not then know, it was enough that he found this to be the fact on reaching the city. It was an after-thought to fly to Europe with his ill-gotten spoils; and whatever may have appeared a politic course to the criminal, would be a probable conjecture in the mind of him by whom he was suspected. The whole story is one of strong probabilities which happened to be verified; and, if proving anything, proves only that which we know—that James Grayling was a man of remarkably sagacious judgment, and quick, daring imagination. This quality of imagination, by the way, when possessed very strongly in connexion with shrewd common sense and well-balanced general faculties, makes that particular kind of intellect which, because of its promptness and powers of creation and combination, we call genius. It is genius only which can make ghosts, and James Grayling was a genius. He never, my son, saw any other ghosts than those of his own making!"

I heard my father with great patience to the end, though he seemed very tedious. He had taken a great deal of pains to destroy one of my greatest sources of pleasure. I need not add that I continued to believe in the ghost, and, with my grandmother, to reject the philosophy. It was more easy to believe the one than to comprehend the other.

The Two Camps
A Legend of The Old North State

"These, the forest born
And forest nurtured—a bold, hardy race,
Fearless and frank, unfettered, with big souls
In hour of danger."

I

It is frequently the case, in the experience of the professional novelist or tale-writer, that his neighbor comes in to his assistance when he least seeks, and, perhaps, least desires any succor. The worthy person, man or woman, however,—probably some excellent octogenarian whose claims to be heard are based chiefly upon the fact that he himself no longer possesses the faculty of hearing,—has some famous incident, some wonderful fact, of which he has been the eye-witness, or of which he has heard from his great-grandmother, which he fancies is the very thing to be woven into song or story. Such is the strong possession which the matter takes of his brain, that, if the novelist whom he seeks to benefit does not live within trumpet-distance, he gives him the narrative by means of post, some three sheets of stiff foolscap, for which the hapless tale-writer, whose works are selling in cheap editions at twelve or twenty cents, pays a sum of one dollar sixty-two postage. Now, it so happens, to increase the evil, that, in ninety-nine cases in the hundred, the fact thus laboriously stated is not worth a straw—consisting of some simple deed of violence, some mere murder, a downright blow with gun-butt or cudgel over the skull, or a hidden thrust, three inches deep, with dirk or bowie knife, into the abdomen, or at random among the lower ribs. The man dies and the murderer gets off to Texas, or is prematurely caught and stops by the way—and still stops by the way! The thing is fact, no doubt. The narrator saw it himself, or his brother saw it, or—more solemn, if not more certain testimony still—his grandmother saw it, long before he had eyes to see at all. The circumstance is attested by a cloud of witnesses—a truth solemnly sworn to—and yet, for the purposes of the tale-writer, of no manner of value. This assertion may somewhat conflict with the received opinions of many, who, accustomed to find deeds of violence recorded in almost every work of fiction, from the time of Homer to the present day, have rushed to the conclusion that this is all, and overlook that labor of the artist, by which an ordinary event is made to assume the character of novelty; in other words, to become an extraordinary event. The least difficult thing in the world, on the part of the writer of fiction, is to find the assassin and the bludgeon; the art is to make them appear in the right place, strike at the right time, and so adapt one fact to another, as to create mystery, awaken curiosity, inspire doubt as to the result, and bring about the catastrophe, by processes which shall be equally natural and unexpected. All that class of sagacious persons, therefore, who fancy they have found a mare's nest, when, in fact, they are only gazing at a goose's, are respectfully counselled that no fact—no tradition—is of any importance to the artist, unless it illustrates some history about which curiosity has already been awakened. A mere brutality, in which John beats and bruises Ben, and Ben in turn shoots John, putting eleven slugs, or thereabouts, between his collar-bone and vertebræ—or, maybe, stabs him under his left pap, or any where you please, is just as easily conceived by the novelist, without the help of history. Nay, for that matter, he would perhaps rather not have any precise facts in his way, in such cases, as then he will be able to regard the picturesque in the choice of his weapon, and to put the wounds in such parts of the body, as will better bear the examination of all persons. I deem it right to throw out this hint, just at this moment, as well for the benefit of my order as for my own protection. The times are hard, and the post-office requires all its dues in hard money. Literary men are not proverbially prepared at all seasons for any unnecessary outlay—and to be required to make advances for commodities of which they have on hand, at all times, the greatest abundance, is an injustice which, it is to be hoped, that this little intimation will somewhat lessen. We take for granted, therefore, that our professional brethren will concur with us in saying to the public, that we are all sufficiently provided with "disastrous chances" for some time to come—that our "moving accidents by flood and field" are particularly numerous, and of "hair-breadth 'scapes" we have enough to last a century. Murders, and such matters, as they are among the most ordinary events of the day, are decidedly vulgar; and, for mere cudgelling and bruises, the taste of the belles-lettres reader, rendered delicate by the monthly magazines, has voted them equally gross and unnatural.

But, if the character of the materials usually tendered to the novelist by the incident-mongers, is thus ordinarily worthless as we describe it, we sometimes are fortunate in finding an individual, here and there, in the deep forests,—a sort of recluse, hale and lusty, but white-headed,—who unfolds from his own budget of experience a rare chronicle, on which we delight to linger. Such an one breathes life into his deeds. We see them as we listen to his words. In lieu of the dead body of the fact, we have its living spirit—subtle, active, breathing and burning, and fresh in all the provocations and associations of life. Of this sort was the admirable characteristic narrative of Horse-Shoe Robinson, which we owe to Kennedy, and for which he was indebted to the venerable hero of the story. When we say that the subject of the sketch which follows was drawn from not dissimilar sources, we must beg our readers not to understand us as inviting any reference to that able and national story—with which it is by no means our policy or wish to invite or provoke comparison.

II

There are probably some old persons still living upon the upper dividing line between North and South Carolina, who still remember the form and features of the venerable Daniel Nelson. The old man was still living so late as 1817. At that period he removed to Mississippi, where, we believe, he died in less than three months after his change of residence. An old tree does not bear transplanting easily, and does not long survive it. Daniel Nelson came from Virginia when a youth. He was one of the first who settled on the southern borders of North Carolina, or, at least in that neighborhood where he afterwards passed the greatest portion of his days.

At that time the country was not only a forest, but one thickly settled with Indians. It constituted the favorite hunting-grounds for several of their tribes. But this circumstance did not discourage young Nelson. He was then a stalwart youth, broad-chested, tall, with a fiery eye, and an almost equally fiery soul—certainly with a very fearless one. His companions, who were few in number, were like himself. The spirit of old Daniel Boone was a more common one than is supposed. Adventure gladdened and excited their hearts,—danger only seemed to provoke their determination,—and mere hardship was something which their frames appeared to covet. It was as refreshing to them as drink. Having seen the country, and struck down some of its game,—tasted of its bear-meat and buffalo, its deer and turkey,—all, at that time, in the greatest abundance,—they returned for the one thing most needful to a brave forester in a new country,—a good, brisk, fearless wife, who, like the damsel in Scripture, would go whithersoever went the husband to whom her affections were surrendered. They had no fear, these bold young hunters, to make a home and rear an infant family in regions so remote from the secure walks of civilization. They had met and made an acquaintance and a sort of friendship with the Indians, and, in the superior vigor of their own frames, their greater courage, and better weapons, they perhaps had come to form a too contemptuous estimate of the savage. But they were not beguiled by him into too much confidence. Their log houses were so constructed as to be fortresses upon occasion, and they lived not so far removed from one another, but that the leaguer of one would be sure, in twenty-four hours, to bring the others to his assistance. Besides, with a stock of bear-meat and venison always on hand, sufficient for a winter, either of these fortresses might, upon common calculations, be maintained for several weeks against any single band of the Indians, in the small numbers in which they were wont to range together in those neighborhoods. In this way these bold pioneers took possession of the soil, and paved the way for still mightier generations. Though wandering, and somewhat averse to the tedious labors of the farm, they were still not wholly unmindful of its duties; and their open lands grew larger every season, and increasing comforts annually spoke for the increasing civilization of the settlers. Corn was in plenty in proportion to the bear-meat, and the squatters almost grew indifferent to those first apprehensions, which had made them watch the approaches of the most friendly Indian as if he had been an enemy. At the end of five years, in which they had suffered no hurt and but little annoyance of any sort from their wild neighbors, it would seem as if this confidence in the security of their situation was not without sufficient justification.

But, just then, circumstances seemed to threaten an interruption of this goodly state of things. The Indians were becoming discontented. Other tribes, more frequently in contact with the larger settlements of the whites,—wronged by them in trade, or demoralized by drink,—complained of their sufferings and injuries, or, as is more probable, were greedy to obtain their treasures, in bulk, which they were permitted to see, but denied to enjoy, or only in limited quantity. Their appetites and complaints were transmitted, by inevitable sympathies, to their brethren of the interior, and our worthy settlers upon the Haw, were rendered anxious at signs which warned them of a change in the peaceful relations which had hitherto existed in all the intercourse between the differing races. We need not dwell upon or describe these signs, with which, from frequent narratives of like character, our people are already sufficiently familiar. They were easily understood by our little colony, and by none more quickly than Daniel Nelson. They rendered him anxious, it is true, but not apprehensive; and, like a good husband, while he strove not to frighten his wife by what he said, he deemed it necessary to prepare her mind for the worst that might occur. This task over, he felt somewhat relieved, though, when he took his little girl, now five years old, upon his knee that evening, and looked upon his infant boy in the lap of his mother, he felt his anxieties very much increase; and that very night he resumed a practice which he had latterly abandoned, but which had been adopted as a measure of strict precaution, from the very first establishment of their little settlement. As soon as supper was over, he resumed his rifle, thrust his *couteau de chasse* into his belt, and, taking his horn about his neck, and calling up his trusty dog, Clinch, he proceeded to scour the woods immediately around his habitation. This task, performed with the stealthy caution of the hunter, occupied some time, and, as the night was clear, a bright starlight, the weather moderate, and his own mood restless, he determined to strike through the forest to the settlement of Jacob Ransom, about four miles off, in order to prompt him, and, through him, others of the neighborhood, to the continued exercise of a caution which he now thought necessary. The rest of this night's adventure we propose to let him tell in his own words, as he has been heard to relate it a thousand times in his old age, at a period of life when, with one foot in his grave, to suppose him guilty of falsehood, or of telling that which he did not himself fervently believe, would be, among all those who knew him, to suppose the most impossible and extravagant thing in the world.

III

"Well, my friends," said the veteran, then seventy, drawing his figure up to its fullest height, and extending his right arm, while his left still grasped the muzzle of his ancient rifle, which he swayed from side to side, the butt resting on the floor—"Well, my friends, seeing that the night was cl'ar, and there was no wind, and feeling as how I didn't want for sleep, I called to Clinch and took the path for Jake Ransom's. I knew that Jake was a sleepy sort of chap, and if the red-skins caught any body napping, he'd, most likely, be the man. But I confess, 'twarn't so much for his sake, as for the sake of all,—of my own as well as the rest;—for, when I thought how soon, if we warn't all together in the business, I might see, without being able to put in, the long yellow hair of Betsy and the babies twirling on the thumbs of some painted devil of the tribe,—I can't tell you how I felt, but it warn't like a human, though I shivered mightily like one,—'twas wolfish, as if the hair was turned in and rubbing agin the very heart within me. I said my prayers, where I stood, looking up at the stars, and thinking that, after all, all was in the hands and the marcy of God. This sort o' thinking quieted me, and I went ahead pretty free, for I knew the track jest as well by night as by day, though I didn't go so quick, for I was all the time on the look-out for the enemy. Now, after we reached a place in the woods where there was a gully and a mighty bad crossing, there were two roads to get to Jake's—one by the hollows, and one jest across the hills. I don't know why, but I didn't give myself time to think, and struck right across the hill, though that was rather the longest way.

"Howsomedever, on I went, and Clinch pretty close behind me. The dog was a good dog, with a mighty keen nose to hunt, but jest then he didn't seem to have the notion for it. The hill was a sizeable one, a good stretch to foot, and I began to remember, after awhile, that I had been in the woods from blessed dawn; and that made me see how it was with poor Clinch, and why he didn't go for'ad; but I was more than half way, and wasn't guine to turn back till I had said my say to Jake. Well, when I got to the top of the hill, I stopped, and rubbed my eyes. I had cause to rub 'em, for what should I see at a distance but a great fire. At first I was afeard lest it was Jake's house, but I considered, the next moment, that he lived to the left, and this fire was cl'ar to the right, and it did seem to me as if 'twas more near to my own. Here was something to scare a body. But I couldn't stay there looking, and it warn't now a time to go to Jake's; so I turned off, and, though Clinch was mighty onwilling, I bolted on the road to the fire. I say road, but there was no road; but the trees warn't over-thick, and the land was too poor for undergrowth; so we got on pretty well, considering. But, what with the tire I had had, and the scare I felt, it seemed as if I didn't get for'ad a bit. There was the fire still burning as bright and almost as far off as ever. When I saw this I stopt and looked at Clinch, and he stopped and looked at me, but neither of us had any thing to say. Well, after a moment's thinking, it seemed as if I shouldn't be much of a man to give up when I had got so far, so I pushed on. We crossed more than one little hill, then down and through the hollow, and then up the hill again. At last we got upon a small mountain the Indians called Nolleehatchie, and then it seemed as if the fire had come to a stop, for it was now burning bright, on a little hill below me, and not two hundred yards in front. It was a regular camp fire, pretty big, and there was more than a dozen Indians sitting round it. 'Well,' says I to myself, 'it's come upon us mighty sudden, and what's to be done? Not a soul in the settlement knows it but myself, and nobody's on the watch. They'll be sculped, every human of them, in their very beds, or, moutbe, waken up in the blaze, to be shot with arrows as they run.' I was in a cold sweat to think of it. I didn't know what to think and what to do. I looked round to Clinch, and the strangest thing of all was to see him sitting quiet on his haunches, looking at me, and at the stars, and not at the fire jest before him. Now, Clinch was a famous fine hunting dog, and jest as good on an Indian trail as any other. He know'd my ways, and what I wanted, and would give tongue, or keep it still, jest as I axed him. It was sensible enough, jest then, that he shouldn't bark, but, dang it!—he didn't even seem to see. Now, there warn't a dog in all the settlement so quick and keen to show sense as Clinch, even when he didn't say a word;—and to see him looking as if he didn't know and didn't care what was a-going on, with his eyes sot in his head and glazed over with sleep, was, as I may say, very onnatural, jest at that time, in a dog of any onderstanding. So I looked at him, half angry, and when he saw me looking at him, he jest stretched himself off, put his nose on his legs, and went to sleep in 'arnest. I had half a mind to lay my knife-handle over his head, but I considered better of it, and though it did seem the strangest thing in the world that he shouldn't even try to get to the fire, for warm sake, yet I recollected that dog natur', like human natur', can't stand every thing, and he hadn't such good reason as I had, to know that the Indians were no longer friendly to us. Well, there I stood, a pretty considerable chance, looking, and wondering, and onbeknowing what to do. I was mighty beflustered. But at last I felt ashamed to be so oncertain, and then again it was a needcessity that we should know the worst one time or another, so I determined to push for'ad. I was no slouch of a hunter, as you may suppose; so, as I was nearing the camp, I begun sneaking; and, taking it sometimes on hands and knees, and sometimes flat to the ground, where there was neither tree nor bush to cover me, I went ahead, Clinch keeping close behind me, and not showing any notion of what I was after. It was a slow business, because it was a ticklish business; but I was a leetle too anxious to be altogether so careful as a good sneak ought to be, and I went on rather faster than I would advise any young man to go in a time of war, when the inimy is in the neighborhood. Well, as I went, there was the fire, getting larger and larger every minute, and there were the Indians round it, getting plainer and plainer. There was so much smoke that there was no making out, at any distance, any but their figures, and these, every now and then, would be so wrapt in the smoke that not more than half of them could be seen at the same moment. At last I stopped, jest at a place where I thought I could make out all that I wanted. There was a sizeable rock before me, and I leaned my elbows on it to look. I reckon I warn't more than thirty yards from the fire. There were some bushes betwixt us, and what with the bushes and the smoke, it was several minutes before I could separate man from man, and see what they were all adoing, and when I did, it was only for a moment at a time, when a puff of smoke would wrap them all, and make it as difficult as ever. But when I did contrive to see clearly, the sight was one to worry me to the core, for, in the midst of the redskins, I could see a white one, and that white one a woman. There was no mistake. There were the Indians, some with their backs, and some with their faces to me; and there, a little a-one side, but still among them, was a woman. When the smoke blowed off, I could see her white face, bright like any star, shining out of the clouds, and looking so pale and ghastly that my blood cruddled in my veins to think lest she might be dead from fright. But it couldn't be so, for she was sitting up and looking about her. But the Indians were motionless. They jest sat or lay as when I first saw them—doing nothing—saying nothing, but jest as motionless as the stone under my elbow. I couldn't stand looking where I was, so I began creeping again, getting nigher and nigher, until it seemed to me as if I ought to be able to read every face. But what with the paint and smoke, I couldn't make out a single Indian. Their figures seemed plain enough in their buffalo-skins and blankets, but their faces seemed always in the dark. But it wasn't so with the woman. I could make her out clearly. She was very young; I reckon not more than fifteen, and it seemed to me as if I knew her looks very well. She was very handsome, and her hair was loosed upon her back. My heart felt strange to see her. I was weak as any child. It seemed as if I could die for the gal, and yet I hadn't strength enough to raise my rifle to my shoulder. The weakness kept on me the more I looked; for every moment seemed to make the poor child more and more dear to me. But the strangest thing of all was to see how motionless was every Indian in the camp. Not a word was spoken—not a limb or finger stirred. There they sat, or lay, round about the fire, like so many effigies, looking at the gal, and she looking at them. I never was in such a fix of fear and weakness in my life. What was I to do? I had got so nigh that I could have stuck my knife, with a jerk, into the heart of any one of the party, yet I hadn't the soul to lift it; and before I knew where I was, I cried like a child. But my crying didn't make 'em look about 'em. It only brought my poor dog Clinch leaping upon me, and whining, as if he wanted to give me consolation. Hardly knowing what I did, I tried to set him upon the camp, but the poor fellow didn't seem to understand me; and in my desperation, for it was a sort of madness growing out of my scare, I jumped headlong for'ad, jest where I saw the party sitting, willing to lose my life rather than suffer from such a strange sort of misery.

IV

"Will you believe me! there were no Indians, no young woman, no fire! I stood up in the very place where I had seen the blaze and the smoke, and there was nothing! I looked for'ad and about me—there was no sign of fire any where. Where I stood was covered with dry leaves, the same as the rest of the forest. I was stupefied. I was like a man roused out of sleep by a strange dream, and seeing nothing. All was dark and silent. The stars were overhead, but that was all the light I had. I was more scared than ever, and, as it's a good rule when a man feels that he can do nothing himself, to look to the great God who can do every thing, I kneeled down and said my prayers—the second time that night that I had done the same thing, and the second time, I reckon, that I had ever done so in the woods. After that I felt stronger.

I felt sure that this sign hadn't been shown to me for nothing; and while I was turning about, looking and thinking to turn on the back track for home, Clinch began to prick up his ears and waken up. I clapped him on his back, and got my knife ready. It might be a *painter* that stirred him, for he could scent that beast a great distance. But, as he showed no fright, only a sort of quickening, I knew there was nothing to fear. In a moment he started off, and went boldly ahead. I followed him, but hadn't gone twenty steps down the hill and into the hollow, when I heard something like a groan. This quickened me, and keeping up with the dog, he led me to the foot of the hollow, where there was a sort of pond. Clinch ran right for it, and another groan set me in the same direction. When I got up to the dog, he was on the butt-end of an old tree that had fallen, I reckon, before my time, and was half buried in the water. I jumped on it, and walked a few steps for'ad, when, what should I see but a human, half across the log, with his legs hanging in the water, and his head down. I called Clinch back out of my way, and went to the spot. The groans were pretty constant. I stooped down and laid my hands upon the person, and, as I felt the hair, I knew it was an Indian. The head was clammy with blood, so that my fingers stuck, and when I attempted to turn it to look at the face, the groan was deeper than ever; but 'twarn't a time to suck one's fingers. I took him up, clapped my shoulders to it, and, fixing my feet firmly on the old tree, which was rather slippery, I brought the poor fellow out without much trouble. Though tall, he was not heavy, and was only a boy of fourteen or fifteen. The wonder was how a lad like that should get into such a fix. Well, I brought him out and laid him on the dry leaves. His groans stopped, and I thought he was dead, but I felt his heart, and it was still warm, and I thought, though I couldn't be sure, there was a beat under my fingers. What to do was the next question. It was now pretty late in the night. I had been all day a-foot, and, though still willing to go, yet the thought of such a weight on my shoulders made me stagger. But 'twouldn't do to leave him where he was to perish. I thought, if so be I had a son in such a fix, what would I think of the stranger who should go home and wait till daylight to give him help! No, darn my splinters, said I,—though I had just done my prayers,—if I leave the lad—and, tightening my girth, I give my whole soul to it, and hoisted him on my shoulders. My cabin, I reckoned, was a good three miles off. You can guess what trouble I had, and what a tire under my load, before I got home and laid the poor fellow down by the fire. I then called up Betsy, and we both set to work to see if we could stir up the life that was in him. She cut away his hair, and I washed the blood from his head, which was chopped to the bone, either with a knife or hatchet. It was a God's blessing it hadn't gone into his brain, for it was fairly enough aimed for it, jest above the ear. When we come to open his clothes, we found another wound in his side. This was done with a knife, and, I suppose, was pretty deep. He had lost blood enough, for all his clothes were stiff with it. We knew nothing much of doctoring, but we had some rum in the cabin, and after washing his wounds clean with it, and pouring some down his throat, he began to groan more freely, and by that we knew he was coming to a nateral feeling. We rubbed his body down with warm cloths, and after a little while, seeing that he made some signs, I give him water as much as he could drink. This seemed to do him good, and having done every thing that we thought could help him, we wrapped him up warmly before the fire, and I stretched myself off beside him. 'Twould be a long story to tell, step by step, how he got on. It's enough to say that he didn't die that bout. We got him on his legs in a short time, doing little or nothing for him more than we did at first. The lad was a good lad, though, at first, when he first came to his senses, he was mighty shy, wouldn't look steadily in our faces, and, I do believe, if he could have got out of the cabin, would have done so as soon as he could stagger. But he was too weak to try that, and, meanwhile, when he saw our kindness, he was softened. By little and little, he got to play with my little Lucy, who was not quite six years old; and, after a while, he seemed to be never better pleased than when they played together. The child, too, after her first fright, leaned to the lad, and was jest as willing to play with him as if he had been a cl'ar white like herself. He could say a few words of English from the beginning, and learnt quickly; but, though he talked tolerable free for an Indian, yet I could never get him to tell me how he was wounded, or by whom. His brow blackened when I spoke of it, and his lips would be shut together, as if he was ready to fight sooner than to speak. Well, I didn't push him to know, for I was pretty sure the head of the truth will be sure to come some time or other, if you once have it by the tail, provided you don't jerk it off by straining too hard upon it.

V

"I suppose the lad had been with us a matter of six weeks, getting better every day, but so slowly that he had not, at the end of that time, been able to leave the picket. Meanwhile, our troubles with the Indians were increasing. As yet, there had been no bloodshed in our quarter, but we heard of murders and sculpings on every side, and we took for granted that we must have our turn. We made our preparations, repaired the pickets, laid in ammunition, and took turns for scouting nightly. At length, the signs of Indians got to be thick in our parts, though we could see none. Jake Ransom had come upon one of their camps after they had left it; and we had reason to apprehend every thing, inasmuch as the outlyers didn't show themselves, as they used to do, but prowled about the cabins and went from place to place, only by night, or by close skulking in the thickets. One evening after this, I went out as usual to go the rounds, taking Clinch with me, but I hadn't got far from the gate, when the dog stopped and gave a low bark;—then I knew there was mischief, so I turned round quietly, without making any show of scare, and got back safely, though not a minute too soon. They trailed me to the gate the moment after I had got it fastened, and were pretty mad, I reckon, when they found their plan had failed for surprising me. But for the keen nose of poor Clinch, with all my skill in scouting,—and it was not small even in that early day,—they'd 'a had me, and all that was mine, before the sun could open his eyes to see what they were after. Finding they had failed in their ambush, they made the woods ring with the war-whoop, which was a sign that they were guine to give us a regular siege. At the sound of the whoop, we could see the eyes of the Indian boy brighten, and his ears prick up, jest like a hound's when he first gets scent of the deer, or hears the horn of the hunter. I looked closely at the lad, and was dub'ous what to do. He moutbe only an enemy in the camp, and while I was fighting in front, he might be cutting the throats of my wife and children within. I did not tell you that I had picked up his bow and arrows near the little lake where I had found him, and his hunting-knife was sticking in his belt when I brought him home. Whether to take these away from him, was the question. Suppose I did, a billet of wood would answer pretty near as well. I thought the matter over while I watched him. Thought runs mighty quick in time of danger! Well, after turning it over on every side, I concluded 'twas better to trust him jest as if he had been a sure friend. I couldn't think, after all we had done for him, that he'd be false, so I said to him—'Lenatewá!'—'twas so he called himself—'those are your people!' 'Yes!' he answered slowly, and lifting himself up as if he had been a lord—he was a stately-looking lad, and carried himself like the son of a Micco,* as he was—'Yes, they are the people of Lenatewá—must he go to them?' and he made the motion of going out. But I stopped him. I was not willing to lose the security which I had from his being a sort of prisoner. 'No,' said I; 'no, Lenatewá, not to-night. To-morrow will do. To-morrow you can tell them I am a friend, not an enemy, and they should not come to burn my wigwam.' 'Brother—friend!' said the lad, advancing with a sort of freedom and taking my hand. He then went to my wife, and did the same thing,—not regarding she was a woman,—'Brother—friend!' I watched him closely, watched his eye and his motions, and I said to Betsy, 'The lad is true; don't be afeard!' But we passed a weary night. Every now and then we could hear the whoop of the Indians. From the loopholes we could see the light of three fires on different sides, by which we knew that they were prepared to cut off any help that might come to us from the rest of the settlement. But I didn't give in or despair. I worked at one thing or another all night, and though Lenatewá gave me no help, yet he sat quietly, or laid himself down before the fire, as if he had nothing in the world to do in the business. Next morning by daylight, I found him already dressed in the same bloody clothes which he had on when I found him. He had thrown aside all that I gave him, and though the hunting-shirt and leggins which he now wore, were very much stained with blood and dirt, he had fixed them about him with a good deal of care and neatness, as if preparing to see company. I must tell you that an Indian of good family always has a nateral sort of grace and dignity which I never saw in a white man. He was busily engaged looking through one of the loopholes, and though I could distinguish nothing, yet it was cl'ar that he saw something to interest him mightily. I soon found out that, in spite of all my watchfulness, he had contrived to have some sort of correspondence and communication with those outside. This was a wonder to me then, for I did not recollect his bow and arrows. It seems that he had shot an arrow through one of the loop-holes, to the end of which he had fastened a tuft of his own hair. The effect of this was considerable, and to this it was owing that, for a few hours afterwards, we saw not an Indian. The arrow was shot at the very peep of day. What they were about, in the meantime, I can only guess, and the guess was only easy, after I had known all that was to happen. That they were in council what to do was cl'ar enough. I was not to know

* A prince or chief.

that the council was like to end in cutting some of their own throats instead of ours. But when we did see the enemy fairly, they came out of the woods in two parties, not actually separated, but not moving together. It seemed as if there was some strife among them. Their whole number could not be less than forty, and some eight or ten of these walked apart under the lead of a chief, a stout, dark-looking fellow, one-half of whose face was painted black as midnight, with a red circle round both his eyes. The other party was headed by an old white-headed chief, who couldn't ha' been less than sixty years—a pretty fellow, you may be sure, at his time of life, to be looking after sculps of women and children. While I was kneeling at my loop-hole looking at them, Lenatewá came to me, and touching me on the arm, pointed to the old chief, saying—'Micco Lenatewá Glucco,' by which I guessed he was the father or grandfather of the lad. 'Well,' I said, seeing that the best plan was to get their confidence and friendship if possible,—'Well, lad, go to your father and tell him what Daniel Nelson has done for you, and let's have peace. We can fight, boy, as you see; we have plenty of arms and provisions; and with this rifle, though you may not believe it, I could pick off your father, the king, and that other chief, who has so devilled himself up with paint.' 'Shoot!' said the lad quickly, pointing to the chief of whom I had last spoken. 'Ah! he is your enemy then?' The lad nodded his head, and pointed to the wound on his temple, and that in his side. I now began to see the true state of the case. 'No,' said I; 'no, Lenatewá, I will shoot none. I am for peace. I would do good to the Indians, and be their friend. Go to your father and tell him so. Go, and make him be my friend.' The youth caught my hand, placed it on the top of his head, and exclaimed, 'Good!' I then attended him down to the gate, but, before he left the cabin, he stopped and put his hand on the head of little Lucy,—and I felt glad, for it seemed to say, 'You shan't be hurt—not a hair of your head!' I let him out, fastened up, and then hastened to the loop-hole.

VI

"And now came a sight to tarrify. As soon as the Indians saw the young prince, they set up a general cry. I couldn't tell whether it was of joy, or what. He went for'ad boldly, though he was still quite weak, and the king at the head of his party advanced to meet him. The other and smaller party, headed by the black chief, whom young Lenatewá had told me to shoot, came forward also, but very slowly, and it seemed as if they were doubtful whether to come or go. Their leader looked pretty much beflustered. But they hadn't time for much study, for, after the young prince had met his father, and a few words had passed between them, I saw the finger of Lenatewá point to the black chief. At this, he lifted up his clenched fists, and worked his body as if he was talking angrily. Then, sudden, the war-whoop sounded from the king's party, and the other troop of Indians began to run, the black chief at their head; but he had not got twenty steps when a dozen arrows went into him, and he tumbled for'a'ds, and grappled with the earth. It was all over with him. His party was scattered on all sides, but were not pursued. It seemed that all the arrows had been aimed at the one person, and when he sprawled, there was an end to it: the whole affair was over in five minutes.

VII

"It was a fortunate affair for us. Lenatewá soon brought the old Micco to terms of peace. For that matter, he had only consented to take up the red stick because it was reported by the black chief—who was the uncle of the young Micco, and had good reasons for getting him out of the way—that he had been murdered by the whites. This driv' the old man to desperation, and brought him down upon us. When he knew the whole truth, and saw what friends we had been to his son, there was no end to his thanks and promises. He swore to be my friend while the sun shone, while the waters run, and while the mountains stood, and I believe, if the good old man had been spared so long, he would have been true to his oath. But, while he lived, he kept it, and so did his son when he succeeded him as Micco Glucco. Year after year went by, and though there was frequent war between the Indians and the whites, yet Lenatewá kept it from our doors. He himself was at war several times with our people, but never with our settlement. He put his *totem* on our trees, and the Indians knew that they were sacred. But, after a space of eleven years, there was a change. The young prince seemed to have forgotten our friendship. We now never saw him among us, and, unfortunately, some of our young men—the young men of our settlement—murdered three young warriors of the Ripparee tribe, who were found on horses stolen from us. I was very sorry when I heard it, and began to fear the consequences; and they came upon us when we least looked for it. I had every reason to think that Lenatewá would still keep the warfare from my little family, but I did not remember that he was the prince of a tribe only, and not of the nation. This was a national warfare, in which the whole Cherokee people were in arms. Many persons, living still, remember that terrible war, and how the Carolinians humbled them at last; but there's no telling how much blood was shed in that war, how many sculps taken, how much misery suffered by young and old, men, women, and children. Our settlement had become so large and scattered that we had to build a sizeable blockhouse, which we stored, and to which we could retreat whenever it was necessary. We took possession of it on hearing from our scouts that Indian trails had been seen, and there we put the women and children, under a strong guard. By day we tended our farms, and only went to our families at night. We had kept them in this fix for five weeks or thereabouts, and there was no attack. The Indian signs disappeared, and we all thought the storm had blown over, and began to hope and to believe that the old friendship of Lenatewá had saved us. With this thinking, we began to be less watchful. The men would stay all night at the farms, and sometimes, in the day, would carry with them the women, and sometimes some even the children. I cautioned them agin this, but they mocked me, and said I was gitting old and scary. I told them, 'Wait and see who'll scare first.' But, I confess, not seeing any Indians in all my scouting, I began to feel and think like the rest, and to grow careless. I let Betsy go now and then with me to the farm, though she kept it from me that she had gone there more than once with Lucy, without any man protector. Still, as it was only a short mile and a half from the block, and we could hear of no Indians, it did not seem so venturesome a thing. One day we heard of some very large b'ars among the thickets—a famous range for them, about four miles from the settlement; and a party of us, Simon Lorris, Hugh Darling, Jake Ransom, William Harkless, and myself, taking our dogs, set off on the hunt. We started the b'ar with a rush, and I got the first shot at a mighty big she b'ar, the largest I had ever seen—lamed the critter slightly, and dashed into the thickets after her! The others pushed, in another direction, after the rest, leaving me to finish my work as I could.

"I had two dogs with me, Clap and Claw, but they were young things, and couldn't be trusted much in a close brush with a b'ar. Old Clinch was dead, or he'd ha' made other guess-work with the varmint. But, hot after the b'ar, I didn't think of the quality of the dogs till I found myself in a fair wrestle with the brute. I don't brag, my friends, but that *was* a fight. I tell you my breath was clean gone, for the b'ar had me about the thin of my body, and I thought I was doubled up enough to be laid down without more handling. But my heart was strong when I thought of Betsy and the children, and I got my knife, with hard *jugging*—though I couldn't use my arm above my elbow—through the old critter's hide, and in among her ribs. That only seemed to make her hug closer, and I reckon I was clean gone, if it hadn't been that she blowed out before me. I had worked a pretty deep window in her waist, and then life run out plentiful. Her nose dropped agin my breast, and then her paws; and when the strain was gone, I fell down like a sick child, and she fell on top of me. But she warn't in a humor to do more mischief. She roughed me once or twice more with her paws, but that was only because she was at her last kick. There I lay a matter of half an hour, with the dead b'ar alongside o' me. I was almost as little able to move as she, and I vomited as if I had taken physic. When I come to myself and got up, there was no sound of the hunters. There I was with the two dogs and the b'ar, all alone, and the sun already long past the turn. My horse, which I had fastened outside of the thicket, had slipped his bridle, and, I reckoned, had either strayed off grazing, or had pushed back directly for the block. These things didn't make me feel much better. But, though my stomach didn't feel altogether right, and my ribs were as sore as if I had been sweating under a coating of hickory, I felt that there was no use and no time to stand there grunting. But I made out to skin and to cut up the b'ar, and a noble mountain of fat she made. I took the skin with me, and, covering the flesh with bark, I whistled off the dogs, after they had eat to fill, and pushed after my horse. I followed his track for some time, till I grew fairly tired. He had gone off in a scare and at a full gallop, and, instead of going home, had dashed down the lower side of the thicket, then gone aside, to round some of the hills, and thrown himself out of the track, it moutbe seven miles or more. When I found this, I saw there was no use to hunt him that day and afoot, and I had no more to do but turn about, and push as fast as I could for the block. But this was work enough. By this time the sun was pretty low, and there was now a good seven miles, work it how I could, before me. But I was getting over my b'ar-sickness, and though my legs felt weary enough, my stomach was better, and my heart braver; and, as I was in no hurry, having the whole night before me, and knowing the way by night as well as by light, I began to feel cheerful enough, all things considering. I pushed on slowly, stopping every now and then for rest, and recovering my strength this way. I had some parched meal and sugar in my pouch which I ate, and it helped me mightily. It was my only dinner that day. The evening got to be very still. I wondered I had seen and heard nothing of Jake Ransom and the rest, but I didn't feel at all oneasy about them, thinking that, like all other hunters, they would naterally follow the game to any distance. But, jest when I was thinking about them, I heard a gun, then another, and after that all got to be as quiet as ever. I looked to my own rifle and felt for my knife, and put forward a little more briskly. I suppose I had walked an hour after this, when it came on close dark, and I was still four good miles from the block. The night was cloudy, there were no stars, and the feeling in the air was damp and oncomfortable. I began to wish I was safe home, and felt queerish, almost as bad as I did when the b'ar was 'bracing me; but it warn't so much the body-sickness as the heart-sickness. I felt as if something was going wrong. Jest as this feeling was most worrisome, I stumbled over a human. My blood cruddled, when, feeling about, I put my hand on his head, and found the sculp was gone. Then I knew there was mischief. I couldn't make out who 'twas that was under me, but I reckoned 'twas one of the hunters. There was nothing to be done but to push for'ad. I didn't feel any more tire. I felt ready for fight, and when I thought of our wives and children in the block, and what might become of them, I got wolfish, though the Lord only knows what I was minded to do. I can't say I had any raal sensible thoughts of what was to be done in the business. I didn't trust myself to think whether the Indians had been to the block yet or no; though ugly notions came across me when I remembered how we let the women and children go about to the farms. I was in a complete fever and agy. I scorched one time and shivered another, but I pushed on, for there was now no more feeling of tire in my limbs than if they were made of steel. By this time I had reached that long range of hills where I first saw that strange campfire, now eleven years gone, that turned out to be a deception, and it was nateral enough that the thing should come fresh into my mind, jest at that moment. While I was thinking over the wonder, and asking myself, as I had done over and often before, what it possibly could mean, I reached the top of one of the hills, from which I could see, in daylight, the whole country for a matter of ten miles or more on every side. What was my surprise, do you reckon, when there, jest on the very same hill opposite where I had seen that apparition of a camp, I saw another, and this time it was a raal one. There was a rousing blaze, and though the woods and undergrowth were thicker on this than on the other side, from which I had seen it before, yet I could make out that there were several figures, and them Indians. It sort o' made me easier to see the enemy before, and then I could better tell what I had to do. I was to spy out the camp, see what the red-devils were thinking to do, and what they had already done. I was a little better scout and hunter this time than when I made the same sort o' search before, and I reckoned that I could get nigh enough to see all that was going on, without stirring up any dust among 'em. But I had to keep the dogs back. I couldn't tie 'em up, for they'd howl; so I stripped my hunting-shirt and put it down for one to guard, and I gave my cap and horn to another. I knew they'd never leave 'em, for I had l'arned 'em all that sort of business—to watch as well as to fetch and carry. I then said a sort of short running prayer, and took the trail. I had to work for'ad slowly. If I had gone on this time as I did in that first camp transaction, I'd ha' lost my sculp to a sartainty. Well, to shorten a long business, I tell you that I got nigh enough, without scare or surprise, to see all that I cared to see, and a great deal more than I wished to see; and now, for the first time, I saw the meaning of that sight which I had, eleven years before, of the camp that come to nothing. I saw that first sight over again, the Indians round the fire, a young woman in the middle, and that young woman my own daughter, my child, my poor, dear Lucy!

VIII

"That was a sight for a father. I can't tell you—and I won't try—how I felt. But I lay there, resting upon my hands and knees, jest as if I had been turned into stone with looking. I lay so for a good half hour, I reckon, without stirring a limb; and you could only tell that life was in me, by seeing the big drops that squeezed out of my eyes now and then, and by a sort of shivering that shook me as you sometimes see the canebrake shaking with the gust of the pond inside. I tried to pray to God for help, but I couldn't pray, and as for thinking, that was jest as impossible. But I could do nothing by looking, and for that matter, it was pretty cla'r to me, as I stood, with no help—by myself—one rifle only and knife—I couldn't do much by moving. I could have lifted the gun, and in a twinkle tumbled the best fellow in the gang, but what good was that guine to do me? I was never fond of blood-spilling, and if I could have been made sure of my daughter, I'd ha' been willing that the red devils should have had leave to live for ever. What was I to do? Go to the block? Who know'd if it warn't taken, with every soul in it? And where else was I to look for help? Nowhere, nowhere but to God! I groaned—I groaned so loud that I was dreadful 'feared that they'd hear me; but they were too busy among themselves, eating supper, and poor Lucy in the midst, not eating, but so pale, and looking so miserable—jest as I had seen her, when she was only a child—in the same fix, though 'twas only an appearance—eleven years ago! Well, at last, I turned off. As I couldn't say what to do, I was too miserable to look, and I went down to the bottom of the hill and rolled about on the ground, pulling the hair out of my head and groaning, as if that was to do me any good. Before I knew where I was, there was a hand on my shoulder. I jumped up to my feet, and flung my rifle over my head, meaning to bring the butt down upon the stranger—but his voice stopped me.

" 'Brother,' said he, 'me Lenatewá!'

"The way he talked, his soft tones, made me know that the young prince meant to be friendly, and I gave him my hand; but the tears gushed out as I did so, and I cried out like a man struck in the very heart, while I pointed to the hill—'My child, my child!'

" 'Be man!' said he, 'come!' pulling me away.

" 'But, will you save her, Lenatewá?'

"He did not answer instantly, but led me to the little lake, and pointed to the old tree over which I had borne his lifeless body so many years ago. By that I knew he meant to tell me, he had not forgotten what I had done for him; and would do for me all he could. But this did not satisfy me. I must know how and when it was to be done, and what was his hope; for I could see from his caution, in leading me away from the camp, that he did not command the party, and had no power over them. He then asked me, if I had not seen the paint of the warriors in the camp. But I had seen nothing but the fix of my child. He then described the paint to me, which was his way of showing me that the party on the hill were his deadly enemies. The paint about their eyes was that of the great chief, his uncle, who had tried to murder him years ago, and who had been shot, in my sight, by the party of his father. The young chief now in command of the band on the hill was the son of his uncle, and sworn to revenge the death of his father upon him, Lenatewá. This he made me understand in a few minutes. And he gave me farther to onderstand, that there was no way of getting my child from them onless by cunning. He had but two followers with him, and they were even then busy in making preparations. But of these preparations he either would not or could not give me any account; and I had to wait on him with all the patience I could muster: and no easy trial it was, for an Indian is the most cool and slow-moving creature in the world, unless he's actually fighting, and then he's about the quickest. After awhile, Lenatewá led me round the hill. We fetched a pretty smart reach, and before I knew where I was, he led me into a hollow that I had never seen before. Here, to my surprise, there were no less than twelve or fourteen horses fastened, that these red devils had stolen from the settlement that very day, and mine was among them. I did not know it till the young prince told me.

" 'Him soon move,' said he, pointing to one on the outside, which a close examination showed me to be my own—'Him soon move,'—and these words gave me a notion of his plan. But he did not allow me to have any hand in it—not jest then, at least. Bidding me keep a watch on the fire above, for the hollow in which we stood was at the foot of the very hill the Indians had made their camp on—though the stretch was a long one between—he pushed for'ad like a shadow, and so slily, so silently, that, though I thought myself a good deal of a scout before, I saw then that I warn't fit to hold a splinter to him. In a little time he had unhitched my horse, and quietly led him farther down the hollow, half round the hill, and then up the opposite hill. There was very little noise, the wind was from the camp, and, though they didn't show any alarm, I was never more scary in my life. I followed Lenatewá, and found where he had fastened my nag. He had placed him several hundred yards from the Indians, on his way to the block; and, where we now stood, owing to the bend of the hollow, the camp of the Indians was between us and where they had hitched the stolen horses. When I saw this, I began to guess something of his plan. Meantime, one after the other, his two followers came up, and made a long report to him in their own language. This done, he told me that three of my hunting companions had been sculped, the other, who was Hugh Darling, had got off cl'ar, though fired upon twice, and had alarmed the block and that my daughter had been made prisoner at the farm to which she had gone without any company. This made me a little easier, and Lenatewá then told me what he meant to do. In course, I had to do something myself towards it. Off he went, with his two men, leaving me to myself. When I thought they had got pretty fairly round the hill, I started back for the camp, trying my best, you may be sure, to move as slily as Lenatewá. I got within twenty-five yards, I reckon, when I thought it better to lie by quietly and wait. I could see every head in the huddle, and my poor child among them, looking whiter than a sheet, beside their ugly painted skins. Well, I hadn't long to wait, when there was such an uproar among the stolen horses in the hollow on the opposite side of the hill—such a trampling, such a whinnying and whickering, you never heard the like. Now, you must know, that a stolen horse, to an Indian, is jest as precious as a sweetheart to a white man; and when the rumpus reached the camp, there was a rush of every man among them, for his critter. Every redskin, but one, went over the hill after the horses, and he jumped up with the rest, but didn't move off. He stood over poor Lucy with his tomahawk, shaking it above her head, as if guine to strike every minute. She, poor child—I could see her as plain as the firelight, for she sat jest on one side of it—her hands were clasped together. She was praying, for she must have looked every minute to be knocked on the head. You may depend, I found it very hard to keep in. I was a'most biling over, the more when I saw the red devil making his flourishes, every now and then, close to the child's ears, with his bloody we'pon. But it was a needcessity to keep in till the sounds died off pretty much, so as not to give them any scare this side, till they had dashed ahead pretty far 'pon the other. I don't know that I waited quite as long as I ought to, but I waited as long as my feelings would let me, and then I dropped the sight of my rifle as close as I could fix it on the breast of the Indian that had the keeping of my child. I took aim, but I felt I was a little tremorsome, and I stopped. I know'd I had but one shoot, and if I didn't onbutton him in that one, it would be a bad shoot for poor Lucy. I didn't fear to hit *her*, and I was pretty sure I'd hit him. But it must be a dead shot to do good, for I know'd if I only hurt him, that he'd sink the tomahawk in her head with what strength he had left him. I brought myself to it again, and this time I felt strong. I could jest hear a little of the hubbub of men and horses afar off. I knew it was the time, and, resting the side of the muzzle against a tree, I give him the whole blessing of the bullet. I didn't stop to ask what luck, but run in, with a sort o' cry, to do the finishing with the knife. But the thing was done a'ready. The beast was on his back, and I only had to use the knife in cutting the vines that fastened the child to the sapling behind her. The brave gal didn't scream or faint. She could only say, 'Oh, my father!' and I could only say, 'Oh! my child!' And what a precious hug followed; but it was only for a minute. We had no time to waste in hugging. We pushed at once for the place where I had left the critter, and if the good old nag ever used his four shanks to any purpose, he did that night. I reckon it was a joyful surprise to poor Betsy when we broke into the block. She had given it out for sartin that she'd never see me or the child again, with a nateral sculp on our heads.

IX

"There's no need to tell you the whole story of this war between our people and the redskins. It's enough that I tell you of what happened to us, and our share in it. Of the great affair, and all the fights and burnings, you'll find enough in the printed books and newspapers. What I tell you, though you can't find it in any books, is jest as true, for all that. Of our share in it, the worst has already been told you. The young chief, Oloschottee—for that was his name—the cousin and the enemy of Lenatewá, had command of the Indians that were to surprise our settlements; and though he didn't altogether do what he expected and intended, he worked us quite enough of mischief as it was. He soon put fire to all our farms to draw us out of the block, but finding that wouldn't do, he left us; for an Indian gets pretty soon tired of a long siege where there is neither rum nor blood to git drunk on. His force was too small to trouble us in the block, and so he drawed off his warriors, and we saw no more of him until the peace. That followed pretty soon after General Middleton gave the nation that licking at Echotee,—a licking, I reckon, that they'll remember long after my day. At that affair Lenatewá got an ugly bullet in his throat, and if it hadn't been for one of his men, he'd ha' got a bag'net in his breast. They made a narrow run with him, head foremost down the hill, with a whole swad of the mounted men from the low country at their heels. It was some time after the peace before he got better of his hurt, though the Indians are naterally more skillful in cures than white men. By this time we had all gone home to our farms, and had planted and rebuilt, and begun to forget our troubles, when who should pop into our cabin one day, but Lenatewá. He had got quite well of his hurts. He was a monstrous fine-looking fellow, tall and handsome, and he was dressed in his very best. He wore pantaloons, like one of us, and his hunting shirt was a raally fine blue, with a white fringe. He wore no paint, and was quite nice and neat with his person. We all received him as an old friend, and he stayed with us three days. Then he went, and was gone for a matter of two weeks, when he came back and stayed with us another three days. And so, off and on, he came to visit us, until Betsy said to me one day, 'Daniel, that Indian, Lenatewá, comes here after Lucy. Leave a woman to guess these things.' After she told me, I recollected that the young prince was quite watchful of Lucy, and would follow her out into the garden, and leave us, to walk with her. But then, again, I thought—'What if he is favorable to my daughter? The fellow's a good fellow; and a raal, noble-hearted Indian, that's sober, is jest as good, to my thinking, as any white man in the land.' But Betsy wouldn't hear to it. 'Her daughter never should marry a savage, and a heathen, and a redskin, while her head was hot:'—and while her head was so hot, what was I to do? All I could say was this only, 'Don't kick, Betsy, till you're spurred. 'Twill be time enough to give the young Chief his answer when he asks the question; and it won't do for us to treat him rudely, when we consider how much we owe him.' But she was of the mind that the boot was on the other leg,—that it was he and not us that owed the debt; and all that I could do couldn't keep her from showing the lad a sour face of it whenever he came. But he didn't seem much to mind this, since I was civil and kind to him. Lucy too, though her mother warned her against him, always treated him civilly as I told her; though she naterally would do so, for she couldn't so easily forget that dreadful night when she was a prisoner in the camp of the enimy, not knowing what to expect, with an Indian tomahawk over her head, and saved, in great part, by the cunning and courage of this same Lenatewá. The girl treated him kindly, and I was not sorry she did so. She walked and talked with him jest as if they had been brother and sister, and he was jest as polite to her as if he had been a born Frenchman.

"You may be sure, it was no pleasant sight to my wife to see them two go out to walk. 'Daniel Nelson,' said she, 'do you see and keep an eye on those people. There's no knowing what may happen. I do believe that Lucy has a liking for that redskin, and should they run!'—'Psho!' said I,—but that wouldn't do for her, and so she made me watch the young people sure enough. 'Twarn't a business that I was overfond of, you may reckon, but I was a rough man and didn't know much of woman natur'. I left the judgment of such things to my wife, and did pretty much what she told me. Whenever they went out to walk, I followed them, rifle in hand; but it was only to please

Betsy, for if I had seen the lad running off with the girl, I'm pretty sure, I'd never ha' been the man to draw trigger upon him. As I said before, Lenatewá was jest as good a husband as she could have had. But, poor fellow, the affair was never to come to that. One day, after he had been with us almost a week, he spoke softly to Lucy, and she got up, got her bonnet and went out with him. I didn't see them when they started, for I happened to be in the upper story,—a place where we didn't so much live, but where we used to go for shelter and defense whenever any Indians came about us. 'Daniel,' said my wife, and I knew by the quickness and sharpness of her voice what 'twas she had to tell me. But jest then I was busy, and, moreover, I didn't altogether like the sort of business upon which she wanted me to go. The sneaking after an enimy, in raal warfare, is an onpleasant sort of thing enough; but this sneaking after one that you think your friend is worse than running in a fair fight, and always gave me a sheepish feeling after it. Besides, I didn't fear Lenatewá, and I didn't fear my daughter. It's true, the girl treated him kindly and sweetly, but that was owing to the nateral sweetness of her temper, and because she felt how much sarvice he had been to her and all of us. So, instead of going out after them, I thought I'd give them a look through one of the loop-holes. Well, there they went, walking among the trees, not far from the picket, and no time out of sight. As I looked at them, I thought to myself, 'Would n't they make a handsome couple!' Both of them were tall and well made. As for Lucy, there wasn't, for figure, a finer set girl in all the settlement, and her face was a match for her figure. And then she was so easy in her motion, so graceful, and walked, or sate, or danced,—jest, for all the world, as if she was born only to do the particular thing she was doing. As for Lenatewá, he was a lad among a thousand. Now, a young Indian warrior, when he don't drink, is about the noblest-looking creature, as he carries himself in the woods, that God ever did make. So straight, so proud, so stately, always as if he was doing a great action—as if he knew the whole world was looking at him. Lenatewá was pretty much the handsomest and noblest Indian I had ever seen; and then, I know'd him to be raally so noble. As they walked together, their heads a little bent downwards, and Lucy's pretty low, the thought flashed across me that, jest then, he was telling her all about his feelings; and perhaps, said I to myself, the girl thinks about it pretty much as I do. Moutbe now, she likes him better than any body she has ever seen, and what more nateral? Then I thought, if there is any picture in this life more sweet and beautiful than two young people jest beginning to feel love for one another, and walking together in the innocence of their hearts, under the shady trees,—I've never seen it! I laid the rifle on my lap, and sat down on the floor and watched 'em through the loop until I felt the water in my eyes. They walked backwards and for'ads, not a hundred yards off, and I could see all their motions, though I couldn't hear their words. An Indian don't use his hands much generally, but I could see that Lenatewá was using his,—not a great deal, but as if he felt every word he was saying. Then I began to think, what was I to do, if so be he was raally offering to marry Lucy, and she willing! How was I to do? what was I to say?—how could I refuse him when I was willing? how could I say 'yes,' when Betsy said 'no!'

"Well, in the midst of this thinking, what should I hear but a loud cry from the child, then a loud yell,—a regular war-whoop,—sounded right in front, as if it came from Lenatewá himself. I looked up quickly, for, in thinking, I had lost sight of them, and was only looking at my rifle; I looked out, and there, in the twinkle of an eye, there was another sight. I saw my daughter flat upon the ground, lying like one dead, and Lenatewá staggering back as if he was mortally hurt; while, pressing fast upon him, was an Indian warrior, with his tomahawk uplifted, and striking—once, twice, three times—hard and heavy, right upon the face and forehead of the young prince. From the black paint on his face, and the red ring about his eyes, and from his figure and the eagle feathers in his head, I soon guessed it was Oloschottee, and I then knew it was the old revenge for the killing of his father; for an Indian never forgets that sort of obligation. Of course, I didn't stand quiet to see an old friend, like Lenatewá, tumbled in that way, without warning, like a bullock; and there was my own daughter lying flat, and I wasn't to know that he hadn't struck her too. It was only one motion for me to draw sight upon the savage, and another to pull trigger; and I reckon he dropped jest as soon as the young Chief. I gave one whoop for all the world as if I was an Indian myself, and run out to the spot; but Lenatewá had got his discharge from further service. He warn't exactly dead, but his sense was swimming. He couldn't say much, and that warn't at all to the purpose. I could hear him, now and then, making a sort of singing noise, but that was soon swallowed up in a gurgle and a gasp, and it was all over. My bullet was quicker in its working than Oloschottee's hatchet; he was stone dead before I got to him. As for poor Lucy, she was not hurt, either by bullet or hatchet; but she had a hurt in the heart, whether from the scare she had, or because she had more feeling for the young prince than we reckoned, there's no telling. She warn't much given to smiling after that. But, whether she loved Lenatewá, we couldn't know, and I never was the man to ask her. It's sartain she never married, and she had about as many chances, and good ones, too, as any girl in our settlement. You've seen her—some among you—and warn't she a beauty—though I say it myself—the very flower of the forest!"

The Last Wager;
or, The Gamester of the Mississippi

—"I have set my life upon a cast,
And I will stand the hazard of the die."
Shakespeare

I

Our story will be found to illustrate one of the current commonplaces of the day. Ever since my Lord Byron, in that poem of excellently expressed commonplaces, Don Juan, declared that "truth was stranger than fiction," every newspaper witling rings the changes upon the theme, until there is no relief to its dull-toned dissonance. That truth should frequently be found to be much stranger than any fiction, is neither so strange nor out of course of things; but is just in accordance, if we bestow any thought upon the matter, with the deliberate convictions of every reasoning mind. For, what is fiction, but the nice adaptation, by an artist, of certain ordinary occurrences in life, to a natural and probable conclusion? It is not the policy of a good artist to deal much in the merely extravagant. His real success, and the true secret of it, is to be found in the *naturalness* of his story, its general seemliness, and the close resemblance of its events to those which may or must take place in all instances of individuals subjected to like influences with those who figure in his narrative. The naturalness must be that of life as it is, or with life as it is shown in such picturesque situations as are probable—seemingly real—and such as harmonize equally with the laws of nature, and such as the artist has chosen for his guide. Except in stories of broad extravagance—ghost stories for example—in which the one purpose of the romancer—that of exciting wonder—is declared at the outset—except in such stories, or in others of the broad grin—such as are common and extravagant enough among the frontier *raconteurs* of the West, it were the very worst policy in the world for a writer of fiction to deal much in the marvellous. He would soon wear out the patience of the reader, who would turn away, with a dissatisfaction almost amounting to disgust, from any author who should be found too frequently to employ what is merely possible in human progress. We require as close reasoning, and deductions as logically drawn, in tale and novel, as in a case at law or in equity; much more close, indeed, than is often found to be the case in a Congressional harangue, and a far more tenacious regard to the *interest* of the reader than is shown in the report of a modern secretary. Probability, unstrained, must be made apparent at every step; and if the merely possible be used at all, it must be so used only, as, in looking like the probable, it is made to lose all its ambiguous characteristics. What we show must not only be the truth, but it must also seem like the truth; for, as the skill of the artist can sometimes enable him to make what is false appear true, so it is equally the case, that a want of skill may transmute the most unquestionable truth into something that nine persons in ten shall say, when they behold it, "It looks monstrous like a lie!"

That we are not at liberty to use too freely what is merely possible in the material brought before us, is a fact more particularly known to painters, who have often felt the danger of any attempt to paint the sky as it sometimes appears to them. They dread to offend the suspicious incredulity of the cold and unobserving citizen. They see, with equal amazement and delight—but without daring to delineate—those intenser hues and exquisite gradations of light and shadow, those elaborate and graceful shapes of cloud, born of the rainbow—carnation, green, and purple, which the sun sometimes, in fantastic mood, and as if in equal mockery of human faith and art, makes upon the lovely background of the sky which he leaves at setting. The beautiful vision gone from sight, who would believe the poor artist, whatever his accuracy and felicity of touch and taste, who had endeavored to transfer, before it faded, the vanishing glory to his canvass? Who could suppose, and how admit, that there had ever been such a panorama, of such super-artistical splendor, displayed before his eyes, without commanding his admiration and fixing his attention? The very attempt to impose such an exhibition upon him as natural, would be something of a sarcasm, and a commentary upon the dull eye and drowsy mind which had failed to discern it for themselves. Nay, though the artist grappled the dull citizen by the arm at the very instant, and compelled his gaze upon the glorious vision ere it melted into the thin gray haze of evening, would he not be apt to say, "How strange! how very unnatural!" Certainly, it would be a nature and a truth infinitely more strange than the most audacious fiction that ever grew up at the touch of the most fantastic votary of art.

II

The sketch which I propose will scarcely justify this long digression; and its character will be still less likely to correspond with the somewhat poetic texture of the introduction. It is simply a strange narrative of frontier life; one of those narratives in which a fact will appear very doubtful, unless the artist shall exhibit such sufficient skill in his elaborations, as to keep its rude points from offending too greatly the suspicious judgment of the reader. This is the task before me. The circumstances were picked up, when, a lad of eighteen, I first wandered over the then dreary and dangerous wastes of the Mississippi border. Noble, indeed, though wild and savage, was the aspect of that green forest country, as yet only slightly smitten by the sharp edges of the ranger's axe. I travelled along the great Yazoo wilderness, in frequent proximity with the Choctaw warriors. Most frequently I rode alone. Sometimes, a wayfarer from the East, solitary with myself, turned his horse's head, for a few days' space, on the same track with mine; but, in most cases, my only companion was some sullen Choctaw, or some still more sullen half-breed, who, emerging suddenly from some little foot-path, would leave me half in doubt whether his introduction would be made first with the tomahawk or the tongue. Very few white men were then settled in the country; still fewer were stationary. I rode forty and fifty miles without sign of human habitation, and found my bed and supper at night most generally in the cabin of the half-breed. But there was one, and that a remarkable exception to this universal necessity; and in this exception my story takes its rise. I had at length reached the borders of the nation, and the turbid waters of the Mississippi, at no great distance, flowed down towards the Gulf. The appearances of the white settler, some doubtful glimmerings of a more civilized region, were beginning to display themselves. Evening was at hand. The sun was fast waning along the mellow heights of heaven; and my heart was beginning to sink with the natural sense of loneliness which such a setting is apt to inspire in the bosom of the youthful wanderer. It was also a question with me, where I should find my pillow for the night. My host of the night before, a low, dark-looking white squatter, either was, or professed to be, too ignorant to give me any information on this head, which would render the matter one of reasonable certainty. In this doubtful and somewhat desolate state of mind, I began to prick my steed forward at a more rapid pace, to cast my eyes up more frequently to the fading light among the tree-tops, and, occasionally, to send a furtive glance on either hand, not altogether assured that my road was as safe as it was lonely. The question "Where shall I find my bed to-night?" was beginning to be one of serious uncertainty, when I suddenly caught a glimpse of an opening on my right, a sort of wagon-path, avenue like, and which reminded me of those dear, dim passages in my own Carolina, which always promised the traveller a hot supper and happy conclusion to his wanderings of the day. Warmed with the notion, and without a farther doubt or thought, I wheeled my sorrel into the passage, and pressed him forward with a keener spur. A cheery blast of the horn ahead, and the dull heavy stroke of an axe immediately after, were so many urgent entreaties to proceed; and now the bellow of a cow, and next the smoke above the cottage roof-trees, assured me that my apprehensions were at an end. In a few seconds I stood before one of the snuggest little habitations which ever kindled hope and satisfied hunger.

This was one of those small log-cabins which are common to the country. Beyond its snug, trim and tidy appearance, there was nothing about it to distinguish it from its class. The clearing was small, just sufficient, perhaps, for a full supply of corn and provisions. But the area in front of the dwelling was cleanly swept, and the trees were trimmed, and those which had been left were evergreens, and so like favorite domestics, with such an air of grace, and good-nature, and venerableness about them, that one's heart warmed to see them, as at sight of one of "the old familiar faces." The aspect of the dwelling within consisted happily with that without. Every thing was so neat, and snug, and comfortable.

The windows were sashed and glassed, and hung with the whitest curtains of cotton, with fringes fully a foot deep. The floors were neatly sanded, the hearth was freshly brightened with the red ocherous clay of the country, and chairs and tables, though made of the plainest stuffs, and by a very rude mechanic, were yet so clean, neat and well-arranged, that the eye involuntarily surveyed them again and again with a very pleased sensation. Nor was this all in the shape of unwonted comforts. Some other matters were considered in this cottage, which are scarcely even dreamed of in the great majority. In one corner of the hall stood a hat-stand; in another there were pins for cloaks; above the fireplace hung a formidable rifle, suspended upon tenter-hooks made of three monstrous antlers, probably those of gigantic bucks which had fallen beneath the weapon which they were now made to sustain. Directly under this instrument, and the only object beside which had been honored with a place so conspicuous, *was a pack of ordinary playing cards*—not hung or suspended against the wall, *but nailed to it*;—driven through and through with a tenpenny nail, and so fastened to the solid log, the black head of the nail showing with particular prominence in contrast with the red spot of the ace of hearts, through which it had been driven. Of this hereafter. On this pack of cards hangs my story. It is enough, in this place, to add, that it was only after supper was fairly over, that my eyes were drawn to this very unusual sort of chimney decoration.

At the door of the cottage sat a very venerable old man, between seventy and eighty. His hair was all white, but still thick, betraying the strength of his constitution and the excellence of his health. His skin was florid, glowing through his white beard, which might have been three days old, and his face bore the burden of very few wrinkles. He had a lively, clear blue eye, and good-humor played about his mouth in every movement of his lips. He was evidently one of those fortunate men, whose winters, if frosty, had always proved kindly. A strong man in his youth, he was now but little bent with years; and when he stood up, I was quite ashamed to find he was rather more erect than myself, and quite as tall. This was the patriarch of the family, which consisted of three members besides himself. The first of these was his only son, a man thirty-eight or forty years of age, of whom it will be quite explicit enough to say, that the old man, in his youth, must very nearly have resembled him. Then, there was the wife of the son, and her son, a lad now ten years old, a smart-looking lad enough, but in no wise resembling his male parent. Instead of the lively, twinkling blue eye of his father, he had the dark, deep, oriental sad ones of the mother; and his cheeks were rather pale than rosy, rather thin than full; and his hair was long, black and silky, in all respects the counterpart of his mother's. A brief description of this lady may assist us in our effort to awaken the interest of the reader.

Conducted into the house by the son, and warmly welcomed by the old man as well as himself, I was about to advance with the bold dashing self-possession of a young cavalier, confident in his course, and accustomed to win "golden opinions of all sorts of people." But my bold carriage and sanguine temper were suddenly checked, not chilled, by the appearance of the lady in front of whom I suddenly stood. She sat beside the fireplace, and was so very different a looking person from any I had expected to see in such a region, that the usual audacity of my temperament was all at once abashed. In place of the good, cheerful, buxom, plain country housewife whom I looked to see, mending Jacky's breeches, or knitting the good-man's hose, I found myself confronted by a dame whose aristocratic, high-bred, highly composed, easy and placid demeanor, utterly confounded me. Her person was small, her complexion darkly oriental, her eye flashing with all the spiritual fires of that region; habitually bright and searching, even while the expression of her features would have made her seem utterly emotionless. Never did features, indeed, appear so thoroughly inflexible. Her beauty,—for she was all beauty,—was not, however, the result of any regularity of feature. Beauties of her order, brunette and piquant, are most usually wanting in preciseness, and mutual dependence and sympathy of outline. They are beautiful in spite of irregularity, and in consequence of the paramount exquisiteness of some particular feature. The charm of the face before me grew out of the piercing, deep-set, and singularly black eye, and the wonderful vitality about the lips. Never was mouth so small, or so admirably delineated. There was witchcraft enough in the web of it to make my own lips water. But I speak like the boy I was then, and am no longer.

Let me not be understood to mean that there was any levity, any lightness of character betrayed in the expression of those lips. Very far otherwise. While soft, sweet, beautiful, and full of life, they were the most sacred and sad-looking forms,—drooping blossoms of beauty, mourning, as it would seem, because beauty does not imply immortality; and this expression led me to observe more closely the character of the eye, the glance of which, at first, had only seemed to denote the brilliance of the diamond, shining through an atmosphere of jet. I now discerned that its intense blaze was not its only character. It was marked with the weight of tears, that, freezing as they had birth, maintained their place in defiance of the light to which they were constantly exposed. It was the brightness of the ice palace, in the Northern Saga, which, in reflecting the bright glances of Balder, the God of Day, still gives defiance to the fervor of his beams.

But a truce to these frigid comparisons, which suit any age but ours. Enough to say that the lady was of a rare and singular beauty, with a character of face and feature not common to our country, and with a deportment seldom found in the homely cabin of the woodman or the squatter. The deep and unequivocal sadness which marked her looks, intense as it was, did not affect or impair the heightened aristocratic dignity of her subdued and perfectly assured manner. To this manner did she seem to have been born; and, being habitual, it is easy to understand that she could not be divested of it, except in a very small degree, by the pressure of any form of affliction. You could see that there had been affliction, but its effect was simply to confirm that elevated social tone, familiar to all mental superiority, which seems, however it may feel, to regard the confession of its griefs as perhaps something too merely human to be altogether becoming in a confessedly superior caste. Whether the stream was only frozen over, or most effectually crystallized, it does not suit our purpose to inquire. It is, at all events, beyond my present ability to determine the doubt.

She was introduced to me, by the husband, as Mrs. Rayner. I afterwards discovered that her Christian name was Rachel; a circumstance that tended to strengthen the impression in my mind that she might be of Jewish parents. That she was a Christian herself, I had reason to believe, from her joining freely and devoutly, and on bended knee, in the devotions of the night. She spoke seldom, yet looked intelligent throughout the conversation, which was carried on freely between the old man, the husband, and myself. When she spoke, her words and accents were marked by the most singular propriety. There was nothing in her utterance to lessen the conviction that she was familiar with the most select circles of city life; and I could see that the husband listened to her with a marked deference, and, though himself, evidently, a rough honest backwoodsman, I detected him, in one or two instances, checking the rude phrase upon his lips, and substituting for it some other, more natural to the ear of civilization and society. There was a touching something in the meekness and quiet deportment of the boy who sat by his mother's knee in silence, her fingers turning in his hair, while he diligently pored over some little trophy of juvenile literature, looking up timidly at moments, and smiling sadly, when he met the deep earnest gaze of the mother's eyes, as she seemed to forget all around in the glance at the one object. I need not say that there was something in this family picture so entirely out of the common run of my woodland experience in the South-west, at that early day, that I felt my curiosity equally excited with my pleasure. I felt assured that there was something of a story to be learned, which would amply recompense the listener. The old patriarch was himself a study—the husband a very noble specimen of the sturdy, frank, elastic frontier-man—a race too often confounded with the miserable runagates by whom the first explorations of the country are begun, but who seldom make the real axe-marks of the wilderness. You could see at a glance that he was just the man whom a friend could rely upon and a foe most fear—frank, ardent, firm, resolute in endurance, patient, perhaps, and slow to anger, as are all noble-minded persons who have a just confidence in their own strength; but unyielding when the field is to be fought, and as cheerful in the moment of danger as he was good-humored in that of peace. Every thing in his look, language and bearing, answered to this description; and I sat down at the supper table beside him that night, as familiar and as much at my ease as if we had jumped together from the first moment of existence.

I pass over much of the conversation preceding, and at the evening repast; for, though interesting enough at the time, particularly to me, it would only delay us still longer in the approach to our story. It was after the table had been withdrawn, when the family were all snugly huddled about the fireplace, and the dialogue, which had been rather brisk before, had begun to flag, that I casually looked up over the chimney-place, and discovered, for the first time, the singular ornament of which I have already spoken. Doubtful of what I saw, I rose to my feet, and grasped the object with my fingers. I fancied that some eccentric forest genius, choosing for his subject one of the great agents of popular pastime in the West, might have succeeded in a delineation sufficiently felicitous, as, at a short distance, to baffle any vision. But, palpable, the real—I had almost said, the living—things were there, unlike the dagger of Macbeth, as "sensible to feeling as to sight." A complete pack of cards, none of the cleanest, driven through with a tenpenny nail, the ace of hearts, as before said, being the top card, and very fairly covering the retinue of its own and the three rival houses. The corners of the cards were curled, and the ends smoked to partial blackness. They had evidently been in that situation for several years. I turned inquiringly to my hosts—

"You have a very singular ornament for your mantleplace, Mr. Rayner," was my natural remark, the expression of curiosity in my face being coupled with an apologetic sort of smile. But it met with no answering smiles from any of the family. On the contrary, every face was grave to sadness, and in a moment more Mrs. Rayner rose and left the room. As soon as she was gone, her husband remarked as follows:

"Why, yes, sir, it is uncommon; but there's a reason why it's there, which I'll explain to you after we've gone through prayers."

By this time the wife had returned, bringing with her the family Bible, which she now laid upon a stand beside the venerable elder. He, good old man, with an action that seemed to be perfectly habitual, drew forth the spectacles from the sacred pages, where they seemed to have been left from the previous evening, and commenced reading the third chapter of Ecclesiastes, beginning, "Hear me, your father, O children! and do thereafter, that ye may be safe." Then, this being read, we all sunk devoutly upon our knees, and the patriarch put up as sweet and fervent a prayer as I should ever wish to listen to. The conceited whipster of the school might have found his pronunciation vulgar, and his sentences sometimes deficient in grammatical nicety; but the *thought* was there, and the *heart*, and the ears of perfect wisdom might well be satisfied with the good sense and the true morality of all that was spoken. We rose refreshed, and, after a lapse of a very few moments which were passed in silence, the wife, leading the little boy by the hand, with a kind nod and courtesy took her leave, and retired to her chamber. Sweetness and dignity were most happily blended in her parting movements; but I fancied, as I caught the glance of her eye, that there had been a freshening and overflowing there of the deep and still gathering fountains. Her departure was followed by that of the old man, and the husband and myself were left alone. It was not long after this, before he, himself, without waiting for any suggestion of mine, brought up the subject of the cards, which had been so conspicuously elevated into a mantel ornament.

III

"Stranger," said he, "there is a sort of history in those cards which I am always happy to tell to any young man that's a beginner in the world like yourself. I consider them as a sort of Bible, for, when I look at them and remember all that I know concerning them, I feel as if I was listening to some prime sermon, or may be, hearing just such a chapter as the old man read to us out of the good book to-night. It's quite a long history, and I'll put on a fresh handful of lightwood before I begin."

The interruption was brief, and soon overcome, and the narrative of the husband ran as follows:

"It is now," said he, "going on to twelve years since the circumstances took place which belong to the story of those cards, and I will have to carry you back to that time before you can have a right knowledge of what I want to tell. I was then pretty much such a looking person as you now see me, for I haven't undergone much change. I was a little sprightlier, perhaps—always famous for light-headedness and laughing—fond of fun and frolic, but never doing any thing out of mischief and bad humor. The old man, my father, too, was pretty much the same. We lived here where you find us now, but not quite so snugly off—not so well settled—rather poor, I may say, though still with a plentiful supply to live on and keep warm and feel lively. There was only us two, and we had but two workers, a man and woman, and they had two children, who could do nothing for us and precious little for themselves. But we were snug, and worked steadily, and were comfortable. We didn't make much money, but we always spent less than we made. We didn't have very nice food, but we had no physic to take, and no doctor's bills to pay. We had a great deal to make us happy, and still more to be thankful for; and I trust in God we were thankful for all of his blessings. I think we were, for he gave us other blessings; and for these, stranger, we are trying to be thankful also.

"Well, as I was saying, about twelve years ago, one hot day in August, I rode out a little piece towards the river bluff to see if any goods had been left for us at the landing. We had heard the steamboat gun the night before, or something like it, and that, you know, is the signal to tell us when to look after our *plunder*. When I got there I found a lot of things, some for us, and some for other people. There was a bag of coffee, a keg of sugar, three sacks of salt, and a box of odds and ends for us. But the chaps on board the steamboat—which was gone—had thrown down the stuff any where, and some of the salt was half melted in a puddle of water. I turned in, and hauled it out of the water, and piled it up in a dry place. What was wet belonged chiefly to our neighbors, and the whole of it might have been lost if I had not got there in season. This kept me a good hour, and as I had no help, and some of the sacks were large and heavy, I was pretty nigh tired out when the work was done. So I took a rest of half an hour more in the shade. The heat was powerful, and I had pretty nigh been caught by sleep—I don't know but I did sleep, for in midsummer one's not always sure of himself in a drowsy moment—when I was suddenly roused up by a noise most like the halloo of a person in distress. I took the saddle on the spur, and went off in the quarter that the sound came from. It so happened that my route homeward lay the same way, and on the river road, the only public road in the settlement; and I had only gone two hundred yards or thereabout, when, in turning an elbow of the path, I came plump upon a stranger, who happened to be the person whom I heard calling. He was most certainly in distress. His horse was flat upon her side, groaning powerfully, and the man was on his knees, rubbing the creature's legs with a pretty hard hand. A little way behind him lay a dead rattlesnake, one of the largest I ever did see, counting twenty-one rattles besides the button; and the sight of the snake told me the whole story. I jumped down to see what I could do in the way of help, but I soon discovered that the nag had the spasms, and was swelled up to her loins. I however cut into her leg with my knife, just where she was bitten, and when I had dug out the poisoned flesh, as much as I thought was reasonable, I got on my horse and rode back to the salt bags at full speed, and brought away a double handful of the salt. I rubbed it into the animal's wound, I really believe, a few minutes after she had groaned her last and stiffened out, but I wasn't rubbing very long. She was about the soonest killed of any creature that I ever saw snakebit before.

"It was only after I was done with the mare, that I got a fair look at her owner. He was a small and rather oldish man, with a great stoop of the shoulders, with a thin face, glossy black hair, and eyes black too, but shining as bright, I reckon, as those of the rattlesnake he had killed. They had a most strange and troublesome brightness, that made me look at them whether I would or not. His face was very pale, and the wrinkles were deep, like so many seams, and, as I have said, he was what I would call a rather oldish man; but still he was very nicely dressed, and wore a span-new velvet vest, a real English broadcloth coat, gold watch with gold seals; and every now and then he pulled out a snuff-box made like a horn, with a curl at the end of it, which was also set with a gold rim, and had a cap of the same precious stuff upon it. He was taking snuff every moment while I was doctoring his mare, and when the creature went dead, he offered it to me; but I had always thought it work enough to feed my mouth, and had no notion of making another mouth of my nose, so I refused him civilly.

"He didn't seem to be much worried by the death of his creature, and when I told him how sorry I was on his account, he answered quickly,

" 'Oh! no matter; you have a good horse; you will let me have him; you look like a good fellow.'

"I was a little surprised, you may reckon. I looked at the old man, and then at my creature. He *was* a good creature; and as prime an animal as ever stepped in traces; good at any thing, plough, wagon, or saddle; as easy-going as a girl of sixteen, and not half so skittish. I had no notion of giving him up to a stranger, you may be sure, and didn't half like the cool, easy, impudent manner with which the old man spoke to me. I had no fears—I didn't think of his taking my nag from me by force—but, of a sudden, I almost begun to think he might be a wizard, as we read in Scripture, and hear of from the old people, or mou't be, the old devil himself, and then I did'nt well know what I had to expect. But he soon made the matter clear to me. Perhaps he saw that I was a little beflustered.

" 'Young man,' says he, 'your horse *is* a fine one. Will you sell him? I am willing to pay you a fair price—give you his full value.'

"There was something to consider in that. When did you ever find a Western man unwilling for a horse-barter? Besides, though the creature was a really first-rate nag, he was one more than I wanted. One for the plough, and one for the saddle—as the old man didn't ride often—was enough for us; and we had three. But Rainbow—that was his name—was so sleek an animal! He could a'most do any thing that you'd tell him. I did'nt want to sell him, but I didn't want to keep a mouth too many. You know a horse that you don't want begins by gnawing through your pockets, and ends by eating off his own head. That's the say, at least. But I raised Rainbow, fed him with my own hands, curried him night and morning myself, and looked upon him as a sort of younger brother. I hated powerful bad to part with him; but then there was no reason to keep him when he was of no use. 'Twas a satisfaction, to be sure, to have such a creature; and 'twas a pleasure to cross him, and streak it away, at a brushing canter, of a bright morning, for a good five miles at a stretch; but poor people can't afford such pleasures and satisfactions; and when I thought of the new wagon that we wanted, and such a smart chance of other things about the farm, I looked at the old man and thought better of his offer. I said to him, though a little slowly,

" 'It's a famous fine horse this, stranger.'

" 'I know it,' said he; 'I never saw one that better pleased my eyes. I'll pay you a famous price for him.'

" 'What'll you give?' said I.

" 'Pshaw!' said he, 'speak out like a man. I'm no baby, and you are old enough to know better. What's your price?'

" 'He's low,' said I, 'at one hundred and seventy dollars.'

" 'He is,' said he, 'he's worth more—will you take that?'

" 'Yes.'

" 'You shall have it,' he answered, 'and I'll throw the dead horse into the bargain; she was a famous fine animal too, in her day, and her skin's worth stuffing as a keepsake. You can stuff it and put it up in your stables, as an example to your other horses.'

IV

"All the time he was talking, he was counting out the money, which was almost all in gold. I was a little dub'ous that it wasn't good money; but I smelt it, and it had no smell of brass, and I was a leetle ashamed to let on that I didn't know good money from bad; besides, there was a something about the old gentleman so much like a gentleman, so easy, and so commanding, that I couldn't find the heart to doubt or to dispute any thing he said. And then, every thing about him looked like a gentleman: his clothes, his hat, the watch he wore, the very dead horse and her coverings, saddle, bridle, and so forth, all convinced me that there was nothing of make-believe.

" 'There,' said he, 'my good fellow,' putting the money in my hand, 'I reckon you never handled so much gold in your life before.'

" 'No,' said I, 'to tell you the truth, though I've hearn a good deal of gold, and know it when I see it by what I've hearn, I never set eyes on a single piece till now.'

" 'May it do your eyes good now, then,' said he; 'you look like a good fellow. Your horse is sound?'

" 'Yes,' said I, 'I can answer better for him than I can for your gold.'

" 'That's good.'

" 'Well!' said I, 'I'm not sure that I've dealt fairly with you, stranger. I've asked you a little more than I've been asking other people. My price on Rainbow has been only one hundred and fifty dollars before.'

" 'And your conscience troubles you. You *are* an honest fellow,' said he, 'but never mind, my lad, I'll show you a way to relieve it.'

"With these words he pulled out a buckskin roll from his pocket, and out of this he tumbled a pack of cards; the very cards which you see nailed above my fireplace.

" 'We'll play for that twenty dollars,' said he, throwing down two gold pieces on the body of the dead mare, and beginning to shuffle the cards immediately. Somehow, I did as he did. I put down two ten dollar pieces along with his. I couldn't help myself. He seemed to command me. I felt scared—I felt that I was doing wrong; but he seemed to take every thing so much as a matter of course, that I hadn't the courage to say 'no' to any thing he did or said.

" 'What do you play?' said he, and he named some twenty games of cards, some in French, I believe, and some in Spanish, but no one of which did I know any thing about. He seemed beflustered.

" 'Do you play any thing at all?' he asked.

" 'Yes—a little of *old sledge*—that's all.'

" 'Oh! that will do. A common game enough. I wonder I should have omitted it. Here! you may shuffle them, and we'll cut for deal.'

"I didn't shuffle, but cut at once. He cut after me, and the deal fell to him. He took up and then put the cards down again—put his hand into his pocket, and drew out a little silver box, about the size of a small snuff-box,—that had in it a good many little pills of a dark gray gummy look. One of these he swallowed, then began to deal, his eye growing brighter every moment, and looking into mine till I felt quite dazzled and strange. Our table was the belly of the dead horse. He sat on one of the thighs. I knelt down upon the grass on the opposite side, and though it pained me, I couldn't take my eyes from him to save my life. He asked me a great many questions while he was throwing out the cards—how old I was—what was my name—what family I had—how far I lived—where I came from—every thing, indeed, about me, and my way of life, and what I had and what I knew:—and all this in no time—as fast as I tell it to you. Then he said, 'You are an honest fellow, take up your cards, and let us see if you are as lucky as you are honest.' It seemed as if I was, for I beat him. I played a pretty stiff game of *old sledge*, or as he called it, '*all fours*,' for I used to play, as long as I could remember, with the old man, my father, every night. Old people like these plays, and it's good for them to play. It keeps 'em lively, keeps them from sleeping too much, and from drinking. It's good for them, so long as it makes their own fireside sweet to them. Well! I was lucky. I won the game, and it worried me mightily when I did so. I didn't touch the money.

" 'I suppose,' said the stranger, 'that I must cover those pieces,' and before I could guess what he was about, he flung down four other gold pieces, making forty dollars, in the pile with mine, and began again shuffling the cards. If I was scared and unhappy before, I was twice as much so now. I could scarcely breathe, and why, I can't say exactly. It wasn't from any anxiety about the winning or the losing, for I preferred not to have the stranger's money: but it was his very indifference and unconcern that worried and distressed me. It seemed so unnatural, that I half the time thought that I was dealing with nothing human: and though I could shuffle, and cut, and play, yet it seemed to me as if I did it without altogether knowing why, or how. As luck would have it, I won the second time; and the third time he pulled out his purse and put down as many more pieces as lay there. I looked at the growing heap with a heart that seemed ready to burst. There was eighty dollars before me, and I felt my face grow red when I caught his eye looking steadily at mine. I began to feel sort o' desperate, and flung about the cards like a person in liquor. The old man laughed, a low chuckle like, that made my blood crawl in my veins, half frozen, as it were. But, neither his skill and coolness, nor my fright, altered the luck at all. I again won, and trembled all over, to see the pile, and to see him take out his purse, and empty every thing upon it.

" 'Stranger,' said I, 'don't think of it; keep your money, and let me go home.'

" 'Pshaw!' said he, 'you're a good fellow, and as lucky as you are good. Why shouldn't you be my heir? I prefer that a good fellow should win my money if any body. It'll do your sight good.'

" 'But not my heart, I'm afraid,' was my answer.

" 'That's precisely as you use it,' said he; 'money's a good creature, like every other good creature that God gives us. It's a good thing to be rich, for a rich man's always able to *do* good, when a poor man can only wish to do it. Get money, my lad, and be wise with it; wiser, I trust, than I have been.'

"With these words, he took out his silver box, swallowed another of the pills, and was busy dealing out the cards in another moment. I, somehow, was better pleased with him for what he said. The mention of God convinced me that he wasn't the devil, and what he said seemed very sensible. But I didn't feel any more right and happy than before. I only wanted the strength to refuse him. I couldn't refuse him. I took up the cards as he threw them, and it did seem to me that

I scarcely saw to make out the spots when I played them. I hardly knew how the game was played; I didn't count; I couldn't tell what I made. I only heard him say at the close of the second hand,

" 'The money's yours. You are a lucky fellow.'

"With these words he pushed the gold heap to me, and threw me the empty purse.

" 'There's something to put it in.'

" 'No!' said I; 'no, stranger—I can't take this money.'

" 'Why, pray?'

" 'It's not right. It don't seem to me to be got honestly. I haven't worked for it.'

" 'Worked, indeed! If nobody used money but those who worked for it, many a precious fellow would gnaw his finger ends for a dinner. Put up your money!'

"I pushed it to him, all but the two eagles which I begun with; but he pushed it back. I got up without touching it. 'Stay,' said he, 'you *are* a good fellow! Sit down again; sit down.' I sat down. 'I can't take that money,' said he, 'for it is yours. According to my way of thinking, it is yours—it is none of mine. There is only one way in which it may become mine; only one way in which I could take it or make use of it, and that is by winning it back. That may be done. I will put the horse against the gold.'

V

"My heart beat quicker than ever when he pointed to Rainbow. Not that I expected or wished to win him back, for I would only have taken him back by giving up all the money, or all except the hundred and fifty dollars; but it now seemed to me as if I looked on the old man with such feelings as would have made me consent to almost any thing he wished. I had a strange sort of pity for him. I considered him a sort of kind-hearted, rich old madman. I said, 'Very well;' and he took another pill out of his box, and began again at the cards.

" 'You are a very fortunate fellow,' said he, 'and seem a very good one. I really see no reason why you should not be my heir. You say you are not married.'

" 'No.'

" 'But you have your sweetheart, I suppose. A lad of twenty-five, which I suppose is much about your age, is seldom without one.'

" 'It's not the case with me,' said I. 'In these parts we have mighty few folks and fewer women, and I don't know the girl among them that's ever seemed to me exactly the one that I should be willing to make my wife.'

" 'Why, you're not conceited, I hope? You don't think yourself too fine a fellow for a poor girl, do you?'

" 'No, by no means, stranger; but there's a sort of liking that one must have before he can think of a wife, and I haven't seen the woman yet to touch me in the right way.'

" 'You are hard to please, and properly. Marriage is easier found than lost. A man is too noble an animal to be kept in a mouse-trap. But there *are* women——'

"He stopped short. I waited for him to say something more, but by this time the cards had been distributed, and he was sorting his hand.

" 'There are women!' he said again, though as if he was talking to himself. There he stopt for a minute, then looking up, and fixing his bright eyes upon mine, he continued:

" 'Come, Rayner,' said he, good-humoredly. 'The cards are in your hands, and remember to play your best, for that famous fine horse may become your own again. I warn you, I have a good hand. What do you do?'

" 'Good or not,' said I, something more boldly, 'I will stand on mine.'

"I had a most excellent hand, being sure of high and low, with a strong leading hand for game.

" 'Play then!' he answered; and at the word, I clapped down the ace of hearts, the very ace you see atop of the pack over the chimney now.

" 'You *are* a lucky fellow, Rayner,' said he, as he flung down the Jack upon it, the only heart he held in his hand. The game ended; I was owner of horse and money. But I jumped to my feet instantly.

" 'Stranger,' said I, 'don't think I'm going to rob you of your horse or money. I don't exactly know why I played with you so long, unless it be because you insisted upon it, and did'nt wish to disoblige an old gentleman like yourself. Take your money, and give me my horse; or, if you want the horse, leave me the hundred and fifty, which is a fair price for him, and put the rest in your own pocket. I won't touch a copper more of it.'

" 'You *are* a good fellow, Rayner, but, with some persons, younger and rasher persons than myself, your words would be answered with a bullet. Nay, were I the boy I have been, it would be dangerous for you to speak, *even to me*, in such a manner. Among gentlemen, the obligation to pay up what is lost by cards is sacred. The loser *must* deliver, and the winner *must* receive. *There* is your money and that is your horse again; but I am not yet done with you. As I said before, you *are* a good fellow, and most certainly a lucky one. I like you, though your principles are scarcely fixed yet—not certain! Still, I like you; and there's some chance that you will be my heir yet. A few more trials at the cards must determine that. I suppose you are not unwilling to give me a chance to win back my losses?'

"I caught at the suggestion.

" 'Surely not,' I replied.

" 'Very good,' says he. 'Don't suppose that, because you've emptied my purse, you've cleaned me out quite. I have a diamond ring and a diamond breastpin yet to stake. They are worth something more than your horse and your heap of money. We will place them against your eagles and horse.'

" 'No!' said I quickly. 'I'm willing to put down all the eagles, but not the horse; or I'll put down the horse and all the money, except the hundred and fifty.'

" 'As you please,' said he, 'but, my good fellow, you must take my word for the ring and breastpin. I do not carry them with me. I know it's rather awkward to talk of playing a promised stake against one that we see, but I give you the honor of a gentleman that the diamonds shall be forthcoming if I lose.'

"I began to think that what he said was only a sort of come-off—but I didn't want his money, and was quite willing that he should win it back. If he had said, 'I'll stake my toothpick against the money,' I'd have been just as willing, for all that I now aimed at was to secure my horse or the price of him. I felt very miserable at the thought of winning the man's money—such a heap of it! I had never played cards for money in all my life before, and there's something in the feeling of winning money, for the first time, that's almost like thieving. As I tell you, if he had said his toothpick, or any worthless thing, instead of his diamonds, I'd have been willing. I didn't say so, however, and I thought his offer to stake diamonds that he couldn't show, was pretty much like a come-off. But I was willing enough, for the money seemed to scald my eyes to look upon. He took out a pencil, the case of which I saw was gold also, and wrote on a slip of paper, 'Good for two brilliants, one a ring, the other a breastpin, the latter in form of a

Maltese cross, both set in gold, with an inner rim of silver, valued at seven hundred dollars.' This was signed with two letters only, the initials of his name. I have the paper now. He bade me read it, and when I did so, I thought him madder than a March hare; but if I thought so then, I was more than ever convinced of it, when, a moment after, and when we were about to play, he spoke to this effect:

" 'There's one thing, Rayner. There's a little incumbrance on these jewels.'

" 'Well, sir,' I said.

"I didn't care a fig for the incumbrance, for I didn't believe a word of the jewels.

" 'If you win them, you win a woman along with them. You win a wife.'

"I laughed outright.

" 'Don't laugh,' said he; 'you don't see me laugh. I'm serious; never more so. You are unmarried. You need a wife. Don't you want one?'

" 'Yes! if I could get a good one—one to my liking.'

" 'You *are* a good fellow. You deserve a good wife, Rayner; and such is the very one I propose to give you.'

" 'Ay, ay,' said I; 'but will she be to my liking?'

" 'I hope so; I believe so. She has all the qualities which should command the liking of a sensible and worthy young man. She, too, is sensible; she is intelligent; she has knowledge; she has read books; she has accomplishments; she sings like an angel; plays on several instruments—piano and guitar!'

" 'Piano and guitar!' said I.

"I didn't know what they were. I felt sure that the old fellow was mad, just out of a hospital, perhaps; but then where did he get the money and the gold things? I began to think more suspiciously of him than ever.

" 'Yes, piano and guitar,' said he; 'she draws and paints too, the loveliest pictures—she can make these trees live on canvass; ah! can she not? Money has not been spared, Rayner, to make Rachel what she is.'

" 'Rachel—is that her name?' I asked.

" 'Yes, it is.'

" 'What's the other name?'

" 'You shall know, if you win the diamonds.'

" 'Yes—but how old is she? how does she look? is she young and handsome? I wouldn't want an ugly wife because she happened to be wise. I've heard that your wise women are generally too ugly for any thing else than wisdom.'

" 'You are a fool, Rayner, though a good fellow. But Rachel is beautiful and young—not more than seventeen—the proper age for you. You, I think you say, are twenty-eight. In this climate a man's wife should always be ten or twelve years younger than himself—provided he be a sober and healthy man, and if he be not, he has no business with a wife, nor a wife with him. You are both sober and healthy. You are a good fellow—I see that. I like you, Rayner, and for this reason I am willing to risk Rachel on the cards, playing against you. My loss will probably be her gain, and this makes me rather regardless how it ends. You shall be my heir yet.'

" 'Thank you, old gentleman,' said I, beginning to feel a little bold and saucy, for I now couldn't help thinking that the stranger was no better than a good-natured madman who had got away from his friends. 'Thank you,' said I. 'If Rachel's the girl you make her out to be, you can't bring her along a day too soon. But, may I ask, is she your daughter?'

" 'My daughter!' he answered sharply, and with something of a frown on his face, 'do I look like a man to have children?—to be favored with such a blessing as a daughter?—a daughter like Rachel?'

" 'Now,' said I to myself, 'his fit's coming on,' and I began to look about me for a start.

" 'No, Rayner,' he continued, 'she is no daughter of mine, but she is the daughter of a good man and of honorable parents. You shall have sufficient proof of that. Have you any more questions?'

" 'No, sir.'

" 'And you will take Rachel as your wife? You have heard my description of her. If she comes up to it, I ask you, will you be willing to take her as your wife?'

"I looked at him queerly enough, I reckon. He fixed his keen black eyes upon me, so that I couldn't look on him without shutting my own. I didn't know whether to laugh or to run. But, thinking that he was flighty in the upper story, I concluded it was best to make a short business of it, and to agree with any thing that he wished; so I told him freely 'yes,' and he reached out his hand to mine, which he squeezed nervously for a minute, and then took out his box of pills, swallowed a couple of them, and began dealing out the cards. I had the strangest luck—the same sort of luck that had kept with me from the start. I won the diamonds and won Rachel!

" 'Well,' said he, 'I'm glad, Rayner, that you are the man. I've been long looking for an heir to my diamonds. They are yours—all is yours; and I shall have to be indebted to you for the loan of the horse, in order to go and bring you your wife.'

" 'Ay,' said I, 'stranger, the horse is at your service, and half of the money too. I never thought to take them from you at the first; I shouldn't have felt easy in my conscience to have used the money that I got in this way.'

" 'Pshaw!' said he, gathering up the cards, and wrapping them in the buckskin wallet from which he had taken them. 'Pshaw, you are a fool. I'll borrow your horse, and a few pieces to pay my way.'

" 'Help yourself to the rest,' said I, taking, as I spoke, fifteen of the eagles to myself, and leaving the rest on the dead body of the horse, where they had been growing from our first commencing to play.

" 'You are my heir,' he answered, 'and behave yourself as you should. Between persons so related there should be no paltry money scruples'; and, while he said these words, he stooped to take the money. I turned away that he shouldn't suppose I watched him, but I couldn't help laughing at the strange sort of cunning which he showed in his conceit. Says I to myself, 'You will take precious good care, old fellow, I see that, that I carry off no more than my own poor hundred and fifty.' But he was too quick in mounting and riding off to give me much time to think about it or to change in my disposition. It was only after he was off, out of sight, and in a full gallop, that, looking round upon the dead horse, I saw the eagles still there, nearly all of them, just as I had heaped them up. He had only taken two of them, just enough, as he said, to bear his necessary expenses.

"I was a little surprised, and was now more sure than ever that the stranger had lost his wits. I gathered up the money, and walked home, mighty slowly, thinking all the way of what had taken place. It seemed more like a strange dream than any thing else. Was there any man? Had I played *old sledge* with a stranger? I was almost inclined to doubt; but there was the dead horse. I went back to look at it, and when I thrust my hand down into my breeches pocket, I brought it up full of the precious metal; but was it precious metal? I began to tremble at this thought. It might be nothing better than brass or copper, and my horse was gone—gone off at a smart canter. My heart grew chilled within me at this reflection. I felt wild—scared half out of my wits, and instead of regarding the old man as a witless person escaped from his keepers, I now began to consider him a cunning sharper, who had found one more witless than I had fancied him.

VI

"But such reflections, even if well founded, came too late for remedy. The old man was gone beyond present reach, and when I reflected that he had taken two of the gold pieces for his own expenses, I began to feel a little reassured on the subject of their value. When I got home, I told my father of the sale of the horse, and the price, though I took precious good care to say nothing of the gambling. The old man, though he himself had taught me to play cards, was mighty strict against all play for money. I showed him only the fifteen pieces that I got for Rainbow, and the rest I put away quietly, meaning to spend them by degrees upon the farm, as chances offered, so as to prevent him from ever getting at the real truth. I felt myself pretty safe with regard to the strange gentleman. I never counted on his coming back to blow me, though, sometimes, when I wasn't thinking, an odd sort of fear would come over me, and I would feel myself trembling with the notion that, after all, he might return. I had heard of rich people having strange ways of throwing away their money, and taking a liking for poor people like myself; and then, there was a serious earnest about the strange gentleman, in spite of all his curiousnesses, that made me a little apprehensive, whenever the recollection of him came into my head.

"But regular work, day after day, is the best physic for mind and body; and, after three days had gone by, I almost ceased to bother myself with the affair. I passed the time so actively that I didn't think much about any thing. I took a trip down the river, some eighteen miles, to a wheelwright's, and bought a prime two-horse wagon, for ninety-five dollars, which made a considerable hole in the price of Rainbow; and, one thing with another, the week went by almost without giving me time to count if the right number of days was in it. Sunday followed, and then Monday. That Monday I was precious busy. I was always an industrious man—doing something or other—making this, or mending that. To be doing nothing was always the hardest work for me. But that Monday I out-worked myself, and I was really glad when I saw the sun sink suddenly down behind the woods. I threw down the broad-axe, for I had been hewing out some door-facings for a new corn-crib and fodder-house, and went towards the gallery (piazza) where the old man was sitting, and threw myself, at full-length, along the entrance, just at his feet. I was mighty tired. My jacket was off, my sleeves rolled up, my neck open, and the perspiration standing thick on my breast and forehead. At that very moment, while I was lying in this condition, who should I see ride into the opening, but the strange old gentleman. I knew him at a glance, and my heart jumped up into my mouth as if it was trying to get out of it. Behind him came another person riding upon a pretty little bay filly. Though it was darkening fast, I could make out that this other person was a woman, and I never felt so scared in all my life. I looked up at my father, and he at me. He saw that I was frightened, but he hadn't time to ask me a question, and I shouldn't have had the strength to answer if he had. Up rode the strange old gentleman, and close behind him came the lady. Though I was mightily frightened, I looked curiously at her. I could make out that she was a small and delicate-framed person, but her face was covered with a thick veil. I could see that she carried herself well, sat her horse upright like a sort of queen, and when the old man offered to take her off, yielded herself to him with a slow but graceful stateliness, not unlike that of a young cedar bending to the wind.

"For my part, though I could see this, I was never more confounded in my life. I was completely horror-struck. To see the old gentleman again was a shocking surprise; but that he should really bring the lady that I had won, and that she should catch me in that condition,—my coat off, my breast open, my face covered with dust and perspiration! If the work made me sweat before, this surprise increased it. I got up, and made out to get a few steps towards the strangers. I said something by way of apology for being caught in that shabby fix; but the old gentleman stopped me.

" 'Never mind, no apologies, Mr. Rayner. The proofs of labor are always honorable, and if the heart can show that it works as well as the body, then the laborer is a gentleman. How are you, and—this is your father?'

"I introduced him to the old man as the person who had bought Rainbow, and we conducted them into the house.

" 'My ward, Mr. Rayner,' said the stranger, when we had entered. 'This is the young friend of whom I spoke to you.'

"At these words the young lady threw up her veil. I staggered back at the sight. I won't talk of her beauty, my friend, for two reasons; one of which is, that I haven't got words to say what I thought and felt—what I think and feel now. The other—but I needn't speak of the other reason. This one is sufficient. The old gentleman looked at me inquiringly, and then he looked at my father. I could see that there was a little doubt and anxiety upon his face, but they soon passed away as he examined the face of my father. There was something so good, so meek, so benevolent about the looks of the old man, that nobody could mistrust that all was right in the bottom of his heart. As for my heart, the strange gentleman seemed to see into it quite as quickly as into that of my father. He was not so blunt and abrupt now in his manner of speaking to me as he had been when we first met. His manner was more dignified and reserved. There was something very lofty and noble about it, and in speaking to the lady his voice sunk almost into a whisper.

" 'Mr. Rayner,' said he, looking to my father, 'I trust that you will give my ward a chamber for the night. I have heard of you, sir, and have made bold to presume on your known benevolence of character in making this application.'

" 'Our home is a poor one, stranger,' said the old man; 'but such as it is, it is quite at the service of the young lady.'

" 'Good!' said the other, 'you are the man after my own heart. I am known,' he continued, 'where men speak of me at all, as Mr. Eckhardt. My ward is the daughter of a very near and dear friend. Her name is Herder—Rachel Herder. So much is necessary for convenience in conversation; and now, sir, if you can tell Rachel where she is to find her chamber, so that she may arrange her dress, and get rid of the dust of travel, she will be very much obliged to you.'

"All this was soon arranged and attended to, and while the lady disappeared in our best chamber, Mr. Eckhardt proceeded to disburthen the horses, on both of which were saddle-bags that were stuffed almost to bursting. These were brought into the house, and sent to the chamber after the lady. Then the stranger sat down with my father, the two old men chatting quite briskly together, while I stripped the horses of their saddles, and took them to the stable. When I returned to the house I found them as free-spoken and good-humored as if they had been intimate from the first day of clearing in that country.

VII

"You may suppose what my confusion must have been, for I can't describe it to you. I can only say that I felt pretty much like a drunken man. Every thing swum around me. I was certain of nothing; didn't know what to believe, and half the time really doubted whether I was asleep or awake. But there were the horses—there was Rainbow. I couldn't mistake him, and if I had, he didn't mistake me. When he heard my voice as I led him to the stable, he whinnied with a sort of joy, and pricked up his ears, and showed his feeling as plainly as if he had a human voice to speak it in words. And I reckon, too, it was a more true feeling than many of those that are spoken in words. I threw my arms round the good creature's neck, and if it hadn't been for thinking of Rachel Herder, I reckon I should have kissed him, too, it did me so much good to see him again. But I hadn't much time for this sort of fondness, and when I remembered the whole affair between the strange old gentleman, Mr. Eckhardt, and myself, I was too much worried to think any more of Rainbow. I couldn't bring myself to believe it true about the diamonds and the wife; and when I remembered the sight that I had caught, though a glimpse only, and for a single moment, of the great beauty of the young lady, I couldn't help thinking that the stranger was only making merry with me—running his rigs upon a poor, rough backwoodsman. But this notion roused up my pride and feeling. 'Not so rough,' says I to myself; 'poor it may be, but not mean; not more rough than honest labor makes a man. And poor as you please, and rough as you please, when the heart's right, and the head's no fool's head, the man's man enough for any woman, though she walks in satin!' With this I considered that I ought, at least, to make myself rather decent before I sat down to supper. My cheeks burned me when I looked at myself and remembered how she had caught me. I knew that good soft spring water, and my best suit, would turn me into quite another sort of looking man; but here again was difficulty. It was my chamber which my father had given up to the young lady, and all my clothes were in it. My new coat and blue pantaloons hung upon pegs behind the door; and all my shirts were in an old chest of drawers on which the looking-glass stood; and to get these things without her seeing was impossible. But it had to be done; so I called up the old negro woman servant we had, and told her what to do, and sent her for the clothes, while I waited for them at the back of the house. When she brought them, I hurried down to the branch (brooklet) and made a rapid and plentiful use of the waters. I then got in among the bushes, and made a thorough change in my dress, taking care to hide the old clothes in the hollow of a gum. I combed my hair smoothly over the branch, which answered me at the same time for a looking-glass, and had the effect of making me much more satisfied with my personal appearance. I needn't blush, my friend, at my time of life, to say that I thought myself then, and was, a tolerable comely fellow; and I couldn't help feeling a sneaking secret notion that the young lady would think so too. Well, I got in time enough for supper. Mr. Eckhardt looked at me, as I thought, with real satisfaction. He and my father had been keeping company all the time I was gone, and I could see among other things, that they were mightily pleased with one another. By and by, supper was brought in, and Rachel Herder came out of her chamber. If I thought her beautiful before, I thought her now ten times more so. Once I caught her eyes fixed upon me, but she turned them away without any flurry or confusion, and I don't think that I saw her look at me in particular once again that night. This worried me, I confess. It seemed to show that she wasn't thinking of me; and, moreover, it seemed to show that Mr. Eckhardt hadn't said a word to her about the business; and this made me more ready to believe that he had only been running his rigs upon me. Yet there was something about his looks and in his words, whenever he spoke to me—something so real, serious, earnest, that I couldn't help believing, after all, that the affair wasn't altogether over. Nor was it, as you will see directly.

"Supper went forward. You know what a country supper is, out here in Mississippi, so I don't need to tell you that cornbread, and a little eggs and bacon, and a smart bowl of milk, was pretty much the amount of it. The young lady ate precious little, took a little milk, I believe, and a corn biscuit. As for me, I'm very sure I ate still less. My heart was too much in my mouth to suffer me to put in any thing more; for, whichever way I thought of the matter, I was worried half to death. If the old gentleman was serious, it was still a mighty terrifying thing to have a wife so suddenly forced upon a body,—a wife that you never saw before and didn't know any thing about; and if he wasn't serious, it was very hard to lose so lovely a creature; just too after your heart had been tantalized and tempted by the promise that she was all for yourself. As I tell you, my friend, whichever way I could think of it, I was still worried half to death.

"After supper, Mr. Eckhardt asked me to walk out with him; so, leaving the young lady with my father,—who, by the way, had already grown mightily pleased with her,—off we went into the woods. We hadn't gone very far when the old gentleman spoke, pretty abruptly:

" 'Well, Rayner, my lad, you've seen the lady whom I intend as your wife. Does she suit you?'

" 'Why, sir, you're rather quick. I can answer for her beauty: she's about the beautifullest creature I ever did see, but it's not beauty altogether that makes a good wife, and I ha'n't had time yet to judge whether she'll suit me.'

" 'How much time do you want?' said he shortly.

" 'Well, I can't say.'

" 'Will a week or ten days answer?'

" 'That's as it happens,' said I. 'Some men you can understand in an hour, just as if you had been with 'em all your life. I'm pretty much such a person myself,—but with some you can't get on so rapidly. You'll be with them a year, and know just as little of their hearts at the end of it, as you did at the beginning.'

" 'Humph! and whose fault will that be but your own? There's an eye to see, Rayner, as well as a thing to be seen. It depends very much upon the seeker whether he shall ever find. But enough. There's no need in this case for much philosophy. You are easily read, and so is Rachel. A week will answer to make you both acquainted, and I'll leave her with you for that time.'

" 'But are you serious?' I asked.

" 'Serious! But your question is natural. I am a man of few words, Rayner. You see something in my proceedings which is extraordinary. As the world goes, and acts, and thinks, perhaps it is; but nothing was ever more deliberate or well advised, on my part, than this proceeding. Hear me, lad! this lady is a ward of mine; the daughter of a very dear friend, who gave her to my trust. I swore to do by her as a father. I am anxious to do so; but I am an old man, not long for this world,—an erring man, not always sure of doing right while I am in it. I wish to find the child a protector,—a good man,—a kind man,—a man whom I can trust. This has been my desire for some time. I fancy I have found in you the very person I seek. I am a man to look keenly, judge quickly, and act in the same manner. As you yourself have remarked, you are a person easily understood. I understood you in a little time, and was pleased with what I saw of you. I have chosen you out as the husband of Rachel. She knows nothing yet of my purpose. You, I see, have kept your father in partial ignorance of our adventure. Perhaps you were right in this case, though, as a general rule, such secrecy between two persons placed as you are would have been an error. Well, Rachel shall stay with you a week. I know her so well that I fancy you will in that time become intimate and remain pleased with each other—sufficiently pleased to make the rest easy.'

"There was some more talk between us, as we went toward the house, but this was the substantial part of what was said. Once I made some remark on the strangeness of such a preference shown to me, when in the great cities he might have found so many young men better suited by education for a young lady whom he represented to be so accomplished; but he had his answer for this also; and so quickly uttered, and with such a commanding manner, that, even if I had not been satisfied, I should still have been silenced.

" 'Your remark is natural. Half the world, having such a child to dispose of, would have gone to the great city, and have preferred a fashionable husband. But I know her heart. It is her heart, and not her accomplishments, that I wish to provide for. I want a man, not a dandy,—a frank, noble-hearted citizen, however plain, not a selfish, sophisticated calculator, who looks for a wife through the stock market. Enough, my good fellow; no more words.'

VIII

"That very night Mr. Eckhardt contrived, after the young lady had gone to bed, to let my father know that he would be pleased if his ward could be suffered to remain in his family for a few days, until he should cross the river, in order to look after a man on the west of the Mississippi, who owed him money. He was unwilling to carry her with him into so very wild a region. He made every thing appear so natural to the old man, that he consented out of hand, just as if it had been the most reasonable arrangement in the world; and it was only after Mr. Eckhardt had set out,—which he did by daylight the next morning,—that my father said to me:

" 'It's very strange, William, now I come to think of it, that Mr. Eckhardt should leave the young lady in a family where there's none but men.'

" 'But she's just as safe here, father,' said I, 'as if she had fifty of her own sex about her.'

" 'That's true enough, William,' said the old man, 'and if the child feels herself at home, why there's nothing amiss. I'm thinking she's about the sweetest-looking creature I ever laid eyes on.'

"I thought so too, but I said nothing, and followed the old man into the house, with my feelings getting more and more strange and worrisome at every moment. I was in the greatest whirl of expectation—my checks a-burning,—my heart as cold as ice, and leaping up and down, just as scarily as a rabbit's when he's finding his way through the paling into a garden patch. I felt as if the business now upon my hands was about the most serious and trying I had ever undertaken; and it took all my thinking, I tell you, to bring my courage to the right pitch, so as to steady my eyes while I spoke to the young lady as she came out to the breakfast-table. My father had a message to her from Mr. Eckhardt, telling her of his absence; and though she looked a little anxious when she heard that he was already gone, she soon seemed to become quiet and at ease in her situation. Indeed, for that matter, she was the most resigned and easy person I ever met in my life. She seemed quite too gentle ever to complain, and I may say now, with some certainty, that, whatever might be her hurts of mind or body, she was the most patient to submit, and the most easy to be pacified, of all human beings.

"Now, if you know any thing of a man of my description, if you're any thing of a judge of human nature, you'll readily understand that, if I was scary and bashful at first, in meeting with a young and beautiful creature like her, and knowing what I did know of what was before me, it didn't take very long for the fright to wear off. The man whose feelings are very quick, gets mightily confused at first, but give him time, don't hurry him, and he'll come to his senses pretty soon, and they'll come to him, and they'll be the sharper and the more steady, from the scare they had at first—you can't scare them in the same manner a second time. Before that day was well out, I could sit down and talk with Rachel, and hear her talk, without growing blind, dumb, and deaf in an instant. Her mildness gave me encouragement, and when I got used to the sound of my own voice, just after hers, I then found out, not only that I had a good deal to say, but that she listened very patiently, and I think was pleased to hear it. I found her so mild, so kind, and encouraging, she seemed to take so much interest in every thing she saw, that I was for showing her every thing. Our cows, the little dairy, the new wagon, even to the fields of corn, cotton, and potatoes, were all subjects of examination one after the other. Then, I could carry her along the hill slopes, through as pretty a grove, too, as you would wish to lay eyes on; and down along just such another, even to the river banks; and we had odd things enough to show, here and there, to keep up the spirits and have something to talk about. These rambles we'd take either in the cool of the morning, or towards sunset in the afternoon; and, sometimes the old man would go along with us—but, as he couldn't go very far at one time, we had pretty much the whole chance to ourselves; and what with talking and walking with Rachel, and thinking about her when I wasn't with her, I did precious little work that week. To shorten a long story, my friend, I now began to think that there was nothing wrong in my gambling with Mr. Eckhardt, and to agree in his notion that the loser was always bound to pay, and the winner to receive. Before he got back, which he did not until ten days were fully over, I had pretty much concluded that I should find it the most trying business in nature to have to give up my winnings. I don't mean the diamonds; for them I had not seen, and hadn't cared to see; but I mean the incumbrance that came with them, which, by this time, was more than all the gold or diamonds, in my sight, that the whole world could show.

IX

"I was now as anxious to see Mr. Eckhardt as I had before been afraid of his coming. He overstayed his time a little, being nearer two weeks gone than one. He was a keen-sighted man. His first words, when we were again alone together, were, 'Well, all's right on your part, Rayner. You are a good fellow—I see that you will be my heir. You find that what I said of Rachel is true; and nothing now remains but to see what she will say. Have you been much together?'

" 'Pretty often. I reckon I've done little else than look after her since you've been gone.'

" 'What! you hav'n't neglected your business, Rayner?' said he, with a smile—'the cows, the horses?'

" 'They've had a sort of liberty,' says I.

" 'Bad signs for farming, however good for loving. You must change your habits when you are married.'

" 'Ah! that's not yet,' said I, with a sigh. 'I'm dub'ous, Mr. Eckhardt, that Miss Rachel won't fancy me so soon as I do her!'

"He looked a little anxious, and didn't answer so quickly as usual, and my heart felt as heavy then as if it was borne down by a thousand pounds of lead. It wasn't much lightened when he answered, with a sort of doubting,—

" 'Rachel,' said he, 'has always heeded my counsel. She knows my love for her—she has every confidence in my judgment. You, Rayner, have some of those advantages which young women are apt to admire. You are well made, youthful, manly, and with a masculine grace and beauty which you owe to the hunter life. These are qualities to recommend the young of one sex to the young of the other. You have something more. You are a sensible youth, with a native delicacy of feeling which, more than any thing beside, will be apt to strike Rachel. It struck me. I will not presume to say that you have won either her eye or her heart—the eye of a woman is easy won at all times, the heart slowly. Perhaps it may be safe to say that hearts are not often won till after marriage. But, at all events, with your personal claims, which I think considerable, and the docility of Rachel, I have hopes that I can bring about an arrangement which, I confess to you, I regard as greatly important to my future purposes. We shall see.'

"At that moment I was quite too full of Rachel and my own hopes, to consider the force of the remark which he last made. I never troubled myself to ask what his purposes might be, beyond the single one which we both had in view. When Mr. Eckhardt met with Rachel, and, indeed, while he spoke with me, I could observe that there was a gravity, like sadness, in his voice and manner, which was not usual with him, or at least had not shown itself in our previous meetings. He hesitated more frequently in what he had to say. His eye was less settled, though even brighter than before; and I noted the fact that he took his pills three times as frequently as ever. Even when he spoke with a show of jesting or playfulness, I noted that there was a real sadness in what he looked, and even something of sadness in what he said, or in his manner of saying it. Nothing but this seriousness of look and manner kept me from thinking that he was playing upon my backwoods ignorance, when he was speaking my own good name and good qualities to my teeth. But when I doubted and began to suspicion that he was running rigs upon me, I had only to look into his face and see that he was talking in the way of downright, matter-of-fact business.

"When he came, Rachel went to him and put her hand in his, but she didn't speak. Nor did he at first. He only bent down and kissed her forehead; and so he stood awhile, holding her hand in his, and talking to my father. It was a sight to see them two. I couldn't stand it. There was something in it, I can't tell you what, that looked so sadful. I went out and wiped the water from my eyes. It seemed to me then, as if the old gentleman was meditating something very distressing, and as if poor Rachel was half dub'ous of it herself. After a little while, my father came out and joined me, and we walked off together to the stable.

" 'William,' says the old man, 'these are strange people. They seem very sweet, good people; at least the girl seems very good, and is a very sweet girl; but there's something very strange and very sorrowful about them.'

"I couldn't say any thing, for my heart was very full, and the old man went forward.

" 'Now, what's more strange than for him to leave her here with us? though, to be sure, we wouldn't see her harmed even to the falling of a hair of her head—and I can answer for you, Bill, as I can for myself; but it's not every body that will say for us what we might feel for ourselves, and precious few fathers would leave an only daughter here, in strange woods, with such perfect strangers.'

" 'But she's not his daughter,' said I.

" 'It don't matter. It's very clear that he loves her as if she was his daughter, and I reckon she's never known any other father. Poor girl!—I'm sure I like her already so much that I wish he'd leave her here altogether.'

"These last words of my father seemed to untie my tongue, and I up and told him every syllable of what had taken place between me and Mr. Eckhardt, from my first meeting with him the day when I went to the river landing, up to the very moment when we were talking. I didn't hide any thing, but told the whole story of the cards, the gold, and the diamonds; and ended by letting him know that if he should be so sorry to lose Rachel, now that we both knew so much about her, it would go a mighty deal harder with me. I told him all that Mr. Eckhardt had said since his return, and what hopes I had that all would go as he wished it. But the old man shook his head. He didn't like what he heard about Mr. Eckhardt's gambling, and was very tight upon me for letting myself be tempted to deal with him in the same business. He didn't think the worse of Rachel, of course, but he looked upon it as a sort of misfortune to be in any way connected with a gambler.

"We hadn't much longer time for confabulating, for Mr. Eckhardt now came from the house and joined us. He was a man who always came jump to the business, whatever it was, that he had in hand. But he wasn't a rough man, though a quick one. He had a way of doing the bluntest things without roughing the feelings. When he drew nigh, he took my father's arm to lead him aside, speaking to me at the same time—'Rayner, go to Rachel;—I have prepared her to see you. I will explain every thing to your father, if you have not already done it; and if you have, I still have something to say.'

"You may reckon I didn't stop to count the tracks after that. I verily think that I made the door of the house in a hop-skip-and-jump from the stable. Yet, when I got to the threshold, I stuck—I stuck fast. I heard a low sweet sort of moaning from within, and oh! how my heart smote me when I heard it. I thought to myself, it's so cruel to force this poor girl's inclination. What can she see in me? That was my question to myself, and it made me mighty humble, I tell you, when I asked it. But that very humbleness did me good, and gave me a sort of strength. 'If she don't see any thing in me to favor,' was my thought, 'at least I'll show her that I'm not the mean-spirited creature to take advantage of her necessity'; and when I thought in this manner, I went forward with a bound, and stood before her. I took her hand in mine, and said,—but Lord bless me, it's no use to try and tell you what I said, for I don't know myself. The words poured from me free enough. My heart was very full. I meant to speak kindly and humbly, and do the thing generously, and I reckon that, when the heart means what is right, and has a straight purpose before it, the tongue can't go very far out of the way. Nor did mine, if I am to judge of the effects which followed it. It's enough for me to tell you, that, though the tears wasn't altogether dried up in Rachel's eyes, her lips began to smile; she let her hand rest in mine, and she said something, but what it was, I can't tell you. It's enough to say that she let me know that she thought that all that had been proposed by Mr. Eckhardt was for her good and happiness, and she was willing to consent to whatever he had said. He came in a little while after, and seemed quite satisfied. He talked, as if he himself was particularly pleased, but there was a very great earnestness in his looks that awed and overpowered me. His eyes seemed very much sunk, even in the short time he had been gone, the wrinkles seemed to have doubled in number on his face; his form trembled very much, and I could perceive that he took his pills from the little box of silver twice as often as ever. He didn't give himself or me much time to think over what was to happen, for he hadn't been ten minutes returned to the house, after the matter was understood all round, before he said to me in a whisper:

" 'Rayner, my lad, you are a good fellow; suppose you ride off at once for your parson. You have one, your father tells me, within a few miles. A smart gallop will bring him back with you before sunset, and I would see you married to-night. I shall have to leave you in the morning.'

"Ah! stranger, don't wonder if I made the dust fly after that! That night we were married.

X

"The next morning, just as breakfast was over, Mr. Eckhardt rose and buttoned his coat.

" 'Rachel, my child,' said he, 'I shall now leave you. It will be perhaps some time before I see you again. For that matter, I may never see you again. But I have fulfilled my promise to your dear father. You are the wife of a good man—a gentle and kind-hearted man. He will make you a good husband, I believe and hope. You, I know, will make him a good wife. The seeds of goodness and happiness are here in this cottage—may they grow to fruits. Kiss me, my child! Kiss me! It may be for the last time!'

" 'No!' said she; 'oh, no!' and she caught and she clung to him. It was a time to bring tears, stranger, not to talk. There was a good many words said by all of us, but not much talking. It was a cry and an exclamation like, with poor Rachel, and then she sunk off in the arms of Mr. Eckhardt. I was monstrous frightened; but he carried her into the room and laid her on the bed. 'She will soon get over it,' said he, 'and in the mean time I'll steal away. When she recovers follow me. You will find me——' He told me where to find him—at the place where we had played together on the dead horse—but the sentence he finished in a whisper. Then he stooped and kissed her, gave her one long look, and his lips moved as if he was speaking a blessing over her. After this he turned from me hurriedly, as if to conceal the tear in his eye. But I saw it. It couldn't be concealed. It was about the largest tear I ever did see in the eye of a man, but I reckon there was only that one. He was gone before Rachel come to herself. Till that happened I was about the most miserable creature on earth. When she opened her eyes and found that he was already gone, her troubles somewhat softened; and when I found that, I set off to follow Mr. Eckhardt, as he had directed me. I found him at the place appointed, but he had no horse and no cloak, and didn't appear to have made any of the usual arrangements for travelling. I expressed my surprise. 'Where's your horse?' I demanded.—'I shall need none. Besides, I *have* none. You seem to forget, Rayner, that the horse is yours.'—'Mine!'—'Yes! you won him!'—'But you can't mean, sir——' I was beginning to expostulate, when he put his hand on my mouth. 'Say no more, Rayner. You are a good fellow. The horse *is* yours, whether you have him by your skill or my generosity. Did I not tell you that I intended to make you my heir?'

"I looked bewildered, and felt so, and said, 'Well, you don't intend to leave us then?'—'Yes I do.'—'How do you mean to go—by water?' Remember, the river was pretty near us, and though I didn't myself expect any steamboat, yet I thought it likely he might have heard of one. 'Very possible,' he answered, with something of a smile upon his countenance. He continued, after a short pause, 'It is difficult to say by what conveyance a man goes when he goes out of the world, Rayner. The journey I propose to take is no other. Life is an uncertain business, Rayner. Uncertain as it is, most people seem never to have enough of it. I am of a different thinking. I have had only too much. I am neither well in it, nor fit for it, and I shall leave it. I have made all my arrangements, settled my concerns, and, as I promised, you shall be my heir.' I began to speak and expostulate with him, but he stopped me. 'Rayner, you are a good fellow, but you shouldn't interrupt me. As I have but little time for talking, you should let me enjoy it all. You can say what you have to say when I am gone, and I promise you *I* shall never interrupt *you* then. You have heard me, you understand my words.'

" 'I think I do,' was my answer; 'you mean to take your own life!'

" 'True, Rayner! but you speak as if it was yours I were about to take!'

"I told him I felt almost as bad as if it was, and asked him why he should think of such a deed.

" 'It's a long story, Rayner, and you would probably understand it as thoroughly in ten words as in ten thousand. Perhaps I should say enough in telling you that I am sick of life, and that life sickens me. Every moment that I live humbles and degrades me. I have been the master of three princely fortunes; and now I have only the means to carry me on my last journey. I have had the reputation of talents, wit, and wisdom in high degree, but lack the strength to forbear the companionship of the basest, and the wit to keep from being the victim of the vilest. Had I been the only victim, Rayner! But that poor child, now your wife—the child of a dear relative and friend—entrusted to my guardianship in the confidence of love, which, at dying, demanded of me no pledge, but that which it fancied was speaking through my eyes—that child has been the victim also! Start not! The child is pure as any angel. It was the robbery of her fortune of which I speak. I squandered hers with my own. I did not bring her to beggary, Rayner. No! But I have lived in perpetual dread that I should do so! Now that she is yours, I have no such fears. I know that she is safe—that she will do well—that you will both do well. Do not fancy, my good fellow, when I tell you this, that I have been seeking in vain for a husband for the child. The thing is otherwise. Husbands have sought for her. Men of rank and substance, for whose attentions the mothers of most daughters would have worked their wits and fingers to the bone. But if I squandered Rachel's fortune—mark me—I was resolved that *she* should not be sacrificed. I resolved that I would do her justice, at least in that one respect—that she should never be yielded, if I could help it, to the shallow witling, the profligate, or the brute—let their social rank and worldly possessions be what they might. I knew her, and fancied I could tell what sort of person would suit her. I have found that person in you—so I believe—and my work is ended. The laborer knocks off when his work is done, and so will I. There is one thing, Rayner——'

"He took from his pocket the buckskin roll which contained his pack of cards.

" 'Do you see these? I will not say that they have been my bane. I were a fool to say so. My own weakness was my bane. They were only the unconscious instruments in my hands, as innocent as the dirk or pistol in the hands of the assassin. But they have their dangers, Rayner; and I would protect you against them. Take them; I promised you should be my heir. Take them, but not to play them. Keep them in your eyes as an omen. Show them to your children as a warning. Tell them what I have told you; and while you familiarize their eyes with their forms, familiarize their hearts with their dangers. There! do not lose sight of them. Leave me now. Farewell! You see I am at the bottom of my box.'

"He thrust the cards into my hands, and as he spoke, he drew out his little silver box, and took from it the only pill which remained.

This he swallowed, and then handed me the box also. I refused to take it. 'Pshaw!' said he, 'why not? your refusal to take it can have no effect on my determination! Take it and leave me!' But I still refused. He turned from me, saying: 'You're a foolish fellow, Rayner'; and walked down the road leading to the river. I followed him closely. He turned half round, once or twice, muttered and seemed discontented. I still kept close with him, and began to expostulate. But he interrupted me fiercely; and I now perceived that his eyes began to glisten and to glare very wildly. It had not escaped my observation, that the last pill which he had taken was greatly larger than any he had used before; and I then remembered, that before the marriage ceremony was performed, on the previous night, he had opened the box more than once, in my presence, and I noted that it contained a good many. By this time we reached the banks of the river. He turned full upon me. 'Rayner,' said he, 'you're a good fellow, but you must go home to your wife.'—'It's impossible,' said I, 'to leave you.'—'We'll see to that,' said he, and he turned towards the river. I took it for certain he was going to plunge in, and I jumped forward to seize him, but, just as my arms were extended to embrace him, he wheeled about and clapped a pistol to my head. I started back, quickly enough, as you may suppose; and he exclaimed—'Ah! Rayner, you are a good fellow, but you cannot prevent the journey. Farewell!' With these words he flung me the pistol, which I afterwards found was unloaded, and, before I could speak or think, he sprang from the bluff into the stream. It appeared to me as if I heard the splash before I saw the motion. I ran up the bluff where he had stood, as soon as I could recover myself, and saw where the water-rings were spreading in great circles where he had gone down. I didn't give myself a moment after that. I could swim like a duck and dive like a serpent, and had no fear of the water for myself; so in I jumped, and fished about as long as I could stand it underneath; but I could find nothing of him. He had given himself up to the currents so entirely, that they whirled him out of sight in a minute. When I rose and got to the shore, I saw his hat floating among some bushes on the other shore. But as for poor Mr. Eckhardt, he was gone, sure enough, upon his last journey!

"You see our little family. The boy is very much like him in looks, and I reckon in understanding. He's very thoughtful and smart. We are happy, stranger, and I don't believe that Mr. Eckhardt was wrong in his notion that I would make Rachel happy. She tells me she is, and it makes me happy to believe her. It makes her sad to see the cards, and sad to hear of them, but she thinks it best for our boy that he should hear the story and learn it all by heart; and that makes her patient, and patience brings a sort of peace along with it that's pretty much like happiness. I could tell you more, my friend, but it's not needful, and your eyes look as if they had kept open long enough for one sitting. So come with me, and let me show you where you are to lie down!"

These words roused me! I half suspect that I was drowsing in my chair. I can hardly suppose, dear reader, that you could be capable of an act of like forgetfulness.

The Arm-Chair of Tustenuggee
A Tradition of the Catawba

I

The windy month had set in, the leaves were falling, and the light-footed hunters of Catawba set forth upon the chase. Little groups went off in every direction, and before two weeks had elapsed from the beginning of the campaign, the whole nation was broken up into parties, each under the guidance of an individual warrior. The course of the several hunting bands was taken according to the tastes or habits of these leaders. Some of the Indians were famous for their skill in hunting the otter, could swim as long with head under water as himself, and be not far from his haunches, when he emerged to breathe. These followed the course of shallow waters and swamps, and thick, dense bays, in which it was known that he found his favorite haunts. The bear hunter pushed for the cane brakes and the bee trees; and woe to the black bear whom he encountered with his paws full of honeycomb, which he was unwilling to leave behind him. The active warrior took his way towards the hills, seeking for the brown wolf and the deer; and, if the truth were known, smiled with wholesale contempt at the more timorous who desired less adventurous triumphs. Many set forth in couples only, avoiding with care all the clamorous of the tribe; and some few, the more surly or successful—the inveterate bachelors of the nation—were content to make their forward progress alone. The old men prepared their traps and nets, the boys their blow guns, and followed with the squaws slowly, according to the division made by the hunters among themselves. They carried the blankets and bread stuffs, and camped nightly in noted places, to which, according to previous arrangement, the hunters might repair at evening and bring their game. In this way, some of the tribes followed the course of the Catawba, even to its source. Others darted off towards the Pacolet and Broad rivers, and there were some, the most daring and swift of foot, who made nothing of a journey to the Tiger River, and the rolling mountains of Spartanburg.

There were two warriors who pursued this course. One of them was named Conattee, and a braver man and more fortunate hunter never lived. But he had a wife who was a greater scold than Xantippe. She was the wonder and the terror of the tribe, and quite as ugly as the one-eyed squaw of Tustenuggee, the grey demon of Enoree. Her tongue was the signal for "slinking," among the bold hunters of Turkey-town; and when they heard it, "now," said the young women, who sympathised, as all proper young women will do, with the handsome husband of an ugly wife, "now," said they, "we know that poor Conattee has come home." The return of the husband, particularly if he brought no game, was sure to be followed by a storm of that "dry thunder," so well known, which never failed to be heard at the farthest end of the village.

The companion of Conattee on the present expedition was named Selonee—one of the handsomest lads in the whole nation. He was tall and straight like a pine tree, had proved his skill and courage in several expeditions against the Chowannee red sticks, and had found no young warriors of the Cherokee, though he had been on the war path against them and had stricken all their posts, who could circumvent him in stratagem or conquer him in actual blows. His renown as a hunter was not less great. He had put to shame the best wolf-takers of the tribe, and the lodge of his venerable father, Chifonti, was never without meat. There was no good reason why Conattee, the married man, should be so intimate with Selonee, the single—there was no particular sympathy between the two; but, thrown together in sundry expeditions, they had formed an intimacy, which, strange to say, was neither denounced nor discouraged by the virago wife of the former. She who approved of but few of her husband's movements, and still fewer of his friends and fellowships, forbore all her reproaches when Selonee was his companion. She was the meekest, gentlest, sweetest tempered of all wives whenever the young hunter came home with her husband; and he, poor man, was consequently, never so well satisfied as when he brought Selonee with him. It was on such occasions, only, that the poor Conattee could persuade himself to regard Macourah as a tolerable personage. How he came to marry such a creature—such a termagant, and so monstrous ugly—was a mystery which none of the damsels of Catawba could elucidate, though the subject was one on which, when mending the young hunter's moccasins, they expended no small quantity of conjecture. Conattee, we may be permitted to say, was still quite popular among them, in spite of his bad taste, and manifest unavailableness; possibly, for the very reason that his wife was universally detested; and it will, perhaps, speak something for their charity, if we pry no deeper into their motives, to say that the wish was universal among them that the Opitchi Manneyto, or Black Devil of their belief, would take the virago to himself, and leave to the poor Conattee some reasonable hope of being made happy by a more indulgent spouse.

II

Well, Conattee and Selonee were out of sight of the smoke of "Turkey-town," and, conscious of his freedom as he no longer heard the accents of domestic authority, the henpecked husband gave a loose to his spirits, and made ample amends to himself, by the indulgence of joke and humor, for the sober constraints which fettered him at home. Selonee joined with him in his merriment, and the resolve was mutual that they should give the squaws the slip and not linger in their progress till they had thrown the Tiger River behind them. To trace their course till they came to the famous hunting ground which bordered upon the Pacolet, will scarcely be necessary, since, as they did not stop to hunt by the way, there were necessarily but few incidents to give interest to their movements. When they had reached the river, however, they made for a cove, well known to them on previous seasons, which lay between the parallel waters of the Pacolet, and a little stream called the Thicketty—a feeder of the Eswawpuddenah, in which they had confident hopes of finding the game which they desired. In former years the spot had been famous as a sheltering place for herds of wolves; and, with something like the impatience of a warrior waiting for his foe, the hunters prepared their strongest shafts and sharpest flints, and set their keen eyes upon the closest places of the thicket, into which they plunged fearlessly. They had not proceeded far, before a single boar-wolf, of amazing size, started up in their path; and, being slightly wounded by the arrow of Selonee, which glanced first upon some twigs beneath which he lay, he darted off with a fearful howl in the direction of Conattee, whose unobstructed shaft, penetrating the side beneath the fore shoulders, inflicted a fearful, if not a fatal wound, upon the now thoroughly enraged beast. He rushed upon

Conattee in his desperation, but the savage was too quick for him; leaping behind a tree, he avoided the rashing stroke with which the white tusks threatened him, and by this time was enabled to fit a second arrow to his bow. His aim was true, and the stone blade of the shaft went quivering into the shaggy monster's heart; who, under the pang of the last convulsion, bounded into the muddy waters of the Thicketty Creek, to the edge of which the chase had now brought all the parties. Conattee beheld him plunge furiously forward—twice—thrice—then rest with his nostrils in the water, as the current bore him from sight around a little elbow of the creek. But it was not often that the Indian hunter of those days lost the game which he had stricken. Conattee stripped to it, threw his fringed hunting shirt of buckskin on the bank, with his bow and arrows, his moccasins and leggins beside it, and reserving only his knife, he called to Selonee, who was approaching him, to keep them in sight, and plunged into the water in pursuit of his victim. Selonee gave little heed to the movements of his companion, after the first two or three vigorous strokes which he beheld him make. Such a pursuit, as it promised no peril, called for little consideration from this hardy and fearless race, and Selonee amused himself by striking into a thick copse which they had not yet traversed, in search of other sport. There he startled the she-wolf, and found sufficient employment on his own hands to call for all his attention to himself. When Selonee first came in sight of her, she was lying on a bed of rushes and leaves, which she had prepared under the roots of a gigantic Spanish oak. Her cubs, to the number of five, lay around her, keeping a perfect silence, which she had no doubt enforced upon them after her own fashion, and which was rigidly maintained until they saw him. It was then that the instincts of the fierce beasts could no longer be suppressed, and they joined at once in a short chopping bark, or cry, at the stranger, while their little eyes flashed fire, and their red jaws, thinly sprinkled with the first teeth, were gnashed together with a show of that ferocious hatred of man, which marks their nature, but which, fortunately for Selonee, was too feeble at that time to make his approach to them dangerous. But the dam demanded greater consideration. With one sweep of her forepaw she drew all the young ones behind her, and showing every preparedness for flight, she began to move backward slowly beneath the overhanging limbs of the tree, still keeping her keen, fiery eye fixed upon the hunter. But Selonee was not disposed to suffer her to get off so easily. The success of Conattee had just given him sufficient provocation to make him silently resolve that the she-wolf—who is always more to be dreaded than the male, as, with nearly all his strength, she has twice his swiftness, and, with her young about her, more than twice his ferocity—should testify more completely to his prowess than the victory just obtained by his companion could possibly speak for his. His eye was fixed upon hers, and hers, never for a moment, taken from him. It was his object to divert it, since he well knew, that with his first movement, she would most probably spring upon him. Without lifting his bow,. which he nevertheless had in readiness, he whistled shrilly as if to his dog; and answered himself by a correct imitation of the bark of the Indian cur, the known enemy of the wolf, and commonly his victim. The keen eye of the angry beast looked suddenly around as if fearing an assault upon her young ones from behind. In that moment, the arrow of Selonee was driven through her neck, and when she leaped forward to the place where he stood, he was no longer to be seen.

From a tree which he had thrown between them, he watched her movements and prepared a second shaft. Meanwhile she made her way back slowly to her young, and before she could again turn towards him a second arrow had given her another and severer wound. Still, as Selonee well knew the singular tenacity of life possessed by these fierce animals, he prudently changed his position with every shaft, and took especial care to place himself in the rear of some moderately sized tree, sufficiently large to shelter him from her claws, yet small enough to enable him to take free aim around it. Still he did not, at any time, withdraw more than twenty steps from his enemy. Divided in her energies by the necessity of keeping near her young, he was conscious of her inability to pursue him far. Carrying on the war in this manner, he had buried no less than five arrows in her body, and it was not until his sixth had penetrated her eye, that he deemed himself safe in the nearer approach which he now meditated. She had left her cubs, on receiving his last shot, and was writhing and leaping, blinded, no less than maddened, by the wound, in a vain endeavor to approach her assailant. It was now that Selonee determined on a closer conflict. It was the great boast of the Catawba warriors to grapple with the wolf, and while he yet struggled, to tear the quick quivering heart from his bosom. He placed his bow and arrows behind the tree, and taking in his left hand a chunk or fragment of a bough, while he grasped his unsheathed knife in his right, he leapt in among the cubs, and struck one of them a severe blow upon the head with the chunk.

Its scream, and the confusion among the rest, brought back the angry dam, and though she could see only imperfectly, yet, guided by their clamor, she rushed with open jaws upon the hunter. With keen, quick eyes, and steady resolute nerves, he waited for her approach, and when she turned her head aside, to strike him with her sharp teeth, he thrust the pine fragment which he carried in his left hand, into her extended jaws, and pressing fast upon her, bore back her haunches to the earth. All this while the young ones were impotently gnawing at the heels of the warrior, which had been fearlessly planted in the very midst of them. But these he did not heed. The larger and fiercer combatant called for all his attention, and her exertions, quickened by the spasms of her wounds, rendered necessary all his address and strength to preserve the advantage he had gained. The fierce beast had sunk her teeth by this into the wood, and, leaving it in her jaws, he seized her with the hand, now freed, by the throat, and, bearing her upward, so as to yield him a plain and easy stroke at her belly, he drove the deep knife into it, and drew the blade upwards, until resisted by the bone of the breast. It was then, while she lay writhing and rolling upon the ground in the agonies of death, that he tore the heart from the opening he had made, and hurled it down to the cubs, who seized on it with avidity. This done, he patted and caressed them, and while they struggled about him for the meat, he cut a fork in the ears of each, and putting the slips in his pouch, left the young ones without further hurt, for the future sport of the hunter. The dam he scalped, and with this trophy in possession, he pushed back to the place where he had left the accoutrements of Conattee, which he found undisturbed in the place where he had laid them.

III

But where was Conattee himself during all this period? Some hours had elapsed since he had taken the river after the tiger that he had slain, and it was something surprising to Selonee that he should have remained absent and without his clothes so long. The weather was cold and unpleasant, and it could scarce be a matter of choice with the hunter, however hardy, to suffer all its biting bleaknesses when his garments were within his reach. This reflection made Selonee apprehensive that some harm had happened to his companion. He shouted to him, but received no answer. Could he have been seized with the cramp while in the stream, and drowned before he could extricate himself? This was a danger to which the very best of swimmers is liable at certain seasons of the year, and in certain conditions of the body. Selonee reproached himself that he had not waited beside the stream until the result of Conattee's experiment was known. The mind of the young hunter was troubled with many fears and doubts. He went down the bank of the river, and called aloud with all his lungs, until the woods and waters re-echoed, again and again, the name of Conattee. He received no other response. With a mind filled with increasing fears, each more unpleasant than the last, Selonee plunged into the creek, and struck off for the opposite shore, at the very point at which the tiger had been about to turn, under the influence of the current, when Conattee went in after him. He was soon across, and soon found the tracks of the hunter in the gray sands upon its margin. He found, too, to his great delight, the traces made by the carcass of the tiger—the track was distinct enough from the blood which dropped from the reeking skin of the beast, and Selonee rejoiced in the certainty that the traces which he followed would soon lead him to his friend. But not so. He had scarcely gone fifty yards into the woods when his tracks failed him at the foot of a crooked, fallen tree, one of the most gnarled and complicated of all the crooked trees of the forest; here all signs disappeared. Conattee was not only not there, but had left no sort of clue by which to follow him further. This was the strangest thing of all. The footprints were distinct enough till he came to the spot where lay the crooked tree, but there he lost them. He searched the forest around him, in every direction. Not a copse escaped his search—not a bay—not a thicket—not an island—and he came back to the spot where the tiger had been skinned, faint and weary, and more sorrowful than can well be spoken. At one time he fancied his friend was drowned, at another, that he was taken prisoner by the Cherokees. But there were his tracks from the river, and there were no other tracks than his own. Besides, so far as the latter supposition was concerned, it was scarcely possible that so brave and cunning a warrior would suffer himself to be so completely entrapped and carried off by an enemy, without so much as being able to give the alarm; and, even had that been the case, would it be likely that the enemy would have suffered him to pass without notice? "But," here the suggestion naturally arose in the mind of Selonee, "may they not even now be on the track!" With the suggestion the gallant youth bounded to his feet. "It is no fat turkey that they seek!" he exclaimed, drawing out an arrow from the leash that hung upon his shoulders, and fitting it to his bow, while his busy, glancing eye watched every shadow in the wood, and his keen, quick ear noted every sound. But there were no signs of an enemy, and a singular and mournful stillness hung over the woods. Never was creature more miserable than Selonee. He called aloud, until his voice grew hoarse, and his throat sore, upon the name of Conattee. There was no answer, but the gibing echoes of his own hoarse accents. Once more he went back to the river, once more he plunged into its bosom, and with lusty sinews struck out for a thick green island that lay some quarter of a mile below, to which he thought it not improbable that the hunter might have wandered in pursuit of other game. It was a thickly wooded but small island, which he traversed in an hour. Finding nothing, he made his weary way back to the spot from which his friend had started on leaving him. Here he found his clothes where he had hidden them. The neighborhood of this region he traversed in like manner with the opposite—going over ground, and into places, which it was scarcely on the verge of physical possibility that his friend's person could have gone.

The day waned and night came on, and still the persevering hunter gave not up his search. The midnight found him at the foot of the tree, where they had parted, exhausted but sleepless, and suffering bitterly in mind from those apprehensions which every moment of hopeless search had necessarily helped to accumulate and strengthen. Day dawned, and his labor was renewed. The unhappy warrior went resolutely over all the ground which he had traversed the night before. Once more he crossed the river, and followed, step by step, the still legible foot tracks of Conattee. These, he again noted, were all in the opposite direction to the stream, to which it was evident he had not returned. But, after reaching the place where lay the fallen tree, all signs failed. Selonee looked round the crooked tree, crawled under its sprawling and twisted limbs, broke into the hollow which was left by its uptorn roots, and again shouted, until all the echoes gave back his voice, the name of Conattee, imploring him for an answer if he could hear him and reply. But the echoes died away, leaving him in a silence that spoke more loudly to his heart than before, that his quest was hopeless. Yet he gave it not up until the day had again failed him. That night, as before, he slept upon the ground. With the dawn, he again went over it, and with equally bad success. This done, he determined to return to the camp. He no longer had any spirit to pursue the sports for which alone he had set forth. His heart was full of sorrow, his limbs were weary, and he felt none of that vigorous elasticity which had given him such great renown as a brave and a hunter, among his own and the neighboring nations. He tied the clothes of Conattee upon his shoulders, took his bows and arrows, now sacred in his sight, along with him, and turned his eyes homeward. The next day, at noon, he reached the encampment.

IV

The hunters were all in the woods, and none but the squaws and the papooses left in the encampment. Selonee came within sight of their back settlements, and seated himself upon a log at the edge of the forest with his back carefully turned towards the smoke of the camp. Nobody ventured to approach him while in this situation; but, at night, when the hunters came dropping in, one by one, Selonee drew nigh to them. He called them apart from the women, and then told them his story.

"This is a strange tale which the wolf-chief tells us," said one of the old men, with a smile of incredulity.

"It is a true tale, father," was the reply.

"Conattee was a brave chief!"

"Very brave, father," said Selonee.

"Had he not eyes to see?"

"The great bird, that rises to the sun, had not better," was the reply.

"What painted jay was it that said Conattee was a fool?"

"The painted bird lied, that said so, my father," was the response of Selonee.

"And comes Selonee, the wolf-chief, to us, with a tale that Conattee was blind, and could not see; a coward that could not strike the she-wolf; a fool that knew not where to set down his foot; and shall we not say Selonee lies upon his brother, even as the painted bird that makes a noise in my ears? Selonee has slain Conattee with his knife. See, it is the blood of Conattee upon the war-shirt of Selonee."

"It is the blood of the she-wolf," cried the young warrior, with a natural indignation.

"Let Selonee go to the woods behind the lodges, till the chiefs say what shall be done to Selonee, because of Conattee, whom he slew."

"Selonee will go, as Emathla, the wise chief, has commanded," replied the young warrior. "He will wait behind the lodges, till the chiefs have said what is good to be done to him, and if they say that he must die because of Conattee, it is well. Selonee laughs at death. But the blood of Conattee is not upon the war-shirt of Selonee. He has said it is the blood of the wolf's mother." With these words the young chief drew forth the skin of the wolf which he had slain, together with the tips of the ears taken from the cubs, and leaving them in the place where he had sat, withdrew, without further speech, from the assembly which was about to sit in judgment upon his life.

V

The consultation that followed was close and earnest. There was scarcely any doubt in the minds of the chiefs that Conattee was slain by his companion. He had brought back with him the arms and all the clothes of the hunter. He was covered with his blood, as they thought; and the grief which filled his heart and depressed his countenance, looked, in their eyes, rather like the expression of guilt than suffering. For a long while did they consult together. Selonee had friends who were disposed to save him; but he had enemies also, as merit must have always, and these were glad of the chance afforded them to put out of their reach, a rival of whom they were jealous, and a warrior whom they feared. Unfortunately for Selonee, the laws of the nation but too well helped the malice of his foes. These laws, as peremptory as those of the Medes and Persians, held him liable in his own life for that of the missing hunter; and the only indulgence that could be accorded to Selonee, and which was obtained for him, was, that he might be allowed a single moon in which to find Conattee, and bring him home to his people.

"Will Selonee go seek Conattee—the windy moon is for Selonee—let him bring Conattee home to his people." Thus said the chiefs, when the young warrior was again brought before them.

"Selonee would die to find Conattee," was the reply.

"He will die if he finds him not!" answered the chief, Emathla.

"It is well!" calmly spoke the young warrior. "Is Selonee free to go?"

"The windy moon is for Selonee. Will he return to the lodges if he finds not Conattee?" was the inquiry of Emathla.

"Is Selonee a dog, to fly?" indignantly demanded the warrior. "Let Emathla send a young warrior on the right and on the left of Selonee, if he trusts not what is spoken by Selonee."

"Selonee will go alone, and bring back Conattee."

VI

The confidence thus reposed in one generally esteemed a murderer, and actually under sentence as such, is customary among the Indians; nor is it often abused. The loss of caste which would follow their flight from justice, is much more terrible among them than any fear of death—which an Indian may avoid, but not through fear. Their loss of caste among themselves, apart from the outlawry which follows it, is, in fact, a loss of the soul. The heaven of the great Manneyto is denied to one under outlawry of the nation, and such a person is then the known and chosen slave of the demon, Opitchi-Manneyto. It was held an unnecessary insult on the part of Emathla, to ask Selonee if he would return to meet his fate. But Emathla was supposed to favor the enemies of Selonee.

With such a gloomy alternative before him in the event of his proving unsuccessful, the young hunter retraced his steps to the fatal waters where Conattee had disappeared. With a spirit no less warmly devoted to his friend, than anxious to avoid the disgraceful doom to which he was destined, the youth spared no pains, withheld no exertion, overlooked no single spot, and omitted no art known to the hunter, to trace out the mystery which covered the fate of Conattee. But days passed of fruitless labor, and the last faint slender outlines of the moon which had been allotted him for the search, gleamed forth a sorrowful light upon his path, as he wearily traced it onward to the temporary lodges of the tribe.

Once more he resumed his seat before the council and listened to the doom which was in reserve for him. When the sentence was pronounced, he untied his arrows, loosened the belt at his waist, put a fillet around his head made of the green bark of a little sapling which he cut in the neighboring woods, then rising to his feet, he spoke thus, in language, and with a spirit, becoming so great a warrior.

"It is well. The chiefs have spoken, and the wolf-chief does not tremble. He loves the chase, but he does not weep like a woman, because it is forbidden that he go after the deer—he loves to fright the young hares of the Cherokee, but he laments not that ye say ye can conquer the Cherokee without his help. Fathers, I have slain the deer and the wolf—my lodge is full of their ears. I have slain the Cherokee, till the scalps are about my knees when I walk in the cabin. I go not to the dark valley without glory—I have had the victories of grey hairs, but there is no grey hair in my own. I have no more to say—there is a deed for every arrow that is here. Bid the young men get their bows ready, let them put a broad stone upon their arrows that may go soon into the life—I will show my people how to die."

They led him forth as he commanded, to the place of execution—a little space behind the encampment, where a hole had been already dug for his burial. While he went, he recited his victories to the youths who attended him. To each he gave an arrow which he was required to keep, and with this arrow, he related some incident in which he had proved his valor, either in conflict with some other warrior, or with the wild beasts of the woods. These deeds, each of them was required to remember and relate, and show the arrow which was given with the narrative on occasion of this great state solemnity. In this way, their traditions are preserved. When he reached the grave, he took his station before it, the executioners, with their arrows, being already placed in readiness. The whole tribe had assembled to witness the execution, the warriors and boys in the foreground, the squaws behind them. A solemn silence prevailed over the scene, and a few moments only remained to the victim; when the wife of Conattee darted forward from the crowd bearing in her hands a peeled wand, with which, with every appearance of anger, she struck Selonee over the shoulders, exclaiming as she did so:

"Come, thou dog, thou shalt not die—thou shalt lie in the doorway of Conattee, and bring venison for his wife. Shall there be no one to bring meat to my lodge? Thou shalt do this, Selonee—thou shalt not die."

A murmur arose from the crowd at these words.

"She hath claimed Selonee for her husband, in place of Conattee—well, she hath the right."

The enemies of Selonee could not object. The widow had, in fact, exercised a privilege which is recognized by the Indian laws almost universally; and the policy by which she was governed in the present instance, was sufficiently apparent to all the village. It was evident, now that Conattee was gone, that nobody could provide for the woman who had no sons, and no male relations, and who was too execrably ugly, and too notorious as a scold, to leave it possible that she could ever procure another husband so inexperienced or so flexible as the one she had lost. Smartly striking Selonee on his shoulders, she repeated her command that he should rise and follow her.

"Thou wilt take this dog to thy lodge, that he may hunt thee venison?" demanded the old chief, Emathla.

"Have I not said?" shouted the scold—"Hear you not? The dog is mine—I bid him follow me."

"Is there no friendly arrow to seek my heart?" murmured the young warrior, as, rising slowly from the grave into which he had previously descended, he prepared to obey the laws of his nation, in the commands of the woman who claimed him to replace the husband who was supposed to have died by his hands. Even the foes of Selonee looked on him with lessened hostility, and the pity of his friends was greater now than when he stood on the precipice of death. The young women of the tribe wept bitterly as they beheld so monstrous a sacrifice. Meanwhile, the exulting hag, as if conscious of her complete control over the victim, goaded him forward with repeated strokes of her wand. She knew that she was hated by all the young women, and she was delighted to show them a conquest which would have been a subject of pride to any among them. With this view she led the captive through their ranks. As they parted mournfully, on either hand, to suffer the two to pass, Selonee stopped short and motioned one of the young women who stood at the greatest distance behind the rest, looking on with eyes which, if they had no tears, yet gave forth an expression of desolateness more woeful than any tears could have done. With clasped hands, and trembling as she came, the gentle maiden drew nigh.

"Was it a dream," said Selonee sorrowfully, "that told me of the love of a singing bird, and a green cabin by the trickling waters? Did I hear a voice that said to me sweetly, wait but a little, till the green corn breaks the hill, and Medoree will come to thy cabin and lie by thy side? Tell me, is this thing true, Medoree?"

"Thou sayest, Selonee—the thing is true," was the reply of the maiden, uttered in broken accents that denoted a breaking heart.

"But they will make Selonee go to the lodge of another woman—they will put Macourah into the arms of Selonee."

"Alas! Alas!"

"Wilt thou see this thing, Medoree? Can'st thou look upon it, then turn away, and going back to thy own lodge, can'st thou sing a gay song of forgetfulness as thou goest?"

"Forgetfulness!—Ah, Selonee."

"Thou art the beloved of Selonee, Medoree—thou shalt not lose him. It would vex thy heart that another should take him to her lodge!"

The tears of the damsel flowed freely down her cheeks, and she sobbed bitterly, but said nothing.

"Take the knife from my belt, Medoree, and put its sharp tooth into my heart, ere thou sufferest this thing! Wilt thou not?"

The girl shrunk back with an expression of undisguised horror in her face.

"I will bless thee, Medoree," was the continued speech of the warrior. She turned from him, covering her face with her hands.

"I cannot do this thing, Selonee—I cannot strike thy heart with the knife. Go—let the woman have thee. Medoree cannot kill thee—she will herself die."

"It is well," cried the youth, in a voice of mournful self-abandonment, as he resumed his progress towards the lodge of Macourah.

VII

It is now time to return to Conattee, and trace his progress from the moment when, plunging into the waters, he left the side of Selonee in pursuit of the wolf, whose dying struggles in the stream he had beheld. We are already acquainted with his success in extricating the animal from the water, and possessing himself of its hide. He had not well done this when he heard a rushing noise in the woods above him, and fancying that there was a prospect of other game at hand, and inflated with the hope of adding to his trophies, though without any weapon but his knife, Conattee hastened to the spot. When he reached it, however, he beheld nothing. A gigantic and singularly deformed pine tree, crooked and most irregular in shape, lay prostrate along the ground, and formed such an intricate covering above it, that Conattee deemed it possible that some beast of prey might have made its den among the recesses of its roots. With this thought, he crawled under the spreading limbs, and searched all their intricacies. Emerging from the search, which had been fruitless, he took a seat upon the trunk of the tree, and spreading out the wolf's hide before him, proceeded to pare away the particles of flesh which, in the haste with which he had performed the task of flaying him, had been suffered to adhere to the skin. But he had scarcely commenced the operation, when two gigantic limbs of the fallen tree upon which he sat, curled over his thighs and bound him to the spot. Other limbs, to his great horror, while he strove to move, clasped his arms and covered his shoulders. He strove to cry aloud, but his jaws were grasped before he could well open them, by other branches; and, with his eyes, which were suffered to peer through little openings in the bark, he could see his legs encrusted by like coverings with his other members. Still seeing, his own person yet escaped his sight. Not a part of it now remained visible to himself. A bed of green velvet-like moss rested on his lap. His knees shot out a thorny excrescence; and his hands, flattened to his thighs, were enveloped in as complete a casing of bark as covered the remainder of the tree around him. Even his knife and wolf skin, to his great surprise, suffered in like manner, the bark having contracted them into one of those huge bulging knobs that so numerously deformed the tree. With all his thoughts and consciousness remaining, Conattee had yet lost every faculty of action. When he tried to scream aloud, his jaws felt the contraction of a pressure upon them, which resisted all their efforts, while an oppressive thorn growing upon a wild vine that hung before his face, was brought by every movement of himself or of the tree into his very mouth. The poor hunter immediately conceived his situation—he was in the power of Tustenuggee, the Grey Demon of Enoree. The tree upon which he sat was one of those magic trees which the tradition of his people entitled the "Arm-chair of Tustenuggee." In these traps for the unwary the wicked demon caught his victim, and exulted in his miseries. Here he sometimes remained until death released him; for it was not often that the power into whose clutches he had fallen, suffered his prey to escape through a sudden feeling of lenity and good humor. The only hope of Conattee was that Selonee might suspect his condition; in which event his rescue was simple and easy enough. It was only to hew off the limbs, or pare away the bark, and the victim was uncovered in his primitive integrity. But how improbable that this discovery should be made! He had no voice to declare his bondage. He had no capacity for movement by which he might reveal the truth to his comrade's eyes; and unless some divine instinct should counsel his friend to an experiment which he would scarcely think upon, of himself, the poor prisoner felt that he must die in the miserable bondage into which he had fallen. While these painful convictions were passing through his mind, he heard the distant shoutings of Selonee. In a little while he beheld the youth anxiously seeking him in every quarter, following his trail at length to the very tree in which he was bound, crawling like himself beneath its branches, but not sitting like himself to be caught upon its trunk. Vainly did the poor fellow strive to utter but a few words, however faintly, apprising the youth of his condition. The effort died away in the most imperfect breathing, sounding in his own ears like the faint sigh of some budding flower. With equal ill success did he aim to struggle with his limbs. He was too tightly grasped, in every part, to stir in the slightest degree a single member. He saw the fond search, meanwhile, which his comrade maintained, and his heart yearned the more in fondness for the youth. But it was with consummate horror that he saw him depart as night came on. Miserable, indeed, were his feelings that night. The voice of the Grey Demon alone kept him company, and he and his one-eyed wife made merry with his condition, goading him the livelong night with speeches of cruel gibe and mischievous reflection, such as the following:

"There is no hope for you, Conattee, till some one takes your place. Some one must sit in your lap, whom you are willing to leave behind you, before you can get out of mine," was the speech of the Grey Demon, who, perched upon Conattee's shoulders, bent his huge knotty head over him, while his red eyes looked into the half-hidden ones of the environed hunter, and glared upon him with the exultation of the tyrant at last secure of his prey. Night passed away at length, and, with the dawn, how was the hopeless heart of Conattee refreshed as he again saw Selonee appear! He then remembered the words of Tustenuggee, which told him that he could not escape until some one sat in his lap whom he was willing to leave behind him. The fancy rose in his mind that Selonee would do this; but could it be that he would consent to leave his friend behind him? Life was sweet, and great was the temptation. At one moment he almost wished that Selonee would draw nigh and seat himself after his fatigue. As if the young hunter knew his wish, he drew nigh at that instant; but the better feelings in Conattee's heart grew strong as he approached, and, striving to twist and writhe in his bondage, and laboring at the same time to call out in warning to his friend, he manifested the noble resolution not to avail himself of his friend's position to relieve his own; and, as if the warning of Conattee had really reached the understanding of Selonee, the youth retraced his steps, and once more hurried away from the place of danger. With his final departure the fond hopes of the prisoner sunk within him; and when hour after hour had gone by without the appearance of any of his people, and without any sort of change in his condition, he gave himself up utterly for lost. The mocks and jeers of the Grey Demon and his one-eyed squaw filled his ears all night, and the morning brought him nothing but flat despair. He resigned himself to his fate with the resolution of one who, however unwilling he might be to perish in such a manner, had yet faced death too frequently not to yield him a ready defiance now.

VIII

But hope had not utterly departed from the bosom of Selonee. Perhaps the destiny which had befallen him had made him resolve the more earnestly to seek farther into the mystery of that which hung above the fate of his friend. The day which saw him enter the cabin of Macourah saw him the most miserable man alive. The hateful hag, hateful enough as the wife of his friend, whose ill treatment was notorious, was now doubly hateful to him as his own wife; and now, when, alone together, she threw aside the harsh and termagant features which had before distinguished her deportment, and, assuming others of a more amorous complexion, threw her arms about the neck of the youth and solicited his endearments, a loathing sensation of disgust was coupled with the hate which had previously possessed his mind. Flinging away from her embrace, he rushed out of the lodge with feelings of the most unspeakable bitterness and grief, and bending his way towards the forest, soon lost sight of the encampment of his people. Selonee was resolved on making another effort for the recovery of his friend. His resolve went even farther than this. He was bent never to return to the doom which had been fastened upon him, and to pursue his way into more distant and unknown forests—a self-doomed exile—unless he could restore Conattee to the nation. Steeled against all those ties of love or of country, which at one time had prevailed in his bosom over all, he now surrendered himself to friendship or despair. In Catawba, unless he restored Conattee, he could have no hope; and without Catawba he had neither hope nor love. On either hand he saw nothing but misery; but the worst form of misery lay behind him in the lodge of Macourah. But Macourah was not the person to submit to such a determination. She was too well satisfied with the exchange with which fortune had provided her, to suffer its gift to be lost so easily; and when Selonee darted from the cabin in such fearful haste, she readily conjectured his determination. She hurried after him with all possible speed, little doubting that those thunders—could she overtake him—with which she had so frequently overawed the pliant Conattee, would possess an effect not less influential upon his more youthful successor. Macourah was gaunt as a greyhound, and scarcely less fleet of foot. Besides, she was as tough as a grey-squirrel in his thirteenth year. She did not despair of overtaking Selonee, provided she suffered him not to know that she was upon his trail. Her first movements therefore were marked with caution. Having watched his first direction, she divined his aim to return to the hunting grounds where he had lost or slain his companion; and these hunting grounds were almost as well known to herself as to him. With a rapidity of movement, and a tenacity of purpose, which could only be accounted for by a reference to that wild passion which Selonee had unconsciously inspired in her bosom for himself, she followed his departing footsteps; and when, the next day, he heard her shouts behind him, he was absolutely confounded. But it was with a feeling of surprise and not of dissatisfaction that he heard her voice. He—good youth—regarding Conattee as one of the very worthiest of the Catawba warriors, seemed to have been impressed with an idea that such also was the opinion of his wife. He little dreamed that she had any real design upon himself; and believed that, to show her the evidences which were to be seen, which led to the fate of her husband, might serve to convince her that not only he was not the murderer, but that Conattee might not, indeed, be murdered at all. He coolly waited her approach, therefore, and proceeded to renew his statements, accompanying his narrative with the expression of the hope which he entertained of again restoring her husband to herself and the nation. But she answered his speech only with upbraidings and entreaties; and when she failed, she proceeded to thump him lustily with the wand by which she had compelled him to follow her to the lodge the day before. But Selonee was in no humor to obey the laws of the nation now. The feeling of degradation which had followed in his mind, from the moment when he left the spot where he had stood up for death, having neither fear nor shame, was too fresh in his consciousness to suffer him to yield a like acknowledgment to it now; and though sorely tempted to pummel the Jezabel in return for the lusty thwacks which she had already inflicted upon his shoulders, he forbore, in consideration of his friend, and contented himself with simply setting forward on his progress, determined to elude her pursuit by an exercise of all his vigor and elasticity. Selonee was hardy as the grisly bear, and fleeter than the wild turkey; and Macourah, virago as she was, soon discovered the difference in the chase when Selonee put forth his strength and spirit. She followed with all her pertinacity, quickened as it was by an increase of fury at the presumption which had ventured to disobey her commands; but Selonee fled faster than she pursued, and every additional moment served to increase the space between them. The hunter lost her from his heels at length, and deemed himself fortunate that she was no longer in sight and hearing, when he again approached the spot where his friend had so mysteriously disappeared. Here he renewed his search with a painful care and minuteness, which the imprisoned Conattee all the while beheld. Once more Selonee crawled beneath those sprawling limbs and spreading arms that wrapped up in their solid and coarse rinds the person of the warrior. Once more he emerged from the spot disappointed and hopeless. This he had hardly done when, to the great horror of the captive, and the annoyance of Selonee, the shrill shrieks and screams of the too well-known voice of Macourah rang through the forests. Selonee dashed forward as he heard the sounds, and when Macourah reached the spot, which she did unerringly in following his trail, the youth was already out of sight.

"I can go no further," cried the woman—"a curse on him and a curse on Conattee, since in losing one I have lost both. I am too faint to follow. As for Selonee, may the one-eyed witch of Tustenuggee take him for her dog."

With this delicate imprecation, the virago seated herself in a state of exhaustion upon the inviting bed of moss which formed the lap of Conattee. This she had no sooner done, than the branches relaxed their hold upon the limbs of her husband. The moment was too precious for delay, and sliding from under her with an adroitness and strength which were beyond her powers of prevention, and, indeed, quite too sudden for any effort at resistance, she had the consternation to behold her husband starting up in full life before her, and, with the instinct of his former condition, preparing to take flight. She cried to him, but he fled the faster—she strove to follow him, but the branches which had relaxed their hold upon her husband had resumed their contracted grasp upon her limbs. The brown bark was already forming above her on every hand, and her tongue, allotted a brief term of liberty, was alone free to assail him. But she had spoken but few words when the bark encased her jaws, and the ugly thorn of the vine which had so distressed Conattee, had taken its place at their portals.

IX

The husband looked back but once, when the voice ceased—then, with a shivering sort of joy that his own doom had undergone a termination, which he now felt to be doubly fortunate—he made a wide circuit that he might avoid the fatal neighborhood, and pushed on in pursuit of his friend, whom his eyes, even when he was surrounded in the tree, had followed in his flight. It was no easy task, however, to overtake Selonee, flying, as he did, from the supposed pursuit of the termagant. Great however was the joy of the young warriors when they did encounter, and long and fervent was their mutual embrace. Conattee described his misfortunes, and related the manner in which he was taken; showed how the bark had encased his limbs, and how the intricate magic had even engrossed his knife and the wolf skin which had been the trophy of his victory. But Conattee said not a word of his wife and her entrapment, and Selonee was left in the conviction that his companion owed his escape from the toils to some hidden change in the tyrannical mood of Tustenuggee, or the one-eyed woman, his wife.

"But the skin and the knife, Conattee, let us not leave them," said Selonee, "let us go back and extricate them from the tree."

Conattee showed some reluctance. He soon said, in the words of Macbeth, which he did not use however as a quotation, "I'll go no more." But Selonee, who ascribed this reluctance to very natural apprehensions of the demon from whose clutches he had just made his escape, declared his readiness to undertake the adventure if Conattee would only point out to his eyes the particular excrescence in which the articles were enclosed. When the husband perceived that his friend was resolute, he made a merit of necessity.

"If the thing is to be done," said he, "why should you have the risk, I myself will do it. It would be a woman-fear were I to shrink from the danger. Let us go."

The process of reasoning by which Conattee came to this determination was a very sudden one, and one, too, that will not be hard to comprehend by every husband in his situation. It was his fear that if Selonee undertook the business, an unlucky or misdirected stroke of his knife might sever a limb, or remove some portions of the bark which did not merit or need removal. Conattee trembled at the very idea of the revelations which might follow such an unhappy result. Strengthening himself, therefore, with all his energies, he went forward with Selonee to the spot, and while the latter looked on and witnessed the operation, he proceeded with a nicety and care which amused and surprised Selonee, to the excision of the swollen scab upon the tree in which he had seen his wolf skin encompassed. While he performed the operation, which he did as cautiously as if it had been the extraction of a mote from the eye of a virgin, the beldam in the tree, conscious of all his movements, and at first flattered with the hope that he was working for her extrication, maintained the most ceaseless efforts of her tongue and limbs, but without avail. Her slight breathing, which Conattee knew where to look for, more like the sighs of an infant zephyr than the efforts of a human bosom, denoted to his ears an overpowering but fortunately suppressed volcano within; and his heart leaped with a new joy, which had been unknown to it for many years before, when he thought that he was now safe, and, he trusted, for ever, from any of the tortures which he had been fain to endure patiently so long. When he had finished the operation by which he had re-obtained his treasures, he ventured upon an impertinence which spoke surprisingly for his sudden acquisition of confidence; and looking up through the little aperture in the bark, from whence he had seen every thing while in the same situation, and from whence he concluded she was also suffered to see, he took a peep—a quick, quizzical and taunting peep, at those eyes which he had not so dared to offend before. He drew back suddenly from the contact—so suddenly, indeed, that Selonee, who saw the proceeding, but had no idea of the truth, thought he had been stung by some insect, and questioned him accordingly.

"Let us be off, Selonee," was the hurried answer, "we have nothing to wait for now."

"Yes," replied Selonee, "and I had forgotten to say to you that your wife, Macourah, is on her way in search of you. I left her but a little ways behind, and thought to find her here. I suppose she is tired, however, and is resting by the way."

"Let her rest," said Conattee, "which is an indulgence much greater than any she ever accorded me. She will find me out soon enough, without making it needful that I should go in search of her. Come."

Selonee kindly suppressed the history of the transactions which had taken place in the village during the time when the hunter was supposed to be dead; but Conattee heard the facts from other quarters, and loved Selonee the better for the sympathy he had shown, not only in coming again to seek for him, but in not loving his wife better than he did himself. They returned to the village, and every body was rejoiced to behold the return of the hunters. As for the termagant Macourah, nobody but Conattee knew her fate; and he, like a wise man, kept his secret until there was no danger of its being made use of to rescue her from her predicament. Years had passed, and Conattee had found among the young squaws one that pleased him much better than the old. He had several children by her, and years and honors had alike fallen numerously upon his head, when, one day, one of his own sons, while hunting in the same woods, knocked off one of the limbs of the Chair of Tustenuggee, and to his great horror discovered the human arm which they enveloped. This led him to search farther, and limb after limb became detached under the unscrupulous action of his hatchet, until the entire but unconnected members of the old squaw became visible. The lad knocked about the fragments with little scruple, never dreaming how near was his relation to the form which he treated with so little veneration. When he came home to the lodge and told his story, Selonee looked at Conattee, but said nothing. The whole truth was at once apparent to his mind. Conattee, though he still kept his secret, was seized with a sudden fit of piety, and taking his sons with him, he proceeded to the spot which he well remembered, and, gathering up the bleached remains, had them carefully buried in the trenches of the tribe.

It may properly end this story, to say that Selonee wedded the sweet girl who, though willing to die herself to prevent him from marrying Macourah, yet positively refused to take his life to defeat the same event. It may be well to state, in addition, that the only reason Conattee ever had for believing that Selonee had not kept his secret from every body, was that Medoree, the young wife of the latter, looked on him with a very decided coolness. "But, we will see," muttered Conattee as he felt this conviction. "Selonee will repent of this confidence, since now it will never be possible for him to persuade her to take a seat in the Arm-chair of Tustenuggee. Had he been a wise man he would have kept his secret, and then there would have been no difficulty in getting rid of a wicked wife."

Oakatibbe;
or, The Choctaw Sampson

I

It was in the year 182–, that I first travelled in the vallies of the great south-west. Circumstances, influenced in no slight degree by an "errant disposition," beguiled me to the Choctaw nation, which, at that time, occupied the greater part of the space below the Tennessee line, lying between the rivers Tombeckbe and Mississippi, as low, nearly, as the town of Jackson, then, as now, the capital of the State of Mississippi. I loitered for several weeks in and about this region, without feeling the loss or the weight of time. Yet, the reader is not to suppose that travelling at that day was so simple a matter, or possessed many, if any, of the pleasant facilities of the present. *Au contraire*: It was then a serious business. It meant *travail* rather than *travel*. The roads were few and very hard to find. Indian foot-paths—with the single exception of the great military traces laid out by General Jackson, and extending from Tennessee to Lake Ponchartrain—formed almost the only arteries known to the "Nation;" and the portions of settled country in the neighborhood, nominally civilized only, were nearly in the same condition. Some of the Indian paths, as I experienced, seemed only to be made for the perplexity of the stranger. Like Gray's passages which "led to nothing," they constantly brought me to a stand. Sometimes they were swallowed up in swamps, and, in such cases, your future route upon the earth was to be discovered only by a deliberate and careful survey of the skies above. The openings in the trees over head alone instructed you in the course you were to pursue. You may readily imagine that this sort of progress was as little pleasant as edifying, yet, in some respects, it was not wanting in its attractions, also. To the young and ardent mind, obstacles of this nature tend rather to excite than to depress. They contain the picturesque in themselves, at times, and always bring out the moral in the man. "To learn to rough it," is an educational phrase, in the dialect of the new countries, which would be of great service, adopted as a rule of government for the young in all. To "coon a log"—a mysterious process to the uninitiated—swim a river—experiment, at a guess, upon the properties of one, and the proprieties of another route—parley with an Indian after his own fashion—not to speak of a hundred other incidents which the civilized world does not often present—will reconcile a lad of sanguine temperament to a number of annoyances much more serious than will attend him on an expedition through our frontier countries.

It was at the close of a cloudy day in November, that I came within hail of the new but rude plantation settlements of Colonel Harris. He had but lately transferred his interests to Mississippi, from one of the "maternal thirteen"—had bought largely in the immediate neighborhood of the Choctaw nation, and had also acquired, by purchase from the natives, certain reserves within it, to which he chiefly owes that large wealth, which, at this day, he has the reputation of possessing. In place of the stately residence which now adorns his homestead, there was then but a miserable log-house, one of the most ordinary of the country, in which, unaccompanied by his family, he held his temporary abiding place. His plantation was barely rescued from the dominions of nature. The trees were girdled only the previous winter, for his first crop, which was then upon the ground, and an excellent crop it was for that immature condition of his fields. There is no describing the melancholy aspect of such a settlement, seen in winter, on a cloudy day, and in the heart of an immense forest, through which you have travelled for miles, without glimpse of human form or habitation. The worm-fence is itself a gloomy spectacle, and the girdled trees, erect but dead, the perishing skeletons of recent life, impress you with sensations not entirely unlike those which you would experience in going over some battle-field, from which the decaying forms of man and horse have not yet been removed. The fences of Col. Harris were low in height, though of great extent. They were simply sufficient to protect the fields from the random assaults of cattle. Of his out-houses, the most respectable in size, solidity and security, was the corn crib. His negro-houses, like the log-house in which he himself dwelt, were only so many temporary shanties, covered with poles and thatched with bark and pine-straw. In short, every thing that met my eye only tended the more to frown upon my anticipations of a cheerful fireside and a pleasant arrangement of the creature-comforts. But my doubts and apprehensions all vanished at the moment of my reception. I was met by the proprietor with that ease and warmth of manner which does not seem to be conscious of any deficiencies of preparation, and is resolved that there shall be none which sincere hospitality can remedy. I was soon prepared to forget that there were deficiencies. I felt myself very soon at home. I had letters to Col. Harris, which made me particularly welcome, and in ten minutes we were both in full sail amongst all the shallows and deeps of ordinary conversation.

Not that we confined ourselves to these. Our discourse, after a little while, turned upon a circumstance which I had witnessed on riding through his fields and while approaching his dwelling, which struck me with considerable surprise, and disturbed, in some degree, certain pre-conceived opinions in my mind. I had seen, interspersed with his negro laborers, a goodly number of Indians of both sexes, but chiefly young persons, all equally and busily employed in cotton picking. The season had been a protracted one, and favorable, accordingly, to the maturing of great numbers of the bolls which an early and severe winter must have otherwise destroyed. The crop, in consequence, had been so great as to be beyond the ability, to gather in and harvest, of the "force" by which it was made. This, in the new and fertile vallies of the south-west, is an usual event. In ordinary cases, when this happens, it is the custom to buy other negroes from less productive regions, to consummate and secure the avails of labor of the original "force." The whole of these, united, are then addressed to the task of opening additional lands, which, should they yield as before, necessarily demand a second purchase of an extra number to secure and harvest, in season, the surplus fruits of their industry. The planter is very readily persuaded to make this purchase so long as the seeming necessity shall re-occur; and in this manner has he continued expanding his interests, increasing the volume of his lands, and incurring debt for these and for his slaves, at exorbitant prices, in order to the production of a commodity, every additional bag of which, disparages its own value, and depreciates the productive power, in an estimate of profit, of the industry by which it is produced. It will not be difficult, keeping this fact in mind as a sample of the profligacy of western adventure—to account, in part, for the insolvency and desperate condition of a people in possession of a country naturally the most fertile of any in the world.

The crop of Col. Harris was one of this description. It far exceeded the ability of his "force" to pick it in; but instead of buying additional slaves for the purpose, he conceived the idea of turning to account the lazy Choctaws by whom he was surrounded. He proposed to hire them at a moderate compensation, which was to be paid them weekly. The temptation of gain was greedily caught at by these hungering outcasts, and, for a few dollars, or an equivalent in goods, groceries, and so forth, some forty-five of them were soon to be seen, as busy as might be, in the prosecution of their unusual labors. The work was light and easy—none could be more so—and though not such adepts as the negro, the Indian women soon contrived to fill their bags and baskets, in the course of the day. At dark, you might behold them trudging forward under their burdens to the log-house, where the proprietor stood ready to receive them. Here he weighed their burdens, and gave them credit, nightly, for the number of pounds which they each brought in. The night of my arrival was Saturday, and the value of the whole week's labor was then to be summed up and accounted for. This necessarily made them all punctual in attendance, and nothing could be more amusing than the interest which they severally displayed as Col. Harris took out his memorandum book, and proceeded to make his entries. Every eye was fixed upon him, and an old Indian, who, though he did not work himself, represented the interests of a wife and two able-bodied daughters, planted himself directly behind this gentleman, and watched, with looks of growing sagacity, every stroke that was made in this—to him—volume of more than Egyptian mystery and hieroglyphics. Meanwhile, the squaws stood about their baskets with looks expressive of similar interest, but at the same time of laudable patience. The negroes in the rear, were scarcely less moved by curiosity, though a contemptuous grin might be seen on nearly all their countenances, as they felt their superiority in nearly every physical and intellectual respect, over the untutored savages. Many Indians were present who neither had nor sought employment. Of those employed, few or none were of middle age. But these were not wanting to the assemblage. They might be seen prowling about the rest—watchful of the concerns of their wives, sons and daughters, with just that sort and degree of interest, which the eagle may be supposed to feel, who, from his perch on the tree-top or the rock, beholds the fish-hawk dart into the water in pursuit of that prey which he meditates to rend from his jaws as soon as he shall re-ascend into the air. Their interest was decidedly greater than that of the poor laborer. It was in this manner that these vultures appropriated the fruits of his industry, and there was no remedy. They commonly interfered, the moment it was declared what was due to the *employée*, to resolve the pay into a certain number of gallons of whiskey; so many pounds of tobacco; so much gunpowder and lead. If the employer, as was the case with Col. Harris, refused to furnish them with whiskey, they required him to pay in money. With this, they soon made their way to one of those moral sinks, called a grog-shop, which English civilization is always ready to plant, as its first, most familiar, and most imposing standard, among the hills and forests of the savage.

It may be supposed that this experiment upon the inflexibility of Indian character and habit—for it was an experiment which had been in trial only a single week—was a subject of no little curiosity to me, as it would most probably be to almost every person at all impressed with the humiliating moral and social deterioration which has marked this fast decaying people. Could it possibly be successful? Could a race, proud, sullen, incommunicative, wandering, be persuaded, even by gradual steps, and with the hope of certain compensation, to renounce the wild satisfaction afforded by their desultory and unconstrained modes of life? Could they be beguiled for a season into employments which, though they did not demand any severe labors, at least required pains-taking, regular industry, and that habitual attention to daily recurring tasks, which, to their roving nature, would make life a most monotonous and unattractive possession? How far the lightness of the labor and the simplicity of the employment, with the corresponding recompense, would reconcile them to its tasks, was the natural subject of my inquiry. On this head, my friend, Col. Harris, could only conjecture and speculate like myself. His experiment had been in progress but a few days. But our speculations led us to very different conclusions. He was a person of very ardent character, and sanguine, to the last degree, of the success of his project. He had no question but that the Indian, even at his present stage, might be brought under the influence of a judicious civilization. We both agreed that the first process was in procuring their labor—that this was the preliminary step, without taking which, no other could be made; but how to bring them to this was the question.

"They can be persuaded to this," was his conclusion. "Money, the popular god, is as potent with them as with our own people. They will do any thing for money. You see these now in the field. They have been there, and just as busy, and in the same number, from Monday last."

"How long will they continue?"

"As long as I can employ and pay them."

"Impossible! They will soon be dissatisfied. The men will consume and squander all the earnings of the females and the feeble. The very motive of their industry, money, to which you refer, will be lost to them after the first payment. I am convinced that a savage people, not as yet familiar with the elements of moral prudence, can only be brought to habitual labor, by the one process of coercion."

"We shall see. There is no coercion upon them now, yet they work with wonderful regularity."

"This week will end it. Savages are children in all but physical respects. To do any thing with them, you must place them in that position of responsibility, and teach them that law, without the due employment of which, any attempt to educate a child, must be an absurdity—you must teach them obedience. They must be made to know, at the outset, that they know nothing—that they must implicitly defer to the superior. This lesson they will never learn, so long as they possess the power, at any moment, to withdraw from his control."

"Yet, even were this to be allowed, there must be a limit. There must come a time when you will be required to emancipate them. In what circumstances will you find that time? You cannot keep them under this coercion always; when will you set them free?"

"When they are fit for freedom."

"How is that to be determined? Who shall decide their fitness?"

"Themselves; as in the case of the children of Israel. The children of Israel went out from bondage as soon as their own intellectual advancement had been such as to enable them to produce from their own ranks a leader like Moses:—one whose genius was equal to that of the people by whom they had been educated, and sufficient for their own proper government thereafter."

"But has not an experiment of this sort already been tried in our country?"

"Nay, I think not—I know of none."

"Yes: an Indian boy was taken in infancy from his parents, carried to one of the Northern States, trained in all the learning and habits of a Northern college and society, associated only with whites, beheld no manners, and heard no morals, but those which are known to

Christian communities. His progress was satisfactory—he learned rapidly—was considered something of a prodigy, and graduated with eclât. He was then left, with the same option as the rest enjoyed, to the choice of a profession. And what was his choice? Do you not remember the beautiful little poem of Freneau on this subject? He chose the buck-skin leggins, the moccasins, bow and arrows, and the wide, wild forests, where his people dwelt."

"Freneau's poem tells the story somewhat differently. The facts upon which it is founded, however, are, I believe, very much as you tell them. But what an experiment it was! How very silly! They take a copper-colored boy from his people, and carry him, while yet an infant, to a remote region. Suppose, in order that the experiment may be fairly tried, that they withhold from him all knowledge of his origin. He is brought up precisely as the other lads around him. But what is the first discovery which he makes? That he is a copper-colored boy—that he is, alone, the only copper-colored boy—that wherever he turns he sees no likeness to himself. This begets his wonder, then his curiosity, and finally his suspicion. He soon understands—for his suspicion sharpens every faculty of observation—that he is an object of experiment. Nay, the most cautious policy in the world could never entirely keep this from a keen-thoughted urchin. His fellow pupils teach him this. He sees that, to them, he is an object of curiosity and study. They regard him, and he soon regards himself, as a creature set apart, and separated, for some peculiar purposes, from all the rest. A stern and singular sense of individuality and isolation is thus forced upon him. He asks—Am I, indeed, alone?—Who am I?—What am I?—These inquiries naturally occasion others. Does he read? Books give him the history of his race. Nay, his own story probably meets his eye in the newspapers. He learns that he is descended from a nation dwelling among the secret sources of the Susquehannah. He pries in all corners for information. The more secret his search, the more keenly does he pursue it. It becomes the great passion of his mind. He learns that his people are fierce warriors and famous hunters. He hears of their strifes with the white man—their successful strifes, when the nation could send forth its thousand bow-men, and the whites were few and feeble. Perhaps, the young pale faces around him, speak of his people, even now, as enemies; at least, as objects of suspicion, and perhaps antipathy. All these things tend to elevate and idealize, in his mind, the history of his people. He cherishes a sympathy, even beyond the natural desires of the heart, for the perishing race from which he feels himself, "like a limb, cast bleeding and torn." The curiosity to see his ancestry—the people of his tribe and country—would be the most natural feeling of the white boy, under similar circumstances—shall we wonder that it is the predominant passion in the bosom of the Indian, whose very complexion forces him away from any connection with the rest! My idea of the experiment—if such a proceeding may be called an experiment—is soon spoken. As a statement of facts, I see nothing to provoke wonder. The result was the most natural thing in the world, and a man of ordinary powers of reflection might easily have predicted it, precisely as it happened. The only wonder is, that there should be found, among persons of common education and sagacity, men who should have undertaken such an experiment, and fancied that they were busy in a moral and philosophical problem."

"Why, how would you have the experiment tried?"

"As it was tried upon the Hebrews, upon the Saxons—upon every savage people who ever became civilized. It cannot be tried upon an individual: it must be tried upon a nation—at least upon a community, sustained by no succor from without—having no forests or foreign shores upon which to turn their eyes for sympathy—having no mode or hope of escape—under the full control of an already civilized people—and sufficiently numerous among themselves, to find sympathy, against those necessary rigors which at first will seem oppressive, but which will be the only hopeful process by which to enforce the work of improvement. They must find this sympathy from beholding others, like themselves in aspect, form, feature, and condition, subject to the same unusual restraints. In this contemplation they will be content to pursue their labors under a restraint which they cannot displace. But the natural law must be satisfied. There must be opportunities yielded for the indulgence of the legitimate passions. The young of both sexes among the subjected people, must commune and form ties in obedience to the requisitions of nature and according to their national customs. What, if the Indian student, on whom the "experiment" was tried, had paid his addresses to a white maiden! What a revulsion of the moral and social sense would have followed his proposition in the mind of the Saxon damsel;—and, were she to consent, what a commotion in the community in which she lived! And this revulsion and commotion would have been perfectly natural, and, accordingly, perfectly proper. God has made an obvious distinction between certain races of men, setting them apart, and requiring them to be kept so, by subjecting them to the resistance and rebuke of one of the most jealous sentinels of sense which we possess—the eye. The prejudices of this sense, require that the natural barriers should be maintained, and hence it becomes necessary that the race in subjection, should be sufficiently numerous to enable it to carry out the great object of every distinct community, though, perchance, it may happen to be an inferior one. In process of time, the beneficial and blessing effects of labor would be felt and understood by the most ignorant and savage of the race. Perhaps, not in one generation, or in two, but after the fifth and seventh, as it is written, "of those who keep my commandments." They would soon discover that, though compelled to toil, their toils neither enfeebled their strength nor impaired their happiness—that, on the contrary, they still resulted in their increasing strength, health, and comfort;—that their food, which before was precarious, depending on the caprices of the seasons, or the uncertainties of the chase, was now equally plentiful, wholesome and certain. They would also perceive that, instead of the sterility which is usually the destiny of all wandering tribes, and one of the processes by which they perish—the fecundity of their people was wonderfully increased. These discoveries—if time be allowed to make them—would tacitly reconcile them to that inferior position of their race, which is proper and inevitable, so long as their intellectual inferiority shall continue. And what would have been the effect upon our Indians—decidedly the noblest race of aborigines that the world has ever known—if, instead of buying their scalps at prices varying from five to fifty pounds each, we had conquered and subjected them? Will any one pretend to say that they would not have increased with the restraints and enforced toils of our superior genius?—that they would not, by this time, have formed a highly valuable and noble integral in the formation of our national strength and character? Perhaps their civilization would have been comparatively easy—the Hebrews required four hundred years—the Britons and Saxons, possibly, half that time after the Norman Conquest. Differing in color from their conquerors, though, I suspect, with a natural genius superior to that of the ancient Britons, at the time of the Roman invasion under Julius Cæsar, the struggle between the two races must have continued for some longer time, but the union would have been finally effected, and then, as in the case of the Englishman, we should have possessed a race, in their progeny, which, in moral and physical structure, might have challenged competition with the world."

"Ay, but the difficulty would have been in the conquest."

"True, that would have been the difficulty. The American colonists were few in number and feeble in resource. The nations from which they emerged put forth none of their strength in sending them forth. Never were colonies so inadequately provided—so completely left to themselves; and hence the peculiar injustice and insolence of the subsequent exactions of the British, by which they required their colonies to support their schemes of aggrandizement and expenditure by submitting to extreme taxation. Do you suppose, if the early colonists had been powerful, that they would have ever deigned to treat for lands with the roving hordes of savages whom they found on the continent? Never! Their purchases and treaties were not for lands, but tolerance. They bought permission to remain without molestation. The amount professedly given for land, was simply a tribute paid to the superior strength of the Indian, precisely as we paid it to Algiers and the Musselmen, until we grew strong enough to whip them into respect. If, instead of a few ships and a few hundred men, timidly making their approaches along the shores of Manhattan, Penobscot and Ocracocke, some famous leader, like Æneas, had brought his entire people—suppose them to be the persecuted Irish—what a wondrous difference would have taken place! The Indians would have been subjected—would have sunk into their proper position of humility and dependence; and, by this time, might have united with their conquerors, producing, perhaps, along the great ridge of the Alleghany, the very noblest specimens of humanity, in mental and bodily stature, that the world has ever witnessed. The Indians were taught to be insolent by the fears and feebleness of the whites. They were flattered by fine words, by rich presents, and abundance of deference, until the ignorant savage, but a single degree above the brute—who, until then, had never been sure of his porridge for more than a day ahead—took airs upon himself, and became one of the most conceited and arrogant lords in creation. The colonists grew wiser as they grew stronger; but the evil was already done, and we are reaping some of the bitter fruits, at this day, of seed unwisely sown in that. It may be that we shall yet see the experiment tried fairly."

"Ah, indeed—where?"

"In Mexico—by the Texians. Let the vain, capricious, ignorant, and dastardly wretches who now occupy and spoil the face and fortunes of the former country, persevere in pressing war upon those sturdy adventurers, and their doom is written. I *fear* it may be the sword—I *hope* it may be the milder fate of bondage and subjection.

Such a fate would save, and raise them finally to a far higher condition than they have ever before enjoyed. Thirty thousand Texians, each with his horse and rifle, would soon make themselves masters of the city of Montezuma, and then may you see the experiment tried upon a scale sufficiently extensive to make it a fair one. But your Indian student, drawn from

"Susquehannah's farthest springs,"

and sent to Cambridge, would present you with some such moral picture as that of the prisoner described by Sterne. His chief employment, day by day, would consist in notching upon his stick, the undeviating record of his daily suffering. It would be to him an experiment almost as full of torture, as that of the Scottish Boot, the Spanish Thumb-screw—or any of those happy devices of ancient days, for impressing pleasant principles upon the mind, by impressing unpleasant feelings upon the thews, joints and sinews. I wish that some one of our writers, familiar with mental analysis, would make this poem of Freneau, the subject of a story. I think it would yield admirable material. To develop the thoughts and feelings of an Indian boy, taken from his people, ere yet he has formed such a knowledge of them, or of others, as to have begun to discuss or to compare their differences—follow him to a college such as that of Princeton or Cambridge—watch him within its walls—amid the crowd, but not of it—looking only within himself, while all others are looking into him, or trying to do so—surrounded by active, sharp-witted lads of the Anglo-Norman race; undergoing an hourly repeated series of moral spasms, as he hears them wantonly or thoughtlessly dwell upon the wild and ignorant people from whom he is chosen;—listening, though without seeming to listen, to their crude speculations upon the great problem which is to be solved only by seeing how well he can endure his spasms, and what use he will make of his philosophy if he survives it—then, when the toils of study and the tedious restraints and troubles of prayer and recitation are got over, to behold and describe the joy with which the happy wretch flings by his fetters, when he is dismissed from those walls which have witnessed his tortures—even supposing him to remain (which is very unlikely), until his course of study is pronounced to be complete! With what curious pleasure will he stop in the shadow of the first deep forest, to tear from his limbs those garments which make him seem unlike his people! How quick will be the beating at his heart as he endeavors to dispose about his shoulders the blanket robe in the manner in which it is worn by the chief warrior of his tribe! With what keen effort—should he have had any previous knowledge of his kindred—will he seek to compel his memory to restore every, the slightest, custom or peculiarity which distinguished them when his eyes were first withdrawn from the parental tribe; and how closely will he imitate their indomitable pride and lofty, cold superiority of look and gesture, as, at evening, he enters the native hamlet, and takes his seat in silence at the door of the Council House, waiting, without a word, for the summons of the Elders!"

"Quite a picture. I think with you, that, in good hands, such a subject would prove a very noble one."

"But the story would not finish here. Supposing all this to have taken place, just as we are told it did—supposing the boy to have graduated at college, and to have flung away the distinction—to have returned, as has been described, to his savage costume—to the homes and habits of his people;—it is not so clear that he will fling away all the lessons of wisdom, all the knowledge of facts, which he will have acquired from the tuition of the superior race. A natural instinct, which is above all lessons, must be complied with; but this done—and when the first tumults of his blood have subsided, which led him to defeat the more immediate object of his social training—there will be a gradual resumption of the educational influence in his mind, and his intellectual habits will begin to exercise themselves anew. They will be provoked necessarily to this exercise by what he beholds around him. He will begin to perceive, in its true aspects, the wretchedness of that hunter-state, which, surveyed at a distance, appeared only the embodiment of stoical heroism and the most elevated pride. He will see and lament the squalid poverty of his people; which, his first lessons in civilization must have shown him, is due only to the mode of life and pursuits in which they are engaged. Their beastly intoxication will offend his tastes—their superstition and ignorance—the circumscribed limits of their capacity for judging of things and relations beyond the life of the bird or beast of prey—will awaken in him a sense of shame when he feels that they are his kindred. The insecurity of their liberties will awaken his fears, for he will instantly see that the great body of the people in every aboriginal nation are the veriest slaves in the world; and the degrading exhibitions which they make in their filth and drunkenness, which reduce the man to a loathsomeness of aspect which is never reached by the vilest beast which he hunts or scourges, will be beheld by the Indian student in very lively contrast with all that has met his eyes during that novitiate among the white sages, the processes of which have been to him so humiliating and painful. His memory reverts to that period with feelings of reconciliation. The torture is over, and the remembrance of former pain, endured with manly fortitude, is comparatively a pleasure. A necessary reaction in his mind takes place; and, agreeably to the laws of nature, what will, and what should follow, but that he will seek to become the tutor and the reformer of his people? They themselves will tacitly raise him to this position, for the man of the forest will defer even to the negro who has been educated by the white man. He will try to teach them habits of greater method and industry—he will overthrow the altars of their false gods—he will seek to bind the wandering tribes together under one head and in one nation—he will prescribe uniform laws of government. He will succeed in some things—he will fail in others; he will offend the pride of the self-conceited and the mulish—the priesthood will be the first to declare against him—and he will be murdered most probably, as was Romulus, and afterwards deified. If he escapes this fate, he will yet, most likely, perish from mortification under failure, or, in consequence of those mental strifes which spring from that divided allegiance between the feelings belonging to his savage and those which have had their origin in his Christian schools—those natural strifes between the acquisitions of civilization on the one hand, and those instinct tendencies of the blood which distinguish his connection with the inferior race. In this conflict, he will, at length, when the enthusiasm of his youthful zeal has become chilled by frequent and unexpected defeat, falter, and finally fail. But will there be nothing done for his people? Who can say? I believe that no seed falls without profit by the wayside. Even if the truth produces no immediate fruits, it forms a moral manure which fertilizes the otherwise barren heart, in preparation for the more favorable season. The Indian student may fail, as his teachers did, in realizing the object for which he has striven; and this sort of failure, is, by the way, one of the most ordinary of human allotment. The desires of man's heart, by an especial Providence that always wills him to act for the future, generally aim at something far beyond his own powers of performance. But the labor has not been taken in vain, in the progress of successive ages, which has achieved even a small part of its legitimate purposes. The Indian student has done for his people much more than the white man achieves ordinarily for his generation, if he has only secured to their use a single truth which they knew not before—if he has overthrown only one of their false gods—if he has smitten off the snaky head of only one of their superstitious prejudices. If he has added to their fields of corn a field of millet, he has induced one farther physical step towards moral improvement. Nay, if there be no other result, the very deference which they will have paid him, as the *elèvé* of the white man, will be a something gained of no little importance, towards inducing their more ready, though still tardy, adoption of the laws and guidance of the superior race."

II

I am afraid that my reader will suffer quite as much under this long discussion, as did my excellent companion, Col. Harris. But he is not to suppose that all the views here expressed, were uttered consecutively, as they are above set down. I have simply condensed, for more easy comprehension, the amount of a conversation which lasted some two hours. I may add, that, at the close, we discovered, as is very often the case among disputants, there was very little substantial difference between us. Our dispute, if any, was rather verbal than philosophical. On the subject of his experiment, however, Col. Harris fancied, that, in employing some forty or fifty of the Indians, of both sexes, he had brought together a community sufficiently large for the purposes of a fair experiment. Still, I thought that the argument remained untouched. They were not subordinate; they were not subdued; they could still exercise a free and absolute will, in despite of authority and reason. He could resort to no method for compelling their obedience; and we know pretty well what will result—even among white men—from the option of vagrancy.

"But," I urged, "even if the objections which I have stated, fail of defeating your scheme, there is yet another agent of defeat working against it, in the presence of these elderly Indians, who do not join in the labor, and yet, according to your own showing, still prowl in waiting to snatch from the hands of the industrious all the fruits of their toil. The natural effect of this will be to discourage the industry of those who work; for, unless the laborer is permitted to enjoy a fair proportion of the fruits of his labor, it is morally impossible that he should long continue it."

Our conference was interrupted by the appearance of the laborers, Indians and Negroes, who now began to come in, bringing with them the cotton which they had severally gathered during the day. This was accumulated in the court-yard, before the dwelling; each Indian, man or woman, standing beside the bag or basket which contained the proofs of his industry. You may readily suppose, that, after the dialogue and discussion which is partially reported above, I felt no little interest in observing the proceedings. The parties present were quite numerous. I put the negroes out of the question, though they were still to be seen, lingering in the background, grinning spectators of the scene. The number of Indians, men and women, who had *that day* been engaged in picking, was thirty-nine. Of these, twenty-six were females; three, only, might be accounted men, and ten were boys—none over sixteen. Of the females the number of elderly and young women was nearly equal. Of the men, one was very old and infirm; a second of middle age, who appeared to be something of an idiot; while the third, whom I regarded for this reason with more consideration and interest than all the party beside, was one of the most noble specimens of physical manhood that my eyes had ever beheld. He was fully six feet three inches in height, slender but muscular in the extreme. He possessed a clear, upright, open, generous cast of countenance, as utterly unlike that sullen, suspicious expression of the ordinary Indian face, as you can possibly imagine. Good nature and good sense were the predominant characteristics of his features, and—which is quite as unusual with Indians when in the presence of strangers—he laughed and jested with all the merry, unrestrainable vivacity of a youth of Anglo-Saxon breed. How was it that so noble a specimen of manhood consented to herd with the women and the weak of his tribe, in descending to the mean labors which the warriors were accustomed to despise?

"He must either be a fellow of great sense, or he must be a coward. He is degraded."

Such was my conclusion. The answer of Col. Harris was immediate.

"He is a fellow of good sense, and very far from being a coward. He is one of the best Choctaws that I know."

"A man, then, to be a leader of his people. It is a singular proof of good sense and great mental flexibility, to find an Indian, who is courageous, voluntarily assuming tasks which are held to be degrading among the hunters. I should like to talk with this fellow when you are done. What is his name?"

"His proper name is Oakatibbé; but that by which he is generally known among us—his English name—is Slim Sampson, a name which he gets on the score of his superior strength and great slenderness. The latter name, in ordinary use, has completely superseded the former, even among his own people. It may be remarked, by the way, as another proof of the tacit deference of the inferior to the superior people, that most Indians prefer to use the names given by the whites to those of their own language. There are very few among them who will not contrive, after a short intimacy with white men, to get some epithet—which is not always a complimentary one—but which they cling to as tenaciously as they would to some far more valuable possession."

This little dialogue was whispered during the stir which followed the first arrival of the laborers. We had no opportunity for more.

The rest of the Indians were in no respect remarkable. There were some eight or ten women, and perhaps as many men, who did not engage in the toils of their companions, though they did not seem the less interested in the result. These, I noted, were all in greater or less degree, elderly persons. One was full eighty years old, and a strange fact for one so venerable, was the most confirmed drunkard of the tribe. When the cotton pickers advanced with their baskets, the hangers-on drew nigh also, deeply engrossed with the prospect of reaping the gains from that industry which they had no mood to emulate. These, however, were very moderate, in most cases. Where a negro woman picked from one to two hundred weight of cotton, *per diem*, the Indian woman, at the utmost, gathered sixty-five; and the general average among them, did not much exceed forty-five. Slim Sampson's basket weighed eighty-six pounds—an amount considerably greater than any of the rest—and Col. Harris assured me, that his average during the week had been, at no time, much below this quantity.

The proceedings had gone on without interruption or annoyance for the space of half an hour. Col. Harris had himself weighed every basket, with scrupulous nicety, and recorded the several weights opposite to the name of the picker, in a little memorandum book which he kept exclusively for this purpose; and it was amusing to see with what pleasurable curiosity, the Indians, men and women, watched the record which stated their several accounts. The whole labor of the week was to be settled for that night (Saturday), and hence the unusual gathering of those whose only purpose in being present, was to grasp at the spoils.

Among these hawks was one middle-aged Indian—a stern, sulky fellow, of considerable size and strength—whose skin was even then full of liquor, which contributing to the usual insolence of his character, made him at times very troublesome. He had more than once, during the proceedings, interfered between Col. Harris and his *employées*, in such a manner as to provoke, in the mind of that gentleman, no small degree of irritation. The English name of this Indian, was Loblolly Jack. Loblolly Jack had a treble motive for being present and conspicuous. He had among the laborers, a wife and two daughters. When the baskets of these were brought forward to be weighed, he could no longer be kept in the background, but, resolutely thrusting himself before the rest, he handled basket, book and steelyards in turn, uttered his suspicions of foul play, and insisted upon a close examination of every movement which was made by the proprietor. In this manner, he made it very difficult for him to proceed in his duties; and his conduct, to do the Indians justice, seemed quite as annoying to them as to Col. Harris. The wife frequently expostulated with him, in rather bolder language than an Indian squaw is apt to use to her liege lord; while Slim Sampson, after a few words of reproach, expressed in Choctaw, concluded by telling him in plain English, that he was "a rascal dog." He seemed the only one among them who had no fear of the intruder. Loblolly Jack answered in similar terms, and Slim Sampson, clearing the baskets at a single bound, confronted him with a show of fight, and a direct challenge to it, on the spot where they stood. The other seemed no ways loath. He recoiled a pace, drew his knife—a sufficient signal for Slim Sampson to get his own in readiness—and, thus opposed, they stood, glaring upon each other with eyes of the most determined expression of malignity. A moment more—an additional word of provocation from either—and blows must have taken place. But Col. Harris, a man of great firmness, put himself between them, and calling to one of his negroes, bade him bring out from the house his double-barreled gun.

"Now," said he, "my good fellows, the first man of you that lifts his hand to strike, I'll shoot him down; so look to it. Slim Sampson, go back to your basket, and don't meddle in this business. Don't you suppose that I'm man enough to keep Loblolly Jack in order? You shall see."

It is not difficult for a determined white man to keep an Indian in subordination, so long as both of them are sober. A few words more convinced Loblolly Jack, who had not yet reached the reckless stage in drunkenness, that his wiser course was to give back and keep quiet, which he did. The storm subsided almost as suddenly as it had been raised, and Col. Harris resumed his occupation. Still, the Indian who had proved so troublesome before, continued his annoyances, though in a manner somewhat less audacious. His last proceeding was to get as nigh as he could to the basket which was about to be weighed—his wife's basket—and, with the end of a stick, adroitly introduced into some little hole, he contrived to press the basket downwards, and thus to add so much to the weight of the cotton, that his squaw promised to bear off the palm of victory in that day's picking. Nobody saw the use to which the stick was put, and for a few moments no one suspected it. Had the cunning fellow been more moderate, he might have succeeded in his attempt upon the steelyards; but his pressure increased with every approach which was made to a determination of the weight, and while all were wondering that so small a basket should be so heavy, Slim Sampson discovered and pointed out the trick to Col. Harris, who suddenly snatching the stick from the grasp of the Indian, was about to lay it over his head. But this my expostulation prevented; and, after some delay, the proceedings were finally ended; but in such a manner as to make my friend somewhat more doubtful than he had been before, on the subject of his experiment. He paid off their accounts, some in cloths and calicoes, of which he had provided a small supply for this purpose; but the greater number, under the evil influence of the idle and the elder, demanded and received their pay in money.

III

It was probably about ten o'clock that evening. We had finished supper, and Col. H. and myself had resumed the subject upon which we had been previously engaged. But the discussion was languid, and both of us were unquestionably lapsing into that state, when each readily receives an apology for retiring for the night, when we were startled from our drowsy tendencies by a wild and terrible cry, such as made me thrill instinctively with the conviction that something terrible had taken place. We started instantly to our feet, and threw open the door. The cry was more distinct and piercing, and its painful character could not be mistaken. It was a cry of death—of sudden terror, and great and angry excitement. Many voices were mingled together—some expressive of fury, some of fear, and many of lamentation. The tones which finally prevailed over, and continued long after all others had subsided, were those of women.

"These sounds come from the shop of that trader. Those rascally Choctaws are drunk and fighting, and ten to one but somebody is killed among them!" was the exclamation of Col. H. "These sounds are familiar to me. I have heard them once before. They signify murder. It is a peculiar whoop which the Indians have, to denote the shedding of blood—to show that a crime has been committed."

The words had scarcely been uttered, before Slim Sampson came suddenly out into the road, and joined us at the door. Col. H. instantly asked him to enter, which he did. When he came fully into the light, we discovered that he had been drinking. His eyes bore sufficient testimony to the fact, though his drunkenness seemed to have subsided into something like stupor. His looks were heavy, rather than calm. He said nothing, but drew nigh to the fireplace, and seated himself upon one corner of the hearth. I now discovered that his hands and hunting shirt were stained with blood. His eyes beheld the bloody tokens at the same time, and he turned his hand curiously over, and examined it by the fire-light.

"Kurnel," said he, in broken English, "me is one dog fool!"

"How, Sampson?"

"Me drunk—me fight—me kill Loblolly Jack! Look ya! Dis blood 'pon my hands. 'Tis Loblolly Jack blood! He dead! I stick him wid de knife!"

"Impossible! What made you do it?"

"Me drunk! Me dog fool!—Drink whiskey at liquor shop—hab money—buy whiskey—drunk come, and Loblolly Jack dead!"

This was the substance of the story, which was confirmed a few moments after, by the appearance of several other Indians, the friends of the two parties. From these it appeared that all of them had been drinking, at the shop of Ligon, the white man; that, when heated with liquor, both Loblolly Jack and Slim Sampson had, as with one accord, resumed the strife which had been arrested by the prompt interference of Col. H.; that, from words they had got to blows, and the former had fallen, fatally hurt, by a single stroke from the other's hand and knife.

The Indian law, like that of the Hebrews, is eye for eye, tooth for tooth, life for life. The fate of Slim Sampson was ordained. He was to die on the morrow. This was well understood by himself as by all the rest. The wound of Loblolly Jack had proved mortal. He was already dead; and it was arranged among the parties that Slim Sampson was to remain that night, if permitted, at the house of Col. H., and to come forth at early sunrise to execution. Col. H. declared his willingness that the criminal should remain in his house; but, at the same time, disclaimed all responsibility in the business; and assured the old chief, whose name was "Rising Smoke," that he would not be answerable for his appearance.

"He won't run," said the other, indifferently.

"But you will not put a watch over him—I will not suffer more than the one to sleep in my house."

The old chief repeated his assurance that Slim Sampson would not seek to fly. No guard was to be placed over him. He was expected to remain quiet, and come forth to execution at the hour appointed.

"He got for dead," continued Rising Smoke—"he know the law. He will come and dead like a man. Oakatibbé got big heart." Every word which the old fellow uttered went to mine.

What an eulogy was this upon Indian inflexibility! What confidence in the passive obedience of the warrior! After a little farther dialogue, they departed,—friends and enemies—and the unfortunate criminal was left with us alone. He still maintained his seat upon the hearth. His muscles were composed and calm—not rigid. His thoughts, however, were evidently busy; and, once or twice, I could see that his head was moved slowly from side to side, with an expression of mournful self-abandonment. I watched every movement and look with the deepest interest, while Col. H., with a concern necessarily deeper than my own, spoke with him freely, on the subject of his crime. It was, in fact, because of the affair of Col. H. that the unlucky deed was committed. It was true, that, for this, the latter gentleman was in no wise responsible, but that did not lessen, materially, the pain which he felt at having, however unwittingly, occasioned it. He spoke with the Indian in such terms of condolence as conventional usage among us has determined to be the most proper. He proffered to buy off the friends and relatives of the deceased, if the offence could be commuted for money. The poor fellow was very grateful, but, at the same time, told him that the attempt was useless.—The tribe had never been known to permit such a thing, and the friends of

Loblolly Jack were too much his enemies, to consent to any commutation of the penalty.

Col. H., however, was unsatisfied, and determined to try the experiment. The notion had only suggested itself to him after the departure of the Indians. He readily conjectured where he should find them, and we immediately set off for the grog-shop of Ligon. This was little more than a quarter of a mile from the plantation. When we reached it, we found the Indians, generally, in the worst possible condition to be treated with. They were, most of them, in the last stages of intoxication. The dead body of the murdered man was stretched out in the piazza, or gallery, half covered with a bear-skin. The breast was bare—a broad, bold, manly bosom—and the wound, a deep narrow gash, around which the blood stood, clotted, in thick, frothy masses. The nearer relations of the deceased, were perhaps the most drunk of the assembly. Their grief necessarily entitled them to the greatest share of consolation, and this took the form of whiskey. Their love of excess, and the means of indulgence, encouraged us with the hope that their vengeance might be bought off without much difficulty, but we soon found ourselves very much deceived. Every effort, every offer, proved fruitless; and after vainly exhausting every art and argument, old Rising Smoke drew us aside to tell us that the thing was impossible.

"Oakatibbé hab for die, and no use for talk. De law is make for Oakatibbé, and Loblolly Jack, and me, Rising Smoke, and all, just the same. Oakatibbé will dead to-morrow."

With sad hearts, we left the maudlin and miserable assembly. When we returned, we found Slim Sampson employed in carving with his knife upon the handle of his tomahawk. In the space thus made, he introduced a small bit of flattened silver, which seemed to have been used for a like purpose on some previous occasion. It was rudely shaped like a bird, and was probably one of those trifling ornaments which usually decorate the stocks of rifle and shot-gun. I looked with increasing concern upon his countenance. What could a spectator—one unacquainted with the circumstances—have met with there? Nothing, surely, of that awful event which had just taken place, and of that doom which now seemed so certainly to await him. He betrayed no sort of interest in our mission. His look and manner denoted his own perfect conviction of its inutility; and when we told him what had taken place, he neither answered nor looked up.

It would be difficult to describe my feelings and those of my companion. The more we reflected upon the affair, the more painful and oppressive did our thoughts become. A pain, little short of horror, coupled itself with every emotion. We left the Indian still beside the fire. He had begun a low chanting song just before we retired, in his own language, which was meant as a narrative of the chief events of his life. The death song—for such it was—is neither more nor less than a recital of those deeds which it will be creditable to a son or a relative to remember. In this way the valor of their great men, and the leading events in their history, are transmitted through successive ages. He was evidently refreshing his own memory in preparation for the morrow. He was arranging the narrative of the past, in proper form for the acceptance of the future.

We did not choose to disturb him in his vocation, and retired. When we had got to our chamber, H., who already had one boot off, exclaimed suddenly—"Look you, S., this fellow ought not to perish in this manner. We should make an effort to save him. We must save him!"

"What will you do?"

"Come—let us go back and try and urge him to flight. He can escape easily while all these fellows are drunk. He shall have my best horse for the purpose."

We returned to the apartment.

"Slim Sampson."

"Kurnel!" was the calm reply.

"There's no sense in your staying here to be shot."

"Ugh!" was the only answer, but in an assenting tone.

"You're not a bad fellow—you didn't mean to kill Loblolly Jack—it's very hard that you should die for what you didn't wish to do. You're too young to die. You've got a great many years to live. You ought to live to be an old man and have sons like yourself; and there's a great deal of happiness in this world, if a man only knows where to look for it. But a man that's dead is of no use to himself, or to his friends, or his enemies. Why should you die—why should you be shot?"

"Eh?"

"Hear me; your people are all drunk at Ligon's—blind drunk—deaf drunk—they can neither see nor hear. They won't get sober till morning—perhaps not then. You've been across the Mississippi, hav'nt you? You know the way?"

The reply was affirmative.

"Many Choctaws live over the Mississippi now—on the Red River, and far beyond, to the Red Hills. Go to them—they will take you by the hand—they will give you one of their daughters to wife—they will love you—they will make you a chief. Fly, Sampson, fly to them—you shall have one of my horses, and before daylight you will be down the country, among the white people, and far from your enemies.—Go, my good fellow, it would be a great pity that so brave a man should die."

This was the substance of my friend's exhortation. It was put into every shape, and addressed to every fear, hope, or passion which might possibly have influence over the human bosom. A strong conflict took place in the mind of the Indian, the outward signs of which were not wholly suppressible. He started to his feet, trod the floor hurriedly, and there was a tremulous quickness in the movement of his eyes, and a dilation of their orbs, which amply denoted the extent of his emotion. He turned suddenly upon us, when H. had finished speaking, and replied in language very nearly like the following:

"I love the whites—I was always a friend to the whites. I believe I love their laws better than my own. Loblolly Jack laughed at me because I loved the whites, and wanted our people to live like them. But I am of no use now. I can love them no more. My people say that I must die. How can I live?"

Such was the purport of his answer. The meaning of it was simple. He was not unwilling to avail himself of the suggestions of my friend—to fly—to live—but he could not divest himself of that habitual deference to those laws to which he had given implicit reverence from the beginning. Custom is the superior tyrant of all savage nations.

To embolden him on this subject, was now the joint object of Col. H. and myself. We spared no argument to convince him that he ought to fly. It was something in favor of our object, that the Indian regards the white man as so infinitely his superior; and, in the case of Slim Sampson, we were assisted by his own inclinations in favor of those customs of the whites, which he had already in part begun to adopt. We discussed for his benefit that which may be considered one of the leading elements in civilization—the duty of saving and keeping life as long as we can—insisted upon the morality of flying from any punishment which would deprive us of it; and at length had the satisfaction of seeing him convinced. He yielded to our arguments and solicitations, accepted the horse, which he promised voluntarily to find some early means to return, and, with a sigh—perhaps one of the first proofs of that change of feeling and of principle which he had just shown, he declared his intention to take the road instantly.

"Go to bed, Kurnel. Your horse will come back." We retired, and a few moments after heard him leave the house. I am sure that both of us felt a degree of light-heartedness which scarcely any other event could have produced. We could not sleep, however. For myself I answer—it was almost dawn before I fell into an uncertain slumber, filled with visions of scuffling Indians—the stark corpse of Loblolly Jack, being the conspicuous object, and Slim Sampson standing up for execution.

IV

Neither Col. H. nor myself arose at a very early hour. Our first thoughts and feelings at waking were those of exultation. We rejoiced that we had been instrumental in saving from an ignominious death, a fellow creature, and one who seemed so worthy, in so many respects. Our exultation was not a little increased, as we reflected on the disappointment of his enemies; and we enjoyed a hearty laugh together, as we talked over the matter while putting on our clothes. When we looked from the window the area in front of the house was covered with Indians. They sat, or stood, or walked, all around the dwelling. The hour appointed for the delivery of Slim Sampson had passed, yet they betrayed no emotion. We fancied, however, that we could discern in the countenances of most among them, the sentiment of friendship or hostility for the criminal, by which they were severally governed. A dark, fiery look of exultation—a grim anticipation of delight—was evident in the faces of his enemies; while, among his friends, men and women, a subdued concern and humbling sadness, were the prevailing traits of expression.

But when we went below to meet them—when it became known that the murderer had fled, taking with him the best horse of the proprietor, the outbreak was tremendous. A terrible yell went up from the party devoted to Loblolly Jack; while the friends and relatives of Slim Sampson at once sprang to their weapons, and put themselves in an attitude of defence. We had not foreseen the effects of our interposition and advice. We did not know, or recollect, that the nearest connection of the criminal, among the Indian tribes, in the event of his escape, would be required to suffer in his place; and this, by the way, is the grand source of that security which they felt the night before, that flight would not be attempted by the destined victim. The aspect of affairs looked squally. Already was the bow bent and the tomahawk lifted. Already had the parties separated, each going to his own side, and ranging himself in front of some one opponent. The women sunk rapidly into the rear, and provided themselves with billets or fence-rails, as they occurred to their hands; while little brats of boys, ten and twelve years old, kept up a continual shrill clamor, brandishing aloft their tiny bows and *blow-guns*, which were only powerful against the lapwing and the sparrow. In political phrase, "a great crisis was at hand." The stealthier chiefs and leaders of both sides, had sunk from sight, behind the trees or houses, in order to avail themselves of all the arts of Indian strategy. Every thing promised a sudden and stern conflict. At the first show of commotion, Col. H. had armed himself. I had been well provided with pistols and bowie knife, before leaving home; and, apprehending the worst, we yet took our places as peacemakers, between the contending parties.

It is highly probable that all our interposition would have been fruitless to prevent their collision; and, though our position certainly delayed the progress of the quarrel, yet all we could have hoped to effect by our interference would have been the removal of the combatants to a more remote battle ground. But a circumstance that surprised and disappointed us all, took place, to settle the strife forever, and to reconcile the parties without any resort to blows. While the turmoil was at the highest, and we had despaired of doing any thing to prevent bloodshed, the tramp of a fast galloping horse was heard in the woods, and the next moment the steed of Col. H. made his appearance, covered with foam, Slim Sampson on his back, and still driven by the lash of his rider at the top of his speed. He leaped the enclosure, and was drawn up still quivering in every limb, in the area between the opposing Indians. The countenance of the noble fellow told his story. His heart had smitten him by continual reproaches, at the adoption of a conduct unknown in his nation; and which all its hereditary opinions had made cowardly and infamous. Besides, he remembered the penalties which, in consequence of his flight, must fall heavily upon his people. Life was sweet to him—very sweet! He had the promise of many bright years before him. His mind was full of honorable and—speaking in comparative phrase—lofty purposes, for the improvement of himself and nation. We have already sought to show that, by his conduct, he had taken one large step in resistance to the tyrannous usages of custom, in order to introduce the elements of civilization among his people. But he could not withstand the reproaches of a conscience formed upon principles which his own genius was not equal to overthrow. His thoughts, during his flight, must have been of a very humbling character; but his features now denoted only pride, exultation and a spirit strengthened by resignation against the worst. By his flight and subsequent return, he had, in fact, exhibited a more lively spectacle of moral firmness, than would have been displayed by his simple submission in remaining. He seemed to feel this. It looked out from his soul in every movement of his body. He leaped from his horse, exclaiming, while he slapped his breast with his open palm:

"Oakatibbé heard the voice of a chief, that said he must die. Let the chief look here—Oakatibbé is come!"

A shout went up from both parties. The signs of strife disappeared. The language of the crowd was no longer that of threatening and violence. It was understood that there would be no resistance on behalf of the condemned. Col. H. and myself, were both mortified and disappointed. Though the return of Slim Sampson, had obviously prevented a combat *à outrance*, in which a dozen or more might have been slain, still we could not but regret the event. The life of such a fellow seemed to both of us, to be worth the lives of any hundred of his people.

Never did man carry with himself more simple nobleness. He was at once surrounded by his friends and relatives. The hostile party, from whom the executioners were to be drawn, stood looking on at some little distance, the very pictures of patience. There was no sort of disposition manifested among them, to hurry the proceedings. Though exulting in the prospect of soon shedding the blood of one whom they esteemed an enemy, yet all was dignified composure and forbearance. The signs of exultation were no where to be seen. Meanwhile, a conversation was carried on in low, soft accents, unmarked by physical action of any kind, between the condemned and two other Indians. One of these was the unhappy mother of the criminal—the other was his uncle. They rather listened to his remarks, than made any of their own. The dialogue was conducted in their own language. After a while this ceased, and he made a signal which seemed to be felt, rather than understood, by all the Indians, friends and enemies. All of them started into instant intelligence. It was a sign that he was ready for the final proceedings. He rose to his feet and they surrounded him. The groans of the old woman, his mother, were now distinctly audible, and she was led away by the uncle, who, placing her among the other women, returned to the condemned, beside whom he now took his place. Col. H. and myself, also drew nigh. Seeing us, Oakatibbé simply said, with a smile:

"Ah, Kurnel, you see, Injun man ain't strong like white man!"

Col. H. answered with emotion.

"I would have saved you, Sampson."

"Oakatibbé hab for dead!" said the worthy fellow, with another, but a very wretched smile.

His firmness was unabated. A procession was formed, which was headed by three sturdy fellows, carrying their rifles conspicuously upon their shoulders. These were the appointed executioners, and were all near relatives of the man who had been slain. There was no mercy in their looks. Oakatibbé followed immediately after these. He seemed pleased that we should accompany him to the place of execution. Our way lay through a long avenue of stunted pines, which conducted us to a spot where an elevated ridge on either hand produced a broad and very prettily defined valley. My eyes, in all this progress, were scarcely ever drawn off from the person of him who was to be the principal actor in the approaching scene. Never, on any occasion, did I behold a man with a step more firm—a head so unbent—a countenance so sweetly calm, though grave—and of such quiet unconcern, at the obvious fate in view. Yet there was nothing in his deportment of that effort which would be the case with most white men on a similar occasion, who seek to wear the aspect of heroism. He walked as to a victory, but he walked with a staid, even dignity, calmly, and without the flush of any excitement on his cheek. In his eye there was none of that feverish curiosity, which seeks for the presence of his executioner, and cannot be averted from the contemplation of the mournful paraphernalia of death. His look was like that of the strong man, conscious of his inevitable doom, and prepared, as it is inevitable, to meet it with corresponding indifference.

The grave was now before us. It must have been prepared at the first dawn of the morning. The executioners paused, when they had reached a spot within thirty steps of it. But the condemned passed on, and stopped only on the edge of its open jaws. The last trial was at hand with all its terrors. The curtain was about to drop, and the scene of life, with all its hopes and promises and golden joys—even to an

Indian golden—was to be shut forever. I felt a painful and numbing chill pass through my frame, but I could behold no sign of change in him. He now beckoned his friends around him. His enemies drew nigh also, but in a remoter circle. He was about to commence his song of death—the narrative of his performances, his purposes, all his living experience. He began a low chant, slow, measured and composed, the words seeming to consist of monosyllables only. As he proceeded, his eyes kindled, and his arms were extended. His action became impassioned, his utterance more rapid, and the tones were distinguished by increasing warmth. I could not understand a single word which he uttered, but the cadences were true and full of significance. The rise and fall of his voice, truly proportioned to the links of sound by which they were connected, would have yielded a fine lesson to the European teacher of school eloquence. His action was as graceful as that of a mighty tree yielding to and gradually rising from the pressure of a sudden gust. I felt the eloquence which I could not understand. I fancied, from his tones and gestures, the play of the muscles of his mouth, and the dilation of his eyes, that I could detect the instances of daring valor, or good conduct, which his narrative comprised. One portion of it, as he approached the close, I certainly could not fail to comprehend. He evidently spoke of his last unhappy affray with the man whom he had slain. His head was bowed—the light passed from his eyes, his hands were folded upon his heart, and his voice grew thick and husky. Then came the narrative of his flight. His glance was turned upon Col. H. and myself, and, at the close, he extended his hand to us both. We grasped it earnestly, and with a degree of emotion which I would not now seek to describe. He paused. The catastrophe was at hand. I saw him step back, so as to place himself at the very verge of the grave—he then threw open his breast—a broad, manly, muscular bosom, that would have sufficed for a Hercules—one hand he struck upon the spot above the heart, where it remained—the other was raised above his head. This was the signal. I turned away with a strange sickness. I could look no longer. In the next instant I heard the simultaneous report, as one, of the three rifles, and when I again looked, they were shoveling in the fresh mould, upon the noble form of one, who, under other more favoring circumstances, might have been a father to his nation.

Ephraim Bartlett,
The Edisto Raftsman

I resume my narrative. In my last, we had just hurried across the common road, once greatly travelled, leading along the Ashley, to the ancient village of Dorchester. Something was said of the fine old plantations along this river. It was the aristocratic region during the Revolution; and when the Virginians and Marylanders, at the close of the war, who had come to the succor of Carolina against the British, drew nigh to Charleston, their hearts were won and their eyes ravished, by the hospitalities and sweets of this neighborhood. Many brave fellows found their wives along this river, which was bordered by flourishing farms and plantations, and crowned by equal luxury and refinement. Here, too, dwelt many of those high-spirited and noble dames whose courage and patriotism contributed so largely to furnish that glorious chapter in Revolutionary history, which has been given to the women of that period. The scene is sadly changed at this season. The plantations along the Ashley are no longer flourishing as then. The land has fallen in value, not exhausted, but no longer fertile and populous. The health of the country is alleged to be no longer what it was. This I regard as all absurdity. The truth is that the cultivation was always inferior; and the first fertile freshness of the soil being exhausted, the opening of new lands in other regions naturally diverted a restless people from their old abodes. The river is still a broad and beautiful one, navigable for steamers and schooners up to Dorchester, which, by land, is twenty-one miles from Charleston. There is abundant means for restoring its fertility. Vast beds of marl, of the best quality, skirt the river all along the route, and there is still a forest growth sufficiently dense to afford the vegetable material necessary to the preparation of compost. As for the health of the neighborhood, I have no sort of question, that, with a dense population, addressed to farming, and adequate to a proper drainage, it would prove quite as salubrious as any portion of the country. Staple culture has been always the curse of Carolina. It has prevented thorough tillage, without which no country can ever ascertain its own resources, or be sure of its health at any time.

Cooper River, on the right, is at a greater distance from us. This, too, was a prosperous and well cultivated region in the Revolution. In a considerable degree it still remains so, and is distinguished by flourishing country seats, which their owners only occupy during spring and winter. The cultivation is chiefly rice, and the rice plantation is notoriously and fatally sickly, except among the negroes. They flourish in a climate which is death to the European. But of this river hereafter. I may persuade you, in future pages, to a special journey in this quarter, when our details and descriptions may be more specific. Between the two rivers the country is full of interest and full of game, to those who can delay to hunt for it. He who runs over the railroad only, sees nothing and can form no conception of it. A few miles further, on the right, there is a stately relic of the old British parochial establishment, a church edifice dedicated to St. James, which modern veneration has lately restored with becoming art, and re-awakened with proper rituals. Built of brick, with a richly painted interior and tesselated aisles, surrounded by patriarchal oaks, and a numerous tentantry of dead in solemn tomb and ivy-mantled monument, you almost fancy yourself in the midst of an antiquity which mocks the finger of the historian. In this neighborhood flourished a goodly population. Large estates and great wealth were associated with equally large refinement and a liberal hospitality, and the land was marked by peculiar fertility. The fertility is not wanting now, but the population is gone—influenced by similar considerations with those which stripped the sister river of its thousands.

Until late years, the game was abundant in this region. The swamps which girdled the rivers afforded a sure refuge, and the deer stole forth to the ridges between, to browse at midnight, seeking refuge in the swamps by day. We have just darted through an extensive tract named Izard's Camp, which used to be famous hunting-ground for the city sportsmen. Twenty years ago I have cracked away at a group of deer, myself, in these forest pastures, and even now you may rouse the hunt profitably in the ancient ranges. There are a few sportsmen who still know where to seek with certainty for the buck at the proper season. The woods, though mostly pine, have large tracts of oak and hickory. The scrubby oak denotes a light sandy soil, of small tenacity, and, most usually, old fields which have been abandoned. Along the smaller water-courses, the creeks and branches, long strips of fertile territory may be had; and the higher swamp lands only need drainage to afford tracts of inexhaustible fertility, equal to any Mississippi bottom. The introduction of farming culture will find these and reclaim them, and restore the poorer regions.

A thousand stories of the Revolution, peculiar to this country, would reward the seeker. Nor is it wanting in other sources of interest. Traditions are abundant which belong more to the spiritual nature of the people than their national history. The poorer classes in the low country of the South were full of superstition. Poverty, for that matter, usually is so, but more particularly when it dwells in a region which is distinguished by any natural peculiarities. Thus the highlands of Scotland cherish a faith in spectral forms that rise in the mist and vapor of the mountain; and the Brownie is but the grim accompaniment of a life, that, lacking somewhat in human association, must seek its companions among the spiritual; and these must derive their aspects from the gloomy fortunes of the seeker. The Banshee of Ireland is but the finally speaking monitor of a fate that has always more or less threatened the fortunes of the declining family; and the Norwegian hunting demons are such as are equally evoked by the sports which he pursues and the necessities by which he is pursued himself. In the wild, deep, dark, and tangled masses of a Carolina swamp region, where, even by daylight, mystic shadows harbor and walk capriciously with every change of the always doubtful sunlight, the mind sees and seeks a spiritual presence, which, though it may sometimes oppress, always affords company. Here, solitude, which is the source of the spiritual and contemplative, is always to be found; and forces herself—certainly at one season of the year—upon the scattered forester and farmer. The man who lives by pursuit of the game, the deer or turkey, will be apt to conjure up, in the silent, dim avenues through which he wanders, some companion for his thought, which will, in time, become a presence to his eye; and, in the secluded toils of the farmer, on the borders of swamp and forest, he will occasionally find himself disturbed by a visitor or spectator which his own loneliness of life has extorted from his imagination, which has shaped it to a becoming aspect with the scene and climate under which he dwells. Many of these wild walkers of the wood are supposed to have been gods and spirits of the Indian tribes, who have also left startling memories behind them; and though reluctant to confess his superstitions—for the white hunter and forester dread ridicule more than anything beside—yet a proper investigation might find treasures of superstition and grim tradition among our people of this region, such as would not discredit any of the inventions of imagination.

One of these traditions occurs to me at this moment, the scene of which is at hand but a short distance from us, but not visible from the railroad. Here is not only a haunted house, but a haunted tract of forest. The tale was told me many years ago, as derived from the narrative of a raftsman of the Edisto. The Edisto, of which we may speak hereafter, is the great *lumber* river of South Carolina. Its extent is considerable, penetrating several district divisions of the State, and upon its two great arms or arteries, and its tributary creeks or branches, it owns perhaps no less than one hundred and fifty mills for sawing lumber. It supplies Charleston, by a sinuous route, almost wholly; and large shipments of its timber are made to the island of Cuba, to Virginia, and recently to New York, and other places. Its navigation is difficult, and, as it approaches the sea, somewhat perilous. Many of its rafts have been driven out to sea and lost, with all on board. It requires, accordingly, an experienced pilot to thread its intricacies, and such an one was Ephraim Bartlett, a worthy fellow, who has passed pretty much out of the memories of the present generation.

Ephraim was a good pilot of the Edisto, one of the best; but he had an unfortunate faith in whiskey, which greatly impaired his standing in society. It did not injure his reputation, however, as a pilot; since it was well known that Ephraim never drank on the voyage, but only on the return; and as this was invariably by land, no evil could accrue from his bad habit to anybody but himself. He rewarded himself for his abstinence on the river, by free indulgence when on shore. His intervals of leisure were given up wholly to his potations; and between the sale of one fleet of rafts, and the preparation for the market of another, Ephraim, I am sorry to say, was a case which would have staggered the temperance societies. But the signal once given by his employers, he would shake himself free from the evil spirit, by a plunge into the river. Purification followed—his head was soon as clear for business as ever; and, wound about with a bandanna handkerchief of flaming spot in place of a hat, it would be seen conspicuous on the raft, making for the city. With cheerful song and cry he made his way down, pole in hand, to ward off the overhanging branches of the trees, or to force aside the obstructions. Accompanied by a single negro, still remembered by many as old 'Bram Geiger, his course was usually prosperous. His lumber usually found the best market, and Ephraim and 'Bram, laying in their little supplies in Charleston, with a sack over their shoulders, and staff or gun in hand, would set out from the city on their return to Lexington, the district of country from which they descended. On these occasions, Ephraim never forgot his jug. This was taken with him empty on the raft, but returned filled, upon his or 'Bram's shoulders. They took turns in carrying it, concealing it from too officious observers by securing it in one end of the sack. In the other might be found a few clothes, and a fair supply of tobacco.

On the particular occasion when Ephraim discovered for himself that the ancient house and tract were haunted, it happened that he left the city about mid-day. It was Saturday, at twelve or one o'clock, according to his account, when they set out, laden as usual. They reached the house, which was probably twelve or thirteen miles from town, long before sundown; and might have stretched away a few miles farther, but for a cramp in the stomach, which seized upon Old 'Bram. Ephraim at once had resort to his jug, and a strong noggin was prepared for the relief of the suffering negro. At the same time, as 'Bram swore that he must die, that nothing could possibly save him under such sufferings as he experienced, Ephraim concluded to take lodgings temporarily in the old house, which happened to be within a few hundred yards of the spot, and to lie by for the rest of the day. The building was of brick, two stories in height, but utterly out of repair—doors and windows gone, floors destroyed, and the entire fabric within quite dismantled. It was a long time before 'Bram was relieved from his suffering and fright. Repeated doses of the potent beverage were necessary to a cure; and, by the time this was effected, the old fellow was asleep. In the meantime, Ephraim had built a rousing fire in the old chimney: had gathered *lightwood* (resinous pine) sufficient to keep up the fire all night; had covered the old negro with his own blanket, which he bore strapped beneath the sack upon his shoulders; and had opened his wallet of dried meat and city bread for his supper. Meanwhile, the fumes of the whiskey had ascended gratefully to his own nostrils; and it seemed only reasonable that he should indulge himself with a dram, having bestowed no less than three upon his companion. He drank accordingly, and as he had no coffee to his supper, he employed the whiskey, which he thought by no means a bad substitute. He may have swallowed three several doses in emulation of 'Bram, and in anticipation of a similar attack, before he had quite finished supper. He admits that he certainly drank again when his meal was ended, by way of washing down the fragments. 'Bram, meanwhile, with the blazing fire at his feet, continued to sleep on very comfortably. When Ephraim got to sleep is not so certain. He admits that he was kept awake till a late hour by the fumes of the whiskey, and by strange noises that reached him from the forest. He recalled to memory the bad character of the dwelling and neighborhood as haunted; and is not so sure, but thinks it possible that this recollection prompted him to take another draught, a stirrup cup, as it were, before yielding himself to sleep. But he denies that he was in any way affected by the whiskey. To use his own language, he had none of the "how-come-you-so" sensation upon him, but insists that he said his prayers, rationally, like any other Christian, put several fresh brands upon the fire, and sank into the most sober of all mortal slumbers.

I am the more particular in stating these details, since a question has been made in regard to them. 'Bram had his story also. He admits that he was sick, and physicked as described—that Ephraim had gathered the fuel, made the fire, and covered him with his blanket, while he slept—but he alleges that he awoke at midnight, when Ephraim himself was asleep, and being still a little distressed in the abdominal region, he proceeded to help himself out of the jug, without disturbing the repose of his comrade; and he affirms, on his honesty, that he then found the jug fully half emptied, which had been quite full when he left the city; and he insisted that, in giving him his several doses, Ephraim had always been very careful not to make them over strong. 'Bram admits that, when he had occasion to help himself, as the attack was still threatening, he preferred to take an over dose rather than peril his safety by mincing the matter. It is very certain, from the united testimonies of the two, the whiskey had, one half of it, most unaccountably disappeared before the night was half over. I must suffer Ephraim to tell the rest of the story for himself, and assert his own argument.

"Well, now, you see, my friends," telling his story to a group, "as I said afore, it was mighty late that night afore I shut my eyes. I reckon twarn't far from day-peep when I slipped off into a hearty sleep, and then I slept like a cat after a supper. Don't you be thinking now 'twas owing to the whiskey that I was wakeful, or that I slept so sound at last. 'Bram's troubles in the stomach made me oneasy, and them strange noises in the woods helped the matter."

"But what were the noises like, Ephraim?"

"Oh! like a'most any thing and every thing. Horns a-blowing, horses a-snorting, cats a-crying, and then sich a rushing and a trampling of four-footed beasts, that I could 'a-swore it was a fox hunt for all the world. But it warn't that! No! 'Twas a hunt agin natur'. The hounds, and horses, and horns that made that racket, warn't belonging to this world. I felt suspicions about it then, and I reckon I knows it now, if such a matter ever is to be made known. Well, as I was a-saying, I got to sleep at last near upon day-light. How long I did sleep there's no telling. 'Twas mighty late when I waked, and then the noise was in my ears again. I raised myself on end, and sat up in my blanket. The fire was gone out clean, and I was a little coldish. 'Bram, the nigger, had scruged himself into the very ashes, and had quite kivered up his head in the blanket. How he drawed his breath there's no telling, since the tip of his nose warn't to be seen nowhere. Says I, ' 'Bram, do you hear them noises?' But never a word did he answer. Says I, to myself, 'the nigger's smothered.' So I onwrapt him mighty quick, and heard him grunt. Then I know'd there was no harm done. The nigger was only drunk."

"Nebber been drunk dat time," was the usual interruption of 'Bram, whenever he was present at the narration.

"'Bram, you was most certainly drunk, sense I tried my best to waken you, and couldn't get you up."

"Ha! da's 'cause I bin want for sleep, so I nebber consent for ye'r (hear). I bin ye'r berry well all de time; but a man wha's bin trouble wid 'fliction in the stomach all night, mus' hab he sleep out in de morning. I bin ye'r well enough, I tell you."

"You old rascal, if I had thought so, I'd ha' chunk'd you with a lightwood knot!—but the nigger *was* asleep, my friends, in a regular drunk sleep, if ever he was; for when I hearn the noises coming nigh—the hounds and the horses—I drawed him away from the ashes by the legs, and laid him close up agin' the wall t'other side of the fire-place, and pretty much out of sight. I kivered him snug with the blanket, and let him take his sleep out, though I was beginning to be more and more jub'ous about them noises. You see, 'twas the regular noises of a deer-hunt. I could hear the drivers beating about in the thick; then the shout; then the dogs, yelping out whenever they struck upon the trail; I know'd when they nosed the cold trail, and when the scent got warm; and then I heerd the regular rush, when the deer was started, all the dogs in full blast, and making the merriest music. Then I heerd the crack of the gun—first one gun, then another, then another, and another, a matter of four shots—and I felt sure they must ha' got the meat. The horns sounded; the dogs were stopped, and, for a little while, nothing but silence. Oh! I felt awful all over, and monstrous jub'ous of something strange!"

"But why should you feel awful, and what should there be so strange about a deer-hunt near Izard's Camp—a place where you may start deer even at this day?"

"Why, 'twas Sunday, you see, and nobody now, in our times, hunts deer, or anything, a-Sundays; and it 'twan't till after midnight on Saturday that I heer'd the noises. That was enough to make me jub'ous. But when I remember'd how they used to tell me of the rich English gentleman, named Lumley, that once lived in the neighborhood, long afore the old Revolution; what a wicked man he was, and how he used to hunt a-Sundays; and how a judgment come upon him; and how he was lost, in one of his huntings, for a matter of six months or more; and when he was found, 'twas only his skeleton. Well I reckon, to think of all that, was enough to give me a bad scare—and it did. People reckoned he must have been snake-bit, for there were the bones of the snake beside him, with the rattles on, eleven and the button; he must have killed the snake after he was struck. But it didn't help him. He never got away from the spot till they found his skileton, and they know'd him by the ring upon his finger, and his knife, and horn, and gun; but all the iron was ruined, eaten up by the rust. Well, when I heer'd the horns a-Sunday, I recollected all about Squire Lumley, and his wickedness; and, before I seed anything, I was all over in a shiver. Well, presently I heerd the horns blowing merrily again, and the sounds come fresher than ever to my ears. I was oneasy enough, and I made another trial to wake up 'Bram, but 'twas of no use. He was sounder than ever."

"I 'speck I bin sleep den, for true," was the modest interruption of 'Bram, at this stage of the narrative. With a grave shake of the head, Ephraim continued—

"I went out then in front of the house, and the horns were coming nigher from behind it. I was a-thinking to run and hide in the bushes, but I was so beflustered that I was afeer'd I should run right into the jaws of the danger. Though, when I thought of the matter agin', I got a little bolder, and I said to myself, 'what's the danger, I wonder. I'm in a free country. I'm troubling no man's property. I've let down no man's fence. I've left no man's gate open to let in the cattle. This old house nobody lives in, and I wouldn't ha' troubled it, ef so be 'Bram hadn't been taken sick in his bowels. What's the danger?' When I thought, in this way, to myself, I went in and took a sup of whiskey—a small sup—only a taste—by way of keeping my courage up. I tried to waken 'Bram again, for I said, 'two's always better than one, though one's a nigger,' but 'twas no use; 'Bram's sleep was sounder than ever. It was pretty cl'ar that he had soak'd the whiskey mighty deep that night!"

" 'Ki! Mas Ephraim! How you talk! Ef you nebber been drink more than me, dat night, you nebber been scare wid de hunters dat blessed Sunday morning."

"The nigger will talk!" said Ephraim, contemptuously, as he continued his narrative.

"Well, I felt stronger after I had taken that little sup, and went out again. Just then there came a blast of the horns almost in my very ears, and in the next minute I hear'd the trampling of horses. Soon a matter of twenty dogs burst out of the woods, and pushed directly for the house as if they knowed it; and then came the riders—five in all—four white men and one nigger. Ef I was scared at the sounds afore, the sight of these people didn't make me feel any easier. They were well enough to look at in the face, but, lord bless you, they were dressed in sich an outlandish fashion! Why, even the nigger had on short breeches, reaching only to his knees, and then stockings blue and red streaked, fitting close to his legs;—and sich a leg, all the calf turned in front, and the long part of his foot pretty much where the heel ought to be. Then he had buckles at his knees, and buckles on his shoes, jest for all the world like his master. And he wore a cap like his master, though not quite so handsome, and a great coat of bright indigo blue, with the cuffs and collar trimmed with yellow. His breeches were of a coarse buff, the same color with the gentlemen, only theirs were made with a finer article—the raal buff, I reckon. They had on red coats that were mighty pretty, and all their horns were silver mounted. Our Governor and his officers, nowadays, never had on prettier regimentals. Well, up they rode, never taking any more notice of me than ef I was a dog; and I saw the nigger throw down a fine buck from his saddle. There was only one, but he had a most powerful head of horns. While they were all getting off their horses, and the nigger was taking 'em, I turned quietly into the house ag'in to try if a kick or two could get 'Bram out of his blankets. But, lord have mercy, when I look in, what should I see but another nigger there spreading a table with a cloth as white as the driven snow, and a-setting plates, and knives, and forks, and spoons, and bottles, and salt, and pepper, and mustard, and horse-radish, all as ef he had a cupboard somewhere at his hand. I was amazed, and worse than amazed, when I seed my own jug among the other things. But I hadn't the heart to touch it. For that matter, the nigger that was setting out the things kept as sharp an eye upon me as ef I was a thief. But soon the dishes began to show upon the table. There were the pots upon the fire, the gridiron, the Dutch oven, and everything, and the most rousing fire, and 'Bram still asleep in the corner, and knowing nothing about it. I was all over in a sweat. Soon, the gentlemen began to come in, but they took no sort of notice of me; and I slipped out and looked at their horses; but as the nigger was standing by 'em, and looking so strange, I didn't go too nigh. But the deer was still a-lying where he first threw it, and I thought I'd turn the head over and see the critter fairly, when, as I'm a living man, the antlers slipped through my fingers jest as fast as I tried to take 'em,—like so much water or smoke. There was a feel to me as ef I had touched something, but I couldn't take hold no how, and while I was a-trying, the nigger holla'd, in a gruff voice, from the horses—'Don't you touch Maussa's meat!' I was getting desp'rate mighty fast, and I thought I'd push back, and try what good another sup of whiskey would do. Well, when I went into the house, the gentlemen were all a-setting round the table, and busy with knife and fork, jest as ef they were the commonest people. There was a mighty smart chance for feeding at the table. Ham and turkey, a pair of as fine wild ducks, English, as you ever seed; a beef tongue, potetters (potatoes), cabbage, eggs, and other matters, and all for jest five men and their servants. Jest then, one of the gentlemen set his eyes on me, and p'inted to one of the bottles—says he, jest as if I had been his own servant—

" 'Hand the bottle.'

"And somehow, I felt as ef I couldn't help myself, but must hand it, sure enough. When he had poured out the liquor, which was a mighty deep red, yet clear as the sunshine, he gin me back the bottle, and I thought I'd take a taste of the stuff, jest to see what it was. I got a chance, and poured out a tolerable dram—supposing it was a sort of red bald face (whiskey)—into a cup and tossed it off in a twinkle. But it warn't bald face, nor brandy, nor wine, nor any liquor that I ever know'd before. It hadn't a strong taste, but was something like a cordial, with a flavor like fruit and essence. 'Twarn't strong, I say; so I tried it ag'in an' ag'in, whenever I could git a chance; for I rather liked the flavor; and I warn't mealy-mouthed at helping myself, as they had enough of the critter, and, by this time, they had begun upon my own old bald-face. They seemed to like it well enough. They tried it several times, as if 'twas something new to them, and they didn't find it hard to make the aquaintance. I didn't quarrel with them, you may be sure, for I never was begrudgeful of my liquor; and, besides, wasn't I trying their'n? Well, I can't tell you how long this lasted. 'Twas a good while; and they kept me busy; one after the other on 'em calling out to me to hand 'em this, and hand 'em that, and even the nigger motioning me to help him with this thing and the other. He didn't say much, and always spoke in a whisper. But, it so happened, that, when I was stretching out for one of the bottles, to try another taste of the cordial, one of the cursed dogs would come always in my way. At last, I gin the beast a kick; and, would you believe it, my foot went clean through him—through skin, and ribs, and body, jest the same as if I had kicked the wind or the water. I did not feel him with my foot. I was all over in a trimble; and the dog yelped, jest as if I had hurt him. Sure enough, at this, the great dark-favored man that sot at the head of the table, he fastened his eye upon me and said in a big threatening voice:

" 'Who kick'd my dog?'

"By this time, my blood was up a little. What with the scare I had, and the stuff I'd been a-drinking, I felt a little desperate; and my eye was sot upon the man pretty bold as I said:

" 'I was just reaching for my own liquor,'—(now, that warn't exactly true, I confess, for I was reaching for one of their own bottles)—'when the dog came in my way, and I just brushed him with my foot.'

" 'Nobody shall kick my dog but myself,' said he, more fierce than ever; and looking as if he meant kicking! That made me a sort o' wolfish, and, just then, something put the old story of Lumley and the rattlesnake fresh into my head; and, I couldn't help myself—but I gin him for answer as nice an imitation of a snake's rattle—you know how well I kin do it, my friends—as ever he heerd in his born days.

"Lord! you should have seen the stir and heard the racket. Every fellow was on his feet in a minnit, and before I could dodge, the great dark-featured man, he rose up, and seized my jug by the handle, and whirled it furious about his head, and then he sent it at me, with such a curse, and such a cry, that I thought all the house a-tumbling to pieces. Like a great wind, they all rushed by me, men and dogs, and nigger, throwing me down in the door-way, and going over me as ef I was nothing in the way. Whether it was the jug that hit me, or them rushing over, and trampling me down, I can't say; but there I lay, pretty much stunned and stupefied; not knowing anything for a long time;—and when I opened my eyes, and could look around me, there I was with 'Bram stooping over me and trying to raise me from the ground."

"*Dat's* true!" said 'Bram, laying special emphasis on *dat's* (that's) and shaking his head significantly. Ephraim continued:

"The strangers were all gone in the twinkling of an eye,—they had swept the platters,—carried off every thing clean,—carried off tables and chairs, bottles and cups, plates and dishes, dinner and drink, pots and ovens, and had even put out the fire; sence, when 'Bram waked up, there was not a sign of it to be seen. My jug was broke all to pieces, and lying beside me at the door, and not a drop of liquor to be had. What they didn't drink, they wasted, the spiteful divels, when they broke the jug over my head."

Such was Ephraim's story, grown into a faith with many, of the Haunted Forest and House near Izard's Camp. In Ephraim's presence, 'Bram does not venture to deny a syllable of the story. He only professes to have seen nothing of it, except the full jug when they arrived at the house, and the broken and empty vessel when he awoke from his sleep. In Ephraim's absence, however, he does not scruple to express his doubts wholly of the ghostly visitors and the strange liquor. His notion is, that Ephraim got drunk upon the "*bald-face*" (whiskey) and dreamed the rest. His only subject of difficulty is that the jug should have been broken. He denies, for himself, that he took a drop too much—considering the state of his stomach.—We must resume our journey hereafter.

How Sharp Snaffles Got His Capital and Wife

I

The day's work was done, and a good day's work it was. We had bagged a couple of fine bucks and a fat doe; and now we lay camped at the foot of the "Balsam Range" of mountains in North Carolina, preparing for our supper. We were a right merry group of seven; four professional hunters, and three amateurs—myself among the latter. There was Jim Fisher, Aleck Wood, Sam or Sharp Snaffles, *alias* "Yaou," and Nathan Langford, *alias* the "Pious."

There were our *professional* hunters. Our *amateurs* may well continue nameless, as their achievements do not call for any present record. Enough that we had gotten up the "camp hunt," and provided all the creature comforts except the fresh meat. For this we were to look to the mountain ranges and the skill of our hunters.

These were all famous fellows with the rifle—moving at a trot along the hill-sides, and with noses quite as keen of scent as those of their hounds in rousing deer and bear from their deep recesses among the mountain laurels.

A week had passed with us among these mountain ranges, some sixty miles beyond what the conceited world calls "civilization."

Saturday night had come; and, this Saturday night closing a week of exciting labors, we were to carouse.

We were prepared for it. There stood our tent pitched at the foot of the mountains, with a beautiful cascade leaping headlong toward us, and subsiding into a mountain runnel, and finally into a little lakelet, the waters of which, edged with perpetual foam, were as clear as crystal.

Our baggage wagon, which had been sent round to meet us by

trail routes through the gorges, stood near the tent, which was of stout army canvas.

That baggage wagon held a variety of luxuries. There was a barrel of the best bolted wheat flour. There were a dozen choice hams, a sack of coffee, a keg of sugar, a few thousand of cigars and last, not least, a corpulent barrel of Western uisquebaugh,* vulgarly, "whiskey;" to say nothing of a pair of demijohns of equal dimensions, one containing peach brandy of mountain manufacture, the other the luscious honey from the mountain hives.

Well, we had reached Saturday night. We had hunted day by day from the preceding Monday with considerable success—bagging some game daily, and camping nightly at the foot of the mountains. The season was a fine one. It was early winter, October, and the long ascent to the top of the mountains was through vast fields of green, the bushes still hanging heavy with their huckleberries.

From the summits we had looked over into Tennessee, Virginia, Georgia, North and South Carolina. In brief, to use the language of Natty Bumppo, we beheld "Creation." We had crossed the "Blue Ridge;" and the descending water-courses, no longer seeking the Atlantic, were now gushing headlong down the western slopes, and hurrying to lose themselves in the Gulf Stream and the Mississippi.

From the eyes of fountains within a few feet of each other we had blended our *eau de vie* with limpid waters which were about to part company forever—the one leaping to the rising, the other to the setting of the sun.

And buoyant, full of fun, with hearts of ease, limbs of health and strength, plenty of venison, and a wagon full of good things, we welcomed the coming of Saturday night as a season not simply of rest, but of a royal carouse. We were decreed to make a night of it.

But first let us see after our venison.

The deer, once slain, is, as soon after as possible, clapped upon the fire. All the professional hunters are good butchers and admirable cooks—of bear and deer meat at least. I doubt if they could spread a table to satisfy Delmonico; but even Delmonico might take some les-

---

* "Uisquebaugh," or the "water of life," is Irish. From the word we have dropped the last syllable. Hence we have "uisque," or, as it is commonly written, "whisky"—a very able-bodied man-servant, but terrible as a mistress or housekeeper.

sons from them in the preparation for the table of the peculiar game which they pursue, and the meats on which they feed. We, at least, rejoice at the supper prospect before us. Great collops hiss in the frying-pan, and finely cut steaks redden beautifully upon the flaming coals. Other portions of the meat are subdued to the stew, and make a very delightful dish. The head of the deer, including the brains, is put upon a flat rock in place of gridiron, and thus baked before the fire—being carefully watched and turned until every portion has duly imbibed the necessary heat, and assumed the essential hue which it should take to satisfy the eye of appetite. This portion of the deer is greatly esteemed by the hunters themselves; and the epicure of genuine stomach for the *haut gout* takes to it as an eagle to a fat mutton, and a hawk to a young turkey.

The rest of the deer—such portions of it as are not presently consumed or needed for immediate use—is cured for future sale or consumption; being smoked upon a scaffolding raised about four feet above the ground, under which, for ten or twelve hours, a moderate fire will be kept up.

Meanwhile the hounds are sniffing and snuffing around, or crouched in groups, with noses pointed at the roast and broil and bake; while their great liquid eyes dilate momently while watching for the huge gobbets which they expect to be thrown to them from time to time from the hands of the hunters.

Supper over, and it is Saturday night. It is the night dedicated among the professional hunters to what is called "The Lying Camp!"

"The Lying Camp!" quoth Columbus Mills, one of our party, a wealthy mountaineer, of large estates, of whom I have been for some time the guest.

"What do you mean by the 'Lying Camp,' Columbus?"

The explanation soon followed.

Saturday night is devoted by the mountaineers engaged in a camp hunt, which sometimes contemplates a course of several weeks, to stories of their adventures—"long yarns"—chiefly relating to the objects of their chase, and the wild experiences of their professional life. The hunter who actually inclines to exaggeration is, at such a period, privileged to deal in all the extravagances of invention; nay, he is *required* to do so! To be literal, or confine himself to the bald and naked truth, is not only discreditable, but a *finable* offense! He is, in such a case, made to swallow a long, strong, and difficult potation! He can not be too extravagant in his incidents; but he is also required to exhibit a certain degree of *art*, in their use; and he thus frequently rises into a certain realm of fiction, the ingenuities of which are made to compensate for the exaggerations, as they do in the "Arabian Nights," and other Oriental romances.

This will suffice for explanation.

Nearly all our professional hunters assembled on the present occasion were tolerable *raconteurs*. They complimented Jim Fisher, by throwing the raw deer-skin over his shoulders; tying the antlers of the buck with a red handkerchief over his forehead; seating him on the biggest boulder which lay at hand; and, sprinkling him with a stoup of whisky, they christened him "The Big Lie," for the occasion. And in this character he complacently presided during the rest of the evening, till the company prepared for sleep, which was not till midnight. He was king of the feast.

It was the duty of the "Big Lie" to regulate proceedings, keep order, appoint the *raconteurs* severally, and admonish them when he found them foregoing their privileges, and narrating bald, naked, and uninteresting truth. They must deal in fiction.

Jim Fisher was seventy years old, and a veteran hunter, the most famous in all the country. He *looked* authority, and promptly began to assert it, which he did in a single word:

"Yaou!"

II

"Yaou" was the *nom de nique* of one of the hunters, whose proper name was Sam Snaffles, but who, from his special smartness, had obtained the farther sobriquet of "*Sharp* Snaffles."

Columbus Mills whispered me that he was called "Yaou" from his frequent use of that word, which, in the Choctaw dialect, simply means "Yes." Snaffles had rambled considerably among the Choctaws, and picked up a variety of their words, which he was fond of using in preference to the vulgar English; and his common use of "*Yaou*," for the affirmative, had prompted the substitution of it for his own name. He answered to the name.

"Ay—yee, Yaou," was the response of Sam. "I was *afeard*, 'Big Lie,' that you'd be hitching me up the very first in your team."

"And what was you afeard of? You knows as well how to take up a crooked trail as the very best man among us; so you go ahead and spin your thread a'ter the best fashion."

"What shill it be?" asked Snaffles, as he mixed a calabash full of peach and honey, preparing evidently for a long yarn.

"Give 's the history of how you got your capital, Yaou!" was the cry from two or more.

"O Lawd! I've tell'd that so often, fellows, that I'm afeard you'll sleep on it; and then agin, I've tell'd it so often I've clean forgot how it goes. Somehow it changes a leetle every time I tells it."

"Never you mind! The Jedge never haird it, I reckon, for one; and I'm not sure that Columbus Mills ever did."

So the "Big Lie."

The "Jedge" was the *nom de guerre* which the hunters had conferred upon me; looking, no doubt, to my venerable aspect—for I had traveled considerably beyond my teens—and the general dignity of my bearing.

"Yaou," like other bashful beauties in oratory and singing, was disposed to hem and haw, and affect modesty and indifference, when he was brought up suddenly by the stern command of the "Big Lie," who cried out:

"Don't make yourself an etarnal fool, Sam Snaffles, by twisting your mouth out of shape, making all sorts of redickilous ixcuses. Open upon the trail at onst and give tongue, or, dern your digestion, but I'll fine you to hafe a gallon at a single swallow!"

Nearly equivalent to what Hamlet says to the conceited player:

"Leave off your damnable faces and begin."

Thus adjured with a threat, Sam Snaffles swallowed his peach and honey at a gulp, hemmed thrice lustily, put himself into an attitude, and began as follows. I shall adopt his language as closely as possible; but it is not possible, in any degree, to convey any adequate idea of his *manner*, which was admirably appropriate to the subject matter. Indeed, the fellow was a born actor.

III

"You see, Jedge," addressing me especially as the distinguished stranger, "I'm a telling this hyar history of mine jest to please *you*, and I'll try to please you ef I kin. These fellows hyar have hearn it so often that they knows all about it jest as well as I do my own self, and they knows the truth of it all, and would swear to it afore any hunters' court in all the county, ef so be the affidavy was to be tooken in camp and on a Saturday night.

"You see then, Jedge, it's about a dozen or fourteen years ago, when I was a young fellow without much beard on my chin, though I was full grown as I am now—strong as a horse, ef not quite so big as a buffalo. I was then jest a-beginning my 'prenticeship to the hunting business, and looking to sich persons as the 'Big Lie' thar to show me how to take the track of b'ar, buck, and painther.

"But I confess I weren't a-doing much. I hed a great deal to l'arn, and I reckon I miss'd many more bucks than I ever hit—that is, jest up to that time—"

"Look you, Yaou," said "Big Lie," interrupting him, "you're gitting too close upon the etarnal stupid truth! All you've been a-saying is jest nothing but the naked truth as I knows it. Jest crook your trail!"

"And how's a man to lie decently onless you lets him hev a bit of truth to go upon? The truth's nothing but a peg in the wall that I hangs the lie upon. A'ter a while I promise that you sha'n't see the peg."

"Worm along, Yaou!"

"Well, Jedge, I warn't a-doing much among the *bucks* yit—jest for the reason that I was quite too eager in the scent a'ter a sartin *doe!* Now, Jedge, you never seed my wife—my Merry Ann, as I calls her; and ef you was to see her *now*—though she's prime grit yit—you would never believe that, of all the womankind in all these mountains, she was the very yaller flower of the forest; with the reddest rose cheeks you ever did see, and sich a mouth, and sich bright curly hair, and so tall, and so slender, and so all over beautiful! O Lawd! when I thinks of it and them times, I don't see how 'twas possible to think of buck-hunting when thar was sich a doe, with sich eyes shining me on!

"Well, Jedge, Merry Ann was the only da'ter of Jeff Hopson and Keziah Hopson, his wife, who was the da'ter of Squire Claypole, whose wife was Margery Clough, that lived down upon Pacolet River—"

"Look you, Yaou, ain't you gitting into them derned facts agin, eh?"

"I reckon I em, 'Big Lie!' 'Scuse me: I'll kiver the pegs *direct-lie*, one a'ter t'other. Whar was I? Ah! Oh! Well, Jedge, poor hunter and poor man—jest, you see, a squatter on the side of a leetle bit of a mountain close on to Columbus Mills, at Mount Tryon, I was all the time on a hot trail a'ter Merry Ann Hopson. I went thar to see her a'most every night; and sometimes I carried a buck for the old people, and sometimes a doe-skin for the gal, and I do think, bad hunter as I then was, I pretty much kept the fambly in deer meat through the whole winter."

"Good for you, Yaou! You're a-coming to it! That's the only fair trail of a lie that you've struck yit!"

So the "Big Lie," from the chair.

"Glad to hyar you say so," was the answer. "I'll git on in time! Well, Jedge, though Jeff Hopson was glad enough to git my meat always, he didn't affection me, as I did his da'ter. He was a sharp, close, money-loving old fellow, who was always considerate of the main chaince; and the old lady, his wife, who hairdly dare say her soul was her own, she jest looked both ways, as I may say, for Sunday, never giving a fair look to me or my chainces, when his eyes were sot on *her*. But 'twa'n't so with my Merry Ann. She hed the eyes for me from the beginning, and soon she hed the feelings; and, you see, Jedge, we sometimes did git a chaince, when old Jeff was gone from home, to come to a sort of onderstanding about our feelings; and the long and the short of it was that Merry Ann confessed to me that she'd like nothing better than to be my wife. She liked no other man but me. Now, Jedge, a'ter that, what was a young fellow to do? That, I say, was the proper kind of incouragement. So I said, 'I'll ax your daddy.' Then she got scary, and said, 'Oh, don't; for somehow, Sam, I'm a-thinking daddy don't like you enough *yit*. Jest hold on a bit, and come often, and bring him venison, and try to make him laugh, which you kin do, you know, and a'ter a time you kin try him.' And so I did—or rether I didn't. I put off the axing. I come constant. I brought venison all the time, and b'ar meat a plenty, a'most three days in every week."

"That's it, Yaou. You're on trail. That's as derned a lie as you've tell'd yit; for all your hunting, in them days, didn't git more meat than you could eat your one self."

"Thank you, 'Big Lie.' I hopes I'll come up in time to the right measure of the camp.

"Well, Jedge, this went on for a long time, a'most the whole winter, and spring, and summer, till the winter begun to come in agin. I carried 'em the venison, and Merry Ann meets me in the woods, and we hes sich a pleasant time when we meets on them little odd chainces that I gits hot as thunder to bring the business to a sweet honey finish.

"But Merry Ann keeps on scary, and she puts me off; ontil, one day, one a'ternoon, about sundown, she meets me in the woods, and she's all in a flusteration. And she ups and tells me how old John Grimstead, the old bachelor (a fellow about forty years old, and the dear gal not yet twenty), how he's a'ter her, and bekaise he's got a good fairm, and mules and horses, how her daddy's giving him the open mouth incouragement.

"Then I says to Merry Ann:

" 'You sees, I kain't put off no longer. I must out with it, and ax your daddy at onst.' And then her scary fit come on again, and she begs me not to—not *jist yit*. But I swears by all the Hokies that I won't put off another day; and so, as I haird the old man was in the house that very hour, I left Merry Ann in the woods, all in a trimbling, and I jist went ahead, detarmined to have the figure made straight, whether odd or even.

"And Merry Ann, poor gal, she wrings her hainds, and cries a smart bit, and she wouldn't go to the house, but said she'd wait for me out thar. So I gin her a kiss into her very mouth—and did it over more than onst—and I left her, and pushed headlong for the house.

"I was jubous; I was mighty oncertain, and a leetle bit scary myself; for, you see, old Jeff was a fellow of tough grit, and with big grinders; but I was so oneasy, and so tired out waiting, and so desperate, and so fearsome that old bachelor Grimstead would get the start on me, that nothing could stop me now, and I jist bolted into the house, as free and easy and bold as ef I was the very best customer that the old man wanted to see."

Here Yaou paused to renew his draught of peach and honey.

IV

"Well, Jedge, as I tell you, I put a bold face on the business, though my hairt was gitting up into my throat, and I was almost a-gasping for my breath, when I was fairly in the big room, and standing up before the old Squaire. He was a-setting in his big squar hide-bottom'd arm-chair, looking like a jedge upon the bench, jist about to send a poor fellow to the gallows. As he seed me come in, looking queer enough, I reckon, his mouth put on a sort of grin, which showed all his grinders, and he looked for all the world as ef he guessed the business I come about. But he said, good-natured enough:

" 'Well, Sam Snaffles, how goes it?'

"Says I:

" 'Pretty squar, considerin'. The winter's coming on fast, and I reckon the mountains will be full of meat before long.'

"Then says he, with another ugly grin, 'Ef 'twas your smoke-house that had it all, Sam Snaffles, 'stead of the mountains, 'twould be better for you, I reckon.'

" 'I 'grees with you,' says I. 'But I rether reckon I'll git my full shar' of it afore the spring of the leaf agin.'

" 'Well, Sam,' says he, 'I hopes, for your sake, 'twill be a big shar'. I'm afeard you're not the pusson to go for a big shar', Sam Snaffles. Seems to me you're too easy satisfied with a small shar'; sich as the fence-squarrel carries onder his two airms, calkilating only on a small corn-crib in the chestnut-tree.'

" 'Don't you be afeard, Squaire. I'll come out right. My cabin sha'n't want for nothing that a strong man with a stout hairt kin git, with good working—enough and more for himself, and perhaps another pusson.'

" 'What other pusson?' says he, with another of his great grins, and showing of his grinders.

" 'Well,' says I, 'Squaire Hopson, that's jest what I come to talk to you about this blessed Friday night.'

"You see, '*twas* Friday!

" 'Well,' says he, 'go ahead, Sam Snaffles, and empty your brain-basket as soon as you kin, and I'll light my pipe while I'm a'hearing you.'

"So he lighted his pipe, and laid himself back in his chair, shet his eyes, and begin to puff like blazes.

"By this time my blood was beginning to bile in all my veins, for I seed that he was jest in the humor to tread on all my toes, and then ax a'ter my feelings. I said to myself:

" 'It's jest as well to git the worst at onst, and then thar'll be an eend of the oneasiness.' So I up and told him, in pretty soft, smooth sort of speechifying, as how I was mighty fond of Merry Ann, and she, I was a-thinking, of me; and that I jest come to ax ef I might hev Merry Ann for my wife.

"Then he opened his eyes wide, as ef he never ixpected to hear sich a proposal from me.

" 'What!' says he. 'You?'

" 'Jest so, Squaire,' says I. 'Ef it pleases you to believe me, and to consider it reasonable, the axing.'

"He sot quiet for a minit or more, then he gits up, knocks all the fire out of his pipe on the chimney, fills it, and lights it agin, and then comes straight up to me, whar I was a-setting on the chair in front of him, and without a word he takes the collar of my coat betwixt the thumb and forefinger of his left hand, and he says:

" 'Git up, Sam Snaffles. Git up, ef you please.'

"Well, I gits up, and he says:

" 'Hyar! Come! Hyar!'

"And with that he leads me right across the room to a big looking-glass that hung agin the partition wall, and thar he stops before the glass, facing it and holding me by the collar all the time.

"Now that looking-glass, Jedge, was about the biggest I ever did see! It was a'most three feet high, and a'most two feet wide, and it had a bright, broad frame, shiny like gold, with a heap of leetle figgers worked all round it. I reckon thar's no sich glass now in all the mountain country. I 'member when first that glass come home. It was a great thing, and the old Squaire was mighty proud of it. He bought it at the sale of some rich man's furniter, down at Greenville, and he was jest as fond of looking into it as a young gal, and whenever he lighted his pipe, he'd walk up and down the room, seeing himself in the glass.

"Well, thar he hed me up, both on us standing in front of this glass, whar we could a'most see the whole of our full figgers, from head to foot.

"And when we hed stood thar for a minit or so, he says, quite solemn like:

" 'Look in the glass, Sam Snaffles.'

"So I looked.

" 'Well,' says I. 'I sees you, Squaire Hopson, and myself, Sam Snaffles.'

" 'Look good,' says he, '*obzarve* well.'

" 'Well,' says I, 'I'm a-looking with all my eyes. I only sees what I tells you.'

" 'But you don't *obzarve*,' says he. 'Looking and seeing's one thing,' says he, 'but obzarving's another. Now *obzarve*.'

"By this time, Jedge, I was getting sort o' riled, for I could see that somehow he was jest a-trying to make me feel redickilous. So I says:

" 'Look you, Squaire Hopson, ef you thinks I never seed myself in a glass afore this, you're mighty mistaken. I've got my own glass at home, and though it's but a leetle sort of a small, mean consarn, it shows me as much of my own face and figger as I cares to see at any time. I never cares to look in it 'cept when I'm brushing, and combing, and clipping off the straggling beard when it's too long for my eating.'

" 'Very well,' says he; 'now obzarve! You sees your own figger, and your face, and you air obzarving as well as you know how. Now, Mr. Sam Snaffles—now that you've hed a fair look at yourself—jest now answer me, from your honest conscience, a'ter all you've seed, ef you honestly thinks you're the sort of pusson to hev *my* da'ter!'

"And with that he gin me a twist, and when I wheeled round he had wheeled round too, and thar we stood, full facing one another.

"Lawd! how I was riled! But I answered, quick:

" 'And why not, I'd like to know, Squaire Hopson? I ain't the handsomest man in the world, but I'm not the ugliest; and folks don't generally consider me at all among the uglies. I'm as tall a man as you, and as stout and strong, and as good a man o' my inches as ever stepped in shoe-leather. And it's enough to tell you, Squaire, whatever *you* may think, that Merry Ann believes in me, and she's a way of thinking that I'm jest about the very pusson that ought to hev her.'

" 'Merry Ann's thinking,' says he, 'don't run all fours with her fayther's thinking. I axed you, Sam Snaffles, to *obzarve* yourself in the glass. I telled you that seeing warn't edzactly obzarving. You seed only the inches; you seed that you hed eyes and mouth and nose and the airms and legs of the man. But eyes and mouth and legs and airms don't make a man!'

" 'Oh, they don't!' says I.

" 'No, indeed,' says he. 'I seed that you hed all them; but then I seed thar was one thing that you hedn't got.'

" 'Jimini!' says I, mighty conflustered. 'What thing's a-wanting to me to make me a man?'

" '*Capital!*' says he, and he lifted himself up and looked mighty grand.

" 'Capital!' says I; 'and what's that?'

" 'Thar air many kinds of capital,' says he. 'Money's capital, for it kin buy every thing. House and lands is capital; cattle and horses and sheep—when thar's enough on 'em—is capital. And as I obzarved you in the glass, Sam Snaffles, I seed that *capital* was the very thing that you wanted to make a man of you! Now I don't mean that any da'ter of mine shall marry a pusson that's not a *parfect* man. I obzarved you long ago, and seed whar you was wanting. I axed about you. I axed your horse.'

" 'Axed my horse!' says I, pretty nigh dumbfoundered.

" 'Yes; I axed your horse, and he said to me: "Look at me! I hain't got an ounce of spar' flesh on my bones. You kin count all my ribs. You kin lay the whole length of your airm betwixt any two on 'em, and it'll lie thar as snug as a black snake betwixt two poles of a log-house." Says he, "Sam's got *no capital!* He ain't got, any time, five bushels of corn in his crib; and he's such a monstrous feeder himself that he'll eat out four bushels, and think it mighty hard upon him to give *me* the other one." Thar, now, was your horse's testimony, Sam, agin you. Then I axed about your cabin, and your way of living. I was curious, and went to see you one day when I knowed you waur at home. You hed but one chair, which you gin me to set on, and you sot on the eend of a barrel for yourself. You gin me a rasher of bacon what hedn't a streak of fat in it. You hed a poor quarter of a poor doe hanging from the rafters—a poor beast that somebody hed disabled—'

" 'I shot it myself,' says I.

" 'Well, it was a-dying when you shot it; and all the hunters say you was a poor shooter at any thing. You cooked our dinner yourself, and the hoe-cake was all dough, not hafe done, and the meat was all done as tough as ef you had dried it for a month of Sundays in a Flurriday sun! Your cabin had but one room, and that you slept in and ate in; and the floor was six inches deep in dirt! Then, when I looked into your garden, I found seven stalks of long collards only, every one seven foot high, with all the leaves stript off it, as ef you wanted 'em for broth; till thar waur only three top leaves left on every stalk. You hedn't a stalk of corn growing, and when I scratched at your turnip-bed I found nothing bigger than a chestnut. Then, Sam, I begun to ask about your fairm, and I found that you was nothing but a squatter on land of Columbus Mills, who let you have an old nigger pole-house, and an acre or two of land. Says I to myself, says I, "This poor fellow's got *no capital*; and he hasn't the head to git *capital*;" and from that moment, Sam Snaffles, the more I obzarved you, the more sartin 'twas that you never could be a man, ef you waur to live a thousand years. You may think, in your vanity, that you air a man; but you ain't, and never will be, onless you kin find a way to git *capital*; and I loves my gal child too much to let her marry any pusson whom I don't altogether consider a man!'

"A'ter that long speechifying, Jedge, you might ha' ground me up in a mill, biled me down in a pot, and scattered me over a manure heap, and I wouldn't ha' been able to say a word!

"I cotched up my hat, and was a-gwine, when he said to me, with his derned infernal big grin:

" 'Take another look in the glass, Sam Snaffles, and obzarve well, and you'll see jest whar it is I thinks that you're wanting.'

"I didn't stop for any more. I jest bolted, like a hot shot out of a shovel, and didn't know my own self, or whatever steps I tuk, tell I got into the thick and met Merry Ann coming towards me.

"I must liquor now!"

V

"Well, Jedge, it was a hard meeting betwixt me and Merry Ann. The poor gal come to me in a sort of run, and hairdly drawing her breath, she cried out:

" 'Oh, Sam! What does he say?'

"What could I say? How tell her? I jest wrapped her up in my airms, and I cries out, making some violent remarks about the old Squaire.

"Then she screamed, and I hed to squeeze her up, more close than ever, and kiss her, I reckon, more than a dozen times, jest to keep her from gwine into historical fits. I telled her all, from beginning to eend.

"I telled her that thar waur some truth in what the old man said: that I hedn't been keerful to do the thing as I ought; that the house *was* mean and dirty; that the horse was mean and poor; that I hed been thinking too much about her own self to think about other things; but that I would do better, would see to things, put things right, git corn in the crib, git 'capital,' ef I could, and make a good, comfortable home for *her*.

" 'Look at me,' says I, 'Merry Ann. Does I look like a man?'

" 'You're all the man I wants,' says she.

" 'That's enough,' says I. 'You shall see what I kin do, and what I *will* do! That's ef you air true to me.'

" 'I'll be true to you, Sam,' says she.

" 'And you won't think of nobody else?'

" 'Never,' says she.

" 'Well, you'll see what I kin do, and what I *will* do. You'll see that I *em* a man; and ef thar's capital to be got in all the country, by working and hunting, and fighting, ef that's needful, we shill hev it. Only you be true to me, Merry Ann.'

"And she throwed herself upon my buzzom, and cried out:

" 'I'll be true to you, Sam. I loves nobody in all the world so much as I loves you.'

" 'And you won't marry any other man, Merry Ann, no matter what your daddy says?'

" 'Never,' she says.

" 'And you won't listen to this old bachelor fellow, Grimstead, that's got the "capital" already, no matter how they spurs you?'

" 'Never!' she says.

" 'Sw'ar it!' says I—'sw'ar it, Merry Ann—that you will be my wife, and never marry Grimstead!'

" 'I sw'ars it,' she says, kissing *me*, bekaize we had no book.

" 'Now,' says I, 'Merry Ann, that's not enough. Cuss him for my sake, and to make it sartin. Cuss that fellow Grimstead.'

" 'Oh, Sam, I kain't cuss,' says she; 'that's wicked.'

" 'Cuss him on my account,' says I—'to my credit.'

" 'Oh,' says she, 'don't ax me. I kain't do that.'

"Says I, 'Merry Ann, if you don't cuss that fellow, some way, I do believe you'll go over to him a'ter all. Jest you cuss him, now. Any small cuss will do, ef you're in airnest.'

" 'Well,' says she, 'ef that's your idee, then I says, "*Drot his skin*,* and drot *my* skin, too, ef ever I marries any body but Sam Snaffles." '

" 'That'll do, Merry Ann,' says I. 'And now I'm easy in my soul and conscience. And now, Merry Ann, I'm gwine off to try my best, and git the "capital." Ef it's the "capital" that's needful to make a man of me, I'll git it, by all the Holy Hokies, if I kin.'

---

* "Drot," or "Drat," has been called an American vulgarism, but it is genuine old English, as ancient as the days of Ben Johnson. Originally the oath was, "God rot it," but Puritanism, which was unwilling to take the name of God in vain, was yet not prepared to abandon the oath, so the pious preserved it in an abridged form, omitting the *G* from God, and using, "Od rot it." It reached its final contraction, "Drot," before it came to America. "Drot it," "Drat it," "Drot your eyes," or "Drot his skin," are so many modes of using it among the uneducated classes.

"And so, after a million of squeezes and kisses, we parted; and she slipt along through the woods, the back way to the house, and I mounted my horse to go to my cabin. But, afore I mounted the beast, I gin him a dozen kicks in his ribs, jest for bearing his testimony agin me, and telling the old Squaire that I hedn't 'capital' enough for a corn crib."

VI

"I was mightily let down, as you may think, by old Squaire Hopson; but I was mightily lifted up by Merry Ann.

"But when I got to my cabin, and seed how mean every thing was there, and thought how true it was, all that old Squaire Hopson had said, I felt overkim, and I said to myself, 'It's all true! How kin I bring that beautiful yaller flower of the forest to live in sich a mean cabin, and with sich poor accommydations? She that had every thing comforting and nice about her.'

"Then I considered all about 'capital;' and it growed on me, ontil I begin to see that a man might hev good legs and arms and thighs, and a good face of his own, and yit not be a parfect and proper man a'ter all! I hed lived, you see, Jedge, to be twenty-three years of age, and was living no better than a three-old-year b'ar, in a sort of cave, sleeping on shuck and straw, and never looking after to-morrow.

"I couldn't sleep all that night for the thinking, and obzarvations. That impudent talking of old Hopson put me on a new track. I couldn't give up hunting. I knowed no other business, and I didn't hafe know that.

"I thought to myself, 'I must l'arn my business so as to work like a master.'

"But then, when I considered how hard it was, how slow I was to git the deers and the b'ar, and what a small chaince of money it brought me, I said to myself:

" 'Whar's the "capital" to come from?'

"Lawd save us! I ate up the meat pretty much as fast as I got it!

"Well, Jedge, as I said, I had a most miserable night of consideration and obzarvation and concatenation accordingly. I felt all over mean, 'cept now and then, when I thought of dear Merry Ann, and her felicities and cordialities and fidelities; and then, the cuss which she gin, onder the kiver of 'Drot,' to that dried up old bachelor Grimstead. But I got to sleep at last. And I hed a dream. And I thought I seed the prettiest woman critter in the world, next to Merry Ann, standing close by my bedside; and, at first, I thought 'twas Merry Ann, and I was gwine to kiss her agin; but she drawed back and said:

" ''Scuse me! I'm not Merry Ann; but I'm her friend and your friend; so don't you be down in the mouth, but keep a good hairt, and you'll hev help, and git the "capital" whar you don't look for it now. It's only needful that you be detarmined on good works and making a man of yourself.'

"A'ter that dream I slept like a top, woke at day-peep, took my rifle, called up my dog, mounted my horse, and put out for the laurel hollows.

"Well, I hunted all day, made several *starts*, but got nothing; my dog ran off, the rascally pup, and, I reckon, ef Squaire Hopson had met him he'd ha' said 'twas bekaise I starved him! Fact is, we hedn't any on us much to eat that day, and the old mar's ribs stood out bigger than ever.

"All day I rode and followed the track and got nothing.

"Well, jest about sunset I come to a hollow of the hills that I hed never seed before; and in the middle of it was a great pond of water, what you call a lake; and it showed like so much purple glass in the sunset, and 'twas jest as smooth as the big looking-glass of Squaire Hopson's. Thar wa'n't a breath of wind stirring.

"I was mighty tired, so I eased down from the mar', tied up the bridle and check, and let her pick about, and laid myself down onder a tree, jest about twenty yards from the lake, and thought to rest myself ontil the moon riz, which I knowed would be about seven o'clock.

"I didn't mean to fall asleep, but I did it; and I reckon I must ha' slept a good hour, for when I woke the dark hed set in, and I could only see one or two right stars hyar and thar, shooting out from the dark of the heavens. But, ef I seed nothing, I haird; and jest sich a sound and noise as I hed never haird before.

"Thar was a rushing and a roaring and a screaming and a plashing, in the air and in the water, as made you think the univarsal world was coming to an eend!

"All that set me up. I was waked up out of sleep and dream, and my eyes opened to every thing that eye could see; and sich another sight I never seed before! I tell you, Jedge, ef there was one wild-goose settling down in that lake, thar was one hundred thousand of em! I couldn't see the eend of 'em. They come every minit, swarm a'ter swarm, in tens and twenties and fifties and hundreds; and sich a fuss as they did make! sich a gabbling, sich a splashing, sich a confusion, that I was fairly conflusterated; and I jest lay whar I was, a-watching 'em.

"You never seed beasts so happy! How they flapped their wings; how they gabbled to one another; how they swam hyar and thar, to the very middle of the lake and to the very edge of it, jest a fifty yards from whar I lay squat, never moving leg or arm! It was wonderful to see! I wondered how they could find room, for I reckon thar waur forty thousand on 'em, all scuffling in that leetle lake together!

"Well, as I watched 'em, I said to myself:

" 'Now, if a fellow could only captivate all them wild-geese—fresh from Canniday, I reckon—what would they bring in the market at Spartanburg and Greenville? Walker, I knowed, would buy 'em up quick at fifty cents a head. Forty thousand geese at fifty cents a head. Thar was "capital!" '

"I could ha' fired in among 'em with my rifle, never taking aim, and killed a dozen or more, at a single shot; but what was a poor dozen geese, when thar waur forty thousand to captivate?

"What a haul 'twould be, ef a man could only get 'em all in one net! Kiver 'em all at a fling!

"The idee worked like so much fire in my brain.

"How kin it be done?

"That was the question!

" 'Kin it be done?' I axed myself.

" 'It kin,' I said to myself; 'and I'm the very man to do it!' Then I begun to work away in the thinking. I thought over all the traps and nets and snares that I hed ever seen or haird of; and the leetle eends of the idee begun to come together in my head; and, watching all the time how the geese flopped and splashed and played and swum, I said to myself:

" 'Oh! most beautiful critters! ef I don't make some "capital" out of you, then I'm not dezarving sich a beautiful yaller flower of the forest as my Merry Ann!'

"Well, I watched a long time, ontil dark night, and the stars begun to peep down upon me over the high hill-tops. Then I got up and tuk to my horse and rode home.

"And thar, when I hed swallowed my bit of hoe-cake and bacon and a good strong cup of coffee, and got into bed, I couldn't sleep for a long time, thinking how I was to git them geese.

"But I kept nearing the right idee every minit, and when I was fast asleep it come to me in my dream.

"I seed the same beautifulest young woman agin that hed given me the incouragement before to go ahead, and she helped me out with the idee.

"So, in the morning, I went to work. I rode off to Spartanburg, and bought all the twine and cord and hafe the plow-lines in town; and I got a lot of great fishhooks, all to help make the tanglement parfect; and I got lead for sinkers, and I got cork-wood for floaters; and I pushed for home jist as fast as my poor mar' could streak it.

"I was at work day and night, for nigh on to a week, making my net; and when 'twas done I borrowed a mule and cart from Columbus Mills, thar;—he'll tell you all about it—he kin make his affidavy to the truth of it.

"Well, off I driv with my great net, and got to the lake about noonday. I knowed 'twould take me some hours to make my fixings parfect, and git the net fairly stretched across the lake, and jest deep enough to do the tangling of every leg of the birds in the very midst of their swimming and snorting and splashing and cavorting! When I hed fixed it all fine, and jest as I wanted it, I brought the eends of my plow-lines up to where I was gwine to hide myself. This was onder a strong sapling, and my calkilation was when I hed got the beasts all hooked, forty thousand, more or less—and I could tell how that was from feeling on the line—why, then, I'd whip the line round the sapling, hitch it fast, and draw in my birds at my own ease, without axing much about their comfort.

" 'Twas a most beautiful and parfect plan, and all would ha' worked beautiful well but for one leetle oversight of mine. But I won't tell you about that part of the business yit, the more pretickilarly as it all turned out for the very best, as you'll see in the eend.

"I hedn't long finished my fixings when the sun suddenly tumbled down the heights, and the dark begun to creep in upon me, and a pretty cold dark it waur! I remember it well! My teeth begun to chatter in my head, though I was boiling over with inward heat, all jest coming out of my hot eagerness to be captivating the birds.

"Well, Jedge, I hedn't to wait overlong. Soon I haird them coming, screaming fur away, and then I seed them pouring, jest like so many white clouds, straight down, I reckon, from the snow mountains off in Canniday.

"Down they come, millions upon millions, till I was sartin thar waur already pretty nigh on to forty thousand in the lake. It waur always a nice calkilation of mine that the lake could hold fully forty thousand, though onst, when I went round to measure it, stepping it off, I was jubous whether it could hold over thirty-nine thousand; but, as I tuk the measure in hot weather and in a dry spell, I concluded that some of the water along the edges hed dried up, and 'twa'n't so full as when I made my first calkilation. So I hev stuck to that first calkilation ever since.

"Well, thar they waur, forty thousand, we'll say, with, it mout be, a few millions and hundreds over. And Lawd! how they played and splashed and screamed and dived! I calkilated on hooking a good many of them divers, in pretickilar, and so I watched and waited, ontil I thought I'd feel of my lines; and I begun leetle by leetle, to haul in, when, Lawd love you, Jedge, sich a ripping and raging, and bouncing and flouncing, and flopping and splashing, and kicking and screaming, you never did hear in all your born days!

"By this I knowed that I hed captivated the captains of the host, and a pretty smart chaince, I reckoned, of the rigilar army, ef 'twa'n't edzactly forty thousand; for I calkilated that some few would get away—run off, jest as the cowards always does in the army, jest when the shooting and confusion begins; still, I reasonably calkilated on the main body of the rigiments; and so, gitting more and more hot and eager, and pulling and hauling, I make one big mistake, and, instid of wrapping the eends of my lines around the sapling that was standing jest behind me, what does I do but wraps 'em round my own thigh—the right thigh, you see—and some of the loops waur hitched round my left arm at the same time!

"All this come of my hurry and ixcitement, for it was burning like a hot fever in my brain, and I didn't know when or how I hed tied myself up, ontil suddently, with an all-fired scream, all together them forty thousand geese rose like a great black cloud in the air, all tied up, tangled up—hooked about the legs, hooked about the gills, hooked and fast in some way in the beautiful leetle twistings of my net!

"Yes, Jedge, as I'm a living hunter to-night, hyar a-talking to you, they riz up all together, as ef they hed consulted upon it, like a mighty thunder-cloud, and off they went, screaming and flouncing, meaning, I reckon, to take the back track to Canniday, in spite of the freezing weather.

"Before I knowed whar I was, Jedge, I was twenty feet in the air, my right thigh up and my left arm, and the other thigh and arm a-dangling useless, and feeling every minit as ef they was gwine to drop off.

"You may be sure I pulled with all my might, but that waur mighty leetle in the fix I was in, and I jest hed to hold on, and see whar the infernal beasts would carry me. I couldn't loose myself, and ef I could I was by this time quite too fur up in the air, and darsn't do so, onless I was willing to hev my brains dashed out, and my whole body mashed to a mammock!

"Oh, Jedge, jest consider my sitivation! It's sich a ricollection, Jedge, that I must rest and liquor, in order to rekiver the necessary strength to tell you what happened next."

VII

"Yes, Jedge," said Yaou, resuming his narrative, "jest stop whar you air, and consider my sitivation!

"Thar I was dangling, like a dead weight, at the tail of that all-fired cloud of wild-geese, head downward, and gwine, the Lawd knows whar—to Canniday, or Jericho, or some other heathen territory beyond the Massissipp, and it mout be, over the great etarnal ocean!

"When I thought of *that*, and thought of the plow-lines giving way, and that on a suddent I should come down plump into the big sea, jest in the middle of a great gathering of shirks and whales, to be dewoured and tore to bits by their bloody grinders, I was ready to die of skeer outright. I thought over all my sinnings in a moment, and I thought of my poor dear Merry Ann, and I called out her name, loud as I could, jest as ef the poor gal could hyar me or help me.

"And jest then I could see we waur a drawing nigh a great thunder-cloud. I could see the red tongues running out of its black jaws; and 'Lawd!' says I, 'ef these all-fired infarnal wild beasts of birds should carry me into that cloud to be burned to a coal, fried, and roasted, and biled alive by them tongues of red fire!'

"But the geese fought shy of the cloud, though we passed mighty nigh on to it, and I could see one red streak of lightning run out of the cloud and give us chase for a full hafe a mile; but we waur too fast for it, and, in a tearing passion bekaise it couldn't ketch us, the red streak struck its horns into a great tree jest behind us, that we hed passed over, and tore it into flinders, in the twink of a musquito.

"But by this time I was beginning to feel quite stupid. I knowed that I waur fast gitting onsensible, and it did seem to me as ef my hour waur come, and I was gwine to die—and die by rope, and dangling in the air, a thousand miles from the airth!

"But jest then I was roused up. I felt something brush agin me; then my face was scratched; and, on a suddent, thar was a stop put to my travels by that conveyance. The geese had stopped flying, and waur in a mighty great conflusteration, flopping their wings, as well as they could, and screaming with all the tongues in their jaws. It was clar to me now that we hed run agin something that brought us all up with a short hitch.

"I was shook roughly agin the obstruction, and I put out my right arm and cotched a hold of a long arm of an almighty big tree; then my legs waur cotched betwixt two other branches, and I rekivered myself, so as to set up a leetle and rest. The geese was a tumbling and flopping among the branches. The net was hooked hyar and thar; and the birds waur all about me, swinging and splurging, but onable to break loose and git away.

"By leetle and leetle I come to my clar senses, and begun to feel my sitivation. The stiffness was passing out of my limbs. I could draw up my legs, and, after some hard work, I managed to onwrap the plow-lines from my right thigh and my left arm, and I hed the sense this time to tie the eends pretty tight to a great branch of the tree which stretched clar across and about a foot over my head.

"Then I begun to consider my sitivation. I hed hed a hard riding, that was sartin; and I felt sore enough. And I hed hed a horrid bad skear, enough to make a man's wool turn white afore the night was over. But now I felt easy, bekaise I considered myself safe. With day-peep I calkilated to let myself down from the tree by my plow-lines, and thar, below, tied fast, warn't thar my forty thousand captivated geese?

" 'Hurrah!' I sings out. 'Hurrah, Merry Ann; we'll hev the "capital" now, I reckon!'

"And singing out, I drawed up my legs and shifted my body so as to find an easier seat in the crutch of the tree, which was an almighty big chestnut oak, when, O Lawd! on a suddent the stump I hed been a-setting on give way onder me. 'Twas a rotten jint of the tree. It give way, Jedge, as I tell you, and down I went, my legs first and then my whole body—slipping down not on the outside, but into a great hollow of the tree, all the hairt of it being eat out by the rot; and afore I knowed whar I waur, I waur some twenty foot down, I reckon; and by the time I touched bottom, I was up to my neck in honey!

"It was an almighty big honey-tree, full of the sweet treacle; and the bees all gone and left it, I reckon, for a hundred years. And I in it up to my neck.

"I could smell it strong. I could taste it sweet. But I could see nothing.

"Lawd! Lawd! From bad to worse; buried alive in a hollow tree with never a chaince to git out! I would then ha' given all the world ef I was only sailing away with them bloody wild-geese to Canniday, and Jericho, even across the sea, with all its shirks and whales dewouring me.

"Buried alive! O Lawd! O Lawd! 'Lawd save me and help me!' I cried out from the depths. And 'Oh, my Merry Ann,' I cried, 'shill we never meet agin no more!' 'Scuse my weeping, Jedge, but I feels all over the sinsation, fresh as ever, of being buried alive in a bee-hive tree and presarved in honey. I must liquor, Jedge."

VIII

Yaou, after a great swallow of peach and honey, and a formidable groan after it, resumed his narrative as follows:

"Only think of me, Jedge, in my sitivation! Buried alive in the hollow of a mountain chestnut oak! Up to my neck in honey, with never no more an appetite to eat than ef it waur the very gall of bitterness that we reads of in the Holy Scripters!

"All dark, all silent as the grave; 'cept for the gabbling and the cackling of the wild-geese outside, that every now and then would make a great splurging and cavorting, trying to break away from their hitch, which was jist as fast fixed as my own.

"Who would git them geese that hed cost me so much to captivate? Who would inherit my 'capital?' and who would hev Merry Ann? and what will become of the mule and cart of Mills fastened in the woods by the leetle lake?

"I cussed the leetle lake, and the geese, and all the 'capital.'

"I cussed. I couldn't help it. I cussed from the bottom of my hairt, when I ought to ha' bin saying my prayers. And thar was my poor mar' in the stable with never a morsel of feed. She had told tales upon me to

Squaire Hopson, it's true, but I forgin her, and thought of her feed, and nobody to give her none. Thar waur corn in the crib and fodder, but it warn't in the stable; and onless Columbus Mills should come looking a'ter me at the cabin, thar waur no hope for me or the mar'.

"Oh, Jedge, you could't jedge of my sitivation in that deep hollow, that cave, I may say, of mountain oak! My head waur jest above the honey, and ef I backed it to look up, my long ha'r at the back of the neck a'most stuck fast, so thick was the honey.

"But I couldn't help looking up. The hollow was a wide one at the top, and I could see when a star was passing over. Thar they shined, bright and beautiful, as ef they waur the very eyes of the angels; and, as I seed them come and go, looking smiling in upon me as they come, I cried out to 'em, one by one:

" 'Oh, sweet sperrits, blessed angels! ef so be thar's an angel sperrit, as they say, living in all them stars, come down and extricate me from this fix; for, so fur as I kin see, I've got no chaince of help from mortal man or woman. Hairdly onst a year does a human come this way; and ef they did come, how would they know I'm hyar? How could I make them hyar me? O Lawd! O blessed, beautiful angels in them stars! O give me help! Help me out!' I knowed I prayed like a heathen sinner, but I prayed as well as I knowed how; and thar warn't a star passing over me that I didn't pray to, soon as I seed them shining over the opening of the hollow; and I prayed fast and faster as I seed them passing away and gitting out of sight.

"Well, Jedge, suddently, in the midst of my praying, and jest after one bright, big star hed gone over me without seeing my sitivation, I hed a fresh skeer.

"Suddent I haird a monstrous fluttering among my geese—my 'capital.' Then I haird a great scraping and scratching on the outside of the tree, and, suddent, as I looked up, the mouth of the hollow was shet up.

"All was dark. The stars and sky waur all gone. Something black kivered the hollow, and, in a minit a'ter, I haird something slipping down into the hollow right upon me.

"I could hairdly draw my breath. I begun to fear that I was to be siffocated alive; and as I haird the strange critter slipping down, I shoved out my hands and felt ha'r—coarse wool—and with one hand I cotched hold of the ha'ry leg of a beast, and with t'other hand I cotched hold of his tail.

" 'Twas a great b'ar, one of the biggest, come to git his honey. He knowed the tree, Jedge, you see, and ef any beast in the world loves honey, 'tis a ba'r beast. He'll go his death on honey, though the hounds are tearing at his very haunches.

"You may be sure, when I onst knowed what he was, and onst got a good gripe on his hindquarters, I warn't gwine to let go in a hurry. I knowed that was my only chaince for gitting out of the hollow, and I do believe them blessed angels in the stars sent the beast, jest at the right time, to give me human help and assistance.

"Now, yer see, Jedge, thar was no chaince for him turning round upon me. He pretty much filled up the hollow. He knowed his way, and slipped down, eend foremost—the latter eend, you know. He could stand up on his hind-legs and eat all he wanted. Then, with his great sharp claws and his mighty muscle, he could work up, holding on to the sides of the tree, and git out a'most as easy as when he come down.

"Now, you see, ef he weighed five hundred pounds, and could climb like a cat, he could easy carry up a young fellow that hed no flesh to spar', and only weighed a hundred and twenty-five. So I laid my weight on him, eased him off as well as I could, but held on to tail and leg as ef all life and etarnity depended upon it.

"Now I reckon, Jedge, that b'ar was pretty much more skeered than I was. He couldn't turn in his shoes, and with something fastened to his ankles, and, as he thought, I reckon, some strange beast fastened to his tail, you never seed beast more eager to git away, and git upwards. He knowed the way, and stuck his claws in the rough sides of the hollow, hand over hand, jest as a sailor pulls a rope, and up we went. We hed, howsomdever, more than one slip back; but, Lawd bless you! I never let go. Up we went, I say, at last, and I stuck jest as close to his haunches as death sticks to a dead nigger. Up we went. I felt myself moving. My neck was out of the honey. My airms were free. I could feel the sticky thing slipping off from me, and a'ter a good quarter of an hour the b'ar was on the great mouth of the hollow; and as I felt that I let go his tail, still keeping fast hold of his leg, and with one hand I cotched hold of the outside rim of the hollow; I found it fast, held on to it; and jest then the b'ar sat squat on the very edge of the hollow, taking a sort of rest a'ter his labor.

"I don't know what 'twas, Jedge, that made me do it. I warn't a-thinking at all. I was only feeling and drawing a long breath. Jest then the b'ar sort o' looked round, as ef to see what varmint it was a-troubling him, when I gin him a mighty push, strong as I could, and he lost his balance and went over outside down cl'ar to the airth, and I could hyar his neck crack, almost as loud as a pistol.

"I drawed a long breath a'ter that, and prayed a short prayer; and feeling my way all the time, so as to be sure agin rotten branches, I got a safe seat among the limbs of the tree, and sot myself down, determined to wait tell broad daylight before I tuk another step in the business."

IX

"And thar I sot. So fur as I could see, Jedge, I was safe. I hed got out of the tie of the flying geese, and thar they all waur, spread before me, flopping now and then and trying to ixtricate themselves; but they couldn't come it! Thar they waur, captivated, and so much 'capital' for Sam Snaffles.

"And I hed got out of the lion's den; that is, I hed got out of the honey-tree and warn't in no present danger of being buried alive agin. Thanks to the b'ar, and to the blessed, beautiful angel sperrits in the stars, that hed sent him thar seeking honey, to be my deliverance from my captivation!

"And thar he lay, jest as quiet as ef he waur a-sleeping, though I knowed his neck was broke. And that b'ar, too, was so much 'capital.'

"And I sot in the tree making my calkilations. I could see now the meaning of that beautiful young critter that come to me in my dreams. I was to hev the 'capital,' but I was to git it through troubles and tribulations, and a mighty bad skeer for life. I never knowed the valley of 'capital' till now, and I seed the sense in all that Squaire Hopson told me, though he did tell it in a mighty spiteful sperrit.

"Well, I calkilated.

"It was cold weather, freezing, and though I had good warm clothes on, I felt monstrous like sleeping, from the cold only, though perhaps the tire and the skeer together had something to do with it. But I was afeard to sleep. I didn't know what would happen, and a man has never his right courage ontil daylight. I fou't agin sleep by keeping on my calkilation.

"Forty thousand wild-geese!

"Thar wa'n't forty thousand, edzactly—very far from it—but thar they waur, pretty thick; and for every goose I could git from forty to sixty cents in all the villages in South Carolina.

"Thar was 'capital!'

"Then thar waur the b'ar.

"Jedging from his strength in pulling me up, and from his size and fat in filling up that great hollow in the tree, I calkilated that he couldn't weigh less than five hundred pounds. His hide, I knowed, was worth twenty dollars. Then thar was the fat and tallow, and the biled marrow out of his bones, what they makes b'ars grease out of, to make chicken whiskers grow big enough for game-cocks. Then thar waur the meat, skinned, cleaned, and all; thar couldn't be much onder four hundred and fifty pounds, and whether I sold him as fresh meat or cured, he'd bring me ten cents a pound at the least.

"Says I, 'Thar's capital!'

" 'Then,' says I, 'thar's my honey-tree! I reckon thar's a matter of ten thousand gallons in this hyar same honey-tree; and if I kint git fifty to seventy cents a gallon for it thar's no alligators in Flurriday!'

"And so I calkilated through the night, fighting agin sleep, and thinking of my 'capital' and Merry Ann together.

"By morning I had calkilated all I hed to do and all I hed to make.

"Soon as I got a peep of day I was bright on the look-out.

"Thar all around me were the captivated geese critters. The b'ar laid down parfectly easy and waiting for the knife; and the geese, I reckon they waur much more tired than me, for they didn't seem to hev the hairt for a single flutter, even when they seed me swing down from the tree among 'em, holding on to my plow-lines and letting myself down easy.

"But first I must tell you, Jedge, when I seed the first signs of daylight and looked around me, Lawd bless me, what should I see but old Tryon Mountain, with his great head lifting itself up in the east! And beyant I could see the house and fairm of Columbus Mills; and as I turned to look a leetle south of that, thar was my own poor leetle log-cabin standing quiet, but with never a smoke streaming out from the chimbley.

" 'God bless them good angel sperrits,' I said, 'I ain't two miles from home!' Before I come down from the tree I knowed edzactly whar I waur. 'Twas only four miles off from the lake and whar I hitched the mule of Columbus Mills close by the cart. Thar, too, I hed left my rifle. Yit in my miserable fix, carried through the air by them wild-geese, I did think I hed gone a'most a thousand miles towards Canniday.

"Soon as I got down from the tree I pushed off at a trot to git the mule and cart. I was pretty sure of my b'ar and geese when I come back. The cart stood quiet enough. But the mule, having nothing to eat, was sharping her teeth upon a boulder, thinking she'd hev a bite or so before long.

"I hitched her up, brought her to my bee-tree, tumbled the b'ar into the cart, wrung the necks of all the geese that waur thar—many hed got away—and counted some twenty-seven hundred that I piled away atop of the b'ar."

"Twenty-seven hundred!" cried the "Big Lie" and all the hunters at a breath. "Twenty-seven hundred! Why, Yaou, whenever you telled of this thing before you always counted them at 3150!"

"Well, ef I did, I reckon I was right. I was sartinly right then, it being all fresh in my 'membrance; and I'm not the man to go back agin his own words. No, fellows, I sticks to first words and first principles. I scorns to eat my own words. Ef I said 3150, then 3150 it waur, never a goose less. But you'll see how to 'count for all. I reckon 'twas only 2700 I fotched to market. Thar was 200 I gin to Columbus Mills. Then thar was 200 more I carried to Merry Ann; and then thar waur 50 at least, I reckon, I kep for myself. Jest you count up, Jedge, and you'll see how to squar' it on all sides. When I said 2700 I only counted what I sold in the villages, every head of 'em at fifty cents a head; and a'ter putting the money in my pocket I felt all over that I hed the 'capital.'

"Well, Jedge, next about the b'ar. Sold the hide and tallow for a fine market-price; sold the meat, got ten cents a pound for it fresh—'twas most beautiful meat; biled down the bones for the marrow; melted down the grease; sold fourteen pounds of it to the barbers and apothecaries; got a dollar a pound for that; sold the hide for twenty dollars; and got the cash for every thing.

"Thar warn't a fambly in all Greenville and Spartanburg and Asheville that didn't git fresh, green wild-geese from me that season, at fifty cents a head, and glad to git, too; the cheapest fresh meat they could buy; and, I reckon, the finest. And all the people of them villages, ef they hed gone to heaven that week, in the flesh, would have carried nothing better than goose-flesh for the risurrection! Every body ate goose for a month, I reckon, as the weather was freezing cold all the time, and the beasts kept week after week, ontil they waur eaten. From the b'ar only I made a matter of full one hundred dollars. First, thar waur the hide, $20; then 450 pounds of meat, at 10 cents, was $45; then the grease, 14 pounds, $14; and the tallow, some $6 more; and the biled marrow, $11.

Well, count up, Jedge; 2700 wild-geese, at 50 cents, you sees, must be more than $1350. I kin only say, that a'ter all the selling—and I driv at it day and night, with Columbus Mills's mule and cart, and went to every house in every street in all them villages—I hed a'most fifteen hundred dollars, safe stowed away onder the pillows of my bed, all in solid gould and silver.

"But I warn't done! Thar was my bee-tree. Don't you think I waur gwine to lose that honey! no, my darlint! I didn't beat the drum about nothing. I didn't let on to a soul what I was a-doing. They axed me about the wild-geese, but I sent 'em on a wild-goose chase; and 'twan't till I hed sold off all the b'ar meat and all the geese that I made ready to git at that honey. I reckon them bees must ha' been making that honey for a hundred years, and was then driv out by the b'ars.

"Columbus Mills will tell you; he axed me all about it; but, though he was always my good friend, I never even telled it to him. But he lent me his mule and cart, good fellow as he is, and never said nothing more; and, quiet enough, without beat of drum, I bought up all the tight-bound barrels that ever brought whisky to Spartanburg and Greenville, whar they hes the taste for that article strong; and day by day I went off carrying as many barrels as the cart could hold and the mule could draw. I tapped the old tree—which was one of the oldest and biggest chestnut oaks I ever did see—close to the bottom, and drawed off the beautiful treacle. I was more than sixteen days about it, and got something over two thousand gallons of the purest, sweetest, yellowest honey you ever did see. I could hairdly git barrels and jimmyjohns enough to hold it; and I sold it out at seventy cents a gallon, which was mighty cheap. So I got from the honey a matter of fourteen hundred dollars.

"Now, Jedge, all this time, though it went very much agin the grain, I kept away from Merry Ann and the old Squaire, her daddy. I sent him two hundred head of geese—some fresh, say one hundred, and another hundred that I hed cleaned and put in salt—and I sent him three jimmyjohns of honey, five gallons each. But I kept away and said nothing, beat no drum, and hed never a thinking but how to git in the 'capital.' And I did git it in!

"When I carried the mule and cart home to Columbus Mills I axed him about a sartin farm of one hundred and sixty acres that he hed to sell. It hed a good house on it. He selled it to me cheap. I paid him down, and put the titles in my pocket. 'Thar's capital!' says I.

"*That* waur a fixed thing for ever and ever. And when I hed moved every thing from the old cabin to the new farm, Columbus let me hev a fine milch cow that gin eleven quarts a day, with a beautiful young caif. Jest about that time thar was a great sale of the furniter of the Ashmore family down at Spartanburg, and I remembered I hed no decent bedstead, or any thing rightly sarving for a young woman's chamber; so I went to the sale, and bought a fine strong mahogany bedstead, a dozen chairs, a chist of drawers, and some other things that ain't quite mentionable, Jedge, but all proper for a lady's chamber; and I soon hed the house fixed up ready for any thing. And up to this time I never let on to any body what I was a-thinking about or what I was a-doing, ontil I could stand up in my own doorway and look about me, and say to myself—this is my 'capital,' I reckon; and when I hed got all that I thought a needcessity to git, I took 'count of every thing.

"I spread the title-deeds of my fairm out on the table. I read 'em over three times to see ef 'twaur all right. Thar was my name several times in big letters, 'to hev and to hold.'

"Then I fixed the furniter. Then I brought out into the stable-yard the old mar'—you couldn't count her ribs *now*, and she was spry as ef she hed got a new conceit of herself.

"Then thar was my beautiful new cow and caif, sealing fat, both on 'em, and sleek as a doe in autumn.

"Then thar waur a fine young mule that I bought in Spartanburg; my cart, and a strong second-hand buggy, that could carry two pussons convenient of two different sexes. And I felt big, like a man of consekence and capital.

"That warn't all.

"I had the shiners, Jedge, besides—all in gould and silver—none of your dirty rags and blotty spotty paper. That was the time of Old Hickory—General Jackson, you know—when he kicked over Nick Biddle's consarn, and gin us the beautiful Benton Mint Drops, in place of rotten paper. You could git the gould and silver jest for the axing, in them days, you know.

"I hed a grand count of my money, Jedge. I hed it in a dozen or twenty little bags of leather—the gould—and the silver I hed in shot-bags. It took me a whole morning to count it up and git the figgers right. Then I stuffed it in my pockets, hyar and thar, every whar, wharever I could stow a bag; and the silver I stuffed away in my saddle-bags, and clapped it on the mar'.

"Then I mounted myself, and sot the mar's nose straight in a bee-line for the fairm of Squaire Hopson.

"I was a-gwine, you see, to supprise him with my 'capital;' but, fust, I meant to give him a mighty grand skeer.

"You see, when I was a-trading with Columbus Mills about the fairm and cattle and other things, I ups and tells him about my courting of Merry Ann; and when I telled him about Squaire Hopson's talk about 'capital,' he says:

" 'The old skunk! What right hes he to be talking big so, when he kain't pay his own debts. He's been owing me three hundred and fifty dollars now gwine on three years, and I kain't git even the *intrust* out of him. I've got a mortgage on his fairm for the whole, and ef he won't let you hev his da'ter, jest you come to me, and I'll clap the screws to him in short order.'

"Says I, 'Columbus, won't you sell me that mortgage?'

" 'You shill hev it for the face of the debt,' says he, 'not considerin' the intrust.'

" 'It's a bargin,' says I; and I paid him down the money, and he signed the mortgage over to me for a vallyable consideration.

"I hed that beautiful paper in my breast pocket, and felt strong to face the Squaire in his own house, knowing how I could turn him out of it! And I mustn't forget to tell you how I got myself a new rig of clothing, with a mighty fine over-coat, and a new fur cap; and as I looked in the glass I felt my consekence all over at every for'a'd step I tuk; and I felt my inches growing with every pace of the mar' on the high-road to Merry Ann and her beautiful daddy!"

X

"Well, Jedge, before I quite got to the Squaire's farm, who should come out to meet me in the road but Merry Ann, her own self! She hed spied me, I reckon, as I crossed the bald ridge a quarter of a mile away. I do reckon the dear gal hed been looking out for me every day the whole eleven days in the week, counting in all the Sundays. In the mountains, you know, Jedge, that the weeks sometimes run to twelve, and even fourteen days, specially when we're on a long camp-hunt!

"Well, Merry Ann cried and laughed together, she was so tarnation glad to see me agin. Says she:

" 'Oh, Sam! I'm so glad to see you! I was afeard you had clean gin me up. And thar's that fusty old bachelor Grimstead, he's a-coming here a'most every day; and daddy, he sw'ars that I shill marry him, and nobody else; and mammy, she's at me too, all the time, telling me how fine a fairm he's got, and what a nice carriage, and all that; and mammy says as how daddy'll be sure to beat me ef I don't hev him. But I kain't bear to look at him, the old griesly!'

" 'Cuss him!' says I. 'Cuss him, Merry Ann!'

"And she did, but onder her breath—the old cuss.

" 'Drot him!' says she; and she said louder, 'and drot me, too, Sam, ef I ever marries any body but you.'

"By this time I hed got down and gin her a long strong hug, and a'most twenty or a dozen kisses, and I says:

" 'You sha'n't marry nobody but me, Merry Ann; and we'll hev the marriage this very night, ef you says so!'

" 'Oh! psho, Sam! How you does talk!'

" 'Ef I don't marry you to-night, Merry Ann, I'm a holy mortar and a sinner not to be saved by any salting, though you puts the petre with the salt. I'm come for that very thing. Don't you see my new clothes?'

" 'Well, you hev got a beautiful coat, Sam; all so blue, and with sich shiny buttons.'

" 'Look at my waistcoat, Merry Ann! What do you think of that?'

" 'Why, it's a most beautiful blue welvet!'

" 'That's the very article,' says I. 'And see the breeches, Merry Ann; and the boots!'

" 'Well,' says she, 'I'm fair astonished, Sam! Why whar, Sam, did you find all the money for these fine things?'

" 'A beautiful young women, a'most as beautiful as you, Merry Ann, come to me the very night of that day when your daddy driv me off with a flea in my ear. She come to me to my bed at midnight—'

" 'Oh, Sam! *ain't* you ashamed!'

" ' 'Twas in a dream, Merry Ann; and she tells me something to incourage me to go for'a'd, and I went for'a'd, bright and airly next morning, and I picked up three sarvants that hev been working for me ever sence.'

" 'What sarvants?' says she.

" 'One was a goose, one was a b'ar, and t'other was a bee!'

" 'Now you're a-fooling me, Sam.'

" 'You'll see! Only you git yourself ready, for by the eternal Hokies, I marries you this very night, and takes you home to *my* fairm bright and airly to-morrow morning.'

" 'I do think, Sam, you must be downright crazy.'

" 'You'll see and believe! Do you go home and git yourself fixed up for the wedding. Old Parson Stovall lives only two miles from your daddy, and I'll hev him hyar by sundown. You'll see!'

" 'But ef I waur to b'lieve you, Sam—'

" 'I've got on my wedding-clothes o' purpose, Merry Ann.'

" 'But *I* hain't got no clothes fit for a gal to be married in,' says she.

" 'I'll marry you this very night, Merry Ann,' says I, 'though you hedn't a stitch of clothing at all!'

" 'Git out, you sassy Sam,' says she, slapping my face. Then I kissed her in her very mouth, and a'ter that we walked on together, I leading the mar'.

"Says she, as we neared the house, 'Sam, let me go before, or stay hyar in the thick, and you go in by yourself. Daddy's in the hall, smoking his pipe and reading the newspapers.'

" 'We'll walk in together,' says I, quite consekential.

"Says she, 'I'm so afeard.'

" 'Don't you be afeard, Merry Ann,' says I; 'you'll see that all will come out jest as I tells you. We'll be hitched to-night, ef Parson Stovall, or any other parson, kin be got to tie us up!'

"Says she, suddently, 'Sam, you're a-walking lame, I'm a-thinking. What's the matter? Hev you hurt yourself any way?'

"Says I, 'It's only owing to my not balancing my accounts even in my pockets. You see I feel so much like flying in the air with the idee of marrying you to-night that I filled my pockets with rocks, jest to keep me down.'

" 'I do think, Sam, you're a leetle cracked in the upper story.'

" 'Well,' says I, 'ef so, the crack has let in a blessed chaince of the beautifulest sunlight! You'll see! Cracked, indeed! Ha, ha, ha! Wait till I've done with your daddy! I'm gwine to square accounts with *him*, and, I reckon, when I'm done with him, you'll guess that the crack's in *his* skull, and not in mine.'

" 'What! you wouldn't knock my father, Sam!' says she, drawing off from me and looking skeary.

" 'Don't you be afeard; but it's very sartin, ef our heads don't come together, Merry Ann, you won't hev me for your husband to-night. And that's what I've swore upon. Hyar we air!'

"When we got to the yard I led in the mar', and Merry Ann she ran away from me and dodged round the house. I hitched the mar' to the post, took off the saddle-bags, which was mighty heavy, and walked into the house stiff enough I tell you, though the gould in my pockets pretty much weighed me down as I walked.

"Well, in I walked, and thar sat the old Squaire smoking his pipe and reading the newspaper. He looked at me through his specs over the newspaper, and when he seed who 'twas his mouth put on that same conceited sort of grin and smile that he ginerally hed when he spoke to me.

" 'Well,' says he, gruffly enough, 'it's you, Sam Snaffles, is it?' Then he seems to diskiver my new clothes and boots, and he sings out, 'Heigh! you're tip-toe fine to-day! What fool of a shop-keeper in Spartanburg have you tuk in this time, Sam?'

"Says I, cool enough, 'I'll answer all them iligant questions a'ter a while, Squaire; but would prefar to see to business fust.'

" 'Business!' says he; 'and what business kin you hev with me, I wants to know?'

" 'You shill know, Squaire, soon enough; and I only hopes it will be to your liking a'ter you l'arn it.'

"So I laid my saddle-bags down at my feet and tuk a chair quite at my ease; and I could see that he was all astare in wonderment at what he thought my sassiness. As I felt I had my hook in his gills, though he didn't know it yit, I felt in the humor to tickle him and play him as we does a trout.

"Says I, 'Squaire Hopson, you owes a sartin amount of money, say $350, with intrust on it for now three years, to Dr. Columbus Mills.'

"At this he squares round, looks me full in the face, and says:

" 'What the old Harry's that to you?'

"Says I, gwine on cool and straight, 'You gin him a mortgage on this fairm for security.'

" What's that to you?' says he.

" 'The mortgage is over-due by two years, Squaire,' says I.

" 'What the old Harry's all that to you, I say?' he fairly roared out.

" 'Well, nothing much, I reckon. The $350, with three years' in-trust at seven per cent., making it now—I've calkelated it all without compounding—something over $425—well, Squaire, that's not much to *you*, I reckon, with your large capital. But it's something to me.'

" 'But I ask you again, Sir,' he says, 'what is all this to you?'

" 'Jist about what I tells you—say $425; and I've come hyar this morning, bright and airly, in hope you'll be able to square up and satisfy the mortgage. Hyar's the dockyment.'

"And I drawed the paper from my breast pocket.

" 'And you tell me that Dr. Mills sent you hyar,' says he, 'to collect this money?'

" 'No; I come myself on my own hook.'

" 'Well,' says he, 'you shill hev your answer at onst. Take that paper back to Dr. Mills and tell him that I'll take an airly opportunity to call and arrange the business with him. You hev your answer, Sir,' he says, quite grand, 'and the sooner you makes yourself scarce the better.'

" 'Much obleeged to you, Squaire, for your ceveelity,' says I; 'but I ain't quite satisfied with that answer. I've come for the money due on this paper, and must hev it, Squaire, or thar will be what the lawyers call *four closures* upon it!'

" 'Enough! Tell Dr. Mills I will answer his demand in person.'

" 'You needn't trouble yourself, Squaire; for ef you'll jest look at the back of that paper, and read the 'signmeant, you'll see that you've got to settle with Sam Snaffles, and not with Columbus Mills!'

"Then he snatches up the dockyment, turns it over, and reads the rigilar 'signmeant, writ in Columbus Mills' own handwrite.

"Then the Squaire looks at me with a great stare, and he says, to himself like:

" 'It's a *bonny fodder* 'signmeant.'

" 'Yes,' says I, 'it's *bonny fodder*—rigilar in law—and the titles all made out complete to me, Sam Snaffles; signed, sealed, and delivered, as the lawyers says it.'

" 'And how the old Harry come you by this paper?' says he.

"I was gitting riled, and I was detarmined, this time, to gin my hook a pretty sharp jerk in his gills; so I says:

" 'What the old Harry's that to *you*, Squaire? Thar's but one question 'twixt us two—air you ready to pay that money down on the hub, at onst, to me, Sam Snaffles?'

" 'No, Sir, I am not.'

" 'How long a time will you ax from me, by way of marciful indulgence?'

" 'It must be some time yit,' says he, quite sulky; and then he goes on agin:

" 'I'd like to know how you come by that 'signmeant, Mr. Snaffles.'

"Mr. Snaffles! Ah! ha!

" 'I don't see any neecessity,' says I, 'for answering any questions. Thar's the dockyment to speak for itself. You see that Columbus Mills 'signs to me for full *con*sideration. That means I paid him!'

" 'And why did you buy this mortgage?'

" 'You might as well ax me how I come by the money to buy any thing,' says I.

" 'Well, I do ax you,' says he.

" 'And I answers you,' says I, 'in the very words from your own mouth, What the old Harry's that to you?'

" 'This is hardly 'spectful, Mr. Snaffles,' says he.

"Says I, ' 'Spectful gits only what 'spectful gives ! Ef any man but you, Squaire, hed been so onrespectful in his talk to me as you hev been I'd ha' mashed his muzzle! But I don't wish to be onrespectful. All I axes is the civil answer. I wants to know when you kin pay this money?'

" 'I kain't say, Sir.'

" 'Well, you see, I thought as how you couldn't pay, spite of all your "capital," as you hedn't paid even the *intrust* on it for three years; and, to tell you the truth, I was in hopes you couldn't pay, as I hed a liking for this fairm always; and as I am jest about to git married, you see—'

" 'Who the old Harry air you gwine to marry?' says he.

" 'What the old Harry's that to you?' says I, giving him as good as he sent. But I went on:

" 'You may be sure it's one of the woman kind. I don't hanker a'ter a wife with a beard; and I expects—God willing, weather premitting, and the parson being sober—to be married this very night!'

" 'To-night!' says he, not knowing well what to say.

" 'Yes; you see I've got my wedding-breeches on. I'm to be married to-night, and I wants to take my wife to her own fairm as soon as I kin. Now, you see, Squaire, I all along set my hairt on this fairm of yourn, and I detarmined, ef ever I could git the "capital," to git hold of it; and that was the idee I hed when I bought the 'signmeant of the mortgage from Columbus Mills. So, you see, ef you kain't pay a'ter three years, you never kin pay, I reckon; and ef I don't git my money this day, why—I kain't help it—the lawyers will hev to see to the *four closures* to-morrow!'

" 'Great God, Sir!' says he, rising out of his chair, and crossing the room up and down, 'do you coolly propose to turn me and my family headlong out of my house?'

" 'Well now,' says I, 'Squaire, that's not edzactly the way to put it. As I reads this dockyment'—and I tuk up and put the mortgage in my pocket—'the house and fairm are *mine* by law. They onst was yourn; but it wants nothing now but the *four closures* to make 'em mine.'

" 'And would you force the sale of property worth $2000 and more for a miserable $400?'

" 'It must sell for what it'll bring, Squaire; and I stands ready to buy it for my wife, you see, ef it costs me twice as much as the mortgage.'

" 'Your wife!' says he; 'who the old Harry is she? You once pertended to have an affection for my da'ter.'

" 'So I hed; but you hedn't the proper affection for your da'ter that I hed. You prefar'd money to her affection, and you driv me off to git "capital!" Well, I tuk your advice, and I've got the capital.'

" 'And whar the old Harry,' said he, 'did you git it?'

" 'Well, I made good tairms with the old devil for a hundred years, and he found me the money.'

" 'It must hev been so,' said he. 'You waur not the man to git capital in any other way.'

"Then he goes on: 'But what becomes of your pertended affection for my da'ter?'

" ' 'Twa'n't pertended; but you throwed yourself betwixt us with all your force, and broke the gal's hairt, and broke mine, so far as you could; and as I couldn't live without company, I hed to look out for myself and find a wife as I could. I tell you, as I'm to be married to-night, and as I've swore a most etarnal oath to hev this fairm, you'll hev to raise the wind to-day, and square off with me, or the lawyers will be at you with the *four closures* to-morrow, bright and airly.'

" 'Dod dern you!' he cries out. 'Does you want to drive me mad!'

" 'By no manner of means,' says I, jest about as cool and quiet as a cowcumber.

"But he was at biling heat. He was all over in a stew and a fever. He filled his pipe and lighted it, and then smashed it over the chimbly. Then he crammed the newspaper in the fire, and crushed it into the blaze with his boot. Then he turned to me, suddent, and said:

" 'Yes, you pertended to love my da'ter, and now you are pushing her father to desperation. Now ef you ever did love Merry Ann, honestly, raally, truly, and *bonny fodder*, you couldn't help loving her yit. And yit, hyar you're gwine to marry another woman, that, perhaps, you don't affection at all.'

" 'It's quite a sensible view you takes of the subject,' says I; 'the only pity is that you didn't take the same squint at it long ago, when I axed you to let me hev Merry Ann. *Then* you didn't valley her affections or mine. You hed no thought of nothing but the "capital" then, and the affections might all go to Jericho, for what you keered! I'd ha' married Merry Ann, and she me, and we'd ha' got on for a spell in a log-cabin, for, though I was poor, I hed the genwine grit of a man, and would come to something, and we'd ha' got on; and yit, without any "capital" your own self, and kivered up with debt as with a winter over-coat, hyar, you waur positive that I shouldn't hev your da'ter, and you waur a-preparing to sell her hyar to an old sour-tempered bachelor, more than double her age. Dern the capital! A man's the best capital for any woman, ef so be he *is* a man. Bekaise, ef he be a man, he'll work out cl'ar, though he may hev a long straining for it through the sieve. Dern the capital! You've as good as sold that gal child to old Grimstead, jest from your love of money!'

" 'But she won't hev him,' says he.

" 'The wiser gal child,' says I. 'Ef you only hed onderstood me and that poor child, I hed it in me to make the "capital"—dern the capital—and now you've ruined her, and yourself, and me, and all; and dern my buttons but I must be married to-night, and jest as soon a'ter as the lawyers can kin fix it I must hev this fairm for my wife. My hairt's set on it, and I've swore it a dozen o' times on the Holy Hokies!'

"The poor old Squaire fairly sweated; but he couldn't say much. He'd come up to me and say:

" 'Ef only you did love Merry Ann!'

" 'Oh,' says I, 'what's the use of your talking that? Ef you only hed ha' loved your own da'ter!'

"Then the old chap begun to cry, and as I seed that I jest kicked over my saddle-bags lying at my feet, and the silver Mexicans rolled out—a bushel on 'em, I reckon—and, O Lawd! how the old fellow jumped, staring with all his eyes at me and the dollars!

" 'It's money!' says he.

" 'Yes,' says I, 'jest a few hundreds of thousands of *my* "capital." ' I didn't stop at the figgers, you see.

"Then he turns to me and says, 'Sam Snaffles, you're a most wonderful man. You're a mystery to me. Whar, in the name of God, hev you been? and what hev you been doing? and whar did you git all this power of capital?'

"I jest laughed, and went to the door and called Merry Ann. She come mighty quick. I reckon she was watching and waiting.

"Says I, 'Merry Ann, that's money. Pick it up and put it back in the saddle-bags, ef you please.'

"Then, says I, turning to the old man, 'Thar's that whole bushel of Mexicans, I reckon. Thar monstrous heavy. My old mar'—ax her about her ribs now!—she fairly squelched onder the weight of me and that money. And I'm pretty heavy loaded myself. I must lighten; with your leave, Squaire.'

"And I pulled out a leetle doeskin bag of gould half eagles from my right-hand pocket and poured them out upon the table; then I emptied my left-hand pocket, then the side pockets of the coat, then the skairt pockets, and jist spread the shiners out upon the table.

"Merry Ann was fairly frightened, and run out of the room; then the old woman she come in, and as the old Squaire seed her, he tuk her by the shoulder and said:

" 'Jest you look at that thar.'

"And when she looked and seed, the poor old hypercritical scamp sinner turned round to me and flung her airms round my neck, and said:

" 'I always said you waur the only right man for Merry Ann.'

"The old spooney!

"Well, when I hed let 'em look enough, and wonder enough, I jest turned Merry Ann and her mother out of the room.

"The old Squaire, he waur a-setting down agin in his airm-chair, not edzactly knowing what to say or what to do, but watching all my motions, jest as sharp as a cat watches a mouse when she is hafe hungry.

"Thar was all the Mexicans put back in the saddle-bags, but he hed seen 'em, and thar was all the leetle bags of gould spread upon the table; the gould—hafe and quarter eagles—jest lying out of the mouths of the leetle bags as ef wanting to creep back agin.

"And thar sot the old Squaire, looking at 'em all as greedy as a fish-hawk down upon a pairch in the river. And, betwixt a whine and a cry and a talk, he says:

" 'Ah, Sam Snaffles, ef you ever did love my leetle Merry Ann, you would never marry any other woman.'

"Then you ought to ha' seed me. I felt myself sixteen feet high, and jest as solid as a chestnut oak. I walked up to the old man, and I tuk him quiet by the collar of his coat, with my thumb and forefinger, and I said:

" 'Git up, Squaire, for a bit.'

"And up he got.

"Then I marched him to the big glass agin the wall, and I said to him: 'Look, ef you please.'

"And he said, 'I'm looking.'

"And I said, 'What does you see?'

"He answered, 'I sees you and me.'

"I says, 'Look agin, and tell me what you *obzarves*.'

" 'Well,' says he, 'I obzarves.'

"And says I, 'What does your *obzarving* amount to? That's the how.'

"And says he, 'I sees a man alongside of me, as good-looking and handsome a young man as ever I seed in all my life.'

" 'Well,' says I, 'that's a correct obzarvation. But,' says I, 'what does you see of *your own self*?'

" 'Well, I kain't edzackly say.'

" 'Look good!' says I. 'Obzarve.'

"Says he, 'Don't ax me.'

" 'Now,' says I, 'that won't edzactly do. I tell you now, look good, and ax yourself ef you're the sawt of looking man that hes any right to be a feyther-in-law to a fine, young, handsome-looking fellow like me, what's got the "capital?" '

"Then he laughed out at the humor of the sitivation; and he says, 'Well, Sam Snaffles, you've got me dead this time. You're a different man from what I thought you. But, Sam, you'll confess, I reckon, that ef I hedn't sent you off with a flea in your ear when I hed you up afore the looking-glass, you'd never ha' gone to work to git in the "capital." '

" 'I don't know *that*, Squaire,' says I. 'Sarcumstances sarve to make a man take one road when he mout take another; but when you meets a man what has the hairt to love a woman strong as a lion, and to fight an inimy big as a buffalo, he's got the raal grit in him. You knowed I was young, and I was poor, and you knowed the business of a hunter is a mighty poor business ef the man ain't born to it. Well, I didn't do much at it jest bekaise my hairt was so full of Merry Ann; and you should ha' make a calkilation and allowed for *that.* But you poked your fun at me and riled me consumedly; but I was detarmined that you shouldn't break *my* hairt or the hairt of Merry Ann. Well, you hed your humors, and I've tried to take the change out of you. And now, ef you raally thinks, a'ter that obzarvation in the glass, that you kin make a respectable feyther-in-law to sich a fine-looking fellow as me, what's got the "capital," jest say the word, and we'll call Merry Ann in to bind the bargain. And you must talk out quick, for the wedding's to take place this very night. I've swore it by the etarnal Hokies.'

" 'To-night!' says he.

" 'Look at the "capital," ' says I; and I pinted to the gould on the table and the silver in the saddle-bags.

" 'But, Lawd love you, Sam,' says he, 'it's so suddent, and we kain't make the preparations in time.'

"Says I, 'Look at the "capital," Squaire, and dern the preparations!'

" 'But,' says he 'we hain't time to ax the company.'

" 'Dern the company!' says I; 'I don't b'lieve in company the very night a man gits married. His new wife's company enough for him ef he's sensible.'

" 'But, Sam,' says he, 'it's not possible to git up a supper by to-night.'

"Says I, 'Look you, Squaire, the very last thing a man wants on his wedding night is supper.'

"Then he said something about the old woman, his wife.

"Says I, 'Jest you call her in and show her the "capital." '

"So he called in the old woman, and then in come Merry Ann, and thar was great hemmings and hawings; and the old woman she said:

" 'I've only got the one da'ter, Sam, and we *must* hev a big wedding! We must spread ourselves. We've got a smart chaince of friends and acquaintances, you see, and 'twon't be decent onless we axes them, and they won't like it! We *must* make a big show for the honor and 'spectability of the family.'

"Says I, 'Look you, old lady! I've swore a most tremendous oath, by the Holy Hokies, that Merry Ann and me air to be married this very night, and I kain't break sich an oath as that! Merry Ann,' says I, 'you wouldn't hev me break sich a tremendous oath as that?'

"And, all in a trimble, she says, 'Never, Sam! No!'

" 'You hyar that, old lady!' says I. 'We marries to-night, by the Holy Hokies! and we'll hev no company but old Parson Stovall, to make the hitch; and Merry Ann and me go off by sunrise to-morrow morning—you hyar?—to my own fairm, whar thar's a great deal of furniter fixing for her to do. A'ter that you kin advartise the whole county to come in, ef you please, and eat all the supper you kin spread! Now hurry up,' says I, 'and git as ready as you kin, for I'm gwine to ride over to Parson Stovall's this minit. I'll be back to dinner in hafe an hour. Merry Ann, you gether up that gould and silver, and lock it up. It's *our* "capital!" As for you, Squaire, thar's the mortgage on your fairm, which Merry Ann shill give you, to do as you please with it, as soon as the parson has done the hitch, and I kin call Merry Ann, Mrs. Snaffles—Madam Merry Ann Snaffles, and so forth, and aforesaid.'

"I laid down the law that time for all parties, and showed the old Squaire sich a picter of himself, and me standing aside him, looking seven foot high, at the least, that I jest worked the business 'cording to my own pleasure. When neither the daddy nor the mammy hed any thing more to say, I jumped on my mar' and rode over to old Parson Stovall.

"Says I, 'Parson, thar's to be a hitch to-night, and you're to see a'ter the right knot. You knows what I means. I wants you over at Squaire Hopson's. Me and Merry Ann, his da'ter, mean to hop the twig to-night, and you're to see that we hop squar', and that all's even, 'cording to the law, Moses, and the profits! I stand treat, Parson, and you won't be the worse for your riding. I pays in gould!'

"So he promised to come by dusk; and come he did. The old lady hed got some supper, and tried her best to do what she could at sich short notice. The venison ham was mighty fine, I reckon, for Parson Stovall played a great stick at it; and ef they hedn't cooked up four of my wild geese, then the devil's an angel of light, and Sam Snaffles no better than a sinner! And thar was any quantity of jimmyjohns, peach and honey considered. Parson Stovall was a great feeder, and I begun to think he never would be done. But at last he wiped his mouth, swallowed his fifth cup of coffee, washed it down with a stiff dram of peach and honey, wiped his mouth agin, and pulled out his prayer-book, psalmody, and Holy Scrip—three volumes in all—and he hemmed three times, and begun to look out for the marriage text, but begun with giving out the 100th Psalm.

" 'With one consent, let's all unite—'

" 'No,' says I, 'Parson; not all! It's only Merry Ann and me what's to unite to-night!'

"Jest then, afore he could answer, who should pop in but old bachelor Grimstead! and he looked round 'bout him, specially upon me and the parson, as ef to say:

" 'What the old Harry's they doing hyar!'

"And I could see that the old Squaire was oneasy. But the blessed old Parson Stovall, he gin 'em no time for ixplanation or palaver; but he gits up, stands up squar', looks solemn as a meat-axe, and he says:

" 'Let the parties which I'm to bind together in the holy bonds of wedlock stand up before me!'

"And, Lawd bless you, as he says the words, what should that old skunk of a bachelor do, but he gits up, stately as an old buck in spring time, and he marches over to my Merry Ann! But I was too much and too spry for him. I puts in betwixt 'em, and I takes the old bachelor by his coat-collar, 'twixt my thumb and forefinger, and afore he knows whar he is, I marches him up to the big looking-glass, and I says:

" 'Look!'

" 'Well,' says he, 'what?'

" 'Look good,' says I.

" 'I'm looking,' says he. 'But what do you mean, Sir?'

"Says I, 'Obzarve! Do you see yourself? Obzarve!'

" 'I reckon I do,' says he.

" 'Then,' says I, 'ax yourself the question, ef you're the sawt of looking man to marry my Merry Ann.'

"Then the old Squaire burst out a-laughing. He couldn't help it.

" 'Capital!', says he.

" 'It's capital,' says I. 'But hyar we air, Parson. Put on the hitch, jest as quick as you kin clinch it; for thar's no telling how many slips thar may be 'twixt the cup and the lips when these hungry old bachelors air about.'

" 'Who gives away this young woman?' axes the parson; and the Squaire stands up and does the thing needful. I hed the ring ready, and before the parson had quite got through, old Grimstead vamoosed.

"He waur a leetle slow in onderstanding that he warn't wanted and warn't, nohow, any party to the business. But he and the Squaire hed a mighty quarrel a'terwards, and ef 't hedn't been for me, he'd ha' licked the Squaire. He was able to do it; but I jest cocked my cap at him one day, and, says I, in the Injin language:

" 'Yaou!' And he didn't know what I meant; but I looked tomahawks at him, so he gin ground; and he's getting old so fast that you kin see him growing downwards all the time.

"All that, Jedge, is jest thirteen years ago; and me and Merry Ann git on famously, and thar's no eend to the capital! Gould breeds like the cows, and it's only needful to squeeze the bags now and then to make Merry Ann happy as a tomtit. Thirteen years of married life, and look at me! You see for yourself, Jedge, that I'm not much the worse for wear; and I kin answer for Merry Ann, too, though, Jedge, we hev hed thirty-six children."

"What!" says I, "thirty-six children in thirteen years!"

The "Big Lie" roared aloud.

"Hurrah, Sharp! Go it! You're making it spread! That last shot will make the Jedge know that you're a right truthful sinner, of a Saturday night, and in the 'Lying Camp.' "

"To be sure! You see, Merry Ann keeps on. But you've only got to do the ciphering for yourself. Here, now, Jedge, look at it. Count for yourself. First we had *three* gal children, you see. Very well! Put down three. Then we had *six* boys, one every year for four years; and then, the fifth year, Merry Ann throwed deuce. Now put down the six boys a'ter the three gals, and ef that don't make thirty-six, thar's no snakes in all Flurriday!

"Now, men," says Sam, "let's liquor all round, and drink the health of Mrs. Merry Ann Snaffles and the thirty-six children, all alive and kicking; and glad to see you, Jedge, and the rest of the company. We're doing right well; but I hes, every now and then, to put my thumb and forefinger on the Squaire's collar, and show him his face in the big glass, and call on him for an *obzarvation*—for he's mighty fond *of going shar's* in my 'capital.' "

"Bald-Head Bill Bauldy,"
And How He Went Through the Flurriday Campaign!—A Legend of the Hunter's Camp

I
Second Saturday Night.

The second week was at an end. Saturday had come! We had toiled, successfully, all the week; but Saturday, had been our crowning glory. We had achieved two bucks, fat as shoats in a fine mast season, a huge she bear, a doe, and two wild turkey gobblers; and had come out, triumphantly, in a hand to hand fight with a saucy panther who gave us battle from the jump; and the sun was yet an hour from his setting!

Our *amateurs* sang cock-a-lory! They, too, had achieved some goodly work, having done most execution in the struggle with the panther.

The Colonel, who was the dandy, the Beau, *par excellence* of our group, and who was supposed to be somewhat effeminate, had shown genuine pluck; and, after giving the panther two mortal shots, had the honor to be knocked over by the dying beast, and of bearing off, as trophies of his valor, three deep scratches on face, arm and bosom. He will swear by these to the day of his death!

All parties were duly exultant! But how to get our "birds" down the mountain to the camp? Our amateurs were puzzled.

Not so the hunters professional. Their ready wit, and long experience, made them equal to all emergencies. The great she bear was slung with leathern straps between two of the mounted men, while panther, bucks and doe, each tasked a single rider; and we made our way down in safety to our lonely hollow, between the gigantic masses, on every hand, of the Balsam Mountains, while our little cataract, sent up to our ears a lively chaunt of welcome and rejoicing, long before we came in sight!

All parties now went to work with a *vim*! It was cold weather, be it remembered, and our amateurs, in spite of furs and flannels, were made to shiver. Rousing fires were soon kindled, and, without taking off our own, we very soon had stripped the jackets from the carcasses of all our victims; and the work of dissection went forward, under the dexterous butchery of the professional hunters, who are all first rate butchers, as well as excellent tanners.

Of course, the peach and honey drams were not forgotten, and these were freely imbibed, at moderate intervals, while the anatomists went on with their work.

It was now a slash in the meat, and now a swallow from the drink, and in the increasing rigors of the evening, no harm followed from the frequency of our potations!

The preparations for supper went on also. Our cook knew his task. The one employed, at present, enjoyed quite a reputation for the excellence of his *cuisine*. He had joined our party during the week; and, as the hunters very soon learn to know in what each person is most an expert, "Bald-Head Bill Bauldy"—otherwise "William Bauldy"—at once received his appointment, as Chief Cook and Bottle Washer during the encampment!

Bald-Head Bill—so called because of a head as clean of hair as the palm of a damsel's hand; the skull polished as marble, and shining bright in the sun, as a sudden moonlight—had distinguished himself in the army; but much more as a cook than a soldier! Of this hereafter.

He wore a wig of monstrous dimensions; a great shaggy mass of reddish brown hair, by which his natural deficiencies of cranium, were concealed. It was only as a favor to the amateurs of the party that he showed his naked skull, to illustrate the truth of the story which he subsequently told us of his experiences and adventures in the "FLURRIDAY WAR." But of all these matters, anon!

Well, you will please suppose supper at an end, and our hunters all happy and at ease, around a roaring fire; that our tent, pitched behind us, is amply supplied with convenient mattresses and any quantity of blankets, shawls and wrappers; that we can lie with our feet to the fire, or sit grouped around it, and spin our yarns to the common merriment; while our baggage wagon, at hand, held its full stores of the creature comforts; the coffee, sugar, bread stuffs, bacon, and the demijohns of peach, honey, and mountain dew; all of which, like the famous cruse of the widow, seemed inexhaustible. At all events, there was no lugubrious party, to look into the faces of the group, and mournfully announce the total evaporation of the spirits!

The hour for the "Lying Camp" had come, and "Big Lie" was duly installed, as before, on the broad stone of patriarchal authority, which he filled with a dignity becoming his *fauteuil.*

Brave old Jim Fisher still held this eminent position, and he was fully equal to any that he undertook. He ordered a stoup of *the* beverage, all round, by way of inauguration, and the ceremonials soon gave way to the tale-tellers.

II
How to Cross an African River.

"Big Lie," after a little "*hemming and hawing,*" apologetic, for the liberty he was about to take, now called upon Major Henry, the oldest of our amateurs, for "a lie that should run like the truth!"

Now, Major Henry was quite a wit and humorist, and almost as famous, as a *raconteur*, as he was in his professional capacity, as a Lawyer. But the good things of the wit and humorist, of a high civilization, and of the purely conventional life of the city, are very apt to be thrown away upon the rude hunters of the mountains, who require the greatly salient in their narrations, and need striking incident to command attention. The quiet humors, the latent fun, and irony, are not so easily perceptible to them;—and the exaggerations of the "Lying Camp," especially, called for the startling, the wild, extravagant; for the droll rather than the wit!

Major Henry was conscious of all this, and was disposed to dodge his responsibility to the circle; but the more he *shied* the duty, the more authoritatively did "Big Lie" insist upon it;—and the Major was forced finally to respond; which he did, by telling an anecdote of a famous African negro, well known as an ancient boatman on the Congaree, who, in process of time, had devolved upon him the task of navigating the flat boat at McCord's Ferry, on that river.

This old African, who claimed to have been a Prince in his own country,—as was the boast of nearly every old African I ever knew,—had grown saucy from age and infirmity. His very impudence finally became so amusing, as to disarm the anger of those who provoked it; and, day by day, Cudjo grew more and more audacious; showing but little reverence for white or black, old or young, man or woman; wagging his tongue with wondrous familiarity in all directions, with a license as free as that of the wind which blows on all it listeth.

That he was a good flat-boatman and did his duty at the ferry, reconciled all parties, in *some* degree, to his impertinences, even where his humor might have failed to do so!——Cudjo, by the way, was not his princely African name, but as he died finally, in the very odor of sanctity with that name, in the bosom of the Fetisch Church of Mumbo Jumbo, we respect his memory too much to declare his regal title or royal claim, as a Prince among the Gullahs!

"We were crossing McCord's Ferry, on the Congaree, on one occasion," said Major Henry, "Col. McCord and myself, when there was a heavy freshet, the waters being very high; so high that polling was difficult; the river was roughened by a heavy blow, and the winds swept our poor little flat about, making it very difficult and indeed, somewhat doubtful, if we should be able to make the opposite shore, or even regain that which we had left. The boat was old and rotten, and one of the poles had broken. Two only remained, and these were managed by Cudjo, and a young assistant negro named Tony, which name was sometimes abridged to 'Scrub.' Cudjo had but little of the strength of youth remaining, and the vigor of his arms bore no sort of proportion to that of his tongue.

"Cudjo was in a strait on the present occasion. All his labors seemed to be fruitless in impelling the flat, which simply whirled about, as it were, in a circle, making no headway; and, after the work of a goodly hour, we found ourselves within a few yards of the point of land from which we had taken our departure.

"Cudjo, suddenly threw down his pole, put his arms akimbo, and confronting McCord, said as abruptly as gruffly,—

" 'Misser McCode, de white people ob dis country, is jis' so many bloody big fool! Dey hab no sense!'

" 'What moves you to think so *now*, Cudjo?'

" 'Wha' moob me, you axes? Enty you kin see for you'saff? Whay de sense, I wants for know, ob trying to cross ribber like dis yer Cong'ree in flat boat, wid long pole wha' can't reach de bottom when de fresh come down. Yer we is now, jis a'turning and a twisting all about; we can't git across and we can't git back; de water takes us one way; de win' takes us anoder way; you can't hole on to de bottom wid de pole, and when you does, de strain ob de water and de win togedder, brecks de pole in you' han'; and dar you air; wid not'ing else for do but set down in de bottom ob de flat, and sing de Hallelujah, when you can't see Jarusalem! Lawd ha' massy! I tell you, Misser Mc-Cord, you buckrah people all so many d——d fool! In my country, we nebber hab flat to cross river! Nebber hab boat! Nebber hab de worry to work de pole, tell your berry eyes is a swimming in de sweat!'

" 'How then, Cudjo, do you cross the river in your country?'

" 'Misser McCode,—you hab no sense? You can't 'tink for you'saff? Hab for tell you ebbry'ting?—Look-a-dar;—out-a-yonder;—on de bank?—Wha' dat you see?'

" 'I see nothing but an alligator.'

" 'Das him! Well, you sees alligator! Das's alligator, I 'speck, 'bout twelve foot long! He's baby to da alligator in my country; but he kin *do*, ef you *mek* 'em do! Da' same alligator, you sees dar, kin carry you 'cross de ribber,—dis berry ribber, Congaree!'

" 'Well, I've no doubt, if he's willing; he's strong enough!'

" 'I don't ax ef he's willing, Misser McCode! I only axes ef he's strong! I *meks* 'em willing! In my country, when I comes to de ribber and wants to git across, I looks 'bout me! I sees de alligators a-sleeping all along de bank ob de ribber! I picks out de biggest ob 'em all, wha's strong enough for carry me! Well, I creeps up to 'em sly as fox at de hen roos'. When I gits close enough, I jumps on he back! Dat wakes 'em up; and de moment he wakes, and feels something heabby on he back, he push for de ribber! I hole on, buckle my leg roun' em so, and 'pur (spur) 'em fast as I kin! Well, wha' den? He push for de ribber, and carry me 'cross! Das's no d—— fool ob a flat, wid long pole, or long rope, and no bodders wid de fresh or de win'. We jis goes ahead, you see, jis as ef he was hoss, or mule, all de same! Ah! Masser Mc-Code, ef de people ob dis country, dis buckrah people, only bin hab sense!'

" 'But Cudjo, how do you *guide* your alligator horse, or boat?' quoth McCord.

"The saucy negro interrupted him with an air of scorn, as he replied,—

" 'Misser McCode, you hab no sense! I hab for tell you ebbry ting! Wha' da dat?'—

"Holding up his right hand thumb.—

" 'That's your thumb!'

" 'Ah! *you* hab t'umb enty! Well, you guide 'em wid dat! You 'tick (stick) your t'umb in he eye! Dat will guide em 'cross de ribber.'

" 'But, suppose Cudjo, I want him to carry me *down* the river?'

" 'Well, wha' den? Ef you wants em to go down de ribber, 'tick you t'umb in he *right* eye! Den he go down.'

" 'But,' says McCord, 'suppose I wish him to go *up* the river, Cudjo?'

" 'My God, Misser McCord, you hab no sense? I hab for tell you ebbry t'ing? Enty you got 'noder t'umb? Well, you want 'em for go *up* de river? 'Tick you udder t'umb in he leff eye; dat shall mek 'em go *up* de ribber!'

" 'But suppose, Cudjo, I want him to go neither up nor down, the river, but to go, just as we wish to go now, straight across;—how then shall I manage him?'

" 'My God! Misser McCode, you hab no sense? You can't 'tink for you seff? I hab for tell you ebbry t'ing? Enty you got *two* t'umb? 'Tick bote t'umb in he eye; dat will mek him carry you 'traight cross de ribber!'

" 'But, Cudjo, suppose he should,—just when we are in the middle of the river,—take it into his head, to go straight down to the bottom?'

"Here the African was at his wits end; his resources were exhausted; he fidgetted; looked dubiously at McCord and then at me, and, having no other alternative, seizing his pole, and working fiercely at the flat, he replied—

" 'Ah! Misser McCord, ef de alligator go *down* to *de bottom*, and hab you on he back;—da berry bad! You hab for swim out de bes' way you kin!'

III

Here Henry's story, or anecdote, reached its final conclusion. While he was telling it, we noted that "Bald-Head Bill" was restless and fidgetting, showing himself somewhat impatient, and evidently, with difficulty, restraining himself from interrupting the narrator. But, as soon as the Major had finished,—he cried out,—

"I'll be dod-derned, Major, but you've got hold of a leetle piece of my history of the campaign I had in Goodwyn's Rigimint in the Flurriday War! You've hearn me tell it, fellows, more'n a dozen times!"

"Yes, to be sure; that's true, Bauldy;" was the cry from several.

"I'm very sorry," said Henry, "to have used up any of your thunder, Bauldy; but, I certainly never heard of your Florida Campaign;

and I reckon there's several others here that never heard it. I move you, 'Big Lie!' that 'Bald-Head Bill' shall tell us his adventures in that same campaign, and we shall then see how much like *his* alligator is to that of my African Prince, Cudjo."

The motion was seconded, and "BIG LIE" gave the order.

Bauldy, so eager before, was now disposed to play the bashful; but, after some petty affectations, he consented, and proceeded after the following fashion.

IV
How Bauldy Volunteers to Fight the Seminoles. First Fight with a Bear.

"Well, fellows and you Gentlemen, you all ricollects, I reckon, about the great Flurriday War, with the Siminole Injins, not quite a hundred years ago. You remember thar was all sorts of great fighting, and skrimaraging in that country, and no great deal of killing on any side, 'cepting the massacr*ee* of Dade's Regiment of 'riglars, that let themselves be cotched in a dern'd ambuscado, when the Ingins chawed 'em up to a man.

"The poor fellows *fit* well, though, but had no chaince; and the Siminoles jist popped 'em down and sculped 'em, as ef they had been so many rabbits in a ring! I dont reckon, with all their cannon and shooting, they killed a single red skin.—

"That warn't all, ef you remember. The Siminoles come mighty nigh to captivating St. Augustine, and sculping all the people, women and children; and so thar was a call for volunteers from Georgy and Sout' Carlina, to go down and save St. Augustine, and whip off the red skins.

"Thar was a grand to do, specially, you see, as that sassy savage, Osceola, had corked up Giniral Gaines in a sort of hollow; and thar was some other ginerals, in pretty nigh the same fix; and, I reckon, of all on 'em, Giniral Clinch, who knowed the country, and the nater of the beasts that waur in it, he did about the best fighting of 'em all! As for the big Giniral Scott, he made a big fuss, and marched his grand army in three columns, and beat his drums, whenever he come nigh to the swamps and thicks, as ef to give fair notis to the Seminoles to lie low and keep dark;—and so they did! They squatted close in the bush and thick, and on the edge of the swamp, and grinned like Chesse-cats, as they seed the big armies marching by, with the big gineral, seven foot in his boots, making the drums beat, and the horns blow, whenever he rode ahead! 'Twas fine marching, I reckon; but marching warn't the thing, and there was no fighting. The grand army did not pick up a single red sculp.

"But I ain't to tell you of the whole war, but only the part that I, Bill Bauldy, had in it.

"Well you must know that I happened to be in Lexington Destrict, South Carolina, when Col. Goodwyn, of Columbia, called for

[*one page of MS missing*]

ways they hev in rigilar armies. We waur over six hundred men; all young fellows like myself, and a stout set of chaps they waur; and, once fairly in a skrimmage, they went at it, with tooth and toe-nail; and sich a hollering as made the woods shiver agin! I confess, I wan't much of a sodger, and hed no more idee of fighting than I had of flying to Heaven on the wings of the wind, as is writ in Holy Scripters. I was always a peaceable man, that only wanted to be let alone; and ef so be I hed pleased, I could have passed myself off for a man past his time of sarvice, seeing that my head was jest as bald of hair as a yallow tarrapin's belly. Besides, I was mighty apt to ketch cold, ef I didn't wear my wig all the time, sleeping and waking. Knowing that, I bought two new wigs from Bedell in Columbia, and stowed 'em, convenient away in my skairt-pockets. Then I was ready for Flurriday, and all blazes!

"And twas mighty soon that the Colonel hed us in marching order; and, almost afore I know'd whar I was, I was down in Flurriday, and hunting up the Ingins. And in the s'arch, which was mighty like hunting for a needle in a haystack, we was in the saddle from morning to night, and sometimes from night to morning; now pushing over the hot sand hills, and now hafe wading, hafe swimming over the lakes, and lagoons; and then agin in great thicks, whar you couldn't see twenty feet before you! Well, we got into some skrimmages on the Withlachoochie and other swampy rivers; but all I seed of the Siminoles was in the hearing of their bullets out of the swamp. Then we'd charge the swamp, and Lawd! they waur no whar!

"Twas in the second skrimmage on the Withlacoochie that my mar', on a suddent, went dead, sprawling right onder me, with a Siminole bullet through her head! I was pitched off, thinking, all the time, twas in my own head that the bullet lodged! I own up; I waur mighty skear'd that time! But that tuk me out of the troop! I hed no money to git another horse, and thar waur none to spar' in the rigiment. I had to go into the infant-*ry*. But I got an adssessment of the vally of my mar', and a sartipcate from the Quarter Master, for a hundred and fifty dollars, that government was to pay me; but, though I sent in my bill and the order to government, by our ripresentative, I never got a copper of money, and haint got it to this day. Our rip (representative) said thar was no use to try, onless I was willing to give a hundred out of the hundred and fifty to sartin high ossifers of government, who always expected two thirds of all the money of the sodgers, to get the rest for 'em. I told him, I'd see all the d——d rogues of Congress in Hell's blazes before I'd give 'em a copper!—And he then tells me a long story of a poor widow woman, one Amy Dardan, who had been trying to get the money from government, for her mar', ever sence the old war of the Revolution; and he said that the very *intrust* on that mar's money, 'cording to the adssessment, would be enough to buy up the whole state of Delawar', or Rhode Island; so, as government would hev to pay so much, they detarmined to pay nothing at all; and so the poor woman never got the hide of her mar' or a copper of her money! A'ter hearing that, I gin it up, and hed no more use for Congress or Washington government!

"Well, a'ter the loss of my mar', I had to go into the infant*ry*, as I tell'd you; and then we hed a few more skrimmages. I own up, I warn't fond of fighting any how; and this gitting shot at, when you couldn't see your inimy, always brought on me an attack of the 'misery,' in my innards!

"So, you see, one of the ossifers said, seeing as how I couldn't keep up with the rigiment when we was on double quick, guine into a skrimmage,—

" 'This fellow Bill Bauldy is not good on a march, and he's no 'count in a fight. What shill we do with him?'

"Another one, that hed a quicker sense of a fellow's vartues, he said,

" 'He looks as ef he mout be a first rate cook! Hev' you ever done any cooking, Bauldy?'

"Well, fellows, you all knows my vartues as a cook by this time, so I spoke up bold, and said,

" 'I'm fust rate at that business. I kin cook any thing from a frog to an alligator terrapin, from a pairch to a blue cat; from a chicken to a turkey gobbler; from a pea to a cabbage! I'm fust rate as a cook!'

" 'We'll try you, my good fellow,' said the Kurnel; 'and ef you only does hafe so well as Rafe Parkinson, you'll do!'

"Now, you see, Rafe Parkinson *was* a good cook enough—nothing to name in the same day with me—but he never could git his belly full of fighting; and soon as he haird an alarum, any thing of a skrimmage guine on, the dern'd fool would drop his gridiron, ketch up his musket, and run, as fast as he could drive, whar he haird the firing; and one day he got a bullet through his body, thet stopt his cooking and fighting the same day together. Twas jest a'ter that, that the oss'fers put me in his place; so I gin up my musket, mighty glad to git shet of it, and took to the gridiron, the sasspan and the spiggot.

"Twant easy work, I tell you, for all the ossfer's mess waur powerful hairty feeders, and thar waur nothing that they could lay hands on that warnt grist to their mill. They ate plentiful: and thar was a mighty fine supply of all things in the pervision wagons! We hed the finest hams, and the best haird-tack; and beef a plenty, and cured fish; and leetle fish in boxes, called 'sartins' and a hundred nice things besides, to say nothing of any quantity of good Monongahely! Them chaps fed well off the government, though I could'nt git a dollar for my mar'! They kept me busy cooking from morning to night, and sometimes, when we waur in camp for rest, pretty much all night! Some on 'em would want something to eat all hours of the night! Then I hed to carry in dinner and breakfast, and supper, and wait upon table; and all I hed to help me was a poor little mangy drummer boy, that couldnt beat, and so they gin him to me for a '*scullion*' as they called it.

"Twas mighty hard work, I tell you; but then I got plenty of fine feed myself; and thar waur sartin 'parquizites,' as they called 'em, in their leavings on table, sich as hafe bottles of wine, and fine Spanish cigars, that I tuk to jist as naterale, as a duck takes to water. Lawd bless you, when they warn't fighting, them fellows lived like fighting cocks! Thar was hairdly nothing that they hedn't got! Some of the kurnels carried their crockery with them, and I've hairn tell of one gineral that carried sartin crockery wessels with him, wharever he marched, sich as no gentleman ever put on his side board! Fact, as I'm a living sinner!

"Well, a'ter dinner always, when the off'sers left the table, I'd begin to pick up, eating as I went. I never missed any of the good things, and I was death on the liquor when I could git it, and never let a hafe bottle, or a cigar pass me, right or left, when they left 'em on the table.

"They had a smart chaince of them big long cigars, they call '*Plantation*,'—a-most a foot long I reckon; jist what them Cuba planters makes for their own smoking. They're the finest as well as the biggest cigars that I ever put betwixt *my* teeth. They waur all smuggled in, when we waur at St. Augustine, and the off'sers shet one eye on the smuggling, and the other they sot on the shares. Twas jist the way to sarve a government that won't pay a man for his gray mar', killed in the sarvice.

"The Cappin' of the schooner had only to count out his hundred boxes, and flip ten on 'em to one side, and then ninety to t'other side, and so we shar'd. Ten in the hundred's mighty good sharing, I tell you, only for shetting your right peeper, and seeing nothing but with the left! And the Cappin' got his market mighty quick for all the rest. Any ten of them boxes, that I hed to stow away in our wagon, would ha' paid for my gray mar'.

"Well, I larne'd, in that school of the kitchen, to smoke cigars instid of Powhatan pipes! And I larned to love 'em mightily! But I durstn't let the offsers see me at it; and so, of an a'ternoon, when they waur all dressing and drilling, and filing and marching, on the parade, I used to slip off to the 'thick,' a-most down to the river, and git under some big tree, hiding away snug, and thar smoke my 'plantation' to my own satisfaction. I never stopt short of three of an a'ternoon, and I swallowed smoke sometimes pretty free at night time, whenever I got a chaince.

"Meantime, I made my little drummer boy, 'Scullion' we called him,—la'rn his business! Ef the little rascal didn't wash up all the plates and dishes, and hev the pots and pans all clean, when I come back from my smoking, I 'gin him Jesse! I thrashed him, ontell I made him larn his lessons!

"Well, 'twas jest in one of these a'ternoons, when the rigiment was a drilling, I slipt off to the 'thick' along the river, and laid myself down and lighted my 'long nine', and gin myself up for a grand smoke! But fust, afore that, I hed drunk up a full hafe bottle of as good liquor, as ever was left to take care of itself on a dinner table. So, when I come to lie down, onder the tree, and got the cigar in my mouth, I felt a leetle overkim,—drowsy like—though I didn't get quite to sleep! And thar' I puffed, and I watched the beautiful blue and white smoke clouds curling upwards all about my head, jest as ef they knowd

I was a-watching em, and loved to see 'em curling up, beautiful in the sun; and I had sweet thoughts, of a thousand things that waur all pleasurable; and I thought to myself, how happy I waur; and ef this sort of life could only last forever, with hairdly nothing to do, 'cept to lick the scullion boy drummer, and make him larn his business; and with jist a plenty always to eat of fine things; and to drink of fine liquors; and to smoke of fine cigars, I would'nt kear to be a King or even a President!

"Well, jist as my head was chock full of this pleasant thinking, a-most like a dream, what should I hear, but pit-a-pat, pit-a-pat, right behind me, as ef a soft foot was sot down upon the dry leaves, making a sort of crinkle. And, says I to myself, ef it should be a beautiful young woman now! Lawd-a-marcy! ef it should only be Susannah Sykes, the prettiest gal in all Lexington Destrict!

"Pit-a-pat! Pit-a-pat!—It come closer and closer; and, at last, I felt a sort of breathing jist over my shoulder. 'Twas my right shoulder. Then, suddent, I haird a sort of snort, and, turning my head a leetle, for I was too lazy to git up, Lawd love you, what should I see but a great big brown b'ar, a-most as big as an elephant, with his great snout jist over my shoulder!

"My hairt jumped into my very mouth. I had no we-pon, and didn't know what to do! The b'ar hed the whip hand of me, I knowd, for he was on his legs, and I hafe stretchd out on my back. But Natur tell'd me what to do. 'Twas all Natur, for I never thought about it, ontell the thing was done; but, suddent, without trying to git up, I tuk the 'long nine' out of my mouth, and clapt the fire eend to his nose!

"Lawd love you! Ef iver you seed a b'ar back out from a skrimmage, you'd ha' seen it then! Soon as he felt the fire at his nose, he snorted deep; then stept backward, about three steps, going tail foremost; then he stopt to rub his nose, with one paw a'ter the other!—

"Soon as I seed that, I sees that I had got the whip-hand of *him*! So I puts the 'long nine' back in my mouth; draws a couple of good whiffs; takes another cigar out of my pocket; lights thet, and puts it in my mouth besides. Then I drawed quick on both cigars, and gits up, and faces the b'ar, and makes at him; puffing, as haird as I could, all the time!

"Soon as he sees me coming at him with two blazing stars in my mouth, he begins to back agin; snorting free, as ef he was still feeling the fire! He went on, waddling backward, tail foremost, clumsy enough and cur'ous to see; and I a'ter him, puffing my cigars hairder than ever! When he sees that, he fairly turns tail and runs; mighty awkward, but mighty fast, as you know a b'ar kin run; and, in three minutes, by the sun, he was out of sight—and kivered up in the 'thick'! I should'nt be afear'd to say that he war rubbing his nose to this very hour! It's mighty sartin, to my thinking, that ef he's living now, he's never forgot that transaction!

"That was my first fight with a b'ar; and I licked him fair, though he did git the whip hand of me at the beginning! And now,—'Big Lie,'—don't you think twould be good to liquor all round, jist to keep the cold wind off a man's stomach?"

V
How Bald-Head Bill Lost His "Sculp."

We liquored all round, every hunter acknowledging the propriety of protecting that delicate region, the stomach, from the atrocious invasion of the east wind, which, even in the days of Abraham, was proverbial for its bad character!— —After wiping his mouth, which he did expertly, with the sleeve of his coat, "Bald-Head Bill" proceeded with the narrative of his experiences in the "Flurriday War," after the following fashion.

"That fight with the B'ar, in which I licked him so fairly, gin me courage for any thing! A'ter that, I begin to see how easy twaur, for a man, ef he'd only set right about it, to lick the whole creation of beasts. I seed that every thing warnt to be done by main force, and strength, but by skill and slight of hand, and knowing a thing or two,—knowing which eend of the cigar to put to your own mouth, and which end to clap to the muzzle of your B'ar! And let me tell you that leetle as that idee may seem to you, fellows, there's ten pussons in every twenty thet kaint come to a right onderstanding about it!

"You may reckon, I spose, that a'ter thet transaction, I believed more in them Spanish cigars than ever; and I only wished our offsers had got the ninety boxes, instid of the ten out of every hundred! I went rigilarly at them every day, and never passed by any hafe bottle of liquor that stood next to 'em convenient for the handling. And every a'ternoon of parade, I jist set my scullion drummer boy at l'arning his business, and went off sly to take my smoke. I was more in love with that one tree in the thick whar I licked the b'ar then ever; and them hours I puff'd away in smoke, jist a hafe sleeping onder that tree, waur about the most heavenly hours I ever hed in all my born days, day or night.

"But, somehow, thar's an eend to every good thing some day, and I've found out, a'ter the trying of forty years, that a man's pleasures don't last any longer than any thing else; and sartinly they never do outlast his liquor! My smoking onder that tree was to come to an eending mighty short and suddent, and more suddent than sweet!

"One hot a'ternoon, when I hed jest swigged pretty nigh on to a pint of good Jamaica, which we got by smuggling as well as the cigars, I gin my 'Scullion' a thundering lickin' to make him l'arn his lessons the quicker.

"And the darn'd dirty little rascal, he runned off, soon as my back was turned, and when I was off for my smoke in the 'thick.' He runned off, and without stopping to clean up a single dish, or plate, or knife, or fork, or nothing thet was needcessary for the supper table thet night! Lawd bless you, and keep you from being sich a fool as to ixpect gratitude from man or beast. A'ter all my lickin's and kickin's of that scullion, to show him how to l'arn the business, he runned away, leaving me to git on eeny how I could!

"But I didn't know nothing 'bout it jest at that time. I went for my smoke. I hed five of them 'long nines' in my pocket, and my skin was jest as full of liquor as it could well hold, without leaking out; and I was jist about as happy that day, as King Nebuchadozzor, jest afore they turned him out to eat grass! I laid down at full length, cigar in mouth, and drawed easy upon it, and I looked up and watched how the creamy and blue clouds of smoke, twirled up and twisted round, and floated among the tree tops and kept going up and up, till I seed them where they stopt to rest, cla'r away up in Heavin! And I hed the sweetest thinkin' at thet time, 'specially about Susannah Sykes, the purtiest white gal in all Lexington Destrict! And it did seem to me as ef I seed her own beautiful self or a beautiful picter of her, coming down to me, through the tree tops, as ef she had jist come down from the blessed skies!

"I own up, I was a-feeling of my liquor, boys. The Jamaica was a working in my brain; and what with the Jamaica, and three of them 'long nines,' I felt a leetle onsartin about the motion of the airth, and more then onst, it did seem to me, as ef twarnt the skies a-coming down to me, but the airth gitting upwards, and swelling onder me, and carrying me up towards the skies; and twas then I seed Susannah, coming through the trees. A'ter thet, come more of them happy thinkin's, and I felt all overish with happiness, when, all on a suddent, I haird an alarum!

"There waur a shouting and a shooting! Thar waur rifle shots and musket shots; and now I haird a yelling; and now a shouting, and then the drums a beating and the bugles a blowing, and I know'd thar waur a sharp scrimmage guine on!

"But, somehow I didn't feel like gitting up to go into it; for, you see, I waur only a cook; and not a sodger; and then, agin, I hed no we'pon! Besides, twouldnt do for the only good cook in the Gineral's mess to be shot down like that chuckleheaded fellow, Rafe Parkinson! You can git any number of sodgers, thet's jest fit to be killed, and not good for nothing else;—but it's not one sodger in a thousand that you kin convart into a decent cook! I know'd all that, and feelin' what a loss twould be to the offsers, ef I was to be shot, I laid low, and kept dark; jest lying whar I was, snug in the 'thick', and drawing my long nine easy with easy breeth!

"And so I let the shooting and the shouting go on, without so much as letting the woods know that I haird any thing about it. And sometimes the noise would come closer and closer; and then I'd feel mighty oncomfortable; but then agin twould go far off; and I could jest make out to hyar the drums; so I begin to think that the darn'd red skins hed got the whip hand of our sodgers, and was a driving them ahead! And that, agin, made me think of the orful massacr*ee* of poor Major Dade's Rigiment, all cut to mammocks, with never a hair left on any man's head for a woman's fingers to play in!—

"Them thinkin's made me mighty oneasy; for, ef our sodgers waur all driv' off, what would bekim of me? Whar would be the 'parquizites'; the cigars, the Jamaica, and the easy time I had of it, after licking the scullion boy, every a'ternoon? And how was I to git to the Rigiment, with the dern'd red skins all between me and them?

"And then, the next, and worst consideration, in that thinking!—'Sposing the red skins should captivate me; wouldn't they massacr*ee* me, jest as ef I waur a part of Dade's Rigiment?

"I begun to be orful skear'd, and to look about me; when, Lawd love you, as I lifted my head, what should I see, but a dern'd infarnal red skin, a'most ten foot high, with his tomhog in one hand and his rifle in t'other, sneaking along through the bushes like a catamount. And the dern'd sharp-eyed fellow seed me jist as I lifted my head, and I seed him, quick as blazes, ketch up his rifle, and p'int!

"When I seed that, I squatted low as I could lie; flat to the ground; and the bullet tore the bush jist right over my head, and I haird the report of the rifle, loud as a seventy six pounder, the minit a'ter!

"I do believe that the dern'd savage tried his best to murder me that very time! I'm sure he did his best to hit me with that bullet.

"Well, he jist missed me, you see; but the thing warn't to eend thar. I know'd he'd be looking a'ter me yet, and what was I to do; without no we'pon to fight; and mighty leetle stomach for it, a'ter eating so hairty a dinner and smoking them long nines!

"I don't know as how I did any much thinking jist then! It was all feelin' and skear! My hairt was in my mouth! But I laid close, flat as a terrapin to the ground, with my head drawed into my shoulders, jist making as leetle show as possible.

"I waited and listened! I haird nothing! But I felt sure the cussed red skin was a-working all round me, like a painther, and feeling his way, leetle by leetle, along my tracks.

"Soon I haird a stick crack, and the dry leaves rattle, but I didn't dar' to look up. But all on a suddent, I felt him plump upon my back! He had jist jumped like a painther upon me, and I know'd my time was up, and I caved in for dead, with all the 'misery' in my innards.

"In another minit, his fingers waur in my wool—that is, in my wig, and I reckon in a minit more I'd ha' felt his knife working round my head; but the wig come off, in his hands, and I haird him cry out—

" 'Hegh!—A-poo-coola chee!'

"And with that he jumped off my back, jist as suddent as he hed jumped on, and I haird him a running.

"Then I looked up, and seed him guine full speed, with the wig in his hand, and he run a'most fifty yards afore I seed him stop and git behind a tree!

"I was a-thinking to git up and driv at him, jist as I was, without any we'pon, thinking, you see, how much I had driv off the b'ar, by a fair skear!

"But I hedn't the hairt for it, and my cigars had gin out! I jist had to lie close and watch for him, with my head jist lifted high enough to see over the bushes. Meantime, as my head begin to feel a leetle bit coolish, I tuk my t'other wig out of my pocket, and clapt it on!

"And so I laid, and waited and watched; and soon I sighted the red rascal sneaking round agin, jist as he did before. But I seed him only for a minit, as he worked his way round the tree, and was kivered by the bushes.

"Well, I reckon, a full quarter of an hour must hev slipt by—I thought it an hour,—when suddently, I felt the savage beast on top of me agin, coming down at a jump. Then I haird him cry out agin—

" 'Hegh!—A-coola-la! Coola-la: Etchee-ma-la-la!'

"In his own sarpent-like way of speaking, twas bekaise he seed I hed as good a head of hair on as ever, in spite of the sculp he tuk before! He jerked agin at my wig, and off it come in his hands, and then he bolted agin, and took fairly to his heels, for another hundred yards.

"By this time, I begin to think how twas. You see, the red rascal thought I was a white witch or wizard, may be, and they're mons'ous afeard of witches.

"Dern his buttons! he hed now got both of my wigs and I hed no more. I could guess that he waur a studying them wigs behind the tree. What his studies come to, I kaint say: but I warn't to git off. He come to me agin, but didn't jump upon me this time. He squatted on me, right across my back, astraddling me, as ef I was a horse, and he poked me in the side with his knife, sticking me a leetle only, but meking me feel mighty oncomfortable.

"Well, I twisted about onder him, and then he laughed like a great frog, and got up and turned me over with his feet, till his face looked fairly into my face!

"Then he made a motion for me to stand up, and when I did so, he tuk one wig a'ter the other, and clapt one on his own head and tother on mine. And oh! Lawd! how the conseeted rascal laughed at the i*deee*!

"But twan't for long! He soon shook his tomhog over my head, and p'inted me to march.

"And so I knowd I was captivated by the Siminoles and I was all over in a trimble, thinking of the captivation of poor Gineral Dade, and all his rigiment, and how they waur all massacr*ee*d.

"But I must licker now! I feel all over, when I think of that time, as ef the cussed knife of that red skin waur about to wipe its way clean round my forehead, sculp or no sculp! I must licker to ease off my feelings! Hyar's to you, fellows, and may you never hev sich a feeling as I hed about that time when I was captivated!"

VI
Bauldy a Captive. How Rescued from the Torture!

Bald-Head Bill, swallowed his liquor, wiped his mouth, groaned bitterly with his memories and resumed.

"We walked on, the cussed red skin pushing me before him, every now and then, when he seed me falling behind, with the sharp eend of his knife. I could hairdly keep my legs, or hold up my head, and thar was a something gathering all the time in my eyes, that a'most blinded me from seeing. And somehow, I tried to think of Polly Hopkins, my mar', and thin agin of Susannah Sykes of Lexington Destrict, jist for a sort of divarsion, and to keep from thinking of Dade's Rigiment; but Lawd love you, I could think of nothing else; for jist as I tried to think of Susannah, I was minded that I, prehaps, would never see her agin! And jist then, I'd feel the sharp p'int of the red skin's knife, poking me for'ard from astarn!

"We marched, as I reckon, about three miles in this way, going down and keeping close to the river-swamp all the time. Then we come to a lagoon, and thar was a dug out. The cussed red skin made me git in and take up the paddles; and he sot a-watching me, with rifle and tomhog and knife ready, ef I didn't work the dug out as he wanted. So he'd p'int to this side and that side, and I paddled him through the lagoon, ontell we got out into the river, and then he p'inted me to cross to t'other side. Thar we got into another lagoon, and run up a bit ontell we got to a sawt of hammocky island. It looked so; as I could see nothing but water all about me.

"And sich a place as twas! The snuggest hiding place in the whole world; a rigilar swamp thick all round about it, so thick, thet you had to pass into the darkness of night before you got to the camp of the red skins; and thar they all was, more than fifty warriors, with twice as many squaws, and a great swarm of boys and papooses, of all sizes and ages, and most of them jist as stark-naked as ef they waur jist then mother born.

"And only three miles off from our campment, whar we had been a-watching, and scouting, marching and counter-marching, for a month and more, in sarch of the red skins, and could never find 'em!

"It was cl'ar to me that thar had been a scrimmage! Thar was a great hubbub among 'em; the warriors having a grand dispute about something, and the old men putting in their palaver to keep 'em quiet.

"But the women made the cussedest racket of all.

"When they seed me, they made a rush at me; but my captivator kept 'em off at arm's length, ontill he hed shown em all how he could pull off my sculp, at a jerk, without drawing a drop of blood. That made 'em all mighty cur'ous; walking all round me, and trying to feel me.

"But when he showed 'em that I hed two sculps, and clapt one a'ter the other on his own head, the hubbub got to be quite an uproar. And the warriors passed the wigs from one to t'other: then they come up to me and felt my head all over, and rubbed it; and oh! how they laughed!

"Them fools thet tell you a red skin never laughs, knows nothing about the matter. I tell you, I've haird more laughing and joking in that Siminole camp, while I was in captivation thar', than I ever haird in any of our camps, the whole time I was on sarvice.

"But, while they waur all busy, looking at my head and feeling of it, and the wigs; on a suddent, a young woman, a bright sassy looking squaw, snatched away one of the wigs, clapt it on her own head and took to her heels.

"She hadnt too much clothing on to keep her from running fast and she show'd as pretty a pair of legs, as ever a trotting horse showed on 'Hampton's Race Course' at Columbya.

"The Ingin that had captivated me tuk a'ter her in double quick time, and a dozen more, men and women, tuk after him. Fast as the gal was, they run her down, and my captivator got back the wig, and 'gin her a sound box on the jaws for her pains.

"Then she and an old woman jumped at him, like two she-tigers; but the old men, they come between and parted them;—the warriors looking on and laughing at the sport without trying to lift a finger. 'Twas a fine race for two hundred yards, I reckon; and I laughed too;—I couldn't help it, though I ixpected every minit to be massa-cr*ee*d!

"And though you sees me hyar this minnit, and hears me talking, I warn't then so fur off from the tomhog as you may think. I sometimes wake up in a dream, and don't feel quite so sartin, remembering that time, that I'm edzackly a living man! The skear was sich, that I feels it now crawling through all my flesh and curdling to my bones. For, you see, them red skins are mighty quick about the business when thar's massacr*ee*ing to be done. They makes mighty short work of it, and don't give a fellow much time, ef its only to say his prayers!

"And so twas with me. A'ter they had tired themselves down with studying my head and wigs, and I reckon that every man, woman, and child, had a feel of my head; they went into a sawt of consult, or counsel, and, a'ter some long and tall talking, they come to me, and they looked into my face and eyes, and walked round me several times; then a sawt of Priest, or Prophet, come along, and he went round me, throwing up his hands and making a great howling.

"Says I to myself, says I—'It's my funeral ceremonies they're a'ter now!'

"Sure enough! Three strong young fellows seized upon me from behind, and in less than three minnits, they had tied me up to a young sapling. The dern'd red skins hed found out that I warn't no wizard, and not much of a sodger; and I'll be dern'd ef one of 'em didn't absolute spit in my face! Oh! how I wanted to knock him down!

"But my airms were tied, you see, and my body was tied, and I was stropped agin the tree, not so tight but I could twist about a leetle.

"Then who should come up but a dozen leetle brats of boys, not one of 'em more than ten years old. And they had their leetle bows and arrows, and they cracked away at me, twelve steps off; and some of the arrows hit me in the breast, and some in the face, and one of 'em a'most brushed my eye; and some of the arrows hed leetle spikes in 'em, and when those touched me, and I'd twist about, and wriggle like, how the leetle red divils would laugh and yell as ef they had done great things!

"They was at me, in this way, for a good half hour, the old warriors looking on and setting 'em on, jist as you'd set a fice-puppy on a rooting pig!

"But, on a suddent, thar was a divarsion in my favor. Before any body could say Jack Robinson, an old squaw, that looked as ef she was a thousand years old,—the ugliest old hag you ever did see,—she comes up, and stands betwixt the boys and me; and behind her comes a young woman, that I reckon was her da'ter, and she carried a papoose on her back, and the old woman, she hits me with her fist three good polks right in my face. Then there was a great grunt from the men, the warriors. And they all cried out—

" 'Hegh!'

"But nobody did nothing. Then the old woman whipt out a knife, and she cut the grape vines that tied me. Then she gin me, I reckon, a dozen sound blows, one a'ter another, all in the face, and she motions me to the young woman and the child. And, without more ado, they strops the leetle red brat on my back, and I knows from that, thet I'm to be a child minder. Oh! I felt so mean!

"But when I considered that I warn't to be burnt alive, or tom-hogged, or shot to misery, by them cussed leetle red skins, I felt easier in my hairt and conscience; and I tuk the child, and thinking to please the old woman and the young one, I made much of the brat, tho' it was about the ugliest, dirtiest little mawmouth that I ever did see; and it smelled, for all the world, like an old pole cat in September!"

VII
How the Alligator Relieves Bauldy of the Papoose.

"Now, my friends, jist you consider, for one minnit, the change in my fortin! Thar was I, only a few months ago, a sprigh young fellow, dashing away among the gals, and preticklarly cavorting about Susannah Sykes, the purttiest critter, of the woman kind, in all Lexington District!—

"Then you sees me next, mounted on my mar', Polly Hopkins, with a bran new coatee and breeches, boots and spurs, cap on my head, and sabre at my side, pushing down with six hundred more handsome fellows, under Col. Goodwyn, to fight the red skins in Flurriday!

"A'ter that, and when the cussed red rascals, shot my mar', you sees me marching on my own two legs, among the infan*try*! Then, bekaise I was a bad hand for foot-walking, when the order was 'double quick,' I was permoted to be Chief Cook, of the Gineral and his staff!—

"And thar', in that honorable cumpassity, you sees me injoying the good things of the grand table, a'ter the ossfers had done;—thar' I had, day by day, the old Jamaica and other lickers, and a good handful of fine Spanish cigars, smuggled all the way from Cuba, to smoke off the misquitars!—

"Warn't I the happiest man!—

"And jist when I was the very happiest man, you sees what a change; with hairdly nothing to eat, fit for a Christian sinner, and a white riprobate, with a cuff on one cheek, and a clip on t'other;—with a red skin to poke me with his knife, when I went too slow; and to shake his tomhog at me, ef I went too fast; and an old woman, ugly as Satan, and I reckon jist as bad, to lay a stick over my shoulders when she was in bad humor;—thar I had to tote the cussed leetle dirty wretch of a red skin papoose, from daylight to dark; and ef the brat cried, I got a whack over my back; and ef I got in any one's way, I got another, with a kick to balance!

"Jist consider, and ax yourselves, if I wasn't about the most unfortunit pusson that ever walked on his naked feet among the snakes, with the tigers driving him from behind, all in full cry! And jist consider, as I did, ef twarn't a thousand times better to have swallowed the bullet of the red skin, and let him take the nateral sculp from my head, instid of the wig!

"Oh, I was the most desprit man!—all day with that brat of a papoose; all day kicked and cuffed about by every body, and never let to have any peace at night! Ef I warnt carrying the brat, I was fetching wood and water for the Fillystines; and they'd rout me up, with a kick, at any hour of the night, to do any dirty sawt of work, that they didn't want to do for themselves!

"I waur desprit, I tell you; and the thought come into my head more than onst, to make a short eending of the misery, by running upon some sharp knife, or jumping plump into the river; or taking some red skin by the throat, jist when he hed his tomhog ready, and gitting myself knocked in the head at onst, and git rid of all the misery.

"But then, you see, when I come to consider, I couldn't bring myself squar' up to any of them *idees*! For, you see, a stick from a sharp knife, even ef it don't kill you, will make you mighty oncomfortable; and gitting drowned is apt to choke a pusson from taking in so much water, without the leetlest drop of licker in it; and as for being tomhogged,—that, you see, would give a pusson gitting the knock, a very great pain in the head; and I 'membered that a pain in the head was always mighty hard upon me to bear.

"But, still them idees come up to me, day a'ter day, though I hed my argyments always ready to put them down. And one day, with the brat of a red skin in my arms, walking by the side of the river, I got the leetle wretch to sleep, and laid it down on the dry leaves at the foot of one tree, and laid down myself in the shadow of another big tree; and thar I sot, thinking of my dreadful, horrid, miserable, owdacious situation, ontell I was all over in a sawt of bloody sweat of agony and rejection! And I looked upon the river;—so smooth and sweet, so cool and comfortable, it flowed along;—I thought to myself—

"Drowning would be better! That's sartin!

"But drowning's very onpleasant, with swallowing and choking with so much water! And then, says I,—I should never see Susannah

Sykes any more; and some other man will git her;—prehaps, some of my own rigiment when he gits back! He'll tell her how I hed to carry a cussed red skin papoose, smelling like a pole cat, and that I drowned myself in misery, and was eat up whole by the Flurriday fishes, that air as big, some of them, as a yearling calf!

"And the poor gal would marry him, as she had no more chaince of me!

"Lawd! Lawd!

"The *idee* was enough to shake the very snakes out of the soul of a sinner!

"And I groaned in the sperrit and the flesh together; and I felt like guine home right away, and thrashing the dern'd lying trooper out of his breeches.—

"And jist then, when I felt all over wolfish, with the hair growing innards, I haird the cussed leetle red skin, pole cat papoose give a great screech, as ef the devil had it on an eend!

"And so he hed!—

"When I looked thar was the leetle wretch snatched up by an alligator, more than two hundred feet long!"

"Two hundred feet!" was the exclamation of one of the groups of listeners—

Bauldy answered impatiently:

"I don't mean edzackly! I never measured the beast! He mout have been only fifty five feet and a few inches. Don't you stop me *now*!

"Yes!" he continued—"Two hundred or fifty five, or it mout be only twenty five or sixty, I kin tell you he was big enough for any pusson hyar, no matter what his gairth might be!

"And thar he was, with the brat in his jaws, moving off for the river, at a double quick. I could see the heels of the leetle red skin, hanging out of one side of his jaws, and the head out of the other; the mouth wide open, and screeching at every squeeze the beast gin it!"

VIII

How the Alligator Runs Away with Bauldy.

Bauldy, here, professing to be quite overcome by his feelings, solicited our sympathies, and we all liquored together.

After a long, deep groan, he resumed as follows:

"You may jedge, men, of my feelin's and sitivation! You sees the dangers of my sitivation! Ef that brat of a papoose was carried off by the alligator, what was to become of me?—What was my chaince, for keeping in the flesh, or holding my soul safe in my body? Jist none at all! I'd be beat, and kicked, and knifed, and sculped, and tomhogged, and shot to death with arrows, and burnt into the airms of etarnity, with pitch pine knots!

"I know'd all this, and, quick as a jerk, I jumped up, and made a'ter the alligator! I screeched too, with the hope to skear him, but that only made him run the faster, holding on to the red papoose, as ef he loved it.

"Fortenittly, I was closer to the river than him, and as I was fast as a runner, though slow at 'double quick,' I double quicked my running, and got up to him, jist as he slipped into the river.

"Right away, I jumped upon his back and straddled him!

"Now, as God's my Jedge, I never haird before that ere story of Major Henry, about Col. McCord, and the Congaree nigger boatman, Cudjo.

"But Natur tell'd me what to do!

"I straddled the beast in the small of his back, doubled my legs onder his belly, and gin him my heels, with all my might. Onluckily, I hed no spurs! I mout ha' done better ef I had! But I did the best!—

"But my seat was a mighty oneasy one, for I hed no purchase of arms or hands, 'cept by hugging him round the neck, and this I tried fust; but, jist then, it flashed across me, as I seed his sharp leetle eyes, looking out from his pine-knotty head, that I could manage him by *gouging*, much better than by spurring. Gouging is a nateral art, you see, wharever a pusson hes got strong fingers and thick nails! I l'arned to use both of 'em at school, but not in writing nor 'rithmetic; and so one a'ter the other, I stuck my fingers into his eyes!

"Now, that made the beast see straight! He bellowed out like a great buffalo bull and made right for the shore agin. By the time he got thar, I could see he was mons'ous sick at the stomach, and jist as he touched the land, he womited the leetle red skinned brat of a papoose, cl'ar out among the bushes;—it bellowing all the time, as ef twaur murdered! and I reckon the sharp teeth of the alligator hed hurt its dilikit feelin's, hyar and thar! I could see the blood a trickling from side and shoulder.

"Well, I was jist making ready to let go and jump off my water-stallion, when Lawd love you, he gives a bellow, wipes his long tail right round me, so as to tie me down to his back, and then pushes off into deep water as fast as he could go!—

IX
Alligator Bull Fight.

"Here was a fix! You'll all say—'That was a fix!' I could git *on*, but I couldn't git *off*! But, my gitting on was down-stream, and jist as rapid as a steam boat. It was jist one long plunge for'ard! But I kept my fingers in the sockets of his eyes, and I worked 'em thar, so as to make him bellow as we went.

"But he went on!—

"Soon, I seed the river a-widening; and I thought ef the dern'd beast, would have twisted his tail off of me, I'd hev tried a swim,—though not much of a swimmer,—before the land got too fur off! But, for all my fingers working in his sockets, he held me fast! I was captivated by him! His tail curled, like a snake, over one of my thighs, fixing it fast, and lapped the other. Ef I only hed a knife now, I could have made him let loose, for I seed just whar to cut through his leather, betwixt the j'ints, but the cussed red skins, when they captivated me, hed tuk my knife, three dollars in gould, my tobacco box and pipe, and I reckon three good long nines! And thar' was a forty-graph of Susannah, and she a gal of only twenty seven. It didn't look a bit like her, hows'ever; so I didn't kear so much for the loss of that!

"But, without my knife, and tied up as I waur, I could do nothing but work my fingers in the cussed brute's sockets. All the time, the land was gitting further and further off, on both sides. But the beast went on guine down stream all the time, and giving out a great bellow, whenever I'd work my thumbs about his peepers.

"But, all on a suddent, he stopt short, and made a motion to wheel about. I soon l'arned what was at the bottom of his change of thinking.

"A terrible great bellow, from another beast, sounded in my ears, close on my left, and then I haird a rush through the waters, jist like fifty wild horses waur a-rushing through the woods!

"Twas another alligator, full speed a'ter my stallion.

"Now, at first, twant easy to say, ef he was a'ter me, or at my alligator! You know that the great king of alligators, has, every one of 'em, a sawt of territory of his own. Thar he rules, and no one dar say—'Who is you?' He's king, I tell you, all thar, in that country!

"Now, from all I could l'arn in the country, the case was this. My water-stallion, not seeing well whar he was guine, had gone down into the enemy's country; and the king of that country was a'ter him with horse, foot artillery, dragoons and the rest.

"The strange King-'Gator, come along rushing,—and bellowing like thunder! At first my stallion tried to turn about and run back, as I tell you; but, I reckon, I was a-hurting his peepers jist then, and keeping him on his track. Finding he couldn't git off, he faced about for a fight. I reckon he was a brave beast, though I rode on his back!

"And the two great bull alligators drove at each other, with a wicked will! Sich a bellowing! Sich a churning of the water! It was all foam, and it splashed up into my eyes and over my face and head and shoulders, jist like a sudden souse coming down from one of our mountain falls, a hundred feet or more!

"And now they rushed agin each other, and I was terribly jostled between 'em when their hard sides come together. The great beast that was attacking us, made a mighty plunge at me, I'm a-thinking, with his jaws stretched wide as the great Cave of Kentucky, and his great white grinders showing like double saws ready to take off a fellow's leg at a single snap! I was dreadful skear'd, thinking he'd hev one of mine. But jist then, my stallion made a wheel, and the other shot past him like a flash, not able to stop himself easy, a'ter he hed made thet desperate start.

"But soon he wheeled about, and was for taking us on 'tother flank, but my nag was too quick for him, and shot round sprigh as a sparrow, and got a leetle headway on the back track, up the river.

"But the other was at him agin, savage as a meat axe; and whether it was me he was a'ter, thinking of his supper all the time, or whether it was only bekaise he had a love for fighting, kaint be said; I only knowed that I was in the misery all the time, thinking of my legs, and I kept 'em doubled-up, close as wax, round the belly of my stallion, and spurring him with my heels, and working his eyes in the sockets, to keep him up on the long stretch!

"But soon to'ther Bull, as they say in the army, changed his tick-tacks, and now fou't with his tail, making a flank movement to do so, and threshing at the starn of my stallion, ontell in self defence, he hed to ontwist, and loose my thigh, that he might put his own tail in fighting order, and to the same usage. And so they jist gin each other the flail, shot a'ter shot, the long tails coming down upon the river jist like thunder!

"At this sort of skrimmaging, I soon seed thet my stallion was a gitting the worst of it, and he felt it too; for, a'ter trying it for five minutes, he fairly begun to run, and now that he hed his tail free, he made pretty good time of it; but the spiteful inimy warn't willing to let him or me off; and he had the heels of my nag, and come up with him mighty soon, steering up close beside him, jist like a ship of war that wants to board at close quarters.

"Well, that gin me a new chaince. I could feel that my stallion was gitting badly whipt, and, as they say in the army, dam moralized! So I watched my chaince, and when the imimy bull was scraping his scaly sides agin my leg, I jist throwed myself over upon him and straddled him instid of my old stallion!

"Twas mighty well done, I tell you. I couldn't jump it, you see; having my feet upon nothing; but jist throw'd myself over him, hugging him round the neck fast, 'tell I could fling my legs over. Soon as I had ixicuted that grand army manoover; taking him in both flanks, and buckling close to his body; I stuck my thumbs into his peepers, without onst axing him, 'by your leave, old Gentleman!'

"With that he squirmed all over, as ef he hed a spasm in his bowels; and then he broke out in sich as bellow as shook the river to its very bottom; and it was c'lar to me that he hed lost all his stomach for the fight, as he let my old stallion make off at the rate, I reckon of fifty miles an hour—more or less!"

X
The Great Bull Alligator Goes Down with Bauldy into the Bottomless Depths.

"Now, my friends, jest consider me in my new sitivation! I do think that was the greatest horse swap that ever I made in all my born and living days! My first stallion was pretty much broke down; and I reckon his eye sight warn't the best! What with the ride he hed taken onder me; and the spurring and gouging; and the fight with the other fellow; who did give him some heavy blows; he was in no fix for much more travel thet night.

"My other stallion, that I got in the swap, was, as I tell you, good for five hundred miles, more or less from day peep to sundown!

"Lawd! It would hev blessed your innards to hev seen how we went down the river under my whip and spur;—thet is under my gouging and kicking! The other stallion warnt a sarcumstance to the new one, and, as we went, shooting away, like a rocket, I begun to feel mighty proud, and to think over my swap, jist as happy, as ef I hed traded off a bloody, sore backed, lazy mule, fourteen years old, for the finest blooded racer that ever old Johnson brought out from old Virginny!

"But whar was I guine, at this grand speed of my stallion? The Lawd only knows; and, heving nothing and nobody else to trust to, why, you see I was forced to lean upon him! I knowd I was guine down stream, not up; and that I was leaving my red skin captivators fur behind me; the cussed old woman, and the etarnal leetle brat of a papoose that smelled so like a polecat! Thar was a satisfaction in them thinkin's!

"But, as I driv on and on, and my alligator stallion didn't onst offer to slack his speed, I begun to be skeary, and to think he was guine to carry me too fur out of my beat, and out of his own! And so I thought of some plan to stop him, jist only that we might take an osservation.

"So, it come to me from Natur, that ef I was to gouge one eye and let to'ther alone, it would make him wheel about, right or left—no matter which,—and run me up on dry land onst more.

"I noticed that the river was spreading out mighty wide, into what peoples calls a Lake, and I noted agin, that the water was so cl'ar that I could see down to the very bottom, and a'most count the shells that was a lying thar. I'm sure, ef you hed dropt a silver picayune thar, I could ha' seed it, lying upon the bottom, all was so beautiful cl'ar in that water, though I reckon it was a thousand foot deep!

"Well, as I considered all things, and seen a beautiful green rising of the shore kivered with almighty big oaks, I gin my stallion a desprit screw in his *right* eye, and it would have done your hairt good to hev haird him.

"How he did bellow!

"How he did turn about and twist about, even ef he didn't jump Jim Crow! But he a'most jumped himself out of the water; then he come down with a thundering squelch; run ahead about twenty feet, and then, O! Lawd,—he went right down, down, down, and carried me onder,—for, in the same minnit, he quiled his tail about my thighs, jist as my t'other stallion, and fastened me close as wax, to his saddle.

"Down! Down! Down! we went, till thar was no more airth, and no more sky, and I begun to feel, all over, what people onderstands by drowning, and hanging, and all sawts of a massacr*ee*."

XI
Out of the Depths.

"How long I lived in thet sitivation, who can tell! I kaint calkilate. I thought it was a month of Sundays; a whole year of holidays, and thar was no fun in Sundays or holidays! My breath was fair stopt short; I know'd thet I couldn't stand it long! I felt death in my head and in my innards! I was a gonner! I know'd I was guine down all the time, on that cussed bull alligator's back, and he holding on to me, never onst letting go, with his rascally scaly tail tying my knee and thigh fast to the saddle.

"I kicked; I twisted; I tried all ways; but nothing would do! I'd ha' givin all in the world jest to get one breath of air: but no! and I jest give in! I could do no more. Says I,—'I'm a gonner at last!' Who'd ha' thought it! And I so young a man! A man what had hairdly seen the world, and had no wife! and Susannah Sykes a widow woman left behind me to git what husband she could—perhaps to marry some dern'd impudent trooper of my old rigiment! Oh! Lawd! O! Lawd! to deliver myself to death, without making any fight of it! Without any chaince to fight! 'Twas mighty haird.

"And then the thinking! Lawd a massy! It did seem to me, as ef every thing wicked I ever did, in all my life, come up to my ricollection; from the time of stealing apples and peaches out of old Geiger's orchard, to the time when Sarah Grimes and me, was caught in the thunder storm, and—

"But thar's no need to be telling about that! She's married off now, and hes three children!—

"Well! But—

"As I was telling you, down I went, on that cussed critter's back, 'tell I thought I was in the very bowels of the airth! and then I stopt short! I couldn't think, nor see, nor breathe, nor do nothing but die! I felt a thousand fingers squeezing my throat. I felt a thousand hands a squeezing in towels down my throat. I felt Death all over! I was dead! dead! dead! and I hed no more feelin' of the sitivation!

"But, all on a suddent, I waked up, and felt my feet a scraping on hard ground! The bull alligator was still onder me; but, he seemed to shuffle me off, and then I haird him bellow out, like the King of all the Buffaloes, onder a misery of the innards.

"And then I haird no more!—

"And then I seemed to be sleeping! and I reckon I did sleep; for I waked up at last;—I warn't dead;—I aint dead yit;—I waked up at last, and found myself on the beautifulest sandy beach of a sawt of island, you ivir did see.

"Whar was I?

"I seed nothing! I haird no alligator! I looked round and listened. Thar warnt a sound. Not a leaf twinkled! Not a breath stirred! Not a bird sang! Not a beast bellowed; and all I could hyar was jest a leetle sawt of onderground singing, like some body that sings softly, and is crying all the time. This, I soon knowed, was the sound of the leetle billows that broke over the sands and whistled in the great conchs that waur scattered all over the beach about me.

"But soon, I haird nothing, not even the waters, for I felt myself suddenly overkim with sleep; and I went off into a doze; into a drowse; and then into a big sleep, thet wrapt me up in its arms, jest as if I was a baby, jest done suck at its mammy's buzzom!"—

XII
Bauldy, After a Series of Serious Experiences, Is Made Captive by the Calypso of Flurriday; a Type Unknown to Ulysses.

"I waked up a'ter a long stretch of sleep, to feel the river jist playing about my feet.

"I felt stronger! But at first, I only crawled away, higher up the sands, to git out of the reach of the water. I hed enough of water a'ready, for one day.

"A'ter awhile, a'ter crawling a hundred yards or so, I sot up, and looked about me. 'Twas jest before sun setting.

"I could see I was on a sawt of island. The sands waur bright and shiny; and they jist sloped up gradywally ontill they come to a grand forest of the biggest trees I ever did see. Thar was oak and laurel among 'em; the tops so high, that you could see the skies fair resting on 'em, jist as ef they hed been so many pillars.

"Soon I felt strong enough to git up and walk, and I pushed for them big trees. Twas beautiful shady, and when I got fairly into the woods, I begin to hyar all sawts of noises, of birds and beasts too, I reckon.

"Thar was all sawts of singing; and soon I seed the beautifulest birds a-flying all around me; birds of all colors; some they called pair-o-kites, and other kinds, I never seed or haird tell of before! Then thar was a continyall barking and bouncing about of the squari'ls; but I seed no harmful beasts, and not even a snake!

"Well, a'ter a pretty tall walk, I gits out of the thick woods, and comes upon palmetto trees, and orange trees, that growd like palmettos in the fields, as ef rigilar laid out. Them palmettos waur standing on leetle sand-hills.

"Walking on, I comes to another beach of sand spread out sloping to a big water, what they called a lake; and, keeping on along the edge of the lake, I gits to the most 'strowdinary place of all.

"First I passed into a hollow, all of white sand, the airth gradywally rising into hills; thet was a'most chalky white; and, as I gits on, I finds the chalk hills meeting a top of me, and kivering me as ef I was in a house. But the pathway was wide and spread with white sand; and now I begins to see conchs and shells, the biggest and beautifullest I ever did see; that growed all along the path; and thar waur leetle breaks, hyar and thar in the hills, and I could see the smooth waters of the lake, shining between them, onder the slanting sunset.

"And in every one of these openings, I seed a most mighty big alligator, that jest stood and looked at me, and never moved, and seemed to stand thar as a sentinel! I gin him the left always, and stood on, between the hills and onder them arches.

"I now seed the hills widen; and the sides of them was stuck full of shiny shells, and great chrystals that gin light; and 'fore I know'd whar I was, I found myself in a most tremendous big hall, all kivered over with shells and chrystals and they gin the light; but, all round, thar was openings to the lake, and they gin light besides.

"And Lawd! to see the alligators, going and coming through them openings, jist as ef they waur on business, carrying messages from one to t'other. Some was big, and some leetle enough, and all of 'em seemed to be busy. They'd look at me, and pass on; and when they'd meet one another, they'd give a grunt or a bellow, jist according to their size and disposition.

"Well, I went on, for this one hall, as I may call it, soon narrowed down to a sawt of gallery or passage, and when I got through thet, thar was another hall, not so big as t'other, but a heap purtier.

"By this time, I was mons'ous cur'ous, and pushed on; and the alligators were guine in and out, through the openings to the lake; but they didn't seem to mind me at all, and I hed nothing to say to them.

"And I was jist on another sawt of chamber opening, when, right ahead of me, stood a most powerful alligator right in the way! I thought I know'd him; and he was one of my stallions, the last I rode on! I knowed him by his sore eyes; and he knowed me too, for jist as soon as he seed me, he bellowed like thunder, and turned tail, and made for the other room beyont!

"That encouraged me. I felt, you see, as ef I had licked him, in a fa'r fight, jist as I did the b'ar. And so I followed him, through a dusky passage, and, Lawd ha' massy, what I then seed, was a wonder to hyar and tell on!

"Now, fellows, it don't much matter whether you does or doesn't believe what I'm guine to tell you. It's so strange and wonderful that I never quarrels with a pusson who says to me,—'I kaint believe that!' I couldn't believe it myself, you see, ef I hedn't seen it with my own mortal sight; and I'll 'scuse any of you, ef you shakes your head, hev-ing no faith, for you know, seeing's believing as they say, and feelin's the naked truth; and as none of you has ever seen these things like me, or been made to feel them like me, so, I shaint quarrel with any of you, even ef you should say,—

" 'Bauldy, you know thet's a lie!'

"But 'taint no lie, I'm telling you, though its mighty strange and onpossible to be believed! Ef you could only onderstand, and hev the right faith;—for its the faith only, you know, that kin ever see the truth;—then you'd find every bit as true as ef twas writ in the Holy Hokies of Nebuchedsneezar; and the 'Columbian orator' to boot!

"You kin believe, as you please, and be the worse off for your onbelieving; but whether you b'lieve or don't, all the same to me. I'll push on with the history.

"Well, as I tell'd you, I followed my big stallion alligator, seeing as how he looked skear'd, and had sore eyes; and I thought, all the time, I hed lick'd him fair, as I did the big b'ar on the Withlacoochie, only with the fire eend of my cigar!

"I followed him, through the dark passage, and on a suddent, came into a great hall, beautiful as ef twas all made of shiny chrystals and beautiful shells. And they gin out sich a light as fair dazzled my eyes. But thar was light coming in from the openings on the lake, be-sides, and, through one of these, like through a great arched window, the sun shined in, and jist over the head of a grand looking woman, that sate a-rocking on a great shell, that I reckon was a living beast out of the sea, for it jist kept heaving her up and down, soft and easy, like a boat rocking on the little billows along the shore!

"When I fixed my eyes on this woman, I was fair dazzled of the peepers; and mighty skeared besides; though, at a distance—for I was at one eend of the hall and she at the other—she looked mighty sweet and beautiful.

"She was built a-most like other women, but she was of a bright reddishy complexion like the Ingins, and she had long black hair that kept floating and playing all round her naked shoulders, as ef she kept up a breeze thar all the time, with nothing else to do! She had'nt much other clothing, I kin tell you, 'cept some thing that spread round her like a wail, made of the finest silk hair; and her figger was sich as to make a fellow's blood churn up to his brain, setting him fairly a fire!

"And I could see, even at that distance that she hed coal black eyes; and when she sot them upon you, it looked as ef they were a shooting little lightning bullets at you, that went through you at every pop!

"Well! I stopt short and did'nt know well what to do; preticklarly as I seed that great bull alligator march up to her very feet, and put out his great tongue as ef to lick her toes. Her feet were bare enough—had neither shoes nor stockings, and they rested on a purty little pavement of shells close fitting together, and mixed together of all colors.

"Well, thar, at the feet of that beautiful strange critter of a woman, thar, that stallion alligator of mine, gin a great bellow; then he wheeled about, wagged his tail like a dog that ixpects his feed, and looked haird at me!

"I seed then that the woman looked at me too; and says I—

" 'What's the to do, now? I wonder ef that great beast and the woman kin onderstand one another.'

"But I reckon they did; for, a minnit a'ter, what does the great beast do, but he twirls his tail about, and actyally carried it up to his eyes, as ef to show that he hed got the infatenzy in 'em! Then he bellowed agin and looked haird at me!

"Now, it's most wonderful to say, but its all true, fellows! I seed that beautiful woman stoop down to the beast and look at his eyes; and she seemed to feel em; she sartainly touched 'em! Then she said something that I couldn't hear, and on a sudden, more than twenty leetle bits of alligators, that I hed'nt seen,—all lying about her, and waiting, jist like little sarvants, they jumped up, and come towards me.

"Lawd love you, how skear'd I was! I was fair fastened to the ground! My feet stuck thar;—my tongue seemed to dry up in my throat! I couldn't talk, and I couldn't walk! I couldn't fight, and I couldn't run; and yit thar was twenty on them leetle devils, big enough, but nothing like my two stallions; they jist come towards me, in three columns, 'minding me of Gineral Scott's grand marching through the Ingin country;—so I reckon the ticktacks of the West P'inters and the stallion alligators must be purty much the same,—that is a'ter a dicklyration of war!

"I ixpected them to dewour me at onst, in a single mouthful. They was enough to do it; but to my wonderment, when they got up to me, they made a sawt of military movement, by files, right and left oblique, spread out like riflemen for a skrimmage, and made a parfect ring around me.

"Says I, to myself, says I—

" 'I'm captivated agin!' "

"But I couldn't move nor speak; but jist kept my eyes rolling from side to side to see what was guine to happen next. And I thought agin of Gineral Scott, when the offsers and the troops made a ring about him, and he made a speech, giving 'em thanks for their sarvices, and telling 'em how beautiful they *could* ha' fout ef only the red skinned innimy hed only gin 'em the chaince!

"But as for my making a speech, Lawd 'a' massy, I warnt then quite sartin that I hed a tongue at all.

"Suddent then, all them little army of leetle alligators begun to bob their heads at me, open their jaws, give a leetle bit of a bellow, and wag their etarnal long tails. This they did three times, as rigilar as ef they hed the word of command and had been under West P'int drill for a hundred years. Twas beautiful to see how they did it!

"Then, without any word of command, they made another army involution, and, half of them in front and half in the rear, they wheeled about and tuk up the line of march to whar the woman sot, watching them all the time, and talking, I reckon, to the great bull alligator. He kept thar close to her feet, and I seed her an'inting his eyes with something that they brought her in a shell.

"Now, one body of them leetle alligators, leading the way before me, and another body, following close behind, was jest the same as saying,

" 'March!'

"And they made me feel it so, when the bloody beasts in the rear, come close up and kept pressing me for'ards, with their horny snouts.

"They did'nt hurt me, that's true—and not one of 'em tried to bite; but, jist as sartin as ef they did, they pressed me on for'ard, showing me what they wanted, ontill, they got me alongside of my big stallion alligator, and at the feet of the strange, queer, astonishing reddish woman, that was, I reckon, a sawt of Queen among the alligators!

"My big stallion wheeled about and looked me full in the face, with his cussed little sharp eyes, bulging out from onder the lightwood knot of horny scales above them.

"But he did'nt offer me any provvication; and, in a minnit, the strange woman, gin out a kind of sound, like a frog's chuckle, and jist as they haird it, all the alligators, big and leetle, my old stallion among 'em, they wheeled about and made off, going through the openings, and all making for the lake, as happy as boys jist let out from school!

"And thar I stood, by my own solitary self, not knowing what was to come next. I seed that I was captivated;—a prisoner, and heving no wepons, and no chaince for escape!

"But all was so wonderful and cur'ous, that I hafe lost the feeling of skear. Says I to myself, says I,—

" 'What's to come next?'

"I didn't hev to wait very long for the answer. The woman she eyed me close, with her bright sharp lightning-like eyes, big and black, and she shook her head till the long hair floated about her as ef the wind was a-rising in it; and I could then see that it was long enough to wrap her body round and round about, close to her feet!

"And she stared at me; and she laughed;—no—not laughed—she made no sound; but she smiled,—and sich an smile! Lawd, love you! She showed through them thick pulpy lips of her'n, sich a double row of the whitest teeth, every one sharp as a dog's grinder, that I begun to think, she would dewour me without turning me over to the cook, or using any salt to the dressing!

"But when I next looked, the smile was sweeter. The mouth was shet. Thar was only the leetlest show of teeth when she smiled agin! And I could see that she had a sawt of loving twinkle in her eye, all the time; and she leaned her head o' one side; and she tossed it; shaking the long hair out, from side to side; then she shot the fire from her eyes, straight into mine; and suddenly when I least ixpicted any sich thing, she flung out from her body, some twenty foot of tail, caught me round the waist, and before I could cry out, or kick, she pulled me into her lap, and gin me such a hug as a she painther might give to the male one who had brought her home a young calf to feed upon."

XIII
Bauldy Discovers the Places of Skulls and Skeletons. Great Excitement. Bauldy Escapes from Captivity in the Midst of War.

"In sich a sitivation as this, I think men, its reasonable that a man should licker."

We all agreed with him and liquored accordingly.

"Well, now," said he, resuming, "Jist you consider my fix! Thar I was, setting in that strange critter's lap, with her tail quiled all about my body, and not able to move, while she hugged me to her buzzom, and kissed me, jist as ef I was her newly married husband!

"Up to that minnit, I hed not seen that she had a tail at all! She looked, for all the world, like a nateral Injin woman, only she was a heap purtier, and a thousand times cleaner than the best on 'em.

"She had kept the tail quiled onder her, jist as a snake quiles himself; and when she throwed it out, it was by a quick jerk, and it worked round me, tight as a thunder snake, when he's got a rattler in his gripe! As I tell you, her body, all on it, was jist as smooth as any Injin woman's; but the tail was raal alligator; it was a scaly tail, scales all over,—only working twenty times more easy than any alligator's.

"And, setting in her lap, tied to it, I may say, she kissed me on my cheeks and mouth, and bit me, every time till the blood come! She had raal genovine dogteeth, or shirk's, I reckon!

"But, she didn't mean to bite or hurt me, that's sartin. She did nothing but squeeze and fondle! And O! Lawd, how I thought upon Susannah Sykes of Lexington Destrict. And, O! Lawd! says I to myself, says I, how dreadful a thing to be married to sich a critter aginst ones will and liking! And O! Lawd! to think that I should be the husband of a Mar'maid!

"I hed hearn tell of Mar'maids before, but I never altogether believed in sich critters; but seeing is believing, and feeling's the naked truth! I knowd now that thar waur sich critters, and that I was captivated by a rigilar Mar'maid!

"Now, fellows, you must'nt ixpect me to tell you all. Thar's some things, you know, not to be mentioned among civil, decent white people! Only onderstand, I was at the marcy of a Mar'maid, the Queen of the alligators, who had a parfect army, a rigiment, I may say, of the most powerful bull alligators always in her sarvice! I jist hed to submit, and say no more about it!

"Now, how long I staid in this sawt of captivation, heving nothing to eat but fish and eystars, and shrimps, and whatever they could catch out of the river and the sea, I kaint tell you. It might have been thirty days or sixty months. I did'nt keep any count of time. The Queen fed me upon shrimps and clams and eystars and all kinds of fish; but everything had to be eat raw. She tried her best, I confess, to make me relish cat and trout, and rock, and sheephead, and cavalli, and other things out of the sea; but twas hard work for me to come it, considerin' that I was a born cook by Nater!

"She picked out the best, biggest and fattest eystars for me, and showed me the nicest fish and the nicest parts of the fish.

"I did l'arn something onder her!

"But twas no go; and when she seed me, picking up sticks and building up a fire, she seemed to onderstand what I was about, and she jist grinned, after her fashion, and said nothing about it! The alligator sarvants brought in the fish.

"When I hed cooked some, a'ter my way, but without no salt, I offered her some, and she tried to eat; but she flung 'em away, and took to the raw baits.

"But I went on cooking for myself; and ef you kin onderstand how a white man kin git on, with fish and eyestars, without never a morsel of bread, why, you may believe me when I tell you, I made out to make a pretty hairty meal every day, and sometimes, three times a day!

"Now, how long I lived in them quarters, onder them sarcumstances, I kaint raally tell you! It may have been twenty one days. I don't think rally twaur more than sixty nine or thirty one. But the days and nights passed away without my counting 'em.

"I hed too much to think about and to worry me. I hed to think about my captivation; and how long I was to be kept away from my people; living in the city of alligators, and with that strange Queen of Mar'maids; jist doing as she pleased, and not able to turn from one side to the other without being watched.

"When she hed'nt got me in her own sight, why she hed a dozen of them dern'd leetle sarvant alligators, that followed me all about, and seed a'ter me; and, go whar I would, they was always hyar and thar, ahead or astarn, or on the flanks of me, and I reckon, ef they hed seen me moving off, they'd ha' mounted me, every mother's son on 'em!

"But how to git off! Thet was the question thet worried me. I didn't know well whar I was. I guessed I was on some island, for, turn which way I would thar was the water. 'Twas wide, too, and spread out jist like a lake; though I could see the trees on t'other side. Twas a mighty beautiful place, and ef I could only hev had Susannah Sykes thar, with jist hafe a dozen of the fambly and neighbors, from old Lexington, I could have spent the rest of my days thar, and never would hev got vexed with the Lawd, if they hed never come to an eending!

"There was some fine hammock land on the island that would hev brought any thing, from corn to cotton, from pindars (ground nuts or ground peas) to potatoes; and one piece of bottomy land, where I'm sure I could make five hundred bushels of rice to the acre! Ef I only hed that island now, in any raal white man's country, I'd live like a fighting cock!

"But 'twant living now that I was. In truth, I felt it was a sawt of dying out from all the world; and the Queen of the Mar'maids pretended to be mighty fond of me, yet she kept me in a contenuyall skear!

"Them teeth of her'n, 'specually when she laughed or tried to laugh,—for twan't nothing better than a grin—they waur all so white and shiny and sharp, that I never seed 'em but I thought of the white double saws in a shirks (shark's) jaws, and the white sharp grinders in the mouth of the great alligator stallion that carried off the Ingin baby. Why, fellows, she never kissed me onst, and she was always awrapping her tail round me, drawing me to her buzzom, and kissing me as ef for dear life, without drawing the blood.

"Well, onst, soon a'ter I was captivated, she made me go with her to the river or lake to swim. She could walk like a human, had legs and feet like ourn, but, all between her toes was webbed, and the toes tied together by the flesh, same as a duck or goose, or any of them water birds. Onst in the water, fellows, Lawd, it was wonderful to see how she could swim; and dive and cavort; throw herself fair out of the water, lash it with her tail into foam; then plunge down, head foremost, into the very depths of the sea and airth, and come up again, and swim off, while her long black hair was spread out over her back, from head to heels, like a great black wail over a woman in mourning!

"It was a most wonderful sight! And when she'd come up from diving, she'd bring up handsfull, of shells from the bottom, and pelt at me, jest as you see boys pelt one another with nuts or apples. And the alligator nation, they'd swim about a'ter her, ten thousand I reckon, but they always keept at a 'spectful distance off, and she never let 'em take any liberties with her; and, in fact, I never seed any of 'em try! It did seem as ef they sawt of worshipt her, as ef she waur their God as well their Queen!

"Well, when she got me into the water onst, I hed a time of it; and I took good kear never to let her catch me in it agin! Why, she'd catch me round the neck and round the middle, and roll over with me, and buckle me to her with her long tail, and then dive down to the bottomless pit of the deep, ontell my breath was a'most gone; and I thought all was over with me!

"I never did like the water, and warn't no great swimmer at the best. I reckon I would ha' been drowned a hundred times over, in her alligator play with me, but that the water of that lake was different from any other. It didn't seem, when you was onst in it, that 'twas much thicker than the air in damp or foggy weather. You could breathe in it, in a sawt of way, and when you was deep down, it didn't lie heavy on your back.

"But I never let her git me in to it but onst, and when she found I didn't like it, she let me alone! She appeared to want to be good natured and coaxing, and she was mighty loving, a'ter her fashion; but it was a coaxing and a loving that somehow kept me in a continuyall skear, and I fought shy of her whenever I could; and when she'd let me, I'd jist wander away, ixploring the island, and finding out all I could; for I seed that twould be a mighty fine place for a leetle settlement, and I calkilated that, ef, I could onst git off, and git among my people, I could git up a good force of twenty stout fellows, and git boats, and cross the river, and captivate the island, and kill off the whole alligator nation in short order!

"Well, one day, when I was a navigating and explorating the island, and when thet Queen of the Mar'maids was taking her a'ternoon swim, I got off about hafe a mile, and when I got to a sartin line, all them leetle spy alligators stopt following a'ter me.

"I couldn't tell what to make of thet, but I warn't sorry to git shet of 'em; so I pushed ahead, and went on, 'tell I got into a thick wood.

"Twas mighty dark and thick, so thick that the sun's blazes

couldn't git in, only hyar and thar, with a faint leetle light that jist sarved to show what a dark and dismal place it was.

"I could hear the squarrls jumping and barking among the trees, and evey now and then an owl, would sweep out, singing his great 'Whoo-Whoo-Whoo! Whoo-Whoo!'

"And then I'd hyar the rush of some big birds with great rattling wings,—I reckon they waur eagles;—and by a leetle pond, I seed more than a hundred great white cranes that walked about the pond and never seemed to mind me; and onst, I seed a beautiful flash of flying birds that looked most like leetle rainbows, and by their cries, I knowed them to be parroquitos.

"But in the midst of my looking, I stumbled over something, and when I picked myself up and looked, what should it be but the skillyton of a man, with the flesh picked off clean to the bone.

"How my flesh did creep at the sight! But how much worser did I feel, when as I could see better, I seed a whole pile of skillytons, more than a hundred, I reckon, all stretched out, and all picked clean to the bones.

"Oh! twas dreadful! Thar, without eyes to see, they seemed to look out from the sockets at me, and I thought I haird them all say at onst,—

" 'You see what you're to come to yit, by that Mar'maid woman!'

"Lawd! Lawd! I could onderstand now, mighty well what them sharp white teeth of my Mar'maid was good for; and my flesh crawled to think how, when she kissed me, she always gin me a bite that drawed the blood. The infarnal critter was a-tasting me all the time, and calculating the meal she was to make of me!—

"I tuk hairt;—some thing told me;—and I squatted down and sarched and examinated the skillytones, and I felt sure that they was all of 'em the skillytones of *white* men like myself; for you see, the skulls were all the skulls of white men, not niggers or Ingins. They waur all broad and high, with big fronts, the eyes setting low onder the foreheads. Now, the nigger you know, hes his eyes high up, and most of his head is on the back of it; and the Ingin's skull is sharp and narrow, and runs back too; not so wide as the nigger's, but longer backward and more like a woman's!—and Ingin and nigger skulls are all mighty thick! Now, all these skulls were thin, and in the front part pretickilarly, some a'most as thin as paper!—

"I got out of that cussed place as soon as I could, and made my way out of that infarnal thick wood; but I fair staggered as I went, with my flesh crawling over me, jest as ef I was gitting on a coating of snakes!

"Now, when I got back to the skairt of wood, whar all the leetle spies of alligators drapt off from me, Lawd! what should I see, but the whole rigiment of 'em, lying squat about and waiting for me.

"And soon as they seed me, they tuk up the line of march, some in front, some in rear, and some on the flanks of me, jist as ef they were a rigilar troop, edicated at West P'int!

"And so we marched on, not heving a word to say to one another, tell jist as we got in sight of the beautiful place where the Queen of the Mar'maids kept me in captivation; they all set up to bellow, with their small v'ices, a sort of howling and singing together, jest as you hyar in a frog pond, in a cloudy night when rain is ixpected!

"By the time we reached the grand hall, the Queen had done her bathing, swimming, playing and cavorting in the river, and thar she sate, shining bright, and with that cussed snake smiling, so like a grin, upon her beautiful wisage. When I stood before, she jist shook her head good humoredly, and one of the leetle alligators, he set up a small bellow, as ef to tell her every thing.

"Then she motioned to me to come to her, and when I did so, suddent she whisked her tail around me, and drawed me into her lap! And then she bussed me, mighty affectionate; drawing the blood from my mouth, for with every buss, she always gin a leetle bite! The infarnal critter was jist a trying to see ef my blood and flesh, feeding as I was, on fish and eysters, was ready for her dewouring! I onderstand it all!

"And, though she hugged me close, and bussed me so keen, I could see that thar was a sawt of twinkle of suspicion in her eyes, as ef she begun to think that I was suspicioning her!

"I was dreadful oneasy, but I did my best to make b'lieve, I was as fond of her as she waur of me! But I hardly sleept a wink that night, thinking of the skillytones, in that dark wood, and what chainces thar waur before *me*, to git out of my perdicament!

"But the Lawd was marciful! The very next a'ternoon, when she went out to bathe, and swim, and cavort, and I hed to go out to see her, though she couldn't git me to come in the water, thar was a mighty change. Some thing happened,—what twas I never could guess,—that put an eend to my captivation and skear.

"When she went down to the river, heving a hundred bull alligators following close a'ter, and jist as many running before, I followed slow behind, the leetle sentinel alligators sticking close to me.

"I jist went down to a leetle sandy flat, kivered by the shade of three big palmettos, and laid myself down, it may be about a hundred yards from the water.

"Then the cussed leetle spy alligators, they laid themselves down all about me. I could see the river, all in front, and I could see the Queen of the Mar'maids, every now and then, as she flashed through the water and cavorted! But I hairdly cared to look; and I was fair blind with thinking of my captivated sitivation, and them thousand skillytons; when, all on a suddent, I haird the greatest uproar in the river.

"Twas the roaring of ten thousand bull alligators; and the whole river was churned into white foam, and the noise was awful!

"And I could see the Queen of the Mar'maids, tossing her long arms in the air; and I could see her tail fairly curling, like a bow over her head; and off she went like a shot from a rifle, pushing down the stream, and followed by a thousand alligator bulls, she was out of sight in a minnit.

"And, jist at the greatest of the outcry, all the leetle sentinel spy alligators, that was a watching me, picked themselves up, and began to bellow; and they too rushed off for the river; and soon I saw their hundred le'ttle pine-knot heads bobbing one a'ter t'other, and going down the river, following, fast as they could, the hundred thousand bull alligators and the Queen.

"Then I ran down to the water side; and, far as I could see, thar they waur, all pushing for dear life, and the whole face of the river was kivered with foam!

"What could be the matter? When they all got out of sight—the Queen of the Mar'maids, and the bull alligators, and the leetle spy alligators,—I could still hear the mighty bellowing below, as ef a thousand battles was a guine on, all at the same time, and prehaps fully five miles off.

"I was mightily conflusterated; but, while I was a looking about me, and wondering what could be the 'casion for the great fuss and uproar and ixcitement—for it was cl'ar to me that thar was some tall fighting guine on below,—what should I see, but a nice new little dug-out, a cypress canoe—come floating across the river, right towards me!

"Oh! how I watched that dug out! As it come nigher and nigher, I could'nt hold myself in!

"I jumped into the river, when it was about thirty yards off, and waded out, 'till I hed to swim; but I got the dug out, and cotch'd fast hold of it! And thar, inside, was a pair of as good new paddles of ash, as you would wish to handle; and thar was a sack and a bundle; by which I knowed that it had been fresh used by somebody thet didn't know, or kear how to make a boat fast to a sapling.

"I didn't wait to say 'good bye' to anybody! I jumped in. There was nobody and nothing to see me. You couldn't see, any whar, a single knot of an alligator's head above water. They waur sartinly all below, and fighting for dear life; for I could hyar the great bellowing; and every now and then a mighty big roar, as ef from the throat of some mighty stallion alligator, some big fellow, sich as I had straddled in my last ixtrimity.

"And as I pushed off, and struck across for t'other side of the river,—I hed seen enough of this side—I thought of the Queen of the Mar'maids, and how she would miss me, ef ever she got back!

"And then I wondered what sawt of fighting she could do ef thar waur a fight sartinly guine on! And then I axed myself, ef evey nation of alligators hed its own Queen; and I begun to consider, what sort of Queen the other was; and ef the two would hitch together in the skrimmage! I could see, in my thinking, what work *my* Queen would do with that tail of her'n, and how she would make them dog teeth meet in the flesh, at every grin!—

"But, when I thought of them teeth, and ricollected how clean all them skillytones had been picked to the bones, I bent and buckled to my paddles, and worked my way, till I sweated like a bull in fly time, pushing up stream.

"Twaur mighty haird work, I tell you;—but, whenever I'd begin to feel faintish, I'd think of them skillytons and them dog teeth of my Mar'maid, and I'd pull the harder!

"When, at last, I struck the shore, and made a landing, I jest had strength enough to make the boat fast to a sapling; to walk into the woods, a leetle way; jist to kiver myself out of sight, and then to throw myself at the bottom of a big tree, say a short prayer, and give myself up to the blessed sleep! I reckon t'want three minnits before it wrapt me up, jist as ef I was in a blanket! But, in them three minnits, Lawd! how I did long for a drink! I'd ha' given a hundred dollars, ef I hed it, jist thin, for a good swallow of peach and honey! And what say you fellows, for a kiss of the sarpent now?—"

A pause while we liquored.

XIV
The Catastrophe. Bauldy's Greatest Miracle of All; and His Escape from Susannah Sykes.

"And now, fellows, the most extonishing part of the history of my campaign in Flurriday, is yet to come; for, I reckon, you'll all say, a'ter you've hairn me out, that nothing could be more strange and surprising, in what's gone before, than what I've got to tell you now!

"How long I slept onder that tree, it's not easy to say. The haird work of paddling up stream, me one and alone,—a matter, I may say, of sixty or twenty miles, more or less, tharabouts, or some whar,—pretty much knock'd me up and knock'd me down too!

"Then the skears I hed; the dangers I went through; the troubles; captivated by the Ingins; sculped; shot at and knifed; and then made to nurse the cussed dirty little red skin papoose; then the ride, first upon one alligator-stallion, then, swapping, and shifting to another; and then the captivation to that Queen of the Mar'maids; then the dreadful sight of the skillitons of our people, chawed up and gnawed to the bone, by that same Queen of the Marmaids, I reckon, with her cussed sharp white dog-teeth;—well, all them dreadsome and fearsome ixperences, they waur enough to knock me down, and make sleep easy to me for a month of Sundays; so, thar's no knowing how long I had been sleeping onder that big tree, on the edge of a mighty great thick of swamp forest.

"But I was suddently waked up by mighty rough usage! First, I felt a kick in my side, and ribs; then I felt myself pulled and jarked about, by the arms and shoulders; and, when I opened my eyes and straightened myself out, to see what alligator hed got hold of me now, what should I see but a squad of four or five of our own Rigiment, all pulling at me at onst!

"And I cried out loud:

" 'Oh! Lawd be praised, I'm safe at last!'

"So I said, though it did seem mighty strange that our own people should handle me so roughly. So I says—

" 'Hello! fellows! Hev' you no sawt of feelin' for a man's ribs, that you kick so haird!'

"With that one kicks me ag'in, and says,—

" 'It's the ribs we're feelin' for you d——d bloody desarter!'

" 'Desarter!' says I.

" 'Yes,' says he, 'a dern'd bloody desarter! We always know'd you was a d——d coward; but nobody ever suspected you of the courage to desart! Git up, you d——d blasted sneak, and git yourself hung as soon as possible! You aint decent enough to be shot!'

"And not a word of ixplanation would they hear to; but jist kept on kicking and hauling at me, 'tell they made me git up, and soon as I did so, they roped my hands behind my back, and the Sargeant, he punched me in the rear, with his sword, 'tell I went ahead. I tried my best to tell 'em every thing, but they gin me no answer 'cept in cusses, and no sawt of satisfaction 'cept in kicks! All they'd say was,

" 'Keep your jabber 'tell you gits before the drum head court martial.'

"And twan't long before they got to camp; and twas a mighty great supprise to me to diskiver that the camp was jis whar I had left it months ago; and, when I calkilated, and looked about me, I was more supprised to find that I had landed jist at a p'int, that took me back to my old tree, whar I used to smoke my long nines on the sly!

"I could now onderstand that, in the scrimmage with the Ingins, they had licked the red devils off, gin 'em chase, and then come back whar the tents were all left standing, onder a rear guard.

"Well, they soon hed me in camp and up before the Gineral and all the off'sers; and thar, right in front of me, stood the cussed leetle dirty scamp of a scullion boy, that I used to lick so, every day, to l'arn him his edication as a cook. The moment I seed him, I smell'd a snake! The ongrateful varmint,—a'ter all I hed done for him to ratify agin me!—

"But I hedn't much time to look at him, or to think of him either; for thar' was the Gineral looking at me, with a great black thunderstorm over his eyes, and them sot upon me, as ef he meant to blast me black with lightning! He did look bigger than ever; and blacker than ever; and his nose was redder than ever; and as much like a great firecoal, hot as blazes; and as he tuk off his great parade hat, with its bunch of feathers, and dashed it down upon the table, he fair snorted at me, like an angry bull at a yaller handkerchief!

"And I fell all over in a heap, wilting up, and running together, and quaking, like a great platter of seablubber, jist brought ashore by the rollers.

"Says he, with a v'ice of thunder—

" 'What hev you got to say for yourself, you scoundrel?'

"That tuk me all aback agin! I hedn't the strength to say nothing; and I shook all over! My tongue was dried up fair, and stuck fast to the roof of my mouth! Then says the Gineral:

" 'He feels his guilt! Read the charges and pacifications, Mr. Adwokit!'

"Then the adwokit, who was no other than Captain Firebrand, he read, and as I haird them charges, I felt the rope growing round my neck, and the bullets going through my bowels!

"What do you think they charged upon me?

"Well, twas a mighty long catalog!

"First, they charged me with desartion from the company. Then they charged me with cowardice; skulking onder an alarum of the inimy; hanging back in an advance; stealing cigars and liquor;—beating the scullion boy cruelly, that he mightn't tell on me; and, Lawd knows how many things besides; among 'em,—would you b'lieve it,—they charged that I did the smuggling at St. Augustine, and kivered up the transactions of Capt. Chubb, of the schooner Sukey Gunja, gitting the ten boxes out of the hundred for *my* pay;—smuggling the boxes, onder hides, in the baggage wagons, and selling cigars and Jamaica, all smuggled, out to the onder offs'ers and soldiers; besides, drinking 'em and smoking 'em myself; and, last of all, they charged me with stealing my own cigars and liquor, and gitting drunk upon the liquor every a'ternoon and night! The very things the d——d raskals had done themselves!—

"I seed what some of it meant. The government hed smelt the rat, and got wind of that smuggling business; and they wanted to put the porkypine saddle upon *my* back! The d——d cunning wipers!

"Then they called up the rascal scullion boy to prove the pacifications, and he swore to a thousand lies! He swore that, when he cotched me drinking the liquor, and carrying off the cigars, I licked him to make him keep a shet mouth; and he told how he followed me, time a'ter time, every a'ternoon, to the edge of the 'thick', where I drunk and smoked by my one self. That I always carried a full bottle; that I never brought it back full or empty; that, if I come in at night, that I never come in quite sober; but sometimes, when I was overdrunk, that I slept in the 'thick' all night! But thar was no eend to it!

"They had other witnesses that swore about the smuggling, a most etarnal pack of lies! And then they brought up the file of soldiers that hed found me sleeping onder the tree; and they said they hed found me, deep, dead drunk asleep; that they hed to kick and punch, and pull, and haul me about to make me open my eyes; and that, when they got me up, I could hairdly walk, and staggered about like a blind man;—that I hed'nt quite slept off the drunk!

"Did you ever hyar sich a cussed story, and jist a'ter I hed gone through all that ixperience of captivation by the Ingins; by the alligators; by the Queen of Mar'maids; and the hard row of two hundred miles, I reckon—more or less—paddling off from the Mar'maid's island, in a poor dug-out, and without a morsel to eat, or a mouthful to drink!

"Them fellows that brought me up, then showed more than a dozen chunk bottles that they said they found in the 'thick' whar I was sleeping;—and they showed five 'long nine' cigars that they swore they tuk out of my pockets;—when, as you all know, I was robbed of them vary last cigars by the cussed red skins when they captivated me!

"I now begin to see that thar was a sawt of conspi*ra*cy agin me to hev me hung, shot, and butcher'd!

"And Lawd love you, I hed no witnesses at all; and I could see, from the looks of all the offsers, that I hedn't no one friend among 'em, to stand up for me, and take my part, and argyfy my defences.

" 'And now, scoundrel!' says the Gineral,—'What have you got to say for yourself?'

"Well, seeing as how twaur pretty much over with me, with every body swearing agin me, and nobody to back me; I was desprit! and, a'ter a leetle time, of trying to settle my thoughts and feelin's, I got the strength, and made bold to tell them the whole of my ixperences and idventures, first about my captivation by the redskin, at the time of the skrimmage—

"With that the Gineral says—

" 'We've hed no scrimmage, in the last seven days.'

" 'Oh!' says I, 'but this was more than a month ago!'

"Then says he, 'What the devil is the fellow talking about? But go on,' says he—'go on!'

"And he squared a one side, looking at me with his left eye, which he could cock wonderful! So I went on to tell about my captivation by the red skin, and how he carried me off, and how he tried to sculp me, and carried off my wigs, and was skear'd at first—

" 'Why, man, what do you talk about,' said the Gineral. 'The wig's on your head now!'

"With that, I felt my head, and, sure enough, thar was the wig.

" 'But,' says I, 'whar's to'ther one?'

" 'Why, to'ther one's in your pocket!' says the sargeant,—'I felt it thar when I sarched you, while you was asleep. Them five cigars was in it!'

"I felt in my pocket, and sure enough, t'other wig was thar! For a minnit, I was dumbfoundered; but, in the next minnit, I seed through it all! They *hed* been scrimmaging with the Ingins; hed killed or captivated the red rascal that captivated me; and found my wigs upon him; and, to fool me, they had clapt one upon my head agin, while I was asleep, and rammed the t'other one in my pocket.

"It was all a cussed trick to make a fool of me, and hev' their fun; and, thinking so, I begun to feel easier, and reckon'd twa'nt so ser'ous a matter a'ter all! I begin to feel twas no hanging or shooting matter; and, from the laughing of the off'sers, I rether thought the whole thing a plan to skear me, and hev their fun out of my skear! Them fellows was up to all sawts of tricks, and thar was no eend to their skylarking when they was off duty.

" 'But,' says the Gineral, 'let him go on with his own redickilous story in his own way. It is a leetle amusing!'

"So I went on, and tell'd the whole; all my idventures; day a'ter day; the captivation among the Ingins; the nussing the d——d leetle dirty papoose; and how he was tuk off by the alligator; and how I jumped on the alligator's back, and rode him, and gouged him, and made him womit up the leetle red skin; and, how he carried me off; and then, how he fought with t'other alligator stallion; and how I swapt hosses, gitting astraddle of the bigger and stronger one; and how he carried me off, through the lake, to the island of the Queen of the Mar'maids; and how she hugged me up and kissed, and bit me; and then how I got off in the dug-out, and got safe back to the old 'thick,' a'ter a captivation of, I reckon, three months, more or less!

"Lawd! how the fellows laughed!

" 'And to think!' says the Gineral, 'that all that stuff should come out of one bottle of Jamaica! Why, Bauldy,' says he, quite good humored, 'How long do you say you were absent from camp?'

" 'Well,' says I, 'Gineral, thar's no keeping right time among the Ingins, or among the Mar'maids either; but I rether reckon, if twarnt two or three months, twaur something over sixty days or thar abouts!'

" 'Now,' says the Gineral, turning to the offsers of the mess;—

" 'Now, Gentlemen, can you remember when Bauldy cooked our last dinner?'

"And, with one v'ice they all answered—

" 'Yisterday, Gineral!'

"Yisterday! was iver hair'd the like of sich bold lying! I was dumbfoundered! They went on:

" 'We missed him only last night, at ten, when we called for supper! Neether he, nor Blox (the scullion boy) was to be found; and thar was nobody to cook breakfast this morning, till Blox come in. He cooked the breakfast.'

"Blox, you see, was the scullion boy; and all the cooking he know'd, he learned from me. And see the thanks I got!—

"Then the off'sers went on, and said, 'Blox put us on the trail, a'ter breakfast, and told how he had followed him, and found out all his tricks. So we diskivered how the liquor and cigars went!'

" 'So, you see, Bauldy, all the stuff you have been telling us, was nothing but a drunken dream! Instead of being absent sixty days, you were not gone sixty hours, and were dead drunk all that time! Now, what ought to be done with a cook that is not forthcoming when we want our supper?—That has no breakfast ready for us in the morning?—This is a dreadful crime, and dezarves ixemplairous punishment! Have you any thing to say in your defence: any thing that may be pleaded in behalf of marcy!'

"I confess I was in sich a fix of bewilderment, and ixtonishment, that I couldn't say nothing! I hed told the truth, and the whole truth; and, by the Hokies, as you knows, fellows, nothing but the truth; for, you see, I've tell'd you every thing jist as it happened, and as I tell'd the off'sers. You'll b'lieve me, though they wouldn't! But they wouldn't b'lieve nothing, though twas the very angels thet come down to tell 'em. They was the ongodliest set of onbelievers I ever sot eyes upon! Says I to 'em—says I—'twas all I could say—says I, 'I've tell'd you every thing:—

" 'I sartinly was sculped and captivated by the Ingin; and had to mind child more than a month of forty days. I reckon.

" 'I sartinly did ride them alligators:

" 'I sartinly was captivated by the Queen of the Mar'maids, and she tuk me to wife, and sartinly hugged and kissed and bit me;—I've got the marks of the bites now on my mouth;—it's all sore yit—'

"And I showed em my sore mouth.

"They laughed, wild fairly, and said twas bekaise I smoked up all their long nine cigars, and then burnt my chops with the Jamaica.

"The onbelieving sinners! They would hyar to nothing and jist laughed at my sufferin's. And so I cried like a baby, and then they laughed the more.

"But, suddent, the Gineral, put on his grand looks, like a thunderstorm, and he clapt on his great parade hat, with all its white feathers; and he said—

" 'Now, Gentlemen, let us dispose of this case. It is cl'ar to you that William Bauldy, otherwise Bald-Head Bill Bauldy, has been found guilty of all the charges, and the pacifications onder them. He as good as pleads guilty; for, you see, all the stuff that he's been telling us is either meant to lead us off his track, or it's nothing but a drunken dream, all born of a bottle of Jamaica. Is he guilty or not guilty!'

" 'Guilty!' was the magnamimous v'ice.

" 'What shall be his punishment?'

" 'Death!' was the answer, all magnamimous together!

" 'How shall he die!'

" 'Shot to death!' says one.

" 'Hung!' says another. 'Shooting's for a brave man.'

"And some went for whipping and branding; and driving out of camp!—

"A'ter they had all done, the Gineral he said—

" 'Gentlemen, I confess to a great onwillingness to put Bauldy to death. I am always onwilling to hang, or shoot any man, ef he's got but a single vartue left in him; for, you see, the vilest sinner may be saved, only give him time; that is,—ef he's got a single vartue to brag upon! Now, we know that Bauldy don't love fighting. We knew *that*, when we tuk him out of the ranks and made a cook of him! Twas for that very reason, that we tuk him out of the ranks and made him cook! Now, as for his desartion, I don't think he meant to desart. But the Jamaica got the better of him and he overstayed his time. Now, I grant you that to overstay his time, and not git our supper, or breakfast, when we put our faith intirely in him, was a great crime, desarving of death; but Jamaica is a great temptationer, and, as he shows you, begits bad dreams. And, I'm afear'd, Bauldy loves to sin with liquor, ef he doesn't love Mar'maids. He's kivered all over with vices, and crimes and temptations; but he's got *one* vartue which you'll all admit; and I'm for letting him off easy, considerin' that one vartue! He's a fust rate cook! He was born to be a cook! It was cl'ar he was never born to be a sodger! Now we've never had sich good cooking, and sich good health, as we've all hed, ontill Bauldy was promoted to be our cook! He's good at a'most every sawt of cookery. Who kin fry a trout, a pairch, or a bream, with Bill Bauldy? Who can bile a bluecat, to make it eat hafe so sweet? and, I never swallows a bowl of his tarrapin soup, but I feels more vartuous and happy a'ter it! Then thar's his tarrapin pies! Now, I'm bold to say, however them Beaufort people may brag about their tarrapin pies, Bauldy's beats them all hollow! A'ter eating one of his pies, I always lies down and sleeps with a good conscience, and rises up with an idee of dinner.

" 'It's a great vartue!' says he, 'to be a cook, and redeems many vices! A great sodger, Gentlemens, is *one* thing, and a great thing; but a great cook is a greater;—he's a sort of life-presarver, and comforter, and saviour of the body, which, you know, is next to being the saviour of the soul! I puts great prophets and great cooks in the same rank, and wants to be marciful to their faults, bekaise of their vartues! And, considerin' *our* case, more than his'n, I'm for taking him to marcy! Ef we don't who'll be the greatest sufferer—We or Him! Ef he's hung, 'twill be only death at last; but ef we kin git no good cooking done, for the rest of this campaign, it's death and darnation both to *us*! I tell you, last night's supper, and this morning's breakfast, both cooked by Blox, waur enough to kill any man's appetite, and distroy his stomach! And I'm clar to let Bauldy off, 'till the eend of the campaign, when you kin do with him what you please! As for Blox, the rascal, who has showed himself so quick to watch his master's vices, without l'arning his vartues, I sentence him to a Baker's dozen, with a hickory on his bare back, well laid on, and order that Bauldy idministers the punishment at onst!'

"Didn't I make them Baker's dozen tell at every crack on the leetle rascal's shoulders!

"That day, we hed caught in camp about two hundred tarrapins more or less! And didn't I do my best. I waited on table, and watched the Gineral, and the mess, as they ate; and ef *they* warn't happy, who was? As the Gineral ate the soup, and swallowed the pie, he took a long breath, wiped his chops with the towel, and said—

" 'Gentlemen, did'nt I tell you so! With all his vices, Bauldy's soul is worth saving. His one vartue is a very great one!'

"And we got on well, to the eend of the campaign, 'cept for one skrimmage, when the Siminoles made a hambush for us, and nearly captivated my baggage wagon, with all the mess kettles, and pots, and pans, and me in the bargin!—But I knocked down one impudent red skin with the frying pan, and driv' the hosses over him. We got *his* sculp; and the Gineral said,

" 'Bauldy's always at home with a frying pan! Ef I was to take him into a battle, he should hev a frying pan or a gridiron, or something of the sawt, instead of a musket!'

At the eend of the campaign, and when we was disbanded, we had *seven* sculps to show; and one was sculped by me;—and they did say thet them *seven* sculps cost the government some twenty four millions of dollars!—Some did go so fur as to say two hundred millions; but I reckon that was an overcount!

"All the time I was with the Brigade, I tried my best to make the off'sers see the truth of my ixperience in captivation to the Ingins; the alligators, and the Mar'maid Queen; but, to the last, they purtended not to believe it! When we was a-parting, for good and all, and the Gineral and the mess was taking the goodbye drink together, the Gineral called me up, and says he—

" 'Bauldy, we won't hang you this time! You're a good fellow, ef you only know'd it, and you've got a great vartue! But Bauldy, you must leave off lying. 'Twont pay! Hyar now, take a pull of this Jamaica! Ef I waur to give you the whole bottle now, you'd see the Queen of the Mar'maids at the bottom!'

" 'Ah, Gineral!' says I, getting bold, a'ter I swallowed, 'that want of faith in you, and the whole mess, will keep you out of Heaven yit! Ef ever I spoke the truth at all, Gineral, it's about that woman; that Queen of the Mar'maids.'

" 'Well,' says he, good natured—'I suppose that story is jist as near the truth as any thing you do say, Bauldy! All your truth, my dear fellow, lies in the kitchen! After eating your tarrapin soup and tarrapin pie, I kin believe equally in you, and the sixty nine particles!'

"What he meant by the sixty nine particles, I never know'd, and I could only think of them things we use in dressing soups and pies, and sich dishes—sich as pepper and spice, and allspice, and nutmeg, and inyons, and Lawd love you, a hundred more things instid of sixty nine!

"I went out of the sarvice poorer than when I went into it. I hed hairdly no clothes left. The sutler's account eat up all my pay before I got it. Government never paid me for my mar' Polly Hopkins; and the worst was last! When I got home to Lexington, I pushed right to see Susannah Sykes; and thar' I found one of our Brigade, playing Cock

Horse, with a Doodle Doo, all about her, and she wouldn't look at me! When I popt the question to her,—which I did desprit,—she turned up her nose and said—

" 'I've hairn all about you, Mr. Bauldy! You may go back to your Queen of the Mar'maids, with her alligator tail! I ain't the pusson you thinks me!'

"The story, you see, had got before me. Jim Crowder hed told her every thing. He was the sergeant that captivated and brought me into camp as a desarter. He got ahead of me. Well, in three weeks a'ter that, she married Jim; and ef I've got any satisfaction in the world, it's the knowing that the two on 'em lives like cat and dog together; and some do say that he threshes her; others says she threshes him! I hopes both stories is true! I'm only glad I'm not the husband! Last time, I seed Susannah, 'twas at church, and she turned up her eyes, like a dying duck in a thunderstorm, and had the impudence to ax me to walk home with her. But she couldn't come it. And, the Lawd be praised, I'm a free white man to this very day!—Amen!"